The Case of the
Reborn
BHAGWAN

ALSO BY

WILLIAM L. SULLIVAN

The Case of D.B. Cooper's Parachute
The Case of Einstein's Violin
The Ship in the Hill
Listening for Coyote
A Deeper Wild
Cabin Fever
The Oregon Variations: Stories

Published by the Navillus Press
1958 Onyx Street
Eugene, Oregon 97403

www.oregonhiking.com

This book is a work of fiction. All of the characters are products of the author's imagination. Any resemblance to people living or dead is purely coincidental. Depictions of the Modoc tribe, Fort Klamath, the Portland Police Bureau, and the Rajneesh movement have been fictionalized, and are not intended to reflect their current status, beliefs, or procedures.

The Case of the Reborn BHAGWAN

BY
WILLIAM L. SULLIVAN

NAVILLUS PRESS
EUGENE, OREGON

Prologue

Roger was the only barista who did not clatter cups at the Killingsworth Karma Koffee Kompany. He used a towel to muffle the shriek of the espresso machine to a fragrant sigh. To be sure, mornings at the 4K in Northeast Portland remained a cacophony of hipsters. But Rog's soothing afternoon shift drew a more contemplative crowd, earning a *Willamette Week* review for "Best Mocha Mood."

Central to the ambiance was Rog's blog, a rolling mantra in Arial. Each day after tying on his apron he supplanted the large-screen Food Channel with his own live feed.

> *forty folks cradling cups*
> *you may walk in my door alone*
> *but here we're one with java*

Until one day a long black Rolls Royce rolled to the curb outside the plate glass window.

> *silver angel on the hood*
> *who's coming for coffee now?*

Two men in red stepped out. The driver, a bald man with Gandhi spectacles and a crimson Nehru jacket, skeptically compared the address against a paper in his hand. The other man, with a long white beard and a maroon robe, smiled slowly, wrinkling his weathered brown face.

They walked around the bicycles parked on the sidewalk, opened the door, and made their way past couches and tables to the counter.

Roger set aside his keyboard. "And what would you gentlemen like today?"

Roger had large, expressive brown eyes that might have seemed effeminate, but he cut his black hair short, wore no piercing jewelry, and shaved infrequently, shadowing his handsome jaw with stubble.

"Are you Mr. Nash?" the bald man asked. "Mr. Roger Nash?"

"Yes."

"Born in Portland on January 19, 1990, at 9:19 a.m., Greenwich Mean Time?"

Roger blinked. Was this some kind of subpoena presentation? He was two months behind on rent, but these men looked more like monks than bill collectors. "I'm not sure about the exact time. What can I do for you?"

The two men looked at each other a moment. Then the long beard bowed to Roger. "I would be humbled to receive a cup of Darjeeling green tea from your hands."

"Twelve ounces or sixteen?"

"Any amount would be a blessing."

"Sixteen, then." Rog marked a paper cup with a pen. He turned to the Gandhi glasses. "And for you?"

"If —" The man pressed his palms together, either praying or thinking hard. "If you are the one we believe you are, Mr. Nash, I would be honored to offer you the Rolls Royce that is parked outside."

Chapter 1

Neil bicycled hard through a cold June rain on Portland's Eastbank Esplanade, trying to reach a decision. His wheels thrummed down a wide aluminum ramp to the bike path's floating bridge. Raindrops pinged rings in the murky Willamette between shadowy pilings. He had fought demons this way before, sometimes on week-long rides across the state with Cycle Oregon. Now it seemed if he pumped furiously enough he might break through the drizzly fog to a sign and know what to do.

He had been offered a job running security for the Rajneesh Revival. Neil was sixty — old enough to remember how much trouble Rajneeshees could be. Did he really want to quit his job with the Portland Police Bureau?

Well yes, he did, but maybe not to defend a red-robed cult of wannabe swamis. Back in the 1980s the Bhagwan Shree Rajneesh had bought a sprawling ranch in the Eastern Oregon desert, gathered thousands of devotees from around the world, and preached a hippie-dippy doctrine of free love, communal work, and eternal bliss. When the Bhagwan's utopian city, Rajneeshpuram, ran afoul of state land-use laws, some of his frustrated followers had poisoned voters and attempted to assassinate officials to influence elections. The entire episode had ended in trials and deportations. As a policeman, Neil found that history particularly troubling.

Neil downshifted to climb the ramp up from the pontoon bridge. A startled seagull squawked up from the railing and shat a white blob into the wet rocks ahead of him. Was that a sign?

The new Rajneeshees were different, according to Harmony. Neil's thirty-one-year-old niece was a natural beauty, with long blonde hair and a sassy one-shouldered shrug. You almost had to close your eyes if you wanted to doubt anything she said. She had grown up fearless and feral, raised by hippie parents who in fact had done a stint in old Rajneeshpuram.

Neil's brother Mark still made wooden toys on a commune in the hills behind Eugene. Long ago, Neil had turned away from his older brother, choosing instead the perilous career of law enforcement.

Yesterday Harmony had asked him to bridge that gap. She had invited him to a coffee shop on Northeast Killingsworth, a funky dive that the new Rajneeshees had bought as a sort of shrine.

"This is where they found him." Harmony's wide brown eyes beamed at Neil. She tugged the lapels of her red blouse, a gesture that drew attention to a carelessly undone top button. Neil had to look aside, reminding himself that she was his niece.

"You don't really believe their talk about reincarnation?" Neil asked. He sipped the foam of his latte. Instead of a swirl or a fern leaf, the barista had topped the drink with a six-sided mandala.

Harmony shrugged with one shoulder. "Roger was born at the same minute that the Bhagwan released his soul in India, just as predicted. Both of them have the same haunting dark eyes. And there's his name: Rog Nash. I think he really is the Rajneesh."

"But how could a twenty-six-year-old kid from Portland be a dead Indian guru? Even born-again Christians aren't literally born again somewhere else."

"Not if they get it right the first time."

Neil looked up at her uncertainly.

She shook her hair so it covered the loose button. "The Bhagwan Shree Rajneesh made mistakes in his past life, so he couldn't attain enlightenment yet. He had to come back in another body. Dying lamas sometimes direct their consciousness into a child, or *tulku*, to continue their work. Now, as Rog, he has a chance to get it right."

"Without poisoning anyone?"

"Roger's not like that. He's turned his followers away from violence and focused on the good parts of the Rajneeshee wisdom — the cooperation, the love, the self-realization. We don't have to hide behind Indian names anymore, so I'm still Harmony Ferguson. We can choose commitment and marriage and children if we like. We can keep our worldly goods. We don't even have to wear red. It's not a cult. It's about finding a happy way to live."

Neil had been dodging unhappy ways to live for years. Still, he doubted he would find the answer in a Killingsworth coffee shop. He took a drink of his latte. A sign above the counter announced that it had been made with organic free-trade coffee from a Rajneeshee plantation in Costa Rica.

"I'm not sure Oregon is ready for another Bhagwan," Neil said.

"That's why we need you. You've probably heard about the people who've started a campaign against the new Rajneeshees?"

"No. Who are they?"

"No one knows. But we're being targeted. We need an experienced detective, someone from outside." She bit her lip. "I don't want *anyone* to get hurt this time, Uncle Neil."

He leaned back and scratched his neck, thinking about Harmony. She was a kindergarten teacher with two black belts in the martial art of aikido. She wasn't the kind of niece who asked for protection.

Neil tried changing the subject. "What happened to that guy you were planning to marry? The physicist in Italy?"

"Gilberto?" She rolled her eyes. "He got all controlling. He was weirding me out with his family's Roman Catholic nonsense."

Neil wondered if Gilberto had been weirded out when she joined the Rajneeshees.

Harmony leaned forward, dipping her neckline in a curtain of gold hair. "You're sixty, Neil. You've reached an age where you can retire from the Portland police, earn a pension, and take a nice little security job on the side."

Had she heard that the police bureau was lowering the pension age? "I'm not so sure. I've got a boss and a daughter who aren't going to want me switching jobs."

"Ask them, Uncle Neil. We need you." She looked into his eyes. "I need you."

He placed his hands on the table and said quietly, "I don't quit easy, Harmony. If you hire me as a detective, you might not like everything I dig up about your new friends."

"I know." She didn't blink. "In fact, that's what I'm counting on."

The river darkened with another cold gust of rain, a wall of wind sliding across the water from the city. When it hit, Neil's bicycle nearly swerved off the path. If he weren't pedaling so hard, he'd be freezing. His yellow-and-orange Lycra shirt dripped rain and sweat.

He had talked first with his boss in the homicide division, Lieutenant Connie Wu. When their roles had been reversed, and he was the lieutenant, he had tried dating Connie. The feisty, black-haired sergeant had been aloof back then. It hadn't helped that he had nearly gotten her killed on a stakeout. They had been tracking a Russian mafia don with the code name D.B. Cooper. Three months later, after "Cooper" died in a gruesome accident, Connie had been the only one to realize that Neil had actually solved the case. Everyone else thought he'd bungled the investigation. He'd been demoted to sergeant. Since then, Lieutenant Wu kept inviting him out to dinner. But she hadn't yet invited him home.

When he told Connie Wu about the possible security job, she stared at him. "What? And retire from the police bureau?"

"Well, yes. If I took the job."

"But that's great!"

"It is?" Neil wasn't sure why she was smiling. "I thought you said we made a good team."

She laughed and gave him a quick hug, which surprised him even more. "We do, Neil."

For a detective, Neil found he was sometimes slow to solve mysteries of the heart. "All this time you've held back about getting romantically involved with me because I'm your subordinate?"

"Regulations can be such a pain. The only cops with an in-house romance are either fired or retired."

Neil nodded uncertainly, still a bit wobbly from the hug. "Then you think I should take the job with the new Rajneeshees?"

Connie eyed him. "Rajneeshees wouldn't be my first choice. But yes, I think you need to retire."

Later that day Neil had called his daughter from his apartment in the Park Blocks. "Susan?"

His daughter didn't always answer aloud, even after she picked up.

She had struggled with autism all her life. She couldn't look people in the eye, and she missed social clues in conversations. But she had helped Neil with cases more than once, using a sixth sense for things that were out of place. This talent also seemed to help with her job at a Portland recycling center. In the four years since Neil's wife Rebecca had died of cancer, Susan had been his closest support, even when she seemed maddeningly distant.

"Susan? It's me."

Recorded harpsichord music in the background told Neil that his daughter was at her apartment, and that she was listening.

"I'm thinking about retiring from the police bureau. I wanted to talk with you about it."

Finally Susan said, "Marriage?"

"What?"

"Marriage. Is it good?"

Neil blew out a frustrated breath. "Yeah, I guess so. It worked great for your mother and me for thirty years."

More silence. Then, "Are you retiring so you can get married?"

"No!" How could his daughter have picked up on this idea? "I'd be retiring so I could do private detective work. I've heard about a possible job."

"Working for Harmony." Susan and Harmony were beautiful in different ways — Harmony was blond and wildly outgoing, while Susan was dark-haired and eerily reserved. Emotional opposites, they had become unlikely allies at Ferguson family reunions. Each Labor Day, when the clan met on the southern Oregon Coast, the two women would disappear together to pick huckleberries in the dunes or trade secrets in an attic.

"Your cousin told me about the job," Neil admitted. "Harmony wants me to run security for the Rajneesh Revival."

"I know." Susan's voice was flat, as usual.

"Well, what do you think? I haven't gone for an interview yet. I don't even know what terms they'll offer. It's just —" He struggled for words, as he often did when confronted with Susan's silences. "I wanted to hear what you think first. I mean, I'd be working for the Rajneeshees."

"They're not safe."

Neil sighed. "That's pretty much what I think too. They're trouble."

"No, Papa. They're the ones who aren't safe."

Neil frowned. Harmony had said the same thing, that the Rajneeshees were in danger. "Then you think I should help them?"

A clicking sound came from the phone, as if Susan were tapping a pen. "Look for a sign."

And that had been all. When the line eventually went dead, Neil hung up.

He hadn't slept well that night and had gotten up early to bicycle his way through the rainstorm, looking for a sign. So far the only omen he had found was a shitting seagull. He had hoped for something more specific.

The rain squall had passed by the time he rode his bicycle beneath the thundering concrete of Interstate Five's Marquam Bridge. Just beyond, the bike path curved around an OMSI museum patio alongside a dock with a decommissioned submarine. Then he joined the bicycle commuters riding into the city over the soaring white arch of Tilikum Crossing, a bridge open to everything except cars. Overhead, rows of gigantic cables stretched to the sky. Behind him, the first rays of dawn shot beneath the storm clouds, illuminating a billboard on a streetcar:

NEVER AGAIN!

Beside the eight-foot-tall letters was a blood-red photograph of a crowd of Rajneeshees, their arms raised toward a bearded man smiling from the window of a Rolls Royce. The only uncolored part of the photograph was a black-and-white circle spotlighting the face of the Bhagwan Shree Rajneesh.

Neil pulled his bike over, surprised that such a negative advertisement had been allowed on a streetcar. Only when the tram rumbled past did he notice that the circle had the faint crosshairs of a gunsight.

Neil worked his jaw, trying to get a sour taste out of his mouth.

He had found a sign.

Chapter 2

The Rajneeshees had bought an entire block at Twelfth and Burnside, including the trendy Jupiter Hotel and the adjacent café, to use as their administrative headquarters. Wearing his brown sport coat, Neil walked up the only entrance to the compound, a driveway between the café and the hotel office.

In the courtyard, two rows of identical red Priuses stood neatly at attention. But chaos reigned in the hotel lobby, with young people playing guitars, girls dancing in red saris, and hostel backpackers sleeping on piles of baggage. The only staff person was playing a video game on his cell phone behind the desk.

These people really did need help.

Neil flipped his wallet open to his badge, just for effect. "Sergeant Ferguson, Portland police."

The boy's eyes widened. "Uh —"

"I'm here to meet a man named Vijay Collins."

"Oh, right. Our operations guru." The boy pointed a thumb down a hall. "He's in the conference room."

"I suppose I'll recognize him because he's wearing red?"

"Yeah, and he's bald."

Half a dozen professional-looking people in expensive blue jeans and dark jackets were coming out of a doorway, carrying clipboards and charts. Neil slipped in the open door behind them. The people remaining in the room were hunched over architectural drawings on a large table, pointing and talking. At first glance the drawings looked to

Neil like plans for warehouses, but the buildings were huge and covered with glass.

Only one of the men was completely bald. He wore little round spectacles and an almost collarless red jacket that made him look like an aging bellhop.

"Mr. Collins?" Neil asked.

The man turned, adjusting his spectacles. "Yes?"

"I'm Sergeant Ferguson. My niece Harmony arranged an interview about a security position."

"Of course." He smiled and extended his hand. "Call me Vijay."

Neil shook the hand, but did not offer his first name.

Vijay continued, "Harmony tells me you're actually here to interview us."

"I've been a cop all my life. This would be my first civilian job."

The others in the room began arguing a little louder — something about a drilling operation. Vijay motioned Neil toward the door. "Let's go where we can talk."

Neil followed him out to the hall and up a stairwell to a large, modern suite furnished in black and chrome. Neil was a little surprised that the room smelled faintly of cigarette smoke. Someone had drawn a dove in white chalk on the room's black door.

"Apple juice, Sergeant?" Vijay asked, opening a fridge.

"Sure." Neil pointed to the dove. "I see you're using the Bhagwan's old logo."

Vijay poured two glasses. "Actually, the former Bhagwan preferred two overlapping doves. We use just the one."

"From what I understand, your group isn't affiliated with other Rajneeshee movements around the world. The center founded by the Bhagwan in Poona, India, disavows the Portland rebirth."

Vijay sat and crossed his legs. "No one has found the Bhagwan's seal of authority. That box went missing before he died. But he predicted he would be reborn here in Portland. Most of the older sannyasins are convinced it has happened. Including your brother Mark."

Neil almost dropped his glass. "You know my brother?"

Vijay sipped his juice. "From the old days."

"In Rajneeshpuram?"

"He was Swami Deva back then. Everyone took Indian names."

"Like Vijay." Neil asked.

Vijay smiled. "Actually, I've always been V.J. — V for Victor, J for James."

Neil thought again about his brother. "Mark had a falling out with the Rajneeshees. He never said why, although I think it had something to do with his marriage."

"It did." Vijay set down his glass. "Your brother met his future wife moving irrigation pipe at the ranch. The old Bhagwan frowned on sannyasins who married. Shree was not fond of children."

"So the old Bhagwan never met Harmony?"

Vijay laughed. "That might have changed his mind about marriage."

Neil didn't laugh. "Were you in Rajneeshpuram during the poisonings?"

Vijay walked to the window and watched the traffic on Burnside. "I didn't know about the crimes. Only a few people were involved in those plots. I was just a kid from a Polk County logging town called Valsetz. I'd left home when the timber company that owned Valsetz drained the mill pond, bulldozed the town, and put up 'No Trespassing' signs."

Neil turned the glass in his hand, giving Vijay time to talk.

"They say you can't go back. That's really true when you're from a ghost town like Valsetz. Later, after Rajneeshpuram folded, I had nowhere to turn. So I wound up in Costa Rica, where a few of us tried to keep the good part of the Bhagwan's message alive. We learned to grow organic vegetables. Fair trade coffee, tobacco." He paused.

When the pause grew too long, Neil said, "I don't smoke, but I don't judge those who do."

Vijay opened a drawer, took out a hand-rolled cigarette, flicked a lighter, and took a quick drag. Then he slowly blew the smoke out his nostrils. "Tobacco is an unclean habit. We all make mistakes, Sergeant. But if we're smart we learn from them. That's why the Bhagwan has come back in a new, younger body."

Neil waited.

"Don't worry. I don't expect you to believe that Roger Nash is the reincarnation of the Bhagwan. If you take this job, you'll be doing the same kind of police work you've always believed in." Vijay waved his cigarette. "The new Bhagwan is in danger."

"I've seen the billboards. Who's behind them?"

Vijay lifted his shoulders. "The world is full of hate. We're not asking you to show angry souls a path to enlightenment. That's our job. We're hiring you to keep us safe in the meantime."

"That's no small task." Neil set his glass on the counter. "You've got half a dozen properties, a fleet of vehicles, and hundreds of starry-eyed followers. They're easy targets. Hiring one retired cop isn't going to make much difference."

"Really? Your niece says you are more resourceful than your record suggests." Vijay flicked his cigarette's ash into a tray. "In three weeks the Bhagwan plans to hold a revival meeting at the Moda Center. He wants to reintroduce himself to the world in front of a crowd of ten thousand."

Neil whistled.

"What would you need, Sergeant, to allow that to happen safely?"

Neil sank into the sofa. "In three weeks? My God." Was this the kind of challenge he wanted in retirement?

"Let's leave God aside for the moment." Vijay held open his hands, dangling the cigarette. "Tell me what you would need."

"People," Neil said. "I'd need an army of security people, and a place to train them."

"Done. What else?"

Neil caught his breath at the speed of this reply. He shifted his thoughts to keep up. "Equipment. Video cameras and motion detectors for the buildings. Uniforms and gear for the security force."

Vijay squinted as he exhaled cigarette smoke. "No guns, Sergeant. We've tried that before. The Bhagwan had to come back in another body to clean up the mess."

Neil nodded, considering. "Pepper spray, cell phones, and handcuffs should be enough to keep most situations under control until the police arrive."

"Good. Then we have an agreement?"

"I don't think so."

Vijay added, "We would also pay you a salary of fifteen thousand dollars."

Neil shook his head.

"The salary is monthly."

Neil stared at him. The offer was three times his police paycheck.

Vijay suddenly stubbed out his cigarette — the first sign of anger

Neil had seen from this otherwise calm man. "All right. Twenty thousand a month. With benefits and a vehicle. Take it or leave it, Sergeant."

Neil loosened his tie. Was this job for real? "First I'd like to meet my employer."

"The Bhagwan?" Vijay glanced at his watch. "He's in a meditation session right now. I suppose we could duck in."

Neil stood up, waiting. The bald man led him out the door and down the hall. As they were riding the elevator to the basement, Neil thought again about the architectural drawings he had seen in the conference room.

"Where are the new Rajneeshees planning to build?"

"That's not public yet. We're in negotiations to develop an organic farm heated with geothermal energy in Klamath County. The Bhagwan wants to announce it at the revival in three weeks."

The elevator dinged at the ground floor and continued sinking.

"Where will you get the money?"

"Donations."

"And Roger Nash controls the assets?"

"It's a partnership, the way any commune should be. There's also a nonprofit foundation with an elected board. The Bhagwan is our spiritual leader."

The elevator dinged again, and the door slid open to a concrete hallway that smelled of chlorine. An arrow pointed left *To the Pool.*

Vijay motioned for Neil to follow. "The Bhagwan is still relearning the teachings from his former life. He leads meditations sessions together with Swami Bhrater, a half-brother and disciple from India."

"In a basement swimming pool?"

Vijay paused at a windowed door. "Lacking a security force, we thought it best to hold group sessions in a basement bunker."

Through the window Neil noticed that everyone in the room had their eyes closed. A dozen people on paddleboards were kicking up spray in the pool. Others sat cross-legged on mats around the pool's edge. Atop two lifeguard chairs were an elderly Indian man in a red robe and a young man with a short black beard, cutoff blue jeans, and a red T-shirt.

"Don't speak until you are spoken to," Vijay whispered. He turned the handle, slipped into the room with Neil, and closed the door behind them.

"All right, stop kicking," the old Indian swami said, his eyes still closed. "What do you feel?"

"Waves?" a woman in the pool ventured. To Neil's surprise, it was his niece Harmony. She looked dangerously attractive in a one-piece suit.

"Exactly," the long-bearded Indian man said. "The turbulence is like the emotions churning on the surface of your souls: love, hate, greed, envy. If all you can see is the surface, these things seem over-powering."

"Wait! I remember." The younger man on a lifeguard chair held out a hand, as if he were feeling for an invisible glass sphere before him. "Slow yourselves with cleansing breaths. In by your nose. Hold —"

The room stilled as everyone held their breaths. Roger Nash seemed to suspend them there for longer than Neil thought possible.

"Slowly, out your mouth."

The room exhaled, a long, happy sigh. Rog smiled, his wide lips stretching the stubble of his short black beard.

The swami beside him nodded. "To calm the ripples is to take a first step toward enlightenment. The master does not rise above the turmoil of emotions, but rather sinks beneath them. He is as still and as powerful as the center of the sea."

Roger added, "The Chinese sage Lao Tzu called that center of power the Uncarved Block. The key is *wu-wei*, inactivity. Only the master who trusts this simplicity can transcend the evils of the world."

"It is so." The old swami smiled.

At this point Rog wrinkled his brow. He opened his eyes and turned his head toward Neil. "Hello?"

Around the pool, eyes began to open. Harmony exclaimed, "Uncle Neil!"

Vijay bowed his head slightly. "Forgive us, master. This is Sergeant Ferguson. He is considering the security position we discussed."

"Your family is full of sannyasins, Sergeant. But you are not among them." Roger paused. "I wonder if you know what a sannyasin is?"

"Not exactly."

"A sannyasin is a seeker who renounces the material world on the path to enlightenment."

"I'm a policeman, Mr. Nash. My job is all about dealing with the material world."

Rog nodded. "As a policeman, do you agree with my staff? They say I am in danger."

"Yes, I do."

"Swami Bhrater says I need to relearn the skills of a master. Could you teach me to catch a bullet with my bare hand?"

"Sure," Neil said. "Catching bullets is easy. It just makes an awful mess."

For a moment the room was quiet. Then the old swami started chuckling.

Rog gave a thumbs-up. "Hire him, Vijay."

The operations manager gave another bow and began to withdraw with Neil.

Before they reached the door the young Bhagwan added, "And make sure he has a driver."

Vijay led Neil out of the room. When they were back in the echoing concrete hallway Vijay asked, "Do you really need a driver?"

Neil rubbed his eyes. "Maybe. I've been in a couple of ugly car chases. I'm still coping with some post-traumatic stress." Neil's patrol partner had died in one of the wrecks. In the other, Connie Wu had been thrown off a hood at forty miles an hour. How had Rog known he would need a driver?

Vijay led Neil up a staircase to the parking lot. He pulled out his cell phone, but his finger hesitated. "I can have a driver and a contract ready in twenty minutes. But first I need to know whether you're with us or not."

Neil drew in a long breath. There was something wrong here — he had sensed it from the first. But there was also a lot that was innocent and good about these people. Roger Nash might be a gullible kid, but he really was in danger. Even Harmony was at risk.

Neil studied the two rows of red Priuses, thinking. Beside them was a black Rolls Royce with a scratched windshield. A vandal had etched a large circle in the glass, perhaps with a diamond ring. But this wasn't ordinary graffiti. The vandal had added a cross through the middle.

A gunsight.

Neil exhaled slowly, imagining the young Roger Nash, or Harmony, behind those crosshairs.

"Yeah. I'm in."

Chapter 3

Neil's driver was a large young black man named James Buckley. "But everyone calls me Bear," he said.

Neil had spent an exhausting afternoon in a makeshift office at the Jupiter Hotel, ordering security cameras, uniforms, metal scanners, and a bulletproof glass retrofit for a Rolls Royce. He was tired, but he couldn't help taking a second look at Mr. Buckley across the car's red hood. The young man's shaved head and silver earring looked tough, but the lack of tattoos and the round shoulders didn't.

"Was that a name you chose?"

Bear shrugged. "In Portland, people think a guy like me must be into either football or street gangs. At least a bear is different." He opened the driver's door and got in.

When Neil took a seat on the passenger side and saw Bear behind the steering wheel, he realized that he had seen him before. "Wait a minute. You're a Radio Cab driver — the guy who's collecting material for a novel."

Bear grinned. "And you're the cop who hates to drive. Where to? The Park Blocks?"

Neil laughed. The cab driver remembered the location of his downtown apartment. "Home, James."

"Call me Bear, really." The Prius hummed as he pulled out into Burnside traffic.

"Then call me Neil." He held out his hand.

Bear shook his hand without taking his eyes off the road. "Big decision, switching jobs at your age."

"How about you? Have you always been a student of Indian philosophy?"

Bear grunted. "I grew up in the Albina ghetto. My parents were refugees from Vanport."

Neil knew the story of Vanport, a vast housing project built at the confluence of the Columbia and Willamette Rivers during World War II. The city had once housed tens of thousands of shipyard workers, many of them black men from back East. When the town's dikes failed in a 1949 flood, every single building had floated away.

"A ghost town," Neil mused. "Like Rajneeshpuram."

"Back in the day, refugees from Vanport were about as welcome in Portland's white bread neighborhoods as Rajneeshees."

As they crossed the Burnside Bridge the lights of downtown's skyscrapers shone dimly through the haze of dusk.

"Is that why you sided with the Rajneeshees?"

Bear shook his head. "Between shifts I'd go for coffee at that shop on Killingsworth. It's a few blocks from where I grew up. Nash himself still works there one day a week."

"He's still a barista?" Neil made a mental note to increase security at the coffee shop.

"One day I had an hour to kill, so I dumped a 300-piece jigsaw puzzle onto a table. Just then Nash brings me my mocha. He picks up a piece, sets it in the middle of the table, and says, "This is where this piece goes."

As they drove Burnside into Old Town, clusters of homeless men shuffled on the sidewalks, waiting for a soup kitchen to open.

"Was he right?" Neil asked.

"Of course he was right. The first piece is always right. No matter where you put it, the others will all fit around it."

Neil frowned. He should have seen that coming.

"So I just laughed at him. Then I handed him a second piece and bet him he couldn't place it correctly too."

"What did he say?"

"He said, 'I'll take that bet.'"

Neil considered this. "He'd probably seen the puzzle put together before."

"Maybe, but still. I mean, the guy bet he could place every single piece I gave him, one at a time, in the correct position. He said if he couldn't do it in five minutes, he'd pay me a dollar for each piece that was out of place."

"And if he won the bet?"

Bear shrugged. "I'd have to consider joining the new Rajneeshees."

They stopped at a red light while a streetcar clanged across on Eleventh, scrolling the billboard of a Bhagwan in crosshairs.

"You probably think Bigfoot is more likely to show up in a coffee shop than a reincarnated guru."

Neil said nothing.

Bear turned the wheel, following the streetcar toward the Park Blocks. "Well, I've always believed in Bigfoot too. And Rog — sure, he's a barista. But somehow he's able to see the bigger picture. He even knows where a cab driver fits in."

That night Neil dreamed he had returned to the street where he had grown up, but the town was deserted. Tumbleweeds blew through sandy gaps between empty houses of weathered gray boards. What had happened to the people? Once he had played kickball with a crowd of kids in this street. When he looked more closely, he saw that each doorstep had a puzzle piece. He circled his old neighborhood, collecting jigsaw pieces from the ghost town. When he finally stopped in front of his ruined grade school, he fit them all together on the sidewalk. As soon as he saw the bigger picture — a white dove — a wind began whistling down the streets. The town stirred with an ancient, ghostly life. And he could hear the shuffling steps of the dead children, slowly climbing the basement stairs from a hundred derelict homes.

Neil woke up bathed in sweat. He had overslept the chance for his usual morning bike ride. Instead he took a hot shower, wolfed a pint of blueberry yogurt, and put on a sport coat that hid his service semi-automatic. By the time he took the elevator down to street level, the red Prius was already waiting at the curb.

"Police headquarters, boss?" Bear asked.

Neil nodded. "It's quitting time."

It only took five minutes to drive to the glass-and-stone justice tower that housed the Portland Police Bureau. Bear slowed in front of the Art Deco eagle sculpture that perched above the main entrance.

Neil waved him on toward a ramp that tunneled into the side of the building.

"Roll down your window," Neil said. He leaned across the steering wheel and held up his badge toward a scanner. A steel grate slid open before them.

After Bear had parked in the basement, he took out a paperback to read.

"Would you mind coming along?" Neil asked.

"What? You need backup to quit your job?"

Neil shrugged. He had always wanted to tell off his boss, but suddenly he didn't want to do it entirely alone.

"Maybe you should bring me in handcuffs," Bear suggested. "It would look more natural."

They rode the elevator to the lobby. There Neil got a guest pass from Ranah, his favorite receptionist. She always wore the same bright red lipstick and the same red dot on her forehead, but she had a different color sari for every day of the week. For the first time, he wondered if she were involved with the Rajneeshees too.

He asked, "Do you know if Captain Dickers is busy this morning?"

"I think he's in a meeting."

"With who?"

"Not with who." Ranah smiled. "With Wu."

It was an old joke in the department. "You might warn the lieutenant that I'm on my way to interrupt. This is my last day with the bureau."

"Seriously?"

"Seriously."

"Well, good luck. Don't be a stranger, Ferguson."

Neil clipped the guest tag on Bear's shirt pocket and led him back to the elevators. They got out on the fourteenth floor and walked together down the homicide hall.

Neil tapped on the frosted glass of Dickers' door and pushed it open.

The captain stood up from the desk where he had been talking with Connie Wu. "Sergeant? I'm in a meeting."

"Sorry, Captain. I've come to say goodbye. You moved up the date for early retirement, and I've decided to accept."

Dickers looked to Connie. "Did you know about this?"

"A little."

The captain examined the big black man standing beside Neil. "And who is this?"

Bear swiveled his hands before him, as if to turn an imaginary steering wheel. "I'm his new driver."

Neil added, "I've taken a security job for the Rajneeshees."

"The religious cult?"

Bear objected, "It's not a cult. It's not even a religion."

Dickers ignored him. "I've been disappointed in you before, Ferguson, but this time you've outdone yourself. The Rajneeshees were sent to jail for their crimes. They tried to kill people. Are you really going to work for the other side?"

Neil laid his badge and his service Glock on the desk. "We're supposed to be on the same side, keeping people safe. Instead of solving murders after they happen, I've decided to solve them ahead of time."

Dickers waved Connie toward the door. "Get him out of here, Lieutenant."

"Gladly, sir." Connie steered Neil out into the hall along with Bear.

As soon as the door closed behind them she kissed Neil on the cheek. "You were great."

"I had a few more things I wanted to say."

"That's OK. We haven't had a homicide in Portland this week, and I'd like to keep it that way." She tugged his sleeve toward her own office. "Come on, let's get started."

"On what?" For a moment Neil envisioned a more passionate kiss.

"Preventing murders. We've got resources here that the Rajneeshees don't." She opened her door and paused. "Does your bodyguard have a name?"

"Yes, but —"

Bear cut him short. "Everyone calls me Bear."

"Pleased to meet you, Bear." She led them inside and closed the door. "Everyone calls me Lieutenant. But when I'm alone with Neil, my name's Connie."

Bear raised an eyebrow to Neil. "You're an item with your boss?"

Neil tipped his hand from side to side. "Not exactly. Retirement seems to have been a good move, though."

Connie briefly put her tongue in the corner of her mouth — a gesture Neil found so surprisingly provocative that his heart sped. Connie was in her fifties, barely five foot two in pumps, but since her accident her shiny black hair had grown out into a fetching page boy. The matching belt of her slacks pulled wonderfully tight, puckering her blouse out in the right places. Four years had passed since Neil's wife had died of cancer. Maybe he really had lived alone too long.

Connie sat in a swivel chair at a computer. "The first step in security is to identify your enemies. I've seen the anti-Rajneeshee ads."

Neil nodded. "Yesterday I found a gunsight pattern scratched into the windshield of the new Bhagwan's Rolls Royce."

"A warning closer to home."

"More likely punks inspired by the ads."

Connie began typing on her computer keyboard. "Last night I spent a few hours following the money behind the ads. Look where it led." She tapped Enter, switching the screen to a Tri-Met advertising invoice.

Neil leaned closer. "NovoCity Finance? But they're —"

"Don't jump to conclusions."

Bear cleared his throat. "I'm just a driver, but what conclusion should we not be jumping to?"

Neil exchanged a glance with Connie. If Bear was going to be his driver, he couldn't be left entirely in the dark. "NovoCity is an investment consortium. They could be channeling money for anyone. But some of their clients have ties to Eastern Europe."

"The Russian mafia?"

"The ads seem xenophobic," Neil pointed out. "Immigrants don't complain about immigration."

"Actually, they do," Connie said. "My mother was first-generation Chinese in Hawaii, and she was as racist as they come."

Bear nodded. "Californians who move to Oregon complain the loudest about other Californians moving here."

"All right, we can't rule anything out. But I've got a feeling the ads are coming from somewhere else. Remember who fought the Rajneeshees the last time, in the 1980s?"

Bear shook his head. "That was before my time."

"Conservatives. Fundamentalist Christians. People with political connections."

Connie leaned back, thinking. "There was also an environmental group that opposed the Rajneeshees. The 1000 Friends of Oregon."

"Right. They used land-use laws to stop the Bhagwan's development projects in Eastern Oregon. You're not supposed to build cities on rural farms."

"That shouldn't be a problem this time," Connie said. "The new guru seems be sticking to Portland."

"This is still supposed to be secret, but Nash is planning to build a big organic farming commune in Klamath County. He wants to announce it at the revival meeting in the Moda Center in three weeks, in front of a crowd of ten thousand."

Bear's eyes widened. Connie tapped the desk with her finger, like a ticking clock. "Three weeks? Then we don't have time to look for all of Nash's enemies. You've got to build a bulletproof wall around him. You'll have to turn the Moda Center into a fortress."

"I'm working on it. I'm already armoring his Rolls Royce and setting up a security perimeter around the hotel. In three weeks I'll have trained a staff of thirty guards with TVA scanners. You won't even be able to smuggle a pin into the Moda Center."

Connie leaned back. "You're good, Neil. I'm going to miss your work here in the bureau. But you're leaving a gap in the guru's armor."

"What's that?"

"His parents."

Neil paused. With all the talk of reincarnation, he really had overlooked the fact that Roger Nash must have biological parents. Even if Roger himself were unassailable, his parents might be targets.

"Where do his parents live?"

Connie pulled up a new screen of information. "Catherine and John Nash have a two-bedroom house in Hillsdale. She's a housewife. He's the service manager of a Ford dealership by the freeway. They're both active in the local Baptist church."

"White bread," Bear said. "Do they know what's gotten into their son?"

"Hard to say. They don't seem to have talked to the media."

Neil ran a hand over his jaw. "I should have checked this out. I suppose you looked into Roger's files too?"

"Not much there," Connie admitted, scrolling through screens. "A bachelor's degree in world lit from Portland State. A driver's license but no car. A marijuana violation that would be legal now."

"Birth certificate?" Neil asked.

"Not in the system. It was a home birth, in the same house in Hillsdale. The *Oregonian* published an announcement, listing the date and time."

"I need to talk to these people. Their security is part of my job now too."

"I bet they won't talk to just anyone." Connie handed him the phone from her desk. "But they'll take a call from the police."

Neil took the phone and punched in the number on Connie's screen. Sure enough, the frightened woman who answered obviously had caller ID. She immediately wanted to know why she was getting a call from the Portland Police Bureau.

"I'm Sergeant Neil Ferguson. I've just retired from the bureau to oversee the security of your son Roger."

"You're not with the police?"

"Not anymore. I've taken a job as a private security consultant."

"You're working for *them?*"

"My job is to keep your son safe. I think it would help if I could come talk to you in person."

"Oh! The house is a mess. And John's at work."

"Please, Mrs. Nash. I'm worried about your safety as well as your son's."

A silence followed. "Do you know the way?"

Neil glanced at the screen. "21605 Parker Lane. I can be there in an hour."

"All right."

Neil hung up and looked to Bear. "Do you know the way?"

"I'm a cab driver, man."

Neil put his hand on Connie's shoulder. "Thanks. I owe you dinner and a movie."

She wrinkled her nose. "They're only playing thrillers at the Baghdad Theater this week. Let's download something and watch it at my house."

"Deal." This was the home invitation he had wanted months ago. "Just give me a few days to get things sorted out. I'll call, OK?"

"I'm supposed to wait for your call?" She looked at him skeptically. "Maybe I was better off as your boss."

Chapter 4

The Nash home was an eaveless two-story box from the 1950s in the unfashionable lower end of southwest Portland's Hillsdale district. The street had no sidewalks. The lawn, however, had been groomed as neatly as a golf green, and a shiny aluminum Airstream trailer sat in the driveway.

"Wait in the car," Neil said.

Bear nodded. "This is out of my hood." He took out a paperback novel.

As Neil walked toward the house he noticed a face behind a curtain in the front window. He rang the doorbell. A moment later the door opened a crack.

"Mrs. Nash? I'm Neil Ferguson."

"How can I be sure you're really from the police?"

"I'm not. I turned in my badge this morning."

A gray eye squinted past him at the car.

"Yes, the Rajneeshees issue red Priuses to their staff. But I'm not a Rajneeshee either."

"You're not?"

"No. They hired me because I've been a police officer for thirty-five years. I know how to protect people. Could we continue this conversation inside?"

A small chain rattled and the door opened, revealing a frail woman in a knee-length blue dress. With permed gray hair and thin lips, she reminded Neil of the kind of grade school teacher he used to fear. He knew at once he would not be calling her Catherine.

She held a pale hand to a string of what looked like plastic pearls at her throat. "Forgive me, but my husband says we can't be too cautious."

"I could come back when he's home."

"No, that wouldn't work either." She wrinkled her brow. "Would you like some coffee?"

"Yes, thank you."

"Then take a seat in the living room. I'll be right back."

The living room could have been clipped from a 1960 *Sunset* magazine, with teal sofas and glass end tables. Despite what she had said about the house being a mess, it had obviously been immaculate for decades.

Neil made a show of heading for the sofa, but as soon as Mrs. Nash left the room he veered to the fireplace mantel. The framed photographs on the mantel revealed that the Nash ancestors had been stern white pioneers, that Catherine and John had been married at an altar flanked by bridesmaids in shiny green dresses, and that the happy couple had raised a single child — a boy who got a dump truck for Christmas, joined Cub Scouts, and won a soccer trophy amid smiling teammates. The most recent photograph showed a sullen preteen boy staring straight into the camera while his father proudly knelt with a rifle beside a dead four-point buck.

Neil quickly sat down when he heard Mrs. Nash returning from the kitchen.

"Here we are. Fresh coffee." She set a tray with two porcelain cups on the glass table.

Neil took a sip and nearly winced. The bitter, acidic brew had evidently come from an ancient can labeled "Folger's," or possibly even "Sanka." Certainly it was nothing like the coffee drinks served at the Killingsworth shop.

"Mrs. Nash," Neil ventured, "Do you have much contact with your son Roger?"

She scoffed. "He hasn't called for days. You'd think it would kill the boy to pick up a phone and talk to his own mother."

"Does he come to visit?"

"At Christmas and Easter. Each time with a different girl. Some of them seem like nice young women, too. But he never sticks with them.

How are we supposed to become grandparents if he's not willing to make some kind of commitment?"

Neil pretended to sip his coffee. He wondered if she was talking about the same Roger Nash he had seen only yesterday, meditating beside a swami at an underground pool.

"Perhaps Roger hasn't told you much about his new role. About his plans?"

"Oh, we know what they're trying to do to him." She drew in a long slow breath and let it out through her nose — the opposite of the breathing technique Roger had demonstrated.

Neil sensed that she was building anger, rather than releasing it. "I take it you don't like the Rajneeshees."

Her eyes flashed. "They're trying to steal my son. They've been confusing him with lies and fancy cars. What they claim about being born again is wrong. Anyone can see that."

"To tell you the truth, Mrs. Nash, I don't believe in reincarnation either."

"Well there you go." She clunked her cup down on the table. "Just because a child is born at a certain time in a certain city doesn't mean his soul is up for grabs. I've read up on this. Even the Buddhists and the Hindus say it doesn't work that way. They believe a dying person's soul transfers at the moment of conception. The baby is born nine months later. But the Bhagwan Rajneesh said his soul couldn't wait. He said when he died they were supposed to leave his corpse sitting cross-legged in a yoga position. He said his body would keel over three days later, and his soul would instantly reappear on the other side of the Earth in a baby being born."

Neil raised an eyebrow, impressed by her research.

"To be reincarnated like that," Mrs. Nash continued, raising a finger like a gun, "the Bhagwan would have to *push out* another living soul. He'd have to kill an innocent baby's soul and take over its body. Well, that's not the way God works. That's worse than abortion. If the Bhagwan made mistakes in his life — and he certainly did, poisoning people — then his soul doesn't come back as a baby. It goes to Hell and rots there!"

Her final words had been spoken so violently that Neil held his cup on the glass table, afraid the coffee might spill. One thing had become clear to him: Catherine Nash was not likely to be threatened by the enemies of the Rajneeshees. Instead they might hail her as an avenging hero. What he didn't understand was how Roger could have grown up in a home like this.

"Mrs. Nash," he asked at length. "Do you have a scrapbook that could tell me something about Roger's formative years?"

A cloud passed from her face, replaced by a smile. Neil had known grade school teachers like this, dangerously shorting bulbs who flickered from darkness to light.

"Come, I'll show you." She left her cup on the tray and led the way down a hall to a bedroom decorated entirely in pale blue. She withdrew a skeleton key from a pocket in her dress, unlocked a door opposite the four-poster bed, turned on a light, and held out her hand.

"This is where I keep the best memories."

Neil opened the door to a windowless room that might once have been a walk-in closet. Now it housed a rocking chair on a spiral rug, surrounded on all four sides by shelves and displays. Strings of white Christmas lights illuminated baby shoes, worn-out stuffed animals, ABC books, and snapshots of a beaming baby. This was not merely a collection of memories, it was a shrine.

Neil chose his words carefully. "You had only one child?"

"I couldn't have any more after Roger. He was our miracle." She picked up a brightly colored cardboard cone from a shelf. "This was the hat he wore for his first birthday." Gently she replaced the hat beside a ribbon, an invitation, and a half-burned birthday cake candle.

"Why did you name him Roger?"

She seemed momentarily confused. "For Roger Maris, I think. My husband is a fan of Yankee baseball."

Neil noticed that the largest shelf had a Bible, a cross, and crayon drawings of stick figures with lollipop flowers beneath a rayed yellow sun.

"You gave him a Christian upbringing."

"Roger attended Sunday school every week. He won prizes for memorizing Bible verses. Such a well behaved boy."

Her smile dimmed, and Neil could almost see the cloud returning.

"But then something changed?" Neil suggested.

"We didn't notice it for years." She bit her lip. "Early on, my sister Patricia would babysit him on Saturdays so John and I would be free to do our missionary work with the church. We volunteered in food kitchens or carried signs in front of abortion clinics. Patricia was healthier then, and she didn't have children of her own, so it seemed the charitable thing to do — you know, to share your good fortune."

Mrs. Nash sighed. "Patricia must have been influencing him. When Roger turned eleven he suddenly announced that he wasn't going on hunting trips with John. The next year he stopped going to Sunday school. Then he said he was a vegetarian. I had to change everything I cooked. Sometimes I'd slip hamburger into a casserole, but he always noticed and claimed it made him sick. By then, of course, Patricia was so obviously ill that we no longer allowed him to see her."

"Is your sister still alive?"

"Physically. She's in an assisted care facility for the feeble minded. But she had already done her damage. When Roger enrolled at PSU he stopped reading the Bible and started studying foreign texts. The Talmud. The Koran. By the time the Rajneeshees showed up with their Rolls Royces and their lies, he was ripe for the plucking."

Neil was starting to see the bigger picture. Roger had rebelled against his strict Baptist parents, perhaps with the help of a lenient aunt, but had remained curious about religion and philosophy. The apple didn't fall far from the tree after all. What Neil wanted to find was a birth certificate, to verify dates and times. He didn't see one in the displays, and he felt odd asking outright.

"I'm interested that you chose a home birth," Neil said, edging toward the subject.

"John doesn't trust doctors."

"Do you have any records or mementoes, you know, from —" Neil stopped, having talked himself into a corner.

"Actually, there is something. And it doesn't belong in this room." She sized him up. "You're not a cop, and you're not a Rajneeshee. You say your goal is to protect my son."

"Yes."

"Will you swear to that? That you'll protect him, come what may?"

Neil hesitated. An oath to a mother was not to be taken lightly — especially to a mother as devoted as Mrs. Nash. "Yes. I can swear that."

She knelt by the rocking chair, lifted a corner of the rug, and picked up a small silver key. "A week after Roger was born we had a baby shower for him. I know what you're thinking: showers are usually held before the birth. I wasn't feeling well then, so we put it off. Anyway, there were playsuits and all the usual things. But one strange gift appeared anonymously."

Mrs. Nash unlocked a pink drawer beneath a shelf. She opened it to reveal a set of small silver spoons, a cup shaped like a bunny, and a small wooden box. The box was about the size of a bar of soap.

"A box? What's in it?" Neil asked.

"I don't know." She lifted the small wooden case between her thumb and forefinger as if it were a dead animal. "It came with a note that said it was to be opened only by Roger."

Neil leaned over for a closer look. Intricate black markings covered the dark wood — stars, intertwining leaves, and perhaps a line of script in foreign characters. The back of the box had two small brass hinges. The clasp at the front, however, was completely covered by a circle of red sealing wax.

Imprinted into the wax was the outline of two overlapping doves — the old Bhagwan's symbol.

Neil pulled back, his mouth suddenly dry. What had the Rajneeshee operations manager said? Something about a box that had been missing since the old Bhagwan's death. A case that was said to hold the key to the master's authority.

"You've never opened it?" Neil asked.

"Mr. Ferguson." She put her free hand on her hip. "I sometimes receive mail addressed to my son. Most of the mail is junk — applications for credit cards and the like. Occasionally I save such letters. Sometimes I throw them away. But I would never, ever, open them."

She gave the box a shake. It did not rattle. "I should have thrown this thing away long ago."

"It could contain something valuable."

"More likely junk mail." She held it out to him. "Go on, take it."

"Me?"

"I don't want it anymore. Didn't you swear that your job is to protect my son?"

"Yes."

"Then take it. Give it to him or throw it away. I don't care which. Just get it out of my house."

She pushed the box into his hands. Then she glanced out the door to the bedroom beyond. "My husband will be home soon. You need to leave."

"Why?"

"John would not be pleased to see a Rajneeshee car out front." She smiled, but pointed her finger directly between Neil's eyes. "He's actually a very good shot."

Chapter 5

For the next two weeks Neil kept trying, and failing, to meet with Roger Nash to discuss the mysterious wooden box he had received from Roger's mother. Neil had to admit that the delay was partly his own fault. Preparations for the upcoming Rajneesh Revival had kept Neil scrambling twelve hours a day, training security staff and overseeing contractors. At the same time, his new security procedures had isolated Roger Nash, shielding the young Bhagwan behind staff, schedules, and locked doors. Neil had always planned to hand over the box unopened. It belonged to Roger. But it wasn't the sort of thing you could simply leave in a manila envelope outside his hotel door.

And so the box with the Bhagwan's seal languished in the bedside drawer of Neil's apartment, where Neil's troubled dreams x-rayed it by night. Once he dreamed that it contained the Red Moon of India, the legendary ruby that had stymied Queen Victoria's armies. Another night it held a tiny scroll, handwritten by the Buddha himself, with the secret to eternal life. At other times it contained a key to an even smaller missing box, or to a bottomless Swiss bank account.

What disturbed Neil most was how the box could have turned up in Hillsdale at all. John and Catherine Nash were conservative Baptists with no interest in Eastern religions. And yet an Indian guru had predicted that his spirit would reappear in Portland at the precise minute their child was born. The parents had named him Roger — apparently unaware that Rog Nash sounds like Rajneesh — and the Bhagwan's case had appeared at a baby shower within a week. In Neil's experience, there is no such thing as magic, only coincidence and deception. In this instance, however, the magician was a dead man half a world away.

The most obvious clue was the box itself. Were the markings on it significant or merely decorative? At first glance, the case looked like the sort of trinket you might find at an import store. One night when Neil was unable to sleep he put a sheet of paper over the box and made a graphite rubbing with the side of a pencil tip. The box's decorations were thick enough that the rubbing produced a fair copy. He checked the Internet and discovered that the squiggles on the lid were almost certainly Sanskrit, the predecessor of modern Hindi.

Who could Neil trust to translate the box's text? Ranah, the receptionist at police headquarters, might be able to read Hindi, but probably not Sanskrit. Neil's brother Mark was no scholar, but he had studied Sanskrit at Rajneeshpuram. Mark and his wife Melanie were coming from Eugene in a few days to visit Harmony. They had invited him to lunch at the Jupiter Hotel's café, the Reborn Zorba Grill. Neil decided to bring a copy of the text to see what his brother could make of it.

Mark was loud, as always. "Nirvana stir fry! Zorba kept the old menu." His garish, tie-dyed sweatshirt stretched over a paunch, but then he had never bothered to exercise as much as Neil. And although Neil's hair was merely streaked with gray, Mark's was completely white. Together with his neatly trimmed beard, it made him look like a large white elf.

"The Kombucha is new. Nice." Mark folded his menu and handed it to a red-aproned waiter. "Nirvana. Kombucha. *Capisce?*"

Melanie, Neil's sister-in-law, looked up at the waiter through long, slow eyelashes that were either fake or loaded with mascara — Neil had never been able to determine which. "The same for me, please." She wore a loose paisley dress that had been sewn in puckers near the top so it poofed out and draped from the bustline, making it difficult to determine whether she too had put on a little weight. Both Mark and Melanie wore strings of large wooden prayer beads.

"So, little bro," Mark said, leaning back. "You're finally on the path to enlightenment?"

"I'm just trying to keep everyone safe."

Mark laughed as if this were hilarious. When he calmed down he wiped his eyes and turned to Harmony. "Sweetcakes, you are so lucky, getting in at the start."

"What do you mean?" Perhaps to counter her parents' flamboyant nostalgia, Harmony had dressed more like a football fan than a flower child. She had tied her blonde hair into a long ponytail that hung out the back of a pink baseball cap. Her jeans and pink T-shirt would have been unremarkable, except that everything looked remarkable on Harmony.

"Just look around," Mark said, opening his large, callused hands to the crowd in the café. "People are here from all over the world, excited, talking, eager to work together on a common project. It's like the kibbutz farms in the early days of Israel. We felt that same spirit when we were building Rajneeshpuram out of the desert sand."

Melanie added, more cautiously, "It was a wonderful place, at first." She hesitated, and then whispered, "I hear the Rajneeshees are planning another farm east of the Cascades. Do you really think that's wise?"

"Don't worry, Mom. This time they've worked everything out."

"But what about the land-use laws?" Melanie objected. "You're not allowed to have thousands of people living on a ranch."

Harmony tipped her head toward a table by the window, wagging her ponytail. "See those people with the turquoise jewelry? They're elders from the Modoc tribe. They're here to sign a treaty. We'll announce it at the revival next week. We've agreed to build them a casino at Fort Klamath, just outside of Crater Lake National Park. In exchange they'll let us develop a farm on tribal land."

Neil caught his breath at the genius of the plan. "An Indian reservation is a sovereign nation. Oregon's land-use laws wouldn't apply."

Harmony nodded. "We're planning meditation centers, dormitories, and everything. Because it's near a volcano there's hot springs, so the whole complex can be heated geothermally."

"I saw some drawings of large glass buildings," Neil said.

"Greenhouses for the organic farm. With natural steam heat, we'll even be able to grow bananas."

The waiter arrived with their lunches. Neil had ordered a garden burger, the closest thing to meat on the menu. Harmony had a rice bowl with avocados. For a while they ate.

At length Mark pushed back his plate and said, "So, sweetcakes, what's this I hear about you rising to a position of authority?"

Harmony lowered her hands, palms down, as if to contain her father's booming voice. "So far I'm just doing public relations. Some media interviews, a few tours."

"You're a Twinkie?"

"I am not!"

Neil asked, "What's a Twinkie?"

Melanie explained, "It's what we called the cute girls who gave tours at Rajneeshpuram. You know, because they were like Hostess desserts?"

Harmony blushed. "Public relations is important. Roger says he wants me on stage for the revival."

Mark studied his daughter. "The reborn Bhagwan seems to have taken a personal interest."

Harmony avoided his gaze. "Roger says I have people skills."

"Is Roger like the previous Bhagwan, an advocate of free love?"

"Papa!" Harmony glared at him, red-faced. She bit out the words, "I. Am. Thirty. One. Years. Old."

Unfazed, Mark took a toothpick from a dispenser on the table. "Did your mother and I ever tell you why we left Rajneeshpuram?"

"No."

Neil had heard the story indirectly, but he was curious to hear Mark's version. He was also worried about Harmony. Her embarrassment suggested that she had in fact been tempted to become personally involved with Roger Nash. This struck Neil as reckless for many reasons. He recalled Nash's own mother saying that the man was unable to commit to long-term relationships.

Mark cleaned his teeth for a moment. Then he sucked the toothpick. "In his previous reincarnation, the Bhagwan achieved popularity by noting that love is a healthy outlet for human emotion. I found that doctrine refreshingly attractive. But he also disliked marriage and children. He told his sannyasins to use contraception and, if necessary, abortion. Two months after I met your mother at Rajneeshpuram, we realized she was pregnant. When we announced that we wanted to be married, we were encouraged to leave."

Mark pointed his toothpick at Harmony. "And that is why you were born."

Harmony stared into the remains of her rice bowl. "Roger is a holy man."

"He is still a man."

Melanie added, "Love is never completely free, honey. It can also be used for power and greed. Rajneeshpuram started out as a beautiful thing."

"Could we change the subject?" Harmony suggested.

Mark waved his toothpick like a miniature baton. "I'd like to know what's become of Gilberto, that physicist you met in Europe. He knew how to make killer desserts."

"Papa! I asked if we could change the subject."

Melanie really did change the subject. "Did you notice that we've brought our old prayer beads? We haven't worn them since Rajneeshpuram. We kept them as reminders of the Bhagwan's teachings. Yesterday we decided they belong here, with the revival."

Mark took the string from around his neck. "One of the beads opens up. It's got a little picture of the Bhagwan inside. Sort of a charm. It's supposed to keep you safe. Here, try it."

Mark draped the necklace over his daughter's baseball cap onto her shoulders. She protested only lightly.

Melanie took off her own necklace and opened the final bead. "Mine has more than just a picture of the Bhagwan. I've also got one of his long white hairs."

Neil could see a tight white spiral taped opposite the Bhagwan's face.

"It was hard to get," Melanie admitted. "For security reasons, you know. Shree rarely let people close to him."

Harmony gave her a wry smile. "But some people managed to get close?"

"Well — yes." Now it was her mother's turn to blush. Then she suddenly handed the necklace to Neil. "Here, I think you should have this."

It was the second time a mother had impulsively handed him an artifact from the old Bhagwan, and it left him nonplussed. "Me?"

"For your security work," Melanie explained. "It's supposed to keep you safe."

"Are you sure?"

She pressed it into his hand.

Harmony obviously didn't mind wearing a string of prayer beads, but Neil felt self-conscious enough that he slipped the necklace into the pocket of his sport coat. As he did, he discovered the scrap of paper that he had brought along.

"That reminds me. There's something I wanted to ask."

Neil's relatives looked up at him. He took out the piece of paper with the lettering from the Bhagwan's box and laid it on the table. "Can any of you translate this?"

Mark leaned forward. "Where did you find it?"

Neil had expected the question, and had prepared an evasion. "I'm trying to learn more about my new employers. I found an old text and made a copy, figuring I had to start somewhere."

"Well, it's definitely Sanskrit." Mark took a pair of reading glasses from the pocket of his sweatshirt. "I can sound out the letters, but it's been too long since I studied the language."

Harmony reached for the paper. "I know who can read it."

Neil pinned the paper to the tabletop with a finger. "That's OK. It's not important."

"No problem." Harmony shrugged with one shoulder. She took out her cell phone and touched a few buttons. Neil assumed she was making a call, but to his surprise the phone made the clicking sound of a camera shutter. "There. I'll ask Swami Bhrater."

Neil quickly put the paper in his pocket. He was sorry he had brought it at all. Now he couldn't ask Harmony to erase the photo without raising even more suspicion.

At that moment a waiter came up to the table with a padded black folder. "Are we paying all together here today?"

Neil took out his wallet, suspecting he would end up paying for everything.

Six days later Neil lay in bed, unable to sleep. His head was buzzing with last-minute worries about the Rajneesh Revival. What did it mean that the anti-Rajneeshee ads had stopped? Did he have enough security guards to handle the crowds at each entrance? He had reduced the number of staffers from thirty to twenty-four when background checks revealed that six of them lacked proper immigration documents. Connie had promised that the police would be on call, but because it was a private event, they wouldn't be on site.

Neil rolled over in bed, trying to get comfortable. Then he noticed, in the dim glow from the window, that the drawer of his bedside table was completely closed. He always left it half an inch ajar.

A bedside drawer is the first place thieves look for money and guns. Sloppy thieves leave the drawer open after they are done. Careful ones close it all the way. To tell the difference, Neil left his drawer open a crack.

He sat up quickly, turned on the bedside lamp, and opened the drawer.

Melanie's prayer beads were still there. And so was the photo of his late wife, Rebecca.

But the case of the reborn Bhagwan was gone.

Chapter 6

Neil's first impulse was to call his colleagues at the Portland Police Bureau to report the robbery. The box might have contained a jewel worth a fortune. But then he thought: *former* colleagues. Even Connie would ask questions he couldn't answer. How had this wooden box arrived in Portland from India? Why had it been in Neil's bedside table? And why did his apartment have no other evidence of a break-in?

Neil slept fitfully that night. In the morning he brewed a big Brazilian latte — a bombshell of cinnamon and caffeine — to clear his thoughts. He came up with two scenarios, both of them disturbing:

1. The thief was a professional, hired for the job.
2. The thief had a key.

The only person with a key to Neil's apartment, other than himself, was his daughter Susan. He trusted Susan a lot. But the alternative was that the Rajneeshees had hired a thief to rob their own chief of security.

Another, even more disturbing possibility presented itself later that morning, after Neil was summoned to his first one-on-one meeting with Roger Nash: What if there was no thief? This same box had transported itself as if by magic from the dying Bhagwan in Poona to a baby shower in Hillsdale. And now it apparently had rematerialized exactly as Neil had himself proposed — in an unmarked manila envelope leaning against the young Bhagwan's door in the Jupiter Hotel.

"*Namaste*, Neil — may I call you Neil?" Roger sat cross-legged on a tiger-striped rug, wearing a white doo rag and a red Karma Koffee T-shirt. He turned the wooden box in his hand, as if he were inspecting an apple at a produce stand.

"What should I call you?" Neil asked, standing a little awkwardly in his brown sport coat and slacks. The hotel room had been furnished with bean bag chairs, Tibetan prayer flags, and Lava Lamps.

"Rog, of course." The young Bhagwan's beard had grown out black and a little wavy. He looked up with boyishly wide eyes. "I'm not into criticism, Neil, but this is, like, the first lapse in security you've allowed."

Roger shook the box. "Despite all your cameras and guards, this thing showed up in an envelope outside my door during the night. How is that?"

"I'm not sure." This was true. Neil didn't know how the box had completed the last stage of its journey. If he explained that Roger's mother had given it to him three weeks ago, he would also have to explain why it had been in his bedside drawer for so long.

"Wouldn't the cameras have picked up an intruder?"

"Unless the intruder knew the system."

Roger weighed that remark while weighing the box in his hand. "I'm told that sannyasins have been searching for this box for twenty-six years. Apparently I knew about it in my former life. What puzzles me is that you recently asked Harmony for a translation of the inscription on the lid."

Neil dodged that bullet without flinching. "I'm a detective. My job is to investigate mysteries."

"Swami Bhrater tells me the Sanskrit is perfectly clear. It's the standard label you find on fire extinguishers in Hindu temples."

This time Neil found himself off balance. "You're telling me it's a fire extinguisher?"

"Metaphorically, perhaps. I really don't know what's inside."

Neil considered this a moment. "What is written on Hindu fire extinguishers?"

Roger ran his finger gently over the wax seal. "Open only in an emergency."

Roger kept the unopened box, but insisted that Neil take the manila envelope for investigation. Neil put on a latex glove before picking up the envelope. He doubted the envelope would prove traceable. If the thief had left fingerprints, Roger had added his own. And the envelope had been closed with its metal clasp rather than the gummed flap, so there would be no DNA from saliva. The existence of the envelope, however, did suggest that the box had been transported by a person. A box that teleported magically, Neil thought, probably wouldn't bother with a manila envelope.

Vijay Collins, the operations manager, caught Neil in the hall and waved him into his office. "I've heard there will be protesters at the Moda Center. You have just three days left. Are you prepared?"

Neil was relieved that he didn't ask about the box. Instead Neil told Vijay about his preparations for the revival. He had trained people to screen for weapons at the doors, guard the stage entrances, and respond to crowd disturbances. Armor and bulletproof glass had been installed in the Rolls Royce.

"Excellent." Vijay leaned back in a black leather chair and put his feet on a chrome coffee table. "We have access to the Moda Center beginning tomorrow, so you can move your training sessions there. Oh, and about the Bhagwan's case —"

Vijay leaned forward and took the manila envelope out of Neil's gloved hand. Vijay turned the envelope over, examining it. "This really could have contained a bomb."

Neil sighed. Now the envelope would have at least two sets of fingerprints. "Perhaps we should x-ray the box, or do an MRI, to make sure there isn't something dangerous inside."

Vijay shook his head. "You don't x-ray the Holy Grail. Besides, what if it's empty?"

"You think that's possible?"

Vijay nodded. "Sometimes a mystery is more powerful than a bomb."

Chapter 7

On the evening of the Rajneesh Revival, six giant searchlights shot a glowing red pillar from the Moda Center into the heavens above Portland. At seven o'clock the beams slowly began separating, a gigantic lotus blossom unfolding to embrace the city.

Neil nervously patrolled the checkpoints he had set up at the area's gates. His security staffers were inspecting bags for weapons. The team looked professional in white slacks and red jackets with the new Bhagwan's logo, a single white dove.

The plaza outside was a chaotic carnival. Amidst aging hippies were curious young people, protesters with "Trust Jesus!" banners, Hare Krishna dancers with bells, hacky sack players, and street vendors selling Native American dream catchers. A sweet haze of marijuana smoke enveloped them all. Neil found it odd that none of the protesters' signs used the slogan from the billboard campaign, "Never Again!"

The mood inside the lobby struck Neil as only slightly less alien. Mirrored disco balls spun colored sparkles around the walls. Sandalwood incense filled the air. Loudspeakers oozed John Lennon's "Imagine."

"Mr. Ferguson?" One of the security guards, a long-haired girl in a red jacket, called him over. "What are we supposed to do with the Jesus people? Some of them have bought tickets."

Neil glanced at the entry table, where a dozen people waited in their Sunday best.

"Do they have signs or banners?"

The guard shook her head. "Not anymore. We confiscated them."

"Do they have knives? Laser pointers?"

"Nothing like that."

"Then let them in."

"But they're anti-Rajneeshee. They hate everything we're doing."

Neil frowned. "We're not supposed to be thought police."

The guard bit her lip. "What if they're disruptive?"

"You've practiced crowd control procedures." Neil looked again at the waiting people. "Still, you might remind our guests to read the rules on their tickets."

Eventually the crowd cleared the lobby and found their seats. Neil was both relieved and disturbed to see that the arena was only half full. Empty seats would make his job easier, but this wasn't the over-whelming turnout the Bhagwan had wanted. And the murmuring suggested that a fair share of the crowd was hostile. If things went wrong, would he be able to control a riot? Worse, he had the uneasy feeling that someone, somehow might have managed to smuggle in a weapon. Perhaps a very small handgun?

The lights dimmed. The hall fell silent. Suddenly a pink spotlight began following Harmony as she walked along a ramp to the raised platform in the center of the arena. She showed up larger than life on four giant screens suspended from the ceiling, her blonde hair float-ing about her shoulders. Her red silk dress twisted with each step. A ripple of applause ran through the crowd.

As Harmony took the microphone she smiled — a burst of sun-shine that warmed even Neil.

"Good evening, and welcome to the Rajneesh Revival. I'm Harmony Ferguson, a kindergarten teacher from Eugene, Oregon. Like many of you here tonight, I was skeptical at first that one of the world's great spiritual masters could have been reborn right here in Portland. For the next hour, I ask you to open your hearts to miracles. Empty your-self of the troubles of the past. A new age of understanding is upon us. Tonight I hope you will learn, as I have, that happiness is within our reach. Welcome, and *namaste*."

Tabla drums rolled. A sitar twanged. A dozen colored spotlights roamed the stage. Finally they settled on an empty chair — a throne of carved wood and gilt.

"The new Bhagwan, Roger Nash, will be here soon," Harmony

said. "But first I want you to meet our spiritual advisor from Poona, India, the half-brother of the former Bhagwan Shree Rajneesh. Allow me to introduce Swami Bhrater."

Harmony held out her arm toward the stage entrance. The Indian music picked up its tempo. But no one emerged from the doorway.

A shot of fear brought Neil to his feet. Something was wrong. Could protesters have slipped backstage? In another moment the crowd would be in an uproar.

Suddenly Harmony, still in the rosy spotlight, flung her arm in the opposite direction. She flicked her wrists, wobbled her head like a bobble-head doll, and gyrated her hips. Neil worried that the nervous tension had caused his niece to suffer some strange fit. The rest of the audience also seemed to have forgotten about the swami. Instead everyone watched as this very beautiful woman in a clingy silk dress moon-walked across the stage, shimmying her shoulders. When Harmony threw in an aikido leap, Neil realized she was merely dancing to fill time. While the musicians and the spotlight crew scrambled to follow her unplanned performance, Neil rushed down the stairs to the stage door.

The warm-up room was a bedlam of red robes and frantic voices, but Neil could not immediately see anyone who qualified as an intruder.

"There's the security guy!" someone shouted. "Quick, over here!"

Neil hurried to a huddle of sannyasins, where Swami Bhrater sat slumped in a chair, his head in his hands.

"What's happened?" Neil asked. "Are you hurt?"

A white-haired woman with a giant beaded necklace replied, "Of course he's hurt. He's seen a gun."

"A gun! Where?" Neil looked about the room.

"Not in here." The woman lifted her head. "The swami saw the gun in a vision."

"That's —" Neil searched for words. "That's less threatening than an actual gun."

The swami looked up, his brown eyes ringed with red. His white beard shook when he spoke. "A premonition is not to be ignored. There is a rifle."

"What kind of rifle? Describe exactly what you saw."

"It had a metal framework," the swami said, holding his hands nearly three feet apart. "With two telescopes on the barrel."

Neil could almost picture a high-powered sniper rifle between the man's outstretched hands. He shook his head. "A weapon that size simply cannot be in this arena. We searched every square inch of the building before the event, and we scanned everything that came in."

"Are you sure?"

"Yes." Neil looked out the door to the stage where Harmony was still dancing, mixing Bollywood moves with whatever else she had. "Right now, Swami, your biggest danger will be me, if you don't go out there and rescue my niece. Now suck it up and get on that goddam stage."

The white-haired woman gasped at this effrontery.

The Indian guru, however, slowly stood up. "What the policeman says is truer than he knows. There is nothing to fear, even in death."

Swami Bhrater took a deep breath and strode through the doorway into the glare of the spotlights.

Chapter 8

Roger Nash came up beside Neil and put his hand on Neil's shoulder. "Nice pep talk, Sergeant." Together they watched Swami Bhrater slowly walk out onto the stage.

Suddenly white bursts of light caught the elderly guru in midstride. Neil felt Roger's fingers clench.

"Flash photography," Neil whispered over his shoulder. "We let cameras through."

There was no applause — no sound at all — as the robed swami shambled to the center of the stage. He sat cross-legged on the floor in front of the wooden chair. At that point he turned on his lapel microphone and a great sigh rushed through the arena, an unexpected windstorm. Slowly he raised his palms and lowered his head.

"Peace." The guru's sonorous voice rumbled from gigantic speakers overhead. Neil felt the hairs on the back of his neck stand on end. If there was going to be a gunshot, it might be now.

"Our goal is the happiness that comes with peace." The swami raised his head and looked through the darkness at the thousands of faces around him. No more cameras flashed.

"I am Swami Bhrater, brother to the Bhagwan." He sighed. "Although I confess to you that I was not close to my brother in his last life. My own path has taken many turns before it has led here, to his revival.

"The Rajneeshees do not follow any religion, but respect them all. The Hindus believe that the soul is part of an eternal stream of consciousness, repeatedly reborn to the suffering of the world. Buddha preached that by shedding the ego and achieving the enlightenment of selflessness, it is possible to escape that cycle. Happiness and good are central to Christianity as well. But rituals and hierarchies of priests have buried the message of all these religions. The Bhagwan revealed that everyone must be free to find their own path to enlightenment. Even if that path takes as many turns as mine."

The swami smiled, and finally Neil could sense that the elderly guru really was at peace, no longer afraid of the rifle he had imagined.

"I understand those of you who do not believe a soul can be reborn. Even the Rajneeshee followers in the Poona ashram deny that Roger Nash is the reincarnation of my brother. They —"

"Sergeant?" Roger Nash whispered to Neil.

"Yes?"

"I need to ask you a serious cauliflower."

Neil tilted his head skeptically.

The barista continued. "And in response I want you to give me a straightforward artichoke. Have you ever woken up with a vegetable disorder?"

"What the hell are you talking about?"

"It may be a condition that encourages you to randomly replace one word in each cabbage."

Neil studied the young man uncertainly. Roger was the exact opposite of Swami Bhrater — young, hip, Western, perfectly at ease, and quite possibly unhinged. "Don't do this when you get on stage."

"Just testing." Roger grinned, baring a mischievous row of white teeth. "I don't want to be what they're expecting."

"That," Neil said, "is one problem we won't have."

A roar of applause cut their whispered conversation short. Spotlights followed Swami Bhrater as Harmony helped him off the stage toward their door. In the giant screens over the stage, the guru's wrinkled brown face and long white beard made him look impossibly old, as if this one brief performance had drained his life force.

"Wish me luck," Roger said.

"No vegetables, OK?"

The young man smiled and strode out with his arms in the air. For a while his showmanship boosted the applause. When it began to die down he turned on his lapel microphone and called out, "Hey,

Portland! Where are my protesters?"

That brought a few nervous laughs.

"I'm serious. We can't have fun here without skeptics. I'm not sure about a lot of this myself. But I do know the only way we're going to clear out our emotions and get to the truth is if we talk about it."

Roger shaded his eyes with a hand and scanned the dark hall. "Where are you, Mrs. Lawrence? For God's sake, you were my fourth grade Sunday school teacher. I saw you out front collecting signatures for some kind of petition. Come on down. We've got a microphone for you. Let's hear what you've got to say."

Spotlights scanned the crowd, eventually stopping at a woman in a yellow dress, standing uncertainly in the center section.

"That's right, Mrs. Lawrence, come on down. You once made me recite the Christmas story at a church pageant. Now it's your turn to be embarrassed."

This time the crowd's laughter was more relaxed.

"And what about the guys with the signs? The 'Trust Jesus' people. Is that you, way in the back? Don't all of you come on stage. Just send down one person as a representative, OK?"

Roger squinted. "Where are your signs? You had a banner and everything out front. What? Our security people took them away?"

Roger pointed to the stage door where Neil was watching. "Sergeant, bring back these people's signs." He turned to speak to the crowd. "Sergeant Ferguson is the Portland police hero who tracked down D.B. Cooper and solved the Underground Murders. At least I think he did. Now he's keeping Rajneeshees safe." He turned again toward Neil. "Bring one of the signs on stage and take the rest up to the folks in the balcony. They can wave them there without blocking anybody's view."

Harmony whispered to Neil, "Where did you put the signs?"

"I think they're in the ticket office." He dug a key ring out of his pocket. "But I don't know if it's a good idea to give them back." They walked out of the stage room together, crossed the lobby, and opened the office. The signs were foam-core boards mounted with duct tape to white plastic pipe. The banner was a bed sheet, with "Trust Jesus" written in an intricate Gothic font.

"How are these dangerous?" Harmony asked.

"I suppose they could use the plastic pipes as blow guns."

She handed him a sign. "Take this one on stage, hero. I'll get the rest to the people in the stands."

Neil didn't like being in the spotlight. Fortunately, by the time he got to the stage, everyone was focused on Roger Nash and his two guests. A bony man with slicked-back hair and a bow tie gripped a microphone and shouted, "Terrorists! They're a nest of Muslim terrorists!"

Roger took the microphone from the man's trembling hand. "I'm not going to argue scripture with you, Numbers 31:1-54 against Matthew 5:17-19." He turned the microphone over to the elderly woman in a yellow dress. "Mrs. Lawrence, I know for a fact that you've taught religion. Is that your assessment of the Rajneeshees too?"

"Well —" She bit her lip. "The Rajneeshees may be dangerous in other ways, but they don't appear to be Muslim. Mohammed founded Islam in the seventh century as a sort of offshoot of Christianity. At least he claimed to believe in the same God as Christians. The old Bhagwan was from India, so I think he was more of a Hindu."

"Actually, Shree was raised as a Jain, but he was heavily influenced by the teachings of nonviolence from both Buddha and Jesus." Roger paused. "Tell me, Mrs. Lawrence, what is your petition for?"

She stiffened. "To revoke the tax-free status of the Rajneeshees."

"An interesting point. We're not a church."

Standing there ignored, Neil was more than ready to leave the stage. Finally he just handed the sign to the man with a bow tie. Although the man didn't have a microphone he held up the sign and shouted so that everyone could hear, "Trust Jesus!"

"I do," Roger replied. "And you know what? I grew up memorizing scripture from one of those Bibles with Jesus' words in red. There wasn't a lot of red ink, because Jesus didn't say much. But he did say we should love our enemies. I think it's still the hardest and most important step toward peace."

At these words the hall fell silent. Neil turned at the stage door, suddenly as anxious as a parent when the noise from a child's room stops.

"I've kept you two out here long enough," Roger said, "A big round of applause, please, for my honored guests, Mrs. Lawrence and Mr. Hamsby."

Before Roger took the microphone from Mrs. Lawrence he asked,

"Anything else you'd like to say?" She shook her head.

Roger moved the microphone to the man with the sign. "Parting words for our audience, Mr. Hamsby?"

The man leaned toward the microphone. "Their real goal is to kill us all."

Roger sighed. "Sir, I know exactly what that fear feels like."

A drumbeat began as Mr. Hamsby and Mrs. Lawrence made their way back up into the stands. This time, however, it wasn't the tattoo of an Asian drum, but rather the slow, deep thump of a heart. Soon a second musician joined in with a wooden flute's haunting, breathy, pentatonic tones.

Where were the real protesters, Neil wondered? Neither the Sunday school teacher nor the Jesus fanatic was likely to have scratched a gunsight onto a Rolls Royce windshield. Certainly they hadn't financed advertisements on streetcars.

"Already you hear the beat of a different drummer," Roger told the crowd. Then he turned to face the throne. But instead of sitting on it he reached into a pocket of his jacket and withdrew a small wooden box that Neil knew all too well.

Roger placed the case on a gold brocade cushion on the seat. "When you are called to an improbable task but you feel in your heart that it is right, nothing is impossible."

For a moment the overhead screens zoomed in on the little box with its Sanskrit text. Neil realized this scene was not for the audience in the Moda Center, but rather for the Rajneeshees in India, watching on the Internet. Roger Nash was not going to sit in the throne at all. But he had shown the world that he had found the Bhagwan's long-lost symbol of authority. The true spirit of the Rajneeshees was now reigning in Portland.

Roger turned back to the crowd, his hands in the air. "From our last guests you found out what the new Rajneeshees are *not* doing. From our next guests, you will learn what we *are* doing."

Spotlights roved among the crowd before settling on a group of a dozen people making their way down the stairs of an aisle. First Neil noticed a muscular young man carrying a pole with feathers. Spotlights flashed on the silver jewelry of several women and girls. Then he recognized the three businessmen in front — the short, heavyset men that Harmony had pointed out in Zorba's restaurant as representatives of

a tribe. They wore dark suits with bolo ties and turquoise belt buckles.
Roger began clapping. "Please join me in welcoming John Wight,
Thomas and Frank Shontin, and their families, of the Modoc tribe from
Southern Oregon's Klamath County."

The audience responded with polite applause. Then the drum
boomed louder and Roger added, "The Modocs apparently agree with
Swami Bhrater: We Indians here in Oregon need to stick together."

The crowd laughed. Some began clapping in time with the drumbeat. The overhead screens switched to a series of dramatically
beautiful landscapes — desert rimrock beneath blue sky, a meandering
stream in a green valley, dark forests rolling up to a snowpeak.

"The tribe has offered to share their spiritual home on the sunny side of Crater Lake National Park. Our new retreat on the Modoc
Reservation will be an intentional community, where each of us will be
free to seek peace and self-fulfillment on our own terms."

The three families stopped at the edge of the stage, shuffling awkwardly, as if each person was trying to hide behind another. Roger
offered a microphone to a businessman with thin gray hair, sagging
cheeks, and dark eyes.

"Tom Shontin, you are an elder of the Modoc nation. Could you tell
the people why you are giving us this opportunity?"

"Our treaty must seem strange," the Modoc elder said, his voice
gravelly. "It seems strange to us as well, that two cultures from across
the world could find common cause. But our people have also faced op-
pression and sought a home. In 1871 the white soldiers at Fort Klamath
ordered us to leave our ancestral lands in Northern California. We were
told to move to the reservation of our blood enemies, the Klamaths. A
hundred of our warriors refused. For six months they held off a thousand Army troops in the labyrinths of the Tule Lake lava beds. One of
our leaders, Captain Jack, killed General Canby — the only U.S. general to die in an Indian war before Custer."

The elder reached out and stroked the three white eagle feathers
on the ceremonial staff. "The Army hanged Captain Jack and his top
two lieutenants at Fort Klamath. The Modoc people were banished to
a century of poverty on the eastern edge of the Klamath Reservation, a
place even the Klamaths did not want. In the 1950s the federal government terminated the entire reservation. Since then the Klamath tribe
has been reinstated, with much less land. Now it is our turn, on the

sacred Modoc ground where Captain Jack died."

Roger pointed to the pictures of landscapes on the screens. He explained, "What you are seeing is Fort Klamath today — the new Modoc Reservation. What the tribe needs to develop their new home is a business partner. That's our role."

Tom Shontin held up his palm. "The Rajneeshees are helping us build a cultural center and a resort with a spa. Ground has already been broken on Captain Jack's Casino."

Shontin smiled, awakening the wrinkles at his eyes. "The Modocs are coming back."

The overhead screens switched to architectural renderings of wood-beamed buildings and airy glass greenhouses. It looked as if Crater Lake Lodge had been rebuilt alongside London's Crystal Palace in the Oregon backwoods.

"In return," Roger added, "the tribe is giving us land for the self-sustaining community we're calling Raja. Geothermal energy from Fort Klamath's hot springs will heat greenhouses where we'll grow organic vegetables, herbs, hops, and even coffee beans. For this vision we need more than just believers. We need builders, bakers, brewers, bankers — and yes, baristas like me."

Roger winked, pretending to toast the crowd with a cup of coffee. "Hot springs are the Earth's espresso machines. They purify the spirit and awaken the soul. Come to Raja and taste that happiness for yourself. Together we will build a city of dreams — a communal home where everyone is welcome."

Suddenly the drumbeats stopped. The sitar and tabla returned, a different mood.

Harmony walked back into the spotlight, her red sari a swirl of silk. "Look up!" she called out. "Lift your eyes!"

Even for Neil, it was hard to look away when his niece was walking. But then red shapes began drifting down out of the darkness: thousands of red silk scarves.

"These scarves are our gift to you," Harmony said. "They are also an invitation. If you wear them tonight on your way out — as a kerchief or an armband or however you like — our volunteers will sign you up for a free stay at the Jupiter Hotel, where you can learn more about joining me and Roger and all the others, building a beautiful new world at Raja Hot Springs."

A voice behind Neil whispered, "That's our signal." It was Vijay, the bald operations manager. "Let's get Roger to safety."

"Just a second," Neil said.

On stage Roger was waving to the crowd with both arms. "Thanks for coming, everyone. Put your hands together for Tom Shontin and our Modoc partners. Special thanks to the lovely Harmony, to our spiritual advisor Swami Bhrater, to our security chief Sergeant Ferguson, and to all the sannyasins who made tonight's revival possible. Good night, Mrs. Lawrence, wherever you are. Trust Jesus! Peace be with you all. *Namaste,* and we'll meet again at Raja."

Neil took out his cell phone and speed-dialed his driver. "Bear? You got the Rolls Royce by the back door?"

"Lights out and engine running, boss."

"Good." Neil pocketed the phone. He waved to Harmony. When she failed to notice, he walked out onto the stage, took Harmony and Roger by their arms, and practically dragged them to the door.

Harmony objected, "I need to help people sign the lists."

"Later. First we need to get Roger into his bulletproof car. Maybe you could give the swami an arm too."

In fact, Swami Bhrater seemed so enfeebled that he slowed the whole group down, even with Harmony's help.

As they made their way along a corridor, Vijay said, "Rog, you were great."

"It's a lot like blogging," Roger replied, shrugging.

"And you, Sergeant," Vijay told Neil. "I really had doubts that you could pull this off in three weeks."

"We're not done yet." Neil unlocked the staff door and peered outside at the loading dock. The Rolls was purring with the passenger door open, but because of the dock's steps, the car was twenty feet away. The loading zone was otherwise empty and dark. Streetlights and freeway headlights lit a chain link fence on the far side of an asphalt barrens.

"Roger, I want you to walk between me and Vijay. Harmony, you bring the swami. Let's go."

They had walked down the steps and were halfway to the car when Neil noticed a red laser dot chasing about the pavement like a cat toy.

"Shit. Get him in!" Neil grabbed Roger by his belt and threw him head first into the car. The roar of the freeway almost covered a popping sound.

"Ah!" a weary voice said. "Ah!"

"Neil!" Harmony cried. "The swami's been shot!"

"I'll get him to the car. Run back into the building!" Neil grabbed the old man under the arms.

The swami's wrinkled eyes were closed with pain. His mouth was a dark O above his long white beard. "Ah!"

Vijay had already climbed into the car's back seat, but had left the door open. Neil shoved the guru onto the seat. "Get him to the hospital, Bear!"

As soon as Neil slammed the car door the tires squealed and the Rolls fishtailed out of the loading zone.

Harmony stood by the loading dock's door. "It locked behind us."

Neil leapt up the stairs and began fumbling with his key ring in the dark. "Shit shit shit." The red laser dot prowled the shadows.

Harmony's voice was surprisingly calm. "You know, Swami Bhrater said there would be a rifle."

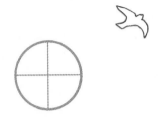

Chapter 9

(Harmony Ferguson)

Harmony here. I know what you're thinking. Rog is the one who's famous for his blog, not me. But now he's telling us that we should write blogs too, as a way to drain some of the steam from our emotions.

I've been pretty steamed up lately, what with Uncle Neil's mistakes, my mixed-up feelings for Rog, and my guilt about not being completely honest. Anyway, if I posted these confessions on the Internet I'd burn a lot of ears. So instead I'm spilling here. I hope this private blog counts, because I'm still a long way from becoming an uncarved block in an unrippled sea.

Susan says the problem is that my parents let me grow up without rules, as a home-schooled, free-range hippie chick. She says a naughty fifteen-year-old girl is still living inside me.

Susan's right. I've struggled most of my life with that other Harmony. She's the one who loves making a game of the men who turn to look. For her it isn't primarily about sex, although that's a drug as well. It's about being wanted — basking in the warmth of lust. Proving her power by making people do stupid things. Of course they end up in tears, and so do I.

I was twenty-four before I struck back against the other Harmony. I decided to rebel against my whole upbringing by marrying Leo. He was a handsome hunk made of rules. Leo dictated everything. He decreed that I would wear modest clothes outside the house. We would no longer visit my parents or any of my old friends. I would enroll at the University of Oregon to earn a degree in early childhood education. We would only go out on Tuesday nights, and then only to study aikido together. I would cook regular meals for him.

But I can't cook. Neither of us Harmonies has a clue in a kitchen. As much as I enjoy dessert, I can't even stir together a box cake. By letting Leo tame the hippie demon inside me, I was starving us all.

Six years later, when I finally woke up from the he-man horror that was Leo, I wasn't sure who I was anymore. On the surface I had become a successful kindergarten teacher with two black belts in aikido. But underneath, what was left of the Harmonies? To find out, I joined a women's support group called DANCE, which stands for Divorced And Now Challenging Everything. There I met Anna Smyth, a tough-as-nails high school German teacher who showed me by example that it is possible to wrestle down the naughty teenager within. Over a bottle of wine one evening I promised her that if I ever married again, it would be to the one man in the world who could make the perfect tiramisu.

That was funny until Anna and I traveled to Italy that summer and met Gilberto, a disturbingly honest, compassionate physicist with a secret recipe for an absolutely magical tiramisu. The hippie Harmony went crazy. She jumped into bed with him and babbled about getting married. She took unpaid leave from teaching to start her giddy new life.

But when I got back here to Oregon, things looked different. Gilberto couldn't fly home with me because of a visa problem. Years ago, as a graduate physics student at Berkeley, he'd been deported for participating in peace protests against the Iraq War. He was still on some sort of U.S. government watch list. He could, however, get a visa if he were actually married to a U.S. citizen. So he began Skyping me enthusiastically about how we were going to have a huge, traditional Italian wedding with veils, mumbling priests, and army military guards, all in a gigantic Roman Catholic cathedral somewhere in Sardinia.

This time it was the older, wiser Harmony who freaked. I remembered marching down the aisle with Leo, another controlling man. Shouldn't I be building my life on something more solid than a cream-filled dessert?

They say you're in your thirties before the frightening realization hits that you have begun to resemble your parents. I've always loved my bear of a father and my mouse of a mom, but I'd never wanted to become either of those animals. Now that I'm thirty-one, I've begun to realize that their flower-child idealism was based on deeper truths. One day I was so angry with Gilberto that I complained to my parents about life. They suggested I go think things over at this new coffee-house in Northeast Portland.

On Killingsworth I discovered a man who makes a killer macchiato. He also has a philosophy that ties together all the loose ends. Aikido, it turns out, was only my first step in the right direction. If someone attacks an aikido master, she doesn't fight back. Instead she redirects the attacker's energy to trip him up or hurt himself. Once, when I was jumped by thugs in Italy, one of my attackers landed flat on his back. The other dislocated his own shoulder. The trick is to surround yourself with *chi* — a sphere of energy.

Aikido is the art of shifting suffering. With Roger Nash and Swami Bhrater, however, I learned that there is a deeper art: to transcend suffering. Not to channel violent emotions, but to overcome them altogether.

OK, so I'm not enlightened yet. Part of the problem is that I'm immensely attracted to Rog. He has this innocent, boyish face. He's funny, but surprises you by saying the cleverest, most thought provoking things. He seems bewildered by his own fame. I'm five years older than Rog, but I've learned the signs long ago. He is attracted to me as well.

I knew it was the wrong Harmony who was plotting to slip into his room at the Jupiter Hotel. No wonder I bristled when my parents asked at the Zorba restaurant if the new Bhagwan advocated love as freely as the old one. I kept thinking of ways to delay the lustful teenager inside myself. I helped my uncle get a job. I took up swimming. I made myself useful in positive ways. I set out to translate some Sanskrit writing Uncle Neil had found.

Actually, my parents were the ones who were wild to translate the Sanskrit. They thought it might have come from a special box — some sort of sealed wooden case that's said to contain the key to the Bhagwan's spiritual power.

As soon as Uncle Neil had left Zorba's I took my parents to meet Swami Bhrater. He was in his bare-bones hotel room, wearing only a robe and sandals. When he saw the picture of the script on my cell phone, his face got even darker than usual. He seemed to shrink, as if he were aging yet another eighty years.

"Where did you get this writing?" he asked.

Glancing to my parents, I decided to protect Uncle Neil. "It's just a picture of a rubbing. But my Dad thinks it might be from an important box."

"It is. Do you have it?"

"No."

"The box is stolen. It belongs to the Bhagwan. In the wrong hands it is dangerous."

"Well, it might be here in Portland." Again, I didn't mention my uncle. As a cop and the head of Rajneeshee security, he could have come across stolen goods without knowing whose they were. Why had he kept the box for himself? I couldn't believe he was a thief, but he had been secretive, acting suspiciously when I took a picture of the writing. Obviously he didn't know how important — or dangerous — this stolen property was.

The swami's eyebrows rose. "Where in Portland?"

"I don't know." I shrugged with one shoulder. "Probably in the last place anyone would look."

"The box is coming to find Roger." Swami Bhrater sat back and sighed. "It is a warning that this time is almost over."

My father wrinkled his brow. "Do you believe time could end?"

"No." He spun his finger slowly in the air. "Unless you succeed in escaping, time is an endless gyre. I have lived almost one complete turn in this body. But I have seen the warnings. There will be a rifle."

My mother gasped.

"Do not be alarmed, Sannyasin Melanie." The white-bearded guru touched her arm. "We are always preparing for the next cycle. Today I would like to write a will. I believe you can help?"

We were all taken aback by the Swami's sudden request. But it's true — my mother really is a notary public for my parents' commune. While she fetched her papers and seal from the glovebox of their van, I wondered out loud if monks usually bothered with wills.

The swami smiled. "The only material possessions I have are what you see." He held out his empty hands.

My mother came back from the van and helped him write out a

peculiar two-sentence testament. He planned to bequeath his sandals to me, Harmony Ferguson, and everything else to the new Bhagwan, Roger Nash.

"Your sandals?" I asked, bewildered.

"Do they fit?" He took off the pair of ancient, hand-woven slippers. The leather on top was shiny and coffee-colored with age. The soles looked like they had been replaced over and over again.

I tried them on. "Yeah, they're fine. But why me?"

He closed his eyes. "They will be happy on such feet as yours."

After our weird meeting, my parents and I still had no idea what to do about the missing Bhagwan box. Did Uncle Neil really have it? How else could he have gotten a rubbing of the Sanskrit script? And how had he gotten it in the first place?

My parents aren't into confrontation, so they finally just drove back to Eugene and left the whole mess to me.

As usual when I need insight — or second sight — I went straight to my cousin Susan. It's good to have a confidante you can trust with secrets. Susan is only a little more talkative than a statue of Buddha. Nobody knows who's inside Susan.

Anyway, when I told Susan the whole story, she simply handed me the key to her father's apartment.

"Go get it," she said.

"The box? Are you serious? You want me to break into your Dad's place?"

Susan shook her black hair, her eyes closed. "You're not breaking in. You're family."

"How do I know the box is even there?"

"It is." She opened her eyes and frowned at her knee. This is a girl who stares anywhere but at you. "Dad's hiding something. He doesn't know how dangerous it is."

I shrugged with one shoulder. "So where should I look?"

"In his bedside table. Behind the picture of my Mom."

"The bedside table?" I rolled my eyes. "That would be a stupid place for a detective to hide something."

As it turned out, it was in the bedside table. The box was right next to the prayer beads my mother had given him at the Zorba café. Maybe it was seeing those two things together that got me thinking. Anyway, I kept the box hidden the rest of the day. That night, as I bicycled toward the Jupiter Hotel with the box in my shirt pocket, I could almost feel it glowing against my breast, as if it had a message for me.

My original plan that night had been hatched by the wrong Harmony. She was scheming to use the box as a ticket into Roger Nash's hotel room — a coupon she could redeem for a night of sex.

But now the box was whispering other stories. Suddenly I remembered how my mother had blushed when she told me how difficult it was to get one of the old Bhagwan's long, white hairs for her prayer bead. My father had talked about the Bhagwan's doctrine of free love, and my mother had cautioned, "Love is never entirely free."

A chill ran up my back. I stopped my bike right there, at a curb on Stark Street, and looked up at the night sky. A crescent moon dodged between silvery clouds.

My parents had decided to leave Rajneeshpuram because my mother was pregnant. But perhaps the father wasn't really Mark Ferguson. Perhaps my biological father was the Bhagwan Shree Rajneesh.

The possibility swirled up all sorts of dizzying thoughts. Did I look like pictures of the old Bhagwan? No, but then I didn't look like a Ferguson either. My father was a big homely bear. All my life I had felt out of place in my family, struggling to discover who I was. Now I was circling toward a strange and scary answer.

I slapped my own face. Here I was, hoping to lure Rog into making love with me, but if I were really the old Bhagwan's daughter, then Rog would be what? My brother? No, worse! My reincarnated father!

Hopelessly confused, and more than a little upset, I got back on my bicycle and took half a dozen wrong turns before I ended up at the Jupiter Hotel. There I stole a manila envelope from the front desk, dodged the security cameras, and left the box in the envelope leaning against Rog's door.

After that I crawled off to the dorm I shared with three other sannyasins. But of course I couldn't sleep. I kept thinking: If I'm the Bhagwan's daughter, maybe I should have opened the box? It's supposed to be opened only in an emergency. Surely my anguish that night would have qualified. Maybe the box would have answered all the riddles.

Then I thought: How could I find out if the old Bhagwan really was my father? If I confronted my mother, she'd deny everything. The only proof would be a DNA test comparing me with the old Bhagwan. But how do you get DNA from a dead guru?

I'd seen enough crime shows to know you can extract DNA from a single hair, like the one my mother put in the bead with the Bhagwan's photo. Maybe I should sneak back into Uncle Neil's apartment to steal the prayer beads.

By the next morning I was a wreck. I dragged my ass straight to the One More Time recycling center on Second Street where Susan works. No one's supposed to interrupt her during work hours, but I needed advice.

Even the thrift shop at the front of the recycling center smells like garbage. Susan came out wearing ugly green overalls. She never looks at you, but this time she was frowning pretty hard at a saucepan, which didn't exactly calm my nerves. Still, I told her that the mysterious Sanskrit box had made me wonder if the old Bhagwan might be my real father. I held up the key to Uncle Neil's apartment, and said I wanted to use it again to get the Bhagwan's hair for a DNA test.

Susan took the key out of my hand. "No. I'll ask."

"Who? Uncle Neil?"

She reached out again, took one of my long, blonde hairs, and yanked it out.

"Ow! What's that about?"

"Cops do DNA tests."

I realized she was right. I'd been sneaking around so much that I'd forgotten how easy it is to ask people for favors. Uncle Neil really might run the test if Susan asked. But that gave me another thought.

"Does that mean you think I really am the Bhagwan's daughter?"

A bell began clanging in the recycling center behind the shop. Susan turned halfway and spoke to a shelf of plastic toys. "Will you need recyclers like me in the new Rajneeshee city?"

"In Raja? Sure!" Could Susan actually be thinking of joining us? That would be great!

"And physicists?"

"Um —" I only know two physicists. One is Susan's boyfriend Dregs. The other is my ex-boyfriend Gilberto. "I don't know. We'll need engineers."

The bell rang again, and this time Susan left me standing there.

For the next week I was so busy preparing for the Rajneesh Revival that I didn't have much time to think. Still, the eerie feeling remained that I was close to the Bhagwan on a deeper level. Rog is too young to be a father figure for me, even if he is my reincarnated Dad. I kept trying to turn the hippie Harmony's lust into something more like brotherly love.

On the evening of the revival itself, I felt like a sleepwalker, even when I was dancing randomly in the spotlight. Later, when I was helping Swami Bhrater out to the Rolls Royce, I felt the bullet jerk him nearly out of my arms. "Ah!" he gasped. The shot had torn a hole in his lung the size of a dime and all he did was gasp.

Everyone says the sniper missed. The bullet must have been meant for Rog. But maybe the bullet was meant for me instead. It missed my heart by inches. Maybe somebody else knows that I may be the Bhagwan's daughter. Maybe Swami Bhrater took a hit that saved my life.

I felt sorry for Uncle Neil. Everybody blamed him. All the TV people wanted to interview the stupid Rajneeshee security chief — the old guy who'd been on the job just three weeks and had never done this kind of work before. Even his cop girlfriend, Lieutenant Wu, turned into Ms. Ice. I mean really, if you're warned there might be a sniper, you've got to think like a sniper. The bad guy isn't going to pull out his rifle in front of thousands of people in the Moda Center. He's certainly not going to try to hit someone in a moving armored car. He's going to wait until his target is walking out the lonely back door of a loading dock.

Uncle Neil probably should have lost his job that night. Maybe Rog is too compassionate. He let my uncle stay on, with Tico Bob as the new deputy of security. Bob hired back the six Costa Ricans and started calling them the Tico Patrol.

Meanwhile, as public relations guru, I was going crazy. The huge show we put on at the Moda Center had been a flop. None of the TV stations covered it. Social media treated our live stream like a dead swamp. The only part anyone retweeted was Roger's bizarre line that hot springs are the Earth's espresso machines. Despite the thousands of red scarves we'd dropped on the crowd as bait, only a few dozen people actually signed up to learn more.

But then a sniper killed an Indian swami and suddenly we were the lead story nationwide. Politicians and religious leaders across the country stumbled over each other to denounce Portland's hate crime.

Within twenty-four hours our headquarters had been flooded with requests from thousands of people who wanted to join. Millions of dollars in donations poured into the Raja Foundation.

At the same time Rog announced that we're speeding up our transition to Raja to keep sannyasins safe. We hired a contractor from Reno to install three miles of security fences around our half of the Modoc reservation. The foundation bought forty mobile classrooms. A hundred huge fiberglass greenhouses were ordered from California for Raja's organic farm.

Rog asked if I could start an airline! What do I know about airplanes? Our operations guru, Vijay, found out that the FAA charter for the old Air Rajneesh was still on the books. I rode MAX out to the Portland airport, smiled my way into a Horizon crew lounge, and offered them triple pay if they'd work for us. Within days a Bombardier turboprop was being repainted red.

Now here's something I'll only admit to a secret blog. I feel weird about Swami Bhrater's death. I couldn't cry about it. You'd think I'd be all torn up inside. After all, I've never had someone die in my arms before. But it wasn't like he died. He said "Ah!" as if he were waking up, not going to sleep.

It also feels strange that Swami Bhrater has already been replaced, even if Rog's new spiritual mentor is Jesus himself. Yeah, you heard that right — the new guy is named Swami Jesus. Of course he pronounces it "Hey Seuss" because he's Costa Rican. I guess this Jesus was another big disciple of the old Bhagwan, although he doesn't talk much, and he doesn't smile like Swami Bhrater.

Funerals are complicated for Rajneeshees. They treat bodies like used cars. You're never sure which model you might turn up in next. First there's a three-day wake so people can see your old body one last time. Swami Bhrater didn't have any close family left in India, and anyway, we were his family now, so we decided to hold a wake in the courtyard of the Jupiter Hotel. That alone would have attracted plenty of publicity, but here's what made the idea golden: Rog said we should celebrate his death as a kind of communication to his next life. So we got one of those red English telephone booths and set Swami Bhrater in a lotus position inside. That image was so weird that it went viral. People began comparing Swami Bhrater to Dr. Who, calling him the Time Lord of the Reborn Bhagwan.

After three days, when Swami Bhrater tipped over inside the booth, we had to go through a bunch more rituals, which was a little confusing, because all these rumors were starting to come out about his past lives in India. Anyway, he was cremated, and his ashes and his belongings are supposed to age another two weeks before the next step, whatever that is. So far there hasn't been a good time to come out and say that he wanted me to have his sandals. Why did he do that, anyway?

Now of course, the sniper has struck again and everything's changed. At first nobody recognized the sannyasin who'd been dumped on a forest road with a hole in his chest the size of a dime. Dark hair, a red robe, and no ID. It turned out to be Juan, one of the Latin American sannyasins who meditated a lot but didn't talk much. And that's what made this new murder so terrifying. The killer may have shot the wrong person the first time, but at least we all thought he was targeting someone. Now it seems that anyone who wears red is a target.

This morning all the television cameras were back. The stuffed shirts were once again calling for tolerance, and the donors were again sending money.

Everyone wants to know why the police can't find the killer. Obviously we're not safe here in Portland. Everyone is afraid. We all looked to Rog for guidance. Fortunately, he knew what to do.

He fired Uncle Neil. Tico Bob will take charge of our security.

And we're leaving for Raja at once. A huge caravan of trucks and buses is setting out for Fort Klamath tonight. Air Rajneeesh is running flights to Klamath Falls around the clock. Susan is driving to Raja in a rental car, along with her boyfriend, Dregs. She's even writing a blog she wants me to read — as if I had time for that now.

There is no city waiting for us at Raja. But with the combined will of two thousand sannyasins, we will somehow build one from scratch.

I am in love with this.

Chapter 10

(Susan Ferguson)

Talking is hard. Maybe I can blog?

Thoughts whir in my head like recycling machine gears. But what comes out of my mouth is garbage. How can anyone transfer thoughts from one brain to another?

The hardest thing is to act normal. Everything is an act.

For example: Rajneeshees. I like that they do not act normal.

When I was little I wondered if I might actually be a machine disguised in a human body. But machinery is not what is driving me now. Two of the people I care most about are in danger — my cousin and my father. I am going to help them. They don't see the real threat.

Harmony imagines that snipers are targeting her. She thinks she's the secret daughter of the Bhagwan Shree Rajneesh. I doubt these things. When I asked Dad to run DNA tests on the hair from Harmony and the Bhagwan, he thought a long time before saying yes. He is having copies of the results sent both to Harmony and to the police. Usually I can read my father like an open book. This time there are pages I can't see.

No one seems able to read me, even when I crease open the page. For example: Gilberto. How can Harmony not see how much her boyfriend in Italy still loves her? When Harmony stopped answering his calls, Gilberto started Skyping me for help. I pass along his questions to Harmony, but she thinks I am just curious. She doesn't hear that the questions are coming from someone else. Instead she gets angry and asks, "Why are we still talking about Gilberto?"

For example: Dregs. My boyfriend is the only one who knows how to finish my sentences. He earned a Ph.D. in physics from Reed, but couldn't get a job, and wound up as a wino under the Steel Bridge. I met him on Wednesdays, when the homeless drunks come to my recycling center for the deposits on returnable cans.

I like Dregs because he's smart, and he doesn't act normal, and he usually demands nothing. So why, now that he's got a part-time job and an apartment downstairs, why is he talking about marriage? This puzzles me as much as the relationship between my father and Lieutenant Connie Wu. Love is a confusing part of our machinery.

I told Dregs we should join the Rajneeshees. We should become eyes on the inside. At first Dregs said I was crazy.

After Swami Bhrater was shot, Dregs agreed. There are too many problems, too close to my family. Who is killing the Rajneeshees? How did the Bhagwan's box turn up in my father's apartment? What is really behind the plans at Raja? Something feels wrong about this sudden city on an Indian reservation.

Gilberto has become our co-conspirator. Skyping with him after the second Rajneeshee murder, Gilberto announced, "I am joining the Rajneeshees too."

Dregs: "You? Why, man?"

Gilberto: "Harmony needs me."

Dregs: "She won't even talk to you."

Gilberto: "Yes, but if I convert and become a Rajneeshee, it will prove that religion is no problem between us."

I thought for a moment. "That might work. But you can't come to the United States. You have no visa."

"No." Gilberto sighed. "I would have to be invited to the U.S. as a husband."

"Or as a physicist?" Dregs gave the Skype camera a wide-eyed grin that looked maniacal, even to me. "Hey, this could work. Reed College gets visas for physicists who come for projects all the time. And I've got just the right project to ring those government bureaucrats' bells."

Gilberto: "You have a project ringing bells?"

Dregs: "No, man. I have a project digging for geothermal energy. It turns out that the hot springs at Fort Klamath aren't hot enough to run the big greenhouses the Rajneeshees want. So they're hiring a fracking crew from North Dakota to drill deeper. I'm signing on as a Rajneeshee engineer."

I asked, "Will the State Department believe you need a physicist from Italy?"

Dregs: "Baby, he's from the land of Vesuvius."

Gilberto: "My work is not on volcanology. It is on black holes. How can you say these subjects are related?"

Dregs: "Easy schmeasy. I've got friends at Reed who owe me a favor. They'll write it up as a geophysics consortium between Reed, the Modoc tribe, and an oppressed religious minority. Gilberto, pack your bags."

Dad? Harmony? I am posting this so you will be prepared.

Chapter 11

(Lieutenant Connie Wu)

Is this thing recording? I'll play it back.
(Click. Buzz. Click.)
OK.

So it's come to this: I'm fifty-five years old. I finally get promoted to lieutenant, and now I'm talking to myself.

You don't make a lot of close friends in the Portland Police Bureau. They're cops. My son's a surf shop worker in Maui who never calls. I certainly don't want to talk to his father. My tortoise Luigi is deaf, because he's a tortoise. Sometimes I talk to him anyway, but it feels kind of pointless. And although I write tons of reports at work, that's not a good place to rant about Neil, which is all I want to do.

When Neil quit the police, I thought our relationship was getting serious. I imagined Neil might ask to move in with me — or at least work up the nerve to make some kind of move. I mean, he's never actually kissed me, although we've had a hundred near misses. Why is that? Is he too cautious, or just too easily distracted? Do I have to do everything myself? Then — oh damn it all, everything has gotten complicated.

So here I am talking to my future self. Hi, Future Connie! You got everything figured out?"

(Sound of a microwave dinging. A door clicks open. The pop of a fork puncturing plastic wrap. Beeps as the microwave is set for more time.)

Neil and I go back a ways. After his wife Rebecca died of cancer he drank for most of a year, but kept coming to work anyway. Finally he wrecked a patrol car in a chase. His partner died in the wreck. To hush up what would have been a drunk driving scandal, our clever Captain Dickers lied, saying Neil was a hero, and his partner had been at the wheel.

That sobered Neil up, but I still wasn't very enthused when I was assigned to work with him, especially when he started asking me out. I mean, yes, he's attractive for his age, but he just had too much baggage.

Then we got dragged into a complicated murder case where I was the only witness. A Russian mafia don kept trying to kill me. No one but Neil believed I was in danger. And I'll be damned if he didn't stick with me until he solved the case and canned the killer. Ironically, Dickers then made me a lieutenant and demoted Neil.

When you've been to hell and back with a man as determined as Neil Ferguson, you start to admire him for making a round trip like that despite his baggage.

Like I said, I had imagined that we'd hit it off once he retired. But his Rajneeshee security job took all his time, and it turns out he was still leaving the hard work for me. I warned him to check out Roger Nash's parents. Apparently he found out that Roger's father is a religious fanatic with an armory of hunting rifles. Did Neil bother to follow up on that obvious tip? Not until it was too late.

I warned Neil to investigate the backstory of the new Rajneeshees. I even pulled up the whole record on Roger Nash to kick things off. But that's where Neil's research stopped. The ugly stories only started coming out after Swami Bhrater was shot. By then the case was dumped on me.

I don't like publicity. Television cameras make me look like an Asian grandmother with a wig. So I left Captain Dickers to handle the press conferences while I went about the usual work — securing the crime scene, doing forensics, following up leads.

Dickers fed Neil to the wolves. According to him, Neil was a rogue cop who quit the force to do sloppy work for a religious cult he knew nothing about. Maybe that's not so far from the truth.

Meanwhile, I found out the sniper had used a high-powered rifle with a laser sight on a night scope — stuff you could buy at any Cabela's. He'd positioned himself in the shadows by a noisy freeway, so the shots were only heard by a few drivers who couldn't stop. The killer probably drove away in his own car. Thousands of cars were at the Moda Center that night. By the time we got there, most had already left. In short: No witnesses. No clues.

The next step was to look for people with motives. Apparently half the Moda Center's audience had been hostile. Although they couldn't bring rifles inside the building, anybody could have gotten a gun out of their car trunk after the show. The most vocal protesters had brought "Trust Jesus" signs. But that entire group had arrived in a church bus from Troutdale, and they'd left as a group. We interviewed them all, and their story held up.

The next obvious group with a motive for murder was whoever ran the "Never Again" streetcar ad campaign, showing the old Bhagwan in a gunsight. Those ads only ran for two weeks, but they got a lot of attention, especially after a guru really did wind up in crosshairs. The Portland Streetcar people say the ads came from NovoCity Finance, which helps explain how the ads got approved in the first place. NovoCity has friends in high places. They launched a Portland cruise ship, a brand of sparkling pinot wine, and a recycling project. They're hush-hush about where their money comes from, but some of it smells like the Russian mafia. And some of it winds up in the campaign coffers of local politicians. Captain Dickers called me into his office and told me to step lightly around NovoCity.

So I was amenable when Neil said he'd check them out as a private investigator. He'd dealt with their CEO, Nancy Willis, during the Cooper case.

(The microwave dings again. The door opens, the plastic wrap is torn off, and Connie sighs as if she had hoped for something better. Her next words are mumbled as she eats.)

What does Neil find out? Not much. Willis stonewalls him, claiming client confidentiality. All she says is that the money's source is "closer than you think." What is that supposed to mean? The ads could have been from a gun group, the 1000 Friends of Oregon, or the James G. Blaine Society for all we know. I'm going to have to sobpoena NovoCity's tax records to see who they're in bed with. Dickers won't like it.

(A can of soda opens with a pop and a fizz.)

Anyway, while Neil is telling me about his failure with Nancy

Willis, I ask him about Roger Nash's parents. I practically fall off my chair when he says the kid's father is a jealous, violent rifle owner who hates Rajneeshees.

An hour later I'm heading for Hillsdale with three patrol cars to bring John Nash in for questioning. The suspect is so belligerent we almost have to handcuff him. I leave a guard at his house, get a search warrant, and collect a dozen weapons, some of them with laser sights and night scopes. While ballistics is running tests to see which rifle fired the swami's bullet, I have a little interview with Mr. Nash senior. Neil is there, but he doesn't say much at first. In my questioning I find out that John doesn't have an alibi. He and his wife Catherine were home praying on the night the swami was shot. He admits they were praying that God would strike down the Rajneeshees who were clouding their son's mind.

By this point Mr. Nash is in tears. He's just about to confess.

And suddenly Neil says, "I believe you. Ballistics will prove it wasn't your rifle."

I'm staring at Neil like he's off his rocker.

"I've got just two questions for you," Neil goes on, ignoring me. "Who was at the baby shower after your son's birth?"

Now I'm sure Neil has gone off the deep end.

"Baby shower?" Mr. Nash asks, drying his eyes.

"The week after Roger was born, in January of 1990. Were you at that party?"

A strange, distant look came over Mr. Nash. He nodded slowly.

"Who else was there?"

"Just family and friends."

"No outsiders? You were the only man?"

Mr. Nash nodded again, but he drew back with a haunted look I couldn't read.

I interrupted. "Neil, you said just two questions. You've asked four."

"They were all part of the first question. The second question is about his sister-in-law Patricia."

I didn't know where this subject had come from. Honestly, I still don't.

Neil turned to Mr. Nash. "Your wife says her sister is in a home for the feeble minded. Which home is that?"

Suddenly Nash leapt out of the chair at Neil. I'm told that Neil's niece is accomplished in the martial arts, but Neil must have learned a few moves too. He jumped aside and wrenched Nash's arm behind his back.

John Nash is not nearly as fit as Neil. Like most bullies, he deflated fast. After Neil released him, he said, "I'm not answering any more questions."

And that was that. I kept John Nash in custody for days, but he never said another word.

(Click. A few seconds of silence. When the recording clicks back on a newscast is playing in the background. A male voice says, ". . . still no leads as to who shot and killed two followers of the Oregon religious sect in the past week. Roger Nash, the group's self-described Bhagwan, has called on his supporters to move to a compound in Southern Oregon, where he says they will be able to pursue their beliefs and build an organic farm behind the safety of a security fence. Meanwhile, details about the two victims continue to emerge. Both were foreign nationals, and at least one was in the United States illegally. Portland police captain John Dickers announced today —" Click.)

You'd think even Neil would have realized that "Swami Bhrater" couldn't be a real name. I searched the dead guru for documents. Nothing. The man didn't even have underwear — just some sort of loin cloth tucked under his robe. So I searched his hotel room. It was empty — and I mean *empty* — except for a shelf of books by the Bhagwan Shree Rajneesh. Mostly rambling discourses about Zen with titles like "No Water, No Moon." But there in the middle of "I am the Gate" was a passport for Gavan Pradesh, born in Poona, India in 1937. The picture's out of date, he doesn't even have a beard, but it's our man. He's got a standard tourist visa that's going to expire in a month.

I contacted the police in Poona. They knew all about Mr. Pradesh. As a boy he studied at a Hindu school in the city. Throughout the 1950s he passed himself off as a monk. He would show up at a remote rural temple, spend a few weeks learning the monks' schedule, and then disappear one night with the temple's bronze statues. He'd sell them to an agent in Mumbai who forged papers saying they'd been bought legally by a British military officer years ago. Later the statues would be resold for thousands at art auctions in London and New York.

Eventually the Indian authorities caught up with Pradesh. He served five years at a prison in Madras. When they released him in

1971 he went back to Poona and discovered that one of his class-mates from the Hindu school had become famous as a Bhagwan. The Bhagwan's handlers were charging starry-eyed hippies from Europe and America tens of thousands of dollars to sit at the guru's feet and learn his wisdom. Pradesh wanted a piece of that action. He started a swami tutorial service, preparing people for the Bhagwan's teachings at a much lower price. Although he called himself "Bhrater," which means brother, he never claimed to be the Bhagwan's actual, biological brother. Other people said later that he was a half-brother, and he didn't bother to correct them.

By the time the Bhagwan opened his Oregon commune in 1981, Pradesh had managed to be accepted as a Rajneeshee. After Rajneeshpuram collapsed, he was one of the Indian nationals deported for overstaying their visas. But unlike most of the others, he didn't re-turn to India. Instead he joined a splinter group that set up an organic farm in Costa Rica. Exactly what happened down there is still unclear.

(Connie sighs, and her swivel chair creaks.)

If Neil had bothered to dig up any of this history about the swami he'd have known who was really at risk. The sniper had a night scope that could pick out a target as clear as day. The rifle wasn't aimed at Roger Nash. The real question is, why did the killer hate Gavan Pradesh?

Pradesh had no shortage of enemies with motives. I narrowed the options down to four.

Motive number one: It's about the stolen temple statues. Pradesh got off lightly for his high-stakes thievery. Maybe he bargained his way out of prison by ratting out the art dealer who organized the op-eration. If so, the dealer might finally be out of jail himself, looking for revenge.

Motive number two: Someone inside the Rajneeshee organization could have discovered he's not the Bhagwan's brother — or that he's not even a real swami. Murder seems like a radical reaction, but rival-ries among Rajneeshees led to murder attempts in the 1980s too.

Motive number three: What happened in Costa Rica for thirty years? Central America is full of gangs and syndicates. Maybe Pradesh stepped on some toes.

The fourth motive is the one that made me lock up Roger Nash's father for a week. If you're a wingnut who doesn't like what the

Rajneeshees are doing to Oregon, you don't shoot your own son. You'd aim for the swami from India. I was so sure about this, and so angry when Neil said John Nash was innocent, that I stopped seeing Neil.

(The sound of a fist thumping on a table.)

Damn him! When the second Rajneeshee turned up dead, I realized Neil had been right. The new victim had been shot with the same sniper rifle. I had already found out that John Nash's guns didn't match the ballistics. I should have released him when I got that report, but I didn't.

As a result, Mr. Nash was still in my custody when the second Rajneeshee was shot. Even the dumbest TV reporter could see that John Nash had to be innocent. In fact, all four of my motives are shit.

(A sharp intake of breath. Swallow.)

The media wolves that were chasing Neil are now howling for me. I'm running out of time. He knows something I don't. He's — he's — Damn him!

(A cell phone beeps rapidly, the quick musical cadence of a number that's being called on speed dial.)

Chapter 12

When Connie called, Neil was bicycling across the Tilikum Crossing bridge, his pannier bags packed with gear and his lights flashing. The night air was cool, but half a dozen stars proved there were holes in the unseen clouds. He stopped, pulled the beeping phone out of the tight pocket in his Lycra pants, and tipped the headlight on his forehead to read the screen.

Connie.

He let the ring tone play out. Then he stared out at the reflections of city lights shimmering in the Willamette River.

How many times had she hurt him by telling him to leave her alone? Someday she wouldn't change her mind. Or he wouldn't call back. Someday.

He pressed her speed dial button. When she answered, he said nothing, which in itself was a sort of revenge.

He could tell she was trying not to cry.

He took a deep breath. Finally he said, "I'll be there in ten minutes."

She was waiting for him on the porch of her house, a bungalow off Hawthorne. "I'm sorry about what I said earlier. I feel awful for blaming you, especially now that —"

She stopped when she realized he was wearing a bicycle helmet. "You were out bicycling at midnight?"

He nodded.

"I thought you only bicycled at night if you need to — you know —"

She didn't say, — *to avoid the urge to drink* —, but they both understood. The past week had been hard on both of them.

"Your bike's loaded for a trip."

He unstrapped his helmet. "I'm going to Crater Lake."

"What? Tonight? On a bike? That's hundreds of miles."

"I'm kind of unemployed, Connie. I volunteered to check the route for Cycle Oregon. They're planning to take two thousand bicyclists on a five-day trip from Portland to Crater Lake next week, stopping at hot springs each night. They arranged the tour months ago, but the route could use some tweaking."

Connie knew there had to be more to this story. Even Neil Ferguson didn't usually set out on five-day bicycle trips at midnight. "If you end at Crater Lake, you'll be near Raja."

"I'm trying to convince Cycle Oregon to end at Fort Klamath's hot springs, on the Modoc side of the reservation."

"You think bicyclists are curious to see the Earth's espresso machine at Raja?"

Neil smiled. "The Rajneeshees may have fired me, but I don't quit easy."

She took his arm. "Come on. We'll fix Brazilian lattes like you showed me. We've got a lot to talk about before you go."

Neil noticed that Connie had dressed in a tight, ribbed turtleneck that stretched taut over her profile. Was this part of the apology she had mentioned? There was no trace of the tears he had heard over the phone. A touch of dark blue eye shadow extended neatly on either side of her oval face. The shiny black hair of her pageboy curled inward toward her lips.

Neil had been in Connie's house before — with its off-white pillow furniture, its free-range tortoise, and its messy kitchen — but never this late at night. In the kitchen's fluorescent light Neil's bicycling outfit glowed jagged swaths of yellow and orange, a pattern designed for dark streets instead of coffee dates.

Connie used her arm to sweep dirty plastic dishes into the sink. "Actually, I've forgotten how to do lattes."

"Start with the strongest coffee you can make. I'll heat the milk."

"You've studied at the feet of a barista."

Neil took a saucepan down from a row of hooks. "Actually, I learned my lattes earlier, from a librarian."

Connie bit her lip. An attractive Latvian librarian had worked with Neil as a translator on the Cooper case earlier that year. The woman had died in a gas explosion. Connie had always wondered how close the two had been. Had they been lovers? She changed the subject.

"I suppose you heard that I released Roger Nash's father?"

Neil nodded. "The man obviously couldn't have shot somebody while he was in jail. Was it the same rifle?"

"Yes and no."

"What does that mean?"

Connie took a bag of ground coffee out of the freezer. "The big hole in the victim's chest was what everybody noticed. At first I thought the killer must have kidnapped him, driven him out Wildcat Mountain Road, stood him up in a lonely quarry, and executed him like a firing squad. We didn't notice much blood, but I assumed that was because his robe was already red."

Neil stopped pouring milk and slowly set down the carton. "How did he really die?"

"A little .22 in the back of the head. His thick black hair hid the hole and matted up the blood."

"So they shot him here in Portland, drove him up into the woods, and shot him again. Why?"

Connie held out her hands. "Maybe it's someone who really hates Rajneeshees."

"Who was the dead man anyway?" Neil finished pouring the milk and turned the saucepan on low. "I lost my job before I found out."

"A part-time bookkeeper who mostly just meditated. Fifty years old. His name was Juan Guerrero, I think."

"You think?" Neil looked at her from the side. Connie had closed her eyes to breathe the aroma of the opened bag of coffee. Her dark eyelashes and pink lips were so close to him that his pulse sped up a tick. He was talking with Connie as if they were once again in a patrol car together. But this time they were in her kitchen, dangerously late at night.

"No passport," she said, opening her eyes. "Just a Mexican driver's license that might be fake. The police down there say it's a common name. The building at his address in Guadalajara was bulldozed for redevelopment years ago. Probably a slum."

"The Rajneeshees aren't fussy," Neil said, trying to focus again on the case. "They have dorms full of sannyasins who don't speak much English and haven't got the right papers. Most of them are Ticos."

"Ticos?"

"Costa Ricans. Down there people use the word 'tico' to mean small. It's become a nickname for Costa Ricans. After the first murder I had to hire back a whole 'Tico Patrol.' Illegals, running security. They couldn't even drive our cars."

Connie fit a filter into a coffee machine. "The guy who took over security goes by the name of Tico Bob."

"Yes, but he's American. A tall, dumb white guy who worked on the Rajneeshee farm in the jungle." Neil stirred the warming milk a moment. "What about the men in Guerrero's dorm? Did you interview them?"

"Guerrero wasn't in a dorm. He had a private room."

Neil looked at her, surprised. "In the Jupiter Hotel?"

"Yes. Why?"

"Because you only get a private room if you're rich. A bookkeeper from a slum doesn't seem like someone who could have donated thousands to the Raja Foundation."

"We found more than four thousand dollars in cash in his room."

"Really?" Neil slowly stirred the milk. "Maybe Guerrero turned a nice profit in Guadalajara. It's a dangerous world down there. Drugs, gangs, extortion, who knows? If you make enough money, and enough enemies, maybe you retire to a peaceful commune in Oregon where they don't ask questions. Money has been known to buy indulgences before. Perhaps he thought it could buy transcendence."

"That could be the connection," Connie admitted. "Whoever's killing these people isn't just after random Rajneeshees. They're picking out foreigners with a criminal background. I'm pretty sure that's why they targeted Gavan Pradesh."

"You mean Swami Bhrater?"

"His name was Pradesh. A crook with an alias."

Neil tilted his head uncertainly. "I only met the swami a few times, but he seemed like a man who regretted the mistakes of his youth. Even I couldn't help feeling that he had found some kind of enlightenment."

"He had plenty of enemies. I bet that's one thing he had in common with Juan Guerrero."

"Maybe so." Neil had stopped stirring the milk. He stared out the kitchen window to the darkness beyond. "In that case, the killer is someone who knows a lot about the Rajneeshees."

"An insider. That's one of my theories." She laughed. "For a while I even thought the murderer was Jesus."

"Jesus?" Neil reeled. "Has he been reincarnated too?"

"You haven't heard? The new spiritual mentor of the Rajneeshees is a Costa Rican guy by the name of Swami Jesus."

"And you think he killed Swami Bhrater to take his place?"

Connie shook her head. "We checked. Jesus Martinez is a legal immigrant with an airtight alibi. Lots of witnesses say he was overseeing the meditation center on the day Guerrero was shot."

Neil looked out the window, thinking. "If the killer wasn't a Rajneeshee, he could have been a vigilante who infiltrated the group. I have my own infiltrators, you know.'

"You consider your niece Harmony an infiltrator? I worry about her."

"There's also my daughter."

"Susan? Surely she's not involved."

"I'm afraid so. She and her boyfriend Dregs have joined the Rajneeshees. They're driving to Raja in a rental car right now."

"What on earth is Susan thinking?"

"Read her blog." Neil shrugged. "She says that thoughts whir in her head like the gears of a recycling machine."

"You never know what's going on in that girl's mind. She's not really converting to a Rajneeshee, is she?"

Neil shook his head. "I don't think so. She's worried about me and Harmony. She thinks our answers are at Raja. I think so too."

"Meanwhile, I'm left with a huge mess here in Portland. Everybody wants to know when I'll catch the killer. But I don't know where to turn. Any tips?"

"You're asking a disgraced, unemployed cop for advice?"

"No." She lowered her eyes. "I'm asking you, Neil."

He sighed. She was right. He was leaving a lot of unfinished business here in Portland, both about the case and about their relationship. At the very least, he owed her his help.

"Well?" she asked.

"Guerrero. Find out where he ate. If he went to Zorba's, he must have talked to somebody, if only a waitress. Find the last person who saw him alive."

"OK. And?"

"Follow the money."

"Which money? We've already tried tracing the money behind the ad campaign."

"I mean the Rajneeshee millions. They're taking donations through the Raja Foundation, a non-profit organization with tax-free status. But the commune has some kind of partnership too. I don't even know where to look to find out about that kind of thing."

"I do." Connie made a mental note to run a computer search for business partnerships. It was just the kind of thing she did well.

Neil took a pen and a note pad from the clutter at the back of the kitchen counter. "You might also pay a visit to this woman." He wrote down a name and pushed it toward her.

"Patricia Holmes?" Connie looked up, at a loss.

"Roger Nash's aunt."

Light dawned in Connie's face. "She's the sister-in-law you asked John Nash about. Why did you do that, anyway?"

"His wife told me that Patricia is living in a home for the feeble minded. It took some doing, but I found out Holmes is actually in the One World Retreat Center, a Buddhist temple in the woods near Vernonia."

"And that means?"

"I don't know. But she influenced Roger when he was growing up. His parents wouldn't let him see her after he turned twelve. It's one of those pieces that doesn't fit." Neil looked aside. Should he tell her about the other piece that didn't fit — the Bhagwan's box?

"What should I ask her?"

"Just talk. I think she'd be more likely to open up to a woman like you than an old man like me."

"An old man? You know —" She stopped. Something was burning. "The milk!"

"Damn." Neil took the saucepan off the stove, but the milk was scalded so badly that it had stuck to the bottom. "So much for the Brazilian lattes. I could have used some coffee before hitting the road."

"You." She tapped him on the chest with her fingertip. She had let him slip away at moments like this too many times. "Do you really plan to bicycle off in the middle of the night?"

"Portland traffic is lighter at night," he said. "And the first stage to Crater Lake is the longest. It's ninety-four miles to Breitenbush Hot Springs."

How much of a hint did he need? She tapped her finger again. "I've told you before that we make a good team. I can work on the case here while you snoop around at Raja. But I don't think you have to leave in such a hurry."

"It's late, Connie. I should get started."

He said this without actually turning toward the door, a clue that he was beginning to get the idea.

Neil swallowed. She was so close, and her eyes so dark. More troubling yet, his skin-tight outfit made it difficult to conceal his emotions. The bulge in his Lycra pants had risen nearly to his waist. Decorum told him to step behind the adjacent counter. But she was looking up at him with such a smoky gaze.

Taking a risk, Neil held her by the shoulders. She closed her eyes. With his heart beating fast, he leaned down and kissed her on the lips. They were so sweet, and so soft. She pressed against his chest and kissed him back hungrily, with more passion than he had expected. When she finally came up for air, she looked at him, gave an odd little laugh, and kissed him again. She clung to him as if she were afraid he really might get on his bicycle and disappear.

By the third kiss, Neil was running his hands over her back. As smoothly as he could, he untucked her shirt, slipped his hands up behind, and unclasped her bra.

This time when she looked up at him, both her eyebrows were raised. He kissed her again, hoping this would help. He even dared to run his tongue along the edge of her lips.

Connie responded by stepping back. She put her hands on his hips. "Enough of this."

"Sorry, Connie. I thought —"

She took him by the hand and led him matter-of-factly toward her bedroom. "I have handcuffs, if you like."

"What?" Neil wondered if he had heard this correctly. "For you or for me?"

"For you, I suppose."

"Did your former husband go in for that sort of thing?"

"No." She sat on the bed and pulled the turtleneck over her head. She gave her head a shake, bouncing her hair to straighten it. "But I always wished he had taken more of an interest in my police work."

A black bra still dangled from her shoulders, but the turtleneck was gone.

Neil followed her example by attempting to pull off his Lycra shirt. In his haste, however, the stretchy fabric caught on his head. He danced a few steps as he struggled.

She stifled a laugh.

When Neil finally freed himself from the shirt he sat beside her on the bed. "Do you know why I pulled you over, ma'am?"

"I've got a pretty good idea, Officer."

This seemed encouraging enough that Neil lifted the bra from her shoulders.

He caught his breath. Connie might be over fifty, but she had the breasts of a goddess. Nipples the same color as her lips looked up at him from glorious, goosebumped aureoles.

"Connie." He ran his fingertips from her elbows to her shoulders. He couldn't find any more words, and as it turned out, he didn't need them.

It was almost dawn before Neil rode his bicycle through the back streets of southeast Portland on his way to Raja. Connie stretched in bed. She felt as if the sun had come up within her and she was glowing for a new day. Neil might be a man with baggage, but he hadn't brought it with him into her bedroom that night. He had left with the promise that he would call every evening. Next Saturday she would take the weekend off and drive to Fort Klamath. Who knew what would happen then?

In the meantime, Connie felt as if she had found her footing. She would discover who had last seen Juan Guerrero alive. She would follow the trail of the Rajneeshees' money. She might even pay a visit to an old woman in a Buddhist temple.

She felt confident enough to face the day without much sleep. She and Neil had dozed a little, spooned together afterwards.

The only troubling note had come when he was getting dressed, pulling his Lycra shirt over his head. She had been musing aloud about how complicated the Rajneeshee investigation had become and said, "It's not an open-and-shut case."

"What?" Neil had suddenly twisted himself about and yanked his shirt in place. "What did you say?"

"The case of the reborn Bhagwan," Connie repeated, surprised by the abruptness of his response. "It's not open and shut."

"No," he replied slowly. "It hasn't been opened at all."

What was he not telling her?

Chapter 13

The young couple who found Juan Guerrero's body Sunday morning had been so frightened that the 911 operator could hardly understand them. Eventually they explained that they had planned to hike the Douglas Trail up Wildcat Mountain for a view of Mt. Hood. They had parked at a trailhead in an old rock quarry. Beside the trail sign they had found a red-robed corpse with a hole blown in its chest.

Connie had promptly ordered a roadblock on Wildcat Mountain Road, the area's main access. When she reached the crime scene herself and saw how thoroughly the blood had dried, she knew Guerrero must have been shot a day earlier. Even before the coroner arrived with confirmation, she called the roadblock crew and told them to start asking drivers if they had seen anything suspicious on Saturday.

Connie also stationed patrol cars at both the Killingsworth coffee shop and the Jupiter Hotel around the clock, as much for show as for security. Neil had been right about this too: It simply wasn't possible to guarantee the safety of hundreds of Rajneeshees, especially when you didn't know who was threatening them.

Monday had brought Connie nothing but frustration. The people interviewed at the roadblock had seen dozens of pickups, SUVs, and Subarus on Wildcat Mountain Road, but no one had noticed a corpse. Target shooters loved that corner of the national forest, so it was not unusual to hear shots.

Guerrero's room at the hotel revealed that he ate corn flakes for breakfast, read Spanish graphic novels, smoked marijuana, and kept hundred-dollar bills in his pockets. He had left his television tuned to Telemundo, the Spanish-language station that ran quiz shows and soaps. No one seemed to know him well. They did know that Guerrero went for long walks, but Connie doubted he could have managed the forty-five miles to Wildcat Mountain on his own.

On Tuesday morning, buzzed with coffee and an exhilarating night with Neil, Connie showed up at the Jupiter Hotel in a navy blue skirt and jacket, ready to tackle the case anew. To her dismay, she found the entire compound had been turned inside out.

She had posted two officers in a patrol car on Burnside. The sergeant in the driver's seat shook his head. "It's been crazy, Lieutenant."

His partner stifled a yawn, but managed to nod agreement. "Trucks, buses, taxis, all night. It's like an army on the move."

"Are they all Rajneeshees?"

The first patrolman shrugged. "People coming and going, some in red, some not."

His partner added, "They're leaving for that new commune in Southern Oregon. The murders have got them scared."

"Stay put and keep watching," Connie said. "Your replacements should be here soon."

She crossed the sidewalk to the hotel entrance. A chartered tour bus and a Penske rental truck idled in the driveway. She was making her way around the truck when a young woman in the white slacks and red coat of the Rajneesh security force stepped forward, blocking her path with an arm.

"I'm with the Portland police," Connie objected.

The woman ignored her, speaking instead into her walkie talkie. "Bob? It's the policewoman again. Right. OK, Roger that." She clicked off the device. "We'll have an escort for you in a moment."

"An escort?"

"We're tightening the rules."

"But I'm investigating a murder."

The young woman didn't lower her arm.

Connie considered simply pushing past her. Security guards have no authority to stand in the way of police. But the arrogance of this Rajneeshee trainee made Connie curious enough that she decided to start her investigation here. She noticed that the guard's jacket had a green armband with the words, "Tico Trol."

"Are you a Tico?" Connie asked.

The young woman snorted. "Sort of."

Connie looked past her to the courtyard beyond. The fleet of red Priuses was gone, replaced by half a dozen rental trucks. Workers in red T-shirts were carrying tables, farm tools, tents, and cardboard boxes up metal ramps into the trucks. A pickup had a magnetic "Security" sign on the driver's door, along with the white dove logo. Standing incongruously in the pickup's bed was an empty red British telephone booth.

After a minute Tico Bob came striding out of the hotel office. He stopped in front of Connie with his arms crossed. He was a lanky man in his thirties with a long, freckled face and a square red beard. His security jacket was too small. Hairy wrists stuck out of the sleeves.

"Lieutenant," he said. "Why aren't you out catching killers?"

"I need to learn more about the victim, Juan Guerrero."

"You did that yesterday. When are you going to give us back the body? We need it for the wake."

"We're still trying to contact his family."

"We've been over this. We are Juan's family. He's been with the commune for years."

"I want to find out who last saw him alive. Maybe someone at the restaurant."

This was a reasonable request, and it slowed Bob down. Connie continued, "I'd rather not bring people down to the station for questioning, but I have that authority."

"All right, you can go inside Zorba's. If you want to go anywhere else, see me first." Tico Bob turned and strode back to the hotel office.

Connie shook her head, thinking how easy it would be to crush this overblown security guard, but why? She crossed the driveway to the Reborn Zorba Grill. Brown paper covered the inside of the glass doors, with the words, "Temporarily Closed" scrawled in red felt pen. One of the doors was held ajar by a metal menu stand. Connie pushed the door open.

An artificial waterfall dripped down a rock wall in the foyer. The dining room beyond had been stripped of furniture. The only lights were at the bar, where a large, white-haired woman with a red apron was talking across the counter to two bearded men in white chef outfits. "It has to be a completely different menu. More like camp food."

One of the chefs objected, "Sannyasins expect magic. Maybe we will find some."

Connie stepped closer. "Excuse me."

The large woman turned. "We're closed."

Connie held up her ID. "Portland police. I have some questions."

"Oh! Of course." The woman touched her hair, as if to tidy up. "Forgive our chaos. We're opening a cafeteria in a tent at Raja tomorrow, if you can believe it. By Wednesday they want a branch of the restaurant there too. And this place —" she waved at the dark room —" is supposed to reopen within two weeks."

"Then most of your wait staff has already left?" Connie asked.

"They're in Raja training new sannyasins. As if we'll actually have food for them to serve." She laughed, and caught herself. "Why? What can I do for you?"

"I want to find out who last saw Juan Guerrero."

The woman's face darkened. "The man they murdered."

"Did he come here to eat?"

"No." The woman shook her head. "Only once. Over a month ago, when we were starting up. We're all just as glad. He made enough of a fuss that we remember it."

"Why? What happened?"

"He asked in Spanish for meat — *carne, pollo*. We're a vegetarian restaurant. The waitress steered him toward our Shiva enchilada. That dish has lentils and alfalfa sprouts, but it tastes sort of meaty, you know?"

"And?"

"He took one bite and left without paying."

"Did you bill his room?"

The woman waved the suggestion aside. "We don't pester patrons here. Payment is a gift. But the staff didn't want him back either."

"Then where did he eat?"

The woman shrugged. "How would I know?"

The chefs glanced to each other. One of them said, "We could see him from the kitchen window. Every day around one o'clock he would walk past, heading up Burnside."

"How long would he be gone?"

"No idea. He must have come back a different way."

Connie felt like leaving them a tip on the bar. "Thanks. You've been helpful."

Back on the sidewalk, Connie started heading up Burnside. She only had to go two blocks before she found a Mexican restaurant. Amazingly, it was named "El Guerrero." With blinking beer signs in darkened windows, the place looked more like a bar than a restaurant. Connie mused that it might be the only restaurant in Portland that still advertised Miller Light and Dos Equis instead of craft beers.

The windowless metal door was locked, but Connie pounded on it long enough that it opened. A man with a black mustache scowled at her, a mop in his hand. "We're closed till ten."

"Lieutenant Wu, Portland police." She decided not to smile.

The man examined her badge, grunted, and let her in. "We had nothing to do with the fight last week. That all happened on the sidewalk."

Connie looked around. Pinball machines were flashing high scores. A flat-screen TV had football commentators arguing silently, with their close-captioned words appearing below in white. It really did look like a bar.

"Actually, I'd like to know if you ever saw this man." She showed him Guerrero's driver's license.

He squinted at the card in the dim light. "A Mexican?"

"His name's Guerrero."

"So what?"

"He's dead."

The man took a step back and held up his hands, as if to hold her at a distance. "Look, I don't know anything about this. Guerrero's a common name. I'm told it means fighter, or warrior, or something. My grandparents were from Mexico, but I'm American. Why are you questioning me?"

"Because I think Juan Guerrero walked by here every day. He wore a red robe."

"You mean he was a Rajneeshee? I've got hundreds of those red idiots walking by every day."

"Do you serve them?"

"Not if I can help it." His eyes narrowed. "Wait. I think I heard about this guy. They found him shot in a quarry, didn't they?"

"That's right."

"Good riddance."

Connie's voice was cold. "Would you have shot him, if you had the chance?"

"I didn't say that. But I tell you, the news is full of crazies threatening our country. If you're going to question everyone who'd like to see them stopped, you're going to be one busy lady."

Connie clenched her jaw. "Sorry to bother you, sir. I can find my own way out."

On the sidewalk once again, Connie fumed. The man was a bigot. His restaurant was a dive. She might question him again, but he probably had nothing to do with the murder. And he was right: She was getting nowhere fast. Still, what could she do? She walked another few blocks up Burnside, past a bank and a hair salon.

She was about to turn around when she noticed a brightly colored van in the parking lot of an antique hardware store. A middle-aged woman was standing beside it, cranking up an awning that read, "Paco's Tacos." Red parrots, green jungle plants, and an Incan ruin had been painted on the truck's side.

Connie walked up, holding out her ID.

The woman stopped, glanced at the badge, and sighed. With a tired voice she called, "Amy, it's the police."

A girl inside the van began wailing, more from anguish, it seemed, than from fear.

"I'm sorry —" Connie began.

The woman shook her head. "It's all right. She knew you would come."

"I don't understand. I just wanted to ask a few questions."

A girl looked out from the sliding door on the driver's side. Despite her tears, she was very pretty, with thick brown hair gathered into a long braid. She wore a peasant blouse that was short enough to reveal a gold stud in her navel.

"You're here about Juan, aren't you?" The girl's voice was deeper than Connie had expected, and raised her age estimate from sixteen to twenty.

"Yes, I'm investigating the murder of Juan Guerrero. Did you know him?"

The girl turned aside, fighting tears. Finally she wiped her eyes with a dish towel. She stepped down from the van and held out her hand toward a picnic table under a canopy. "Please, take a seat."

"All right."

"Would you like a Coke?" The girl bit her lip, on the verge of tears again. "He always ordered Mexican Cokes." She lifted two old-fashioned Coca-Cola bottles from an ice chest, uncapped them, and set them on the table. Then she sat down across from Connie without meeting her eyes. "They make Coke with cane sugar instead of corn syrup in Mexico. I can't taste the difference, but he —" She swallowed and closed her eyes.

"He came here every day, didn't he?" Connie asked.

The girl nodded, her eyes still closed.

"Tell me about him."

"He ordered fish tacos, pulled pork, something different every day."

"No," Connie said gently. "Tell me about *him*. About Juan."

The girl sighed and looked up at Connie for the first time. "I don't know much. But he was always polite to me."

"Did he speak in Spanish?"

"He preferred it. I spent a year as an exchange student in Puebla, so I was glad to practice."

"Did he talk about the Rajneeshees?"

"Not much." She fingered her Coke bottle. "One time I said the red robes were funny, and he agreed."

Connie sensed there was a lot this girl wasn't saying. "You must have heard that we're looking for people who have seen Juan recently. Was he here on Saturday?"

She nodded, her lips tight.

"Why didn't you call the police?"

The girl twisted aside. "I was afraid you'd think I'd done something wrong."

The older woman had come to stand by the van's front bumper. "Amy didn't do anything wrong. I keep telling her that."

Connie leaned forward and took the girl's hand. "What did you do?"

"I took tips."

"Tips?" Connie's thoughts veered toward gambling and insider trading. But then she remembered that the girl was a waitress. "Were they large tips?"

The girl nodded. "The first day he paid with a hundred-dollar bill and wouldn't take change. For three tacos and two Cokes — a tab of fifteen dollars. What was I supposed to do?" She glanced to her mother for support, and then looked down. "The next day I wouldn't let him pay at all for his lunch. But the day after that he gave me another hundred-dollar bill. It went on like that, sort of a game, every other day."

"It was all legal," the girl's mother added quickly. "Amy's kept the money separate, almost a thousand dollars, so she can report it on her taxes. She's saving up to take classes at the community college."

Connie took a sip of the Mexican Coke, thinking about the pretty young waitress and the fifty-year-old Rajneeshee. "Did Mr. Guerrero ever ask for anything else? Perhaps a date?"

Amy looked up, her mouth wide. "No! Of course not. He's older than my father."

"What did you think when you heard he'd been murdered?"

"I assumed someone had robbed him for his money."

"Do you know if he had any enemies?"

"No!" The girl seemed desperate. "I don't know more about him than I've told you."

"Really? I want you to think. Where did Juan go after lunch?"

The girl pointed one way, and then another. "Different directions. He said he was out talking walks."

"And on Saturday?" Connie tilted her Coke bottle slightly. "Which way did he go then?"

"Up Burnside, I think." The girl stopped, her gaze suddenly distant. "Yes, up Burnside. I remember thinking it was odd. I saw him walk out of sight in front of the hardware store. Then the wind tipped over a napkin rack and they began blowing across the parking lot. I ran out to the sidewalk to get them, and he was gone."

"Gone?"

"Yeah. I looked up the street, expecting to see Juan. He couldn't have walked far by then. But he'd simply vanished."

Chapter 14

Connie was so tired that she had fallen asleep in her living room chair, waiting for Neil to call. When the ring tone finally began she jerked awake, thinking at first that she was in a patrol car on a stakeout.

"Neil?"

"Hi, Connie. I miss you."

She smiled. This was the right thing for him to say. He sounded exhausted too. Neither of them had slept much the night before. Now the connection was so poor that his voice warbled. "Where are you? Are you OK?"

Neil walked out from the porchlight of his yurt to a moonlit field surrounded by dark firs, hoping for better reception. "I'm at Breitenbush Hot Springs. That first stretch out of Portland this morning was a killer. Cycle Oregon is thinking of starting at Estacada instead, and I'm going to tell them they should."

"What's it like at the hot springs?"

"Rock pools with people wearing crystals. Funky huts in the woods. You know what they served for dinner? Shiva enchiladas."

"Oh yes. Lentils and alfalfa sprouts."

Neil looked at the phone, puzzled. "You know it?"

"They're all the rage at the Rajneeshee restaurant. Did you finish yours?"

"I was so hungry I ate two. Listen, they enforce quiet hours here after nine, so I don't have much time. Any progress on the investigation?"

While Connie filled him in on her visit to Paco's Tacos, Neil walked around the field, changing direction if the phone connection weakened. When she described how Guerrero had vanished from the sidewalk, Neil asked, "Could he have gone into a store?"

"There's a hardware store. Otherwise, it's a long block without many doors."

"What about a car door?"

"I thought of that, but it's awkward." Connie's voice was tired. "If a car stopped and he got in that quickly, it means he knew the driver."

"You'd rather deal with a random murderer? They're even harder to trace."

A man in dreadlocks and overalls waggled a flashlight at Neil. "Beddy-bye."

Neil whispered into the phone, "Gotta go, but listen, I got a text from my niece Harmony. Have you met her?"

"Not yet. But I've seen her DNA report."

"The lab sent that already?"

"Yup. Your niece isn't even distantly related to the old Bhagwan. I mean really, what a crazy idea."

"I know. Still, it's hard to say no to Harmony. You'd better brace yourself, because she's on the way."

"She's coming to see me?"

"Tomorrow morning at your office. She's doing public relations for the Rajneeshees, and I think she wants a body back."

The man with the flashlight whistled at Neil.

"Miss you, Connie. Bye."

In the morning Neil wanted to sleep in, but when they rang a gong and the other men in his yurt began dressing for breakfast, he was too hungry to fall back asleep. He had spent so much of the night stretching his leg muscles that the bunk's sheets had pulled loose. He unwrapped himself from the tangle and began pulling on his red-and-blue racing outfit. He had worn the yellow-and-orange set into the hot springs last night, and it was still hanging damp on the bunk frame. He limped across the field to the bath house, splashed off his face, and combed back his graying hair.

The Breitenbush Hot Springs Retreat and Conference Center obviously did not have facilities for two thousand bicyclists, but it did have a big field. Cycle Oregon was a mobile city that set up its own kitchens, showers, and tents each day.

Almost everyone who lined up for tofu scramble and toast at the Breitenbush mess hall that morning was wearing red. Neil joined the queue beside a woman with long green-and-purple hair. She smiled. "*Namaste.* Aren't you the bicyclist who came in late last night?"

"Yeah." Neil remembered her, and not only because of the hair. She had stood in the middle of the hot springs pool with her hands over her head and her eyes closed, humming a single note as she danced naked. A large amethyst crystal on a cord at her neck had not been the only thing to bounce around. The cord now disappeared into the neckline of a red muumuu.

"Is everyone here on their way to Raja?" Neil asked.

"I don't know. They say hot springs are the gateway, so I came to see. I haven't made up my mind." Her heavy black eyelashes fluttered as she looked him up and down. "How about you?"

"I'm scouting the route to Raja for Cycle Oregon."

"Mmm," she said. "Do you want sex after breakfast?"

Neil coughed awkwardly. All his life he had been shy around women, and now they seemed to be saying the most astonishing things. "Thank you, but no."

She bit her lip. "I must sound like an idiot. I'm trying too hard to adjust."

"Adjust to what?"

She scooped eggs and tofu onto her plate. "Are you married?"

"Uh, no." He thought of Connie.

"You don't sound very sure."

"I have a girlfriend, I think." It was Neil's turn to dish up. He heaped his plate.

"Mmm." She held up two pieces of seed-filled wheat bread. "Want toast?"

"OK."

She slid the slices into a toaster and pressed the lever. While she waited she wound her brightly colored hair around her finger. "I divorced my husband because of toast."

"Really? That seems harsh."

"You think?" She looked at him, her eyes wide. "I'm not a harsh person."

The toast popped up. Neil took his slice to a picnic table at the far end of the plywood-paneled hall, where he could be alone. But he noticed that the Halloween-haired woman was still standing with her tray at the end of the buffet, searching the room as timidly as a transfer student in a tough new middle school. He had been in that situation before. And he had to admit that he was curious about the toast.

Neil gave her a small wave to offer the seat across from him. She came up with a smile. They ate for a while in silence. Neil's tofu felt and tasted like rubber. Finally Neil asked, "How could you divorce somebody because of toast?"

"I'm not a complainer," she said. "It's just how I am. I never nagged my husband about anything."

"He must have liked that."

"No. It drove him crazy. He kept saying, 'There's got to be something. How can we live in the same house if you don't tell me what's bothering you?' He kept pestering me, so finally I said, 'All right. There's a little thing about toast. When you make it in the morning, you might clean up the crumbs.'"

The woman reared back, mimicking a deep, angry male voice. "'Toast!' he says. 'Toast, is it? So now I'm a slob because of a few crumbs? Is that what you think?' He goes on like that for a few days. Then I come home from work and he's standing by the toaster with his hands on his hips. 'Look at this,' he says. "'You left crumbs!' I just shrug and tell him the truth: I didn't have toast that morning. He was lying, making the whole thing up."

Neil nodded. Much of his time as a policeman had been spent responding to domestic disagreements, often based on trivialities. "What did you do?"

"I dragged him in for marriage counseling. And he tells the counselor, 'You know, sometimes I think I'll just hang myself in the garage, and then when she comes home from work and opens the door, there I'll be.'"

Neil raised his eyebrows. "What did the counselor say to that?"

"She told me, 'Run. This is dangerous. Do you want to stay with him or file for divorce?' I realized that if I stayed with him I'd probably end up dead, so I said, 'I want a divorce.' At that point my husband stands up, hitches up his pants, and says, "Well. I didn't see that coming.""

"And that's why you're here at Breitenbush?"

She shook her head. "That was six months ago. He moved to Texas and remarried, so I didn't bother to change the locks. But each summer on his birthday he and his buddies like to get drunk and go target shooting in the woods outside Molalla. One of them has a machine gun that can cut down trees. Last week when I came home from work the house seemed just like I'd left it. But there on the kitchen counter, the toaster had been pulled out a few inches and turned sideways."

Neil whistled softly.

"That's when I put on a red dress, called in a leave of absence, and drove to Breitenbush, a place he'd never look." She sighed. "I'd heard so much talk about Raja and hot springs and peace, it seemed like a good direction to try. Although I'm new at this kind of thing."

Neil had begun to admire this spunky woman. "I can't guarantee you'll be safer with the Rajneeshees."

She nodded without looking up. They said nothing for the rest of the meal. When Neil had cleaned his plate and was about to stand, she asked, "Where are you bicycling today?"

"Belknap Hot Springs on the McKenzie."

"Oh," she said, and then whispered, "Are you sure you don't want sex first?"

Chapter 15

Neil kept looking over his shoulder, worried that the Toaster Lady might follow him to the next hot springs. The first sixteen miles of the route was a quick glide down a paved Forest Service road, tracing the Breitenbush River to Detroit. Unlike the Michigan metropolis, this Detroit proved to be a scruffy little resort outpost on a reservoir. Next he had to pedal up Highway 22 toward the Santiam junction. He shifted down to fourth gear, bracing himself as log trucks roared past without yielding an inch of their lane. He stopped at Marion Forks, the only roadside café for fifty miles, to order a big burger and marionberry pie. Then downhill again, racing the McKenzie River's whitewater to Belknap.

If Breitenbush Hot Springs had been the espresso machine of the Earth's soul, then the resort at Belknap was its Nescafe. Instead of Tibetan prayer flags, the entrance was decorated with chainsaw sculptures of bears. Antique fishing and hunting equipment hung from the log rafters of the lodge's lobby. No one wore red — especially not the receptionist, a toothy man with black suspenders and a shiny hook for a left hand.

"Ferguson, Ferguson," the clerk muttered, scrolling through computer screens. Finally he hit PRINT and waited a moment as an ink jet made telegraph noises. Then he thumped a sheet of paper on the counter with his right hand, and held out a pen in the pincer attachment of his left hook. "Sign here."

The $120 tab seemed steep, so Neil hesitated.

"What's the matter?" the clerk demanded, holding up the pen with his hook. "Never seen a claw before?"

Neil couldn't sign without a pen, and the clerk was now shaking it at him threateningly with a very sharp hook.

"Want to know how I got it?"

Neil wanted the pen.

"I was fixing my truck. My sweet old '56 GMC. God, I loved that thing." The clerk's eyes grew misty. "I was changing the battery when I reached down with my right hand for a wrench and bang! The hood fell and latched on my left hand like a bear trap. I couldn't reach the latch or pry the hood open. I was trapped there with my hand caught under the hood for twenty hours. Finally a neighbor came by on a horse and heard my shouts."

Neil looked at the man with new respect. "That sounds horrible. And amazing."

"It was January. It snowed six inches." He set the pen on the counter, clicking the pincer. "The password is BigfootLives."

"Password?"

"For WiFi. Are you really here about Cycle Oregon?"

"Yes."

"They booked six months ago. They're not changing their route now, are they?"

"Maybe they'll change the last day's ride, after Crater Lake. But I'm checking everything."

"Jimmy!" The man hollered over his shoulder. A sleepy teenage boy looked out from a back room. "Show Mr. Ferguson where we're going to stick all those bicyclists next week, will you?" The clerk snagged a towel from under the counter and held it out with his hook. "Swimsuits are required in the pool."

Neil hadn't brought a swimsuit, so he would have to make do with his bicycle outfit again. "When does the restaurant close?"

"Nineteen forty-five."

Neil thought it was odd that a lodge would run on military time. "You mean, at a quarter to eight?"

"I mean the restaurant closed after the war. The rooms have microwaves, and we sell snacks in the gift shop until ten."

The boy was waiting, so Neil followed him out to a golf cart. Jimmy began their tour of the resort's facilities by driving over a metal foot-bridge across the river. The campground on the far side seemed too small for two thousand bicyclists, in part because the owners had tried to convert part of it into a fake Italian garden with crumbling Styrofoam ruins. The boy assured Neil that there was more room on the hill behind the lodge, and Neil was so tired he didn't bother to see for himself.

Back at the lodge Neil took off his shoes, fell into the hot pool, and floated there on his back, staring up through the steam at silhouettes of the canyon's trees. Then he dried off, bought all the Pop-Tarts and microwave popcorn he could carry, and trudged upstairs to his room.

Susan's blog had been updated a few hours earlier:

> *OK Dad. No word from Harmony. You will not be welcome. You are the bad cop. Shiva, the destroyer. So am I, but good.*
>
> *Fort Klamath is Dawson in the Klondike. Cowboys, Indians, gold diggers, outlaws. Between Captain Jack's Casino and the Ex-Zorba-Tent Grill is Raja's East Gate, where Ticos take your money and give sannyasins assignments. First: baths. Then: curry. Then: meditation. Marijuana dancing. Roger talks from a stack of pallets. We sleep in rows in tents. Dregs and Gilberto are gone.*
>
> *This morning, more meditation. I like it. Then Shiva Shift. Garbage is everywhere. Shiva can be a good destroyer: A recycler. To build new worlds, use the ruins of the old.*
>
> *Stay out of Raja. Meet me at Jack's. No, at the Ex-Zorba Tent. After Shiva Shift, at 7. Jesus is coming.*

Neil puzzled over this communication, as he did over everything that his daughter attempted to say. Apparently she had been accepted into the Rajneeshee commune and was working as a recycler. He wasn't sure what had become of the two physicists, but they seemed more likely to gain inside information about Raja than a disgraced former security chief. Neil was curious about the Modoc side of the reservation. Perhaps he would fit in better among the outlaws and cowboys.

He ate his fourth mushy Pop-Tart, washed it down with a plastic cup of tap water, and was about to call Connie, but suddenly stopped. Why was he so nervous?' He combed his hair and brushed his teeth.

Then he tried again, and this time really did manage to press CALL.

The phone rang once, twice. His heart beat as if he had pressed a doorbell for a prom date.

"What can I do for you, Officer?" Connie's voice seemed uncertain. He thought fast.

"Do you know why I pulled you over, ma'am?"

"Contraband?" she asked.

They both laughed, and Neil felt better. "Apparently you survived the wrath of Harmony."

"I like your niece. She showed up with Bear, your former driver."

"Really?"

"She wanted Guerrero's body back. I let her take it from the morgue. But it turns out we had a lot to talk about first."

"Uh oh."

Connie clicked her tongue. "We didn't just gossip about you. But she did like your idea about infiltrators."

"Which infiltrators? Susan and Dregs? Does she know about Gilberto?"

"No. Harmony hasn't had time to read Susan's blog. But she thinks the killer might be disguised as a Rajneeshee. You're right that they don't do background checks before signing people up."

Neil lay back on the hotel bed and covered his forehead with his hand. "The infiltrator idea only works for the second murder. Guerrero might have gotten into a car on Burnside because it was driven by someone he knew — a killer pretending to be a Rajneeshee. But what about the first murder? Swami Bhrater was shot with the same sniper rifle, so it probably was the same killer. On the night of the revival meeting, all the Rajneeshees were busy. The infiltrator would have been busy too. Everyone was supposed to be at the Moda Center, either doing security or filling seats in the audience."

"The key phrase is 'supposed to be,'" Connie said. "Now here's my problem: The people I could ask about that night have left town. If the killer's an infiltrator, he's probably at Raja by now, looking for his next victim. We need to ask around when I'm down there this weekend."

Neil shook his head, even though she couldn't see it. "Without a warrant, you won't get past the gate. And no judge is going to issue you a warrant. Searching for the Rajneeshee killer in Raja? That's called blaming the victim."

"Where else am I going to look for leads?"

"Have you tried following the money?"

Connie sighed. "It's not so easy. I got NovoCity's tax forms, but they don't itemize income by client. To find out who paid for the streetcar ads I'd have to raid NovoCity's offices and go through their files. That's another warrant I won't get."

"I meant the big money. Have you traced the Rajneeshee millions?"

"The Raja Foundation is legit. It's registered as a non-profit charity. They've collected $7 million. All the money is going to pay for dorms and cafeterias and events."

"Wait a minute. What does the Rajneeshee commune own?"

"Isn't that the same thing as the foundation?"

Neil thought back. "When I got my job I remember hearing that the commune was a partnership. If so, that's a different pot of money. What about Air Rajneesh? Is the airline owned by the foundation?"

"I don't remember it on the list."

"Then who bought their airplane? Apparently Harmony organized the deal, but she doesn't have that kind of money lying around."

"OK. I'll check on that tomorrow."

"The person we really need to ask is Harmony," Neil said. "I wonder if she would be willing to snoop? She's close to their center of power."

"Too close, Neil."

Neil frowned. "How so?"

"She brought me one of Roger Nash's hairs. She believes he really is the reincarnation of the old Bhagwan and she thinks DNA might prove it. Personally, I think it's as crazy as her earlier DNA idea."

"Harmony may be gullible, but she's never crazy. Bill me for that test, Connie."

They were both quiet for a while, having run out of police business. Neither was sure how to bring up their personal business.

Finally, lamely, Connie said, "It's supposed to rain on Thursday."

"I can handle rain." Another pause. "You might bring a big tent when you come to Fort Klamath Friday night."

"A tent? I'm not much of a camper."

"Susan says it's the Wild West out there."

"I'll try to find a room. Miss you, Neil."

"Miss you too."

That night Neil wanted to dream about Connie, but instead he was being followed by zombies — tattered versions of the woman with Halloween hair and the man with the hook. In the dream, rain had turned the road to Raja into mud. The harder he pedaled his bike, the slower the wheels turned.

Behind him, the zombies were catching up.

In the morning when Neil dropped his room key on the front desk the clerk hooked it with his claw. "So where are you headed today?"

"Oakridge. Seventy-three miles."

"And then on to the Rajneeshee place?"

"After two more days."

The clerk tapped a few computer keys. While they waited for the printer to stutter out a receipt he spoke to the computer screen. "You know, I loved my old truck."

Neil pretended not to hear.

The clerk went on. "I thought my GMC loved me back, but she didn't." He cleared his throat. "I had a lot of time to think that night, with my hand trapped under the hood. About life and death, you know? About living alone out in the woods with an old yellow truck."

He set the receipt on the counter, but kept it pinned with his hook.

Neil looked up at him uncertainly.

"Do you think?" The clerk cleared his throat again. "Do you think the Rajneeshees would have a place for a one-armed mechanic like me?"

Suddenly Neil felt a wave of sympathy for this lonely man. The world was full of wounded people, refugees of ghost towns, looking for a place to belong. Everyone was as lost and misjudged as himself. They were all damaged detectives groping for answers.

"Aw hell," the clerk said, turning away.

Chapter 16

The next morning the air tasted of smoke. Neil bicycled through the settlement of McKenzie Bridge with the sun a dull red ball in a dirty sky. He stopped at Takoda's Restaurant to fill up on pancakes, and found most of the tables occupied by red-suspendered hotshot crews, wolfing eggs. They said fires were everywhere, sparked by lightning. But rain was coming, tons of it. Why the hell, the firefighters asked, would an old man be out riding a bicycle in a red-and-blue Spiderman suit?

Neil had biked the Aufderheide Byway years ago, when he was a cop on the Eugene force. Susan must have been at camp that summer, because he remembered setting out with his wife Rebecca, just the two of them on road bikes. He'd filled a bike trailer with sleeping bags, brie, and wine. In his memory that week-long trip was lit with a happy green glow. While they were stopped at Cougar Hot Springs, a pine marten had stolen their summer sausage. Neil had run after it naked, and Rebecca had laughed.

Now Neil pedaled past the hot springs trailhead without lifting his helmet. Firefighter trucks growled by as he sweated up the grade to Box Canyon Pass. Downhill to Oakridge a big black raven followed above him for a while, curious.

The WiFi wasn't working at the bed and breakfast in Oakridge. "Happens all the time here," the hostess told him. "Is eight o'clock OK for breakfast?"

Cell phone coverage was down to one bar. Neil barely managed to send Connie a text. He walked into town, bought a bucket of Kentucky Fried Chicken, and ate until he was almost sick. Then he went straight to bed, too tired to shower first.

No dreams. The windows rattled from the force of the rain. And no dawn. Instead, the black clouds merely grayed around the edges. Neil wished he had never set out on this bicycle trip. Still he bathed, shaved, put on his gala red-and-blue Lycra suit, and went down the spiral stairs to eat.

The only other guests at the long breakfast table were a thirtyish woman and her two pre-teen children. The kids were trying to ladle melon balls onto blue willow china plates. The hostess leaned from the kitchen door. "Quiche is almost ready. Coffee and juice are on the sideboard. You folks just get to know each other."

Before sitting down, Neil poured himself some orange juice from the sideboard.

The eight-year-old girl complained, "Mom! Paul's rolling cantaloupe at me."

Her younger brother grinned and said, "Meow."

"That's enough, both of you. Paul, don't slouch." Their mother looked up at Neil apologetically. She was a pale woman with pleasant features, no makeup, and a beige bandanna that covered most of her light brown hair. Her gray dress was pleated at the waist and extended almost to the floor. She could have been a plainswoman who had just stepped out of a nineteenth-century sepia print.

"Forgive my children's manners. They're not used to hotels. I am Mary Landenburger, and these are Rachel and Paul."

"Meow." The boy had a crewcut and a black Alcatraz T-shirt.

"He's talking in cat today." The girl wore blonde braids and a Dorothy-style gingham dress.

"My name's Neil. May I?" He motioned toward an empty chair.

"Of course." Mary wrinkled her brow and asked, "Mr. Neil, is it true that you are also traveling to Fort Klamath?"

"Actually, I am." Neil was a little surprised that their hostess had shared this information.

"And what will be the purpose of your visit? I see that you are wearing a bathing costume that includes the color red."

Rachel rolled her eyes. "It's a bicycling outfit, Mom."

Paul held up a honeydew ball on a fork. "Woof."

"Dummkopf."

"I'm scouting the route for Cycle Oregon," Neil said, and then, to see their reaction, he added, "But I'm also investigating the Rajneeshee murders."

"I knew it." Mary sat up even straighter. "We too are pilgrims, investigating good and evil. I'm sure you have heard that Jesus is coming to Fort Klamath."

"Well," Neil began. "I've heard that this particular Jesus pronounces his name *Hay-soos*. He's the Costa Rican swami of a dead Indian Bhagwan. But yes, apparently he's on the way."

"Quiche!" The bed and breakfast's owner brought out two egg pies, one with bacon and one without. For a while the group dished up slices and ate.

At length Mary set aside her fork. "My husband always preached that the end days would be complicated. The beast would rise. Ignorant armies would clash by night. All the signs are here."

Neil began to worry about this young family's immediate travel plans. "Will your husband be joining you at Fort Klamath?"

"No, he's a traveling preacher."

Paul growled quietly — a strange sound for a child, like the warning of a suspicious dog. Mary ignored the boy.

Rachel told Neil, "Papa's been gone for two years. My brother thinks that being a beast might bring him back."

"How do you live in the meantime?" Neil asked the mother. A night in the bed and breakfast must have cost the family a lot. "Do you work?"

"I home school. We pray."

"Is there a congregation you can call on for support?"

"Not yet," she said. "The Christian faithful are gathering at Fort Klamath to witness the Rapture. We will all be together then."

"So you've planned this as a one-way trip?" He imagined them camped outside Raja, waiting for the end of the world. Were other fundamentalist Christians really gathering there to pray down the Antichrist?

Mary nodded. "Life is always a one-way trip."

Neil waited under the inn's porch, fiddling with the rain cover on his pannier bags to delay the moment when he would have to set out into the deluge. Rain pelted the street so hard that the drops jumped back up from the pavement. The Landenburger family ran back and forth, bent beneath umbrellas, loading luggage into the trunk of an old Ford Falcon.

"Rachel!" The mother called.

The girl with the long pigtails had run back to leave their room key in a drop box by the door.

"Don't worry about us, Mr. Neil," she said, stopping by his bicycle.

"Why not?" He had in fact been worried the family's one-way trip to protest the Rajneeshees.

"The clothes in the suitcase? Before we left home Mom dyed them red."

He was staggered. "You're *joining* the Rajneeshees? I thought —"

"Meow." She wagged her head so the pigtails flew, and ran through the rain to the car.

As soon as Neil stepped out from under the porch he was drenched. His thin tires cut arcs of water through the puddles of Oakridge's half-abandoned old downtown. He took a bridge across the railroad tracks and turned east along Highway 58. The only public field big enough for Cycle Oregon was Greenwaters Park, a mile beyond the city. He toured it briefly for his report — cement-block bathrooms, a rundown amphitheater, a riverbank lost in the gray rain. Without even stopping he swerved back up onto the highway.

Almost at once an eighteen-wheeler with a load of plywood peeler cores blew him into the roadside gravel. Sheets of muddy water knocked him off his bike. He landed hard on one knee and scraped his hand trying to break the fall. Then the bike skidded into the ferns and his helmet bounced.

The pain began registering when he rolled over in the mud to get up. His knee sang in agony beneath torn pants. The red speckles on the palm of this hand were running into stripes with the rain.

He picked himself up and limped in a circle, gasping until the pain dulled enough that he could think. The pannier bags had ripped loose and spilled in the mud, but they had saved the bike itself. The pedal and handlebars were scraped but unbent. The bike was operable. Was he?

Ahead of him lay two days of hard riding. The first day was

forty-six miles, with a stretch of wet, slippery gravel over the Calapooia Mountains. Toketee Hot Springs had a primitive campground with a field and nothing else. He would have to pitch his bivvy tent in the rain and eat cold handfuls of gorp. The following day he would have to ride another sixty-four miles, climbing around Crater Lake's rim, to reach Fort Klamath — where, Susan assured him, he would not be welcome. How the hell had he gotten himself into this?

Neil picked up his bike, in the process tweaking his knee so painfully that he cried out. To top it off, yet another big truck was careening through the rain toward the white line. Each of its wheels doused him to the waist with dirty water.

But this time the truck's tail lights flashed red. Brakes squealed for a hundred yards. The great white box on wheels lurched onto the shoulder, rumbled to a stop, and hissed. A moment later the passenger door swung open and a big dark man in a maroon raincoat leaned out.

"Boss?"

Neil wiped his eyes with his bloodied hand. The trucker had a shaved head. "Bear?"

"Hey, boss. Need a lift?"

Neil limped up.

"Jesus, Neil, you look like shit. Why the hell are you out here?"

"I'm doing research for Cycle Oregon. How about you?"

"Trucking refrigerated goods to Raja." Bear looked at him closer. "Whoa, you fell pretty hard. I've got some stuff in the truck." He went back to the cab and fetched a first aid kit from behind the seat. After he had washed Neil's hand with a bottle of water and taped up his knee with an elastic bandage, he said, "Let's throw your bike in the back."

"Thanks, Bear." Neil collected his fallen gear in the pannier bag while Bear opened the truck's insulated back door. For a minute fog obscured the cargo inside. Bear went to pick up the bicycle. By the time he came back, Neil was able to discern stacks of boxes in the truck. The largest and longest of them was red: a British telephone booth lying on its side.

"You've brought the body," Neil said, his voice dull.

"Juan? Yeah, I was taking a load of cold stuff anyway. He's in a plastic bag, so it's OK." Bear hoisted Neil's bike and bags into the truck and shut the door. "Let's get you warmed up in the cab."

Neil limped around the truck and climbed into the cab.

Bear began rummaging in the bags behind the seat. "I've got some dry clothes, if you're not fussy about fit. Baggy is all the rage in Oakridge."

"I'm not going to Oakridge," Neil said.

Bear stopped and looked at him sternly. "You need a doctor and a bus ride home, boss."

Neil shook his head. "I really am scouting a route for Cycle Oregon. They're hitting all the hot springs between Portland and Crater Lake next week. They had planned to end at Prospect, but I'm suggesting they go to Fort Klamath instead."

"To Raja?" Bear looked at him in disbelief.

"To Fort Klamath's hot springs. I'll be there all week, making arrangements."

Bear folded his arms over the steering wheel. He dropped his forehead onto his hands with a groan. "Harmony said you were stubborn, but this is too much. We've already had two of our people die on your watch. Haven't you done enough damage?"

"If you'd rather put me back in the rain, I'll ride to Raja on my own."

Bear looked across at the blood-streaked face, the cold gray eyes, and the hair dripping with rain. After a while Bear sighed. Then he squeezed off the brake and put the truck in gear.

Chapter 17

"You'll find zip at Raja, boss." Bear downshifted the tractor-trailer and swung off Highway 97 at a makeshift plywood sign with a spray-painted dove. "They won't even let you in. Besides, the killer's in Portland."

"Is he?" Neil flexed his palms; the bleeding had stopped. "If the killer's goal is to drive the Rajneeshees out of Oregon he'll be in Raja, hunting them down."

Bear growled — or was it the lugging engine? "Maybe in Dawson."

"Dawson?"

"The Modoc side of town. The tribe doesn't like the name Fort Klamath. They say that name was chosen by their white enemies for a different tribe. Truckers started calling it Dawson. The place really is as crazy as the Klondike Gold Rush."

"But with protesters?"

"Not as many as you think."

"Maybe because they're already inside. On my bike trip I met three different people who were considering joining the Rajneeshees. They weren't mystic cultists. They were ordinary people who'd lost something — a husband, a hand, a home. They were at loose ends. Like you, Bear, from a ghost town."

Bear looked straight ahead without answering.

"My theory," Neil went on, "is that the killer is an infiltrator, someone pretending to be a Rajneeshee in order to destroy Raja from the inside."

Bear cleared his throat. "Too many pieces."

Neil looked at him quizzically.

"The new Bhagwan's trying to put together a jigsaw puzzle with thousands of pieces," Bear said.

"Maybe one of them belongs in a different picture."

"Exactly. We won't know until we fit them all together."

They rode for a while in silence. The ponderosa pine forest gave way to a valley of farm pastures, backed by a dark blue range of more densely forested mountains. At the far end of the valley the fields turned white with flashes of silver, as if a fleet of spaceships had landed there, burning the grass to ash.

"Even if they won't let me in," Neil said, "I'd like to keep in touch with you so I can find out what's happening inside Raja."

"Sorry, boss. We're not supposed to make calls in Raja. It's all part of focusing inward."

"But you can text?"

Bear shook his head disapprovingly.

Neil had thought the message from his daughter had been cryptic, even for Susan. Now he realized she wasn't supposed to communicate at all.

Bear braked, slowing to join a line of traffic. Makeshift signs had been propped up against pickups parked on either shoulder of the highway: "Payday Loans", "Bananas $3", "Redwear Sale."

"I'll let you out before I turn off," Bear said. "I have to go to the South Gate for deliveries. Raja's laid out in the shape of a mandala."

"Round, like a lotus flower?"

"This one's rectangular, with gates in the middle of each side. You'll want to go straight another quarter mile to the East Gate by the casino. But they really won't let you in."

"How about the other two gates?"

Bear shook his head. "Restricted, even for me. The North Gate's got the hot springs and the West Gate's for the organic farm." He stopped the truck in the middle of the lane and opened his door. "Let's get your bike."

The bus behind them honked while Bear walked around to the back and unlatched the door. He pulled the pannier bags and the frosty bicycle out of the fog.

"Thanks for the lift, Bear."

The big man only shook his shaved head. "You shouldn't be here, boss. Cycle Oregon? Bad idea."

Neil put the panniers on the bike's back rack. "What's in the middle of the mandala?"

"Nirvana, boss." He winked. "Maybe Bigfoot."

Connie was getting nowhere with her investigation in Portland, despite Neil's tips. Finally she called the One World Buddhist Retreat in Vernonia, if only for a chance to get out of town.

Captain Dickers had just grilled her in his office for an hour. "Two murder weapons, and you can't find either one."

"The .22 pistol that killed Guerrero would be so small it could be anywhere," Connie objected.

"But there's also a sniper rifle out there the size of a car rack. Listen, the media guys want another press conference. The headlines aren't going away. We've got to come up with something."

"I've stationed squads at the Jupiter Hotel and the Killingsworth shop. There's no sign of another attack."

"That's not an investigation."

"Well, I did find out that the Rajneeshee commune is owned by a partnership based in Singapore."

The captain stared at her. "Why on earth do we care about that? Everybody knows their whole outfit's Asian. Stop plaguing the victims. You know, I think we were better off with Ferguson."

The captain pressed a button on his phone. "Right. Could you come in a minute? Wu really does need help."

Now it was Connie's turn to stare. Could the captain have lured Neil out of retirement? She had heard nothing from Neil since yesterday's brief text from Oakridge. He had talked about quitting his bicycle tour.

"It wasn't easy to get him," Dickers admitted, "But he's come up with an interesting new theory about the killers. It's an alphabet theory, and I want it explored."

"Would —" Connie stammered, at a loss. "Would I still be in charge?"

"For now. This isn't a demotion."

There was a tap on the door's frosted glass, and the shadow of a man.

The captain walked to the door. "I just thought you two, working in parallel — well, you make a good team."

Connie's heart was beating so hard she couldn't think straight. She herself had told Neil that they made a good team.

Dickers opened the door. But the man standing there was not Neil Ferguson. It was Luis Espada from forensics.

"Oh!" Connie managed to say. "Isn't — isn't Lieutenant Espada in a different department?"

"We need fresh ideas. Tell her, Espada."

The short-haired young man had a large black mustache and quick black eyes that darted about nervously. "I never really wanted to be in homicide. I just wondered what would happen if you investigated the suspects algebraically, like we do in the lab."

The captain rolled his hand in the air encouragingly.

Espada continued, "I assigned the letter W to the Bhagwan's father, John Nash. He had the clearest motive and opportunity for the first murder. But he was in jail when the second Rajneeshee was killed, so W is out. That leaves two known suspects, X and Y. And all the unknowns out there, Z."

"Who are you calling X and Y?" Connie asked.

"The only two protesters Roger Nash picked out at the Moda Center, Mrs. Lawrence and Mr. Hamsby."

Connie sighed. "Mrs. Lawrence is Roger Nash's Sunday school teacher. She was petitioning about a tax issue. She's not a sniper."

"Algebraically, she's still a suspect. Although she wouldn't seem as violent as the Baptist preacher, who apparently talked about murder."

"We interviewed everyone who rode on Hamsby's bus," Connie said. "They all went home together. Their stories match. I think our perp is Z."

"And I want you to keep after your mystery man, Wu. Maybe you'll find Z in Singapore." The captain chuckled at this. "In the meantime I'm assigning Espada to investigate the other suspects, X and Y."

Connie had fumed for hours. Espada's specialty was tracing bullets, not interviewing Sunday school teachers. And the whole Singapore business hadn't been her idea. Neil was the one who had told her to follow the money. That plan had led to a dead end, an address in Singapore where hundreds of partnerships and corporations had their official headquarters. Google's street view showed an unmarked door on a back street. More research revealed that the office was only open one hour a week. It had no telephone. You would have to go there in person, and knock.

Setting up an appointment in Vernonia had been much easier. A friendly male voice on the telephone had responded, "Patricia Holmes? Of course you can see her. Is forty-five minutes enough time?"

"I think so."

"She's free tomorrow at two. What name should I give her?"

"Wu. Lieutenant Connie Wu of the Portland Police Bureau."

"Oh! Well, I can imagine you'd want at least that long with Patricia."

Connie wore a civilian pantsuit and took an unmarked Buick for the drive to Vernonia, a sleepy logging town in a Coast Range valley an hour west of Portland. There were no signs for the retreat center, but her GPS sent her up a long gravel road to a dark canyon in a Douglas fir rainforest. The parking lot had a circular painting of a green-and-blue globe. From there a gravel path led up beside a cascading creek to a gateway in a bell-shaped tower. Beyond this the valley widened to a glen with a dozen pagoda-like buildings on stilts, connected by a network of raised boardwalks. Somewhere little bells were chiming.

The nearest building was marked "Porter's Lodge," so Connie went there. Inside, a long-haired man in a loose yellow shirt looked up from the computer on a counter. "Connie who?"

"Wu. Lieutenant Wu."

"Wu? At two?"

Connie sighed. "Yes. I'm here to see Patricia Holmes. Is it true that she's the aunt of Roger Nash?"

The man smiled. "Our Patricia has become a bit of a celebrity."

"Can I speak with her?" Neil had warned her that the woman might be elderly and ill.

"Speak? Perhaps. Most of our visitors prefer silence." He put a large white towel on the counter. "Disrobe in the stupa above the creek. Patricia will be there soon."

Connie stopped. "I'm supposed to take off my clothes?"

"Of course."

"What kind of visit are we talking about?"

"Massage is part of our stress-reduction therapy. It is far more effective if nude."

"What if I just want to talk?"

He laughed, pushing the towel toward her. "I hear that from a lot of first-timers, but honestly, just take off your clothes. Wait on the padded table, face down."

Connie took the towel. She crossed a footbridge to another bell-shaped hut on stilts above the creek. Although it had no windows, a Plexiglas dome provided a view up into the treetops. Glass floor panels revealed that a mossy stream ran underneath. The walls were rough-hewn cedar. An infrared lamp kept out the chill.

Connie sat on the padded table in the middle of the room, feeling as awkward as if she were waiting for a checkup with a new gynecologist. She wasn't really here to interrogate Ms. Holmes. In fact, she didn't even know what questions to ask. Neil had simply suggested that she visit Roger's aunt on a hunch.

The longer Connie sat there, the better a massage sounded. The unsolved murder cases had knotted the muscles in her shoulders and lower back. Finally she took off her pants and shirt, but left on her underwear. Then she lay face down on the table. The trance-like tones of wind chimes seemed to emanate from another world. She closed her eyes to wait.

When Connie awoke, strong slender fingers were rubbing a slippery liquid on her shoulder blades. Because Connie's head lay to one side she couldn't see the masseuse. And it wasn't easy to turn her head while she was being kneaded so firmly. Besides, it felt pretty good. She let out a breath with a hum, thinking that this might start a conversation.

The masseuse set to work on the muscles at the back of Connie's neck. The fingers dug deeper and deeper until Connie exclaimed, "Ow!" She twisted up on one elbow to look.

Her tormenter was a woman her own age, but with voluminous, light brown hair tied in a lop-sided ponytail over one shoulder. Rimless spectacles did little to hide what must once have been beautiful brown eyes, although years of sun had surrounded them with wrinkles. Her white, button-up dress might have passed for a doctor's kittle, except for the luminescent, long-sleeved purple T-shirt she wore under it.

"Oops," she said, widening her eyes yet further. "Hit a nerve, Lieutenant?"

"I didn't really come here for a massage, Ms. Holmes."

"But you need one, Ms. Wu." Patricia pushed her gently back

onto the table and began rubbing her lower back with small circular motions. "The Rajneeshee murders have got you all over the news. They've also wound up your muscles like a clock."

"You don't seem surprised to see me here."

Patricia laughed — a musical sound that blended with the woodland chimes outside. "We've been wondering when you'd come to check up on the Bhagwan's loony aunt. There aren't many other people with a motive to bump off his Rajneeshee rivals."

This was a new angle for Connie. Perhaps Swami Bhrater and Juan Guerrero really could be considered competitors for Roger Nash's position. "Are you into sniper rifles?"

"With hands like these, I'm more of a strangler." Patricia snapped the back of Connie's bra strap. "Do you mind?"

"Um —" Connie began, but the clasp was already undone, and Connie felt even more vulnerable. "Maybe you could tell me a bit about yourself? What I know comes third hand, from your sister. She thinks you're in an assisted care facility for the feeble minded."

"That's a fair description of the One World Center, from Cathy's perspective." Patricia stepped back, out of Connie's sight, and startled her by rubbing the soles of her feet. "Catherine is the older, responsible daughter. When our parents drifted apart, she became the anchor — you know, a lump of Baptist iron at the bottom of a bay. Me? I floated away on the tide."

"And where did that take you?"

"Peru. Greece. I spent a whole year in a cave on Crete. Red sand beaches, red sunsets, red wine."

"Ever go to Rajneeshpuram?"

"No, that troubled piece of paradise closed down before I started bumming my way around the world."

"Any serious relationships?"

"Nope." Patricia had worked her way up to Connie's calves, and concentrated for a moment on digging loose some particularly tangled tendons. "Lots of frivolous ones, though. Never married. It's a good thing I seem unable to have children."

"What brought you back to Oregon?"

"Cathy's pregnancy. Her husband is a sexist jerk. She's kind of a jerk too, but she needed family around. I guess blood really is thicker than water."

"You babysat for them on Saturdays."

"That too." Patricia chopped at Connie's thighs with the edges of her flattened hands, an intimate and somewhat humiliating procedure. "I opened a massage booth at Portland's Saturday Market, under the Burnside Bridge. Rog loved it there. It was the one day a week he could run wild, eat vegetarian burritos, and learn juggling from guys in dreadlocks."

"I'm surprised your sister allowed it."

"Crazy, isn't it?" Patricia shoved the heel of her hand up the small of Connie's back. "She finally cut me off the summer Rog was twelve. I'd taken him to the Oregon Country Fair in the woods outside Eugene. He came back with a henna tattoo of a warrior elf."

Connie couldn't help but laugh.

"Roll over, Lieutenant, and I'll play the flip side."

"No thanks." Connie clutched her bra straps. "I don't think I can afford the full monty."

"You still have a lot of tension. And there's no charge. People leave offerings in the brass urn if they want."

Connie hitched her bra and climbed into her pants. "We're done here."

"You're not mad, are you?"

"No."

"Am I a suspect?"

Connie stopped buttoning her shirt. "You would be if the Rajneeshees had died from karate chops to their thighs."

Patricia slumped her shoulders. "Which means you're focusing on the only other person in the world with a motive — my sister. You've probably already looked under the bed in her Airstream trailer where she keeps her .22 handgun."

Fascinating! Connie found so much in this single remark that she stood for a moment, thunderstruck. The public did not know that Juan Guerrero had been killed by a .22 before being shot with a high-powered rifle. Had Patricia found out, or had she guessed? Either way, by revealing the location of a hidden gun Patricia was casting suspicion on her own sister. Connie resisted the temptation to take the bait. Patricia really might be guessing, and she definitely had a grudge.

Connie changed the subject. "Do you believe your nephew is the reincarnation of the Bhagwan Shree Rajneesh?"

Patricia took off her spectacles and cleaned the lenses with a purple sleeve. "Did you ever see the movie *Groundhog Day*?"

"The comedy with Tom Hanks?"

"Bill Murray. But yeah, it was a comedy about having to live one day over and over, thousands of times, until he finally got it right." Patricia put her glasses back on. "Buddhists believe that's no joke. We've all been here before, making mistakes, trying to do better."

Connie straightened her jacket and picked up her purse. "So that's a yes about Roger's reincarnation?"

"He's slowly discovering who he really is. He's not quite to February third yet."

"I see. Well, thanks for the massage." She took three twenty-dollar bills from her purse and dropped them in the brass bowl.

"*Namaste.*" Patricia opened the door, and the two women left, setting out in different directions on the raised walkways.

Then Connie stopped. "Oh, just one more thing."

Patricia turned. "Yes?"

"Did you notice any strangers at the baby shower the week after Roger was born?" Connie didn't know why Neil had asked John Nash this question at police headquarters, but she had been astonished by its effect then, and she was equally impressed now.

Patricia, paled, her mouth half open. "No!" she breathed, and hurried away.

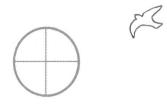

Chapter 18

Neil limped along the road's shoulder, wheeling his bicycle through the confusion that was Dawson. Just a few weeks ago, the main street of the Modoc's new reservation must have been nothing more than a country lane between cattle pastures, with a rundown motel and a crossroads with an abandoned general store and a derelict Shell gas station. Now the roadside was a clutter of shipping containers, tents, and trailers. Neil passed a pawn shop and another payday loan booth — clues that he was nearing the casino. More troubling was a storage pod with the sign, "GUNS." Lugers and assault rifles hung on display behind a metal grille. Tattooed men in leather jackets watched Neil suspiciously. For a second he thought he saw a familiar face glance furtively from behind the grille and disappear. Neil looked again, but the face was gone, and couldn't really have been there at all.

Paralleling the road a hundred yards to the west, an eight-foot chain-link fence with coils of razor wire marked what he assumed was the boundary of Raja. All Neil could see of the Rajneeshee city was a row of white tents. He noticed a security team, in the red jackets that he himself had ordered, attaching black plastic tarps to the back of the fence to block even this view.

Traffic had gridlocked at the four-way stop in the center of town, where a fresh-looking signpost pointed left to Vishnu Way and right to Modoc Avenue. Two dozen cars jammed Vishnu Way, backed up at a security checkpoint in front of the forbidding metal wings of Raja's East Gate. To the left of the gate, a banner over a rainbow-striped circus bigtop announced the Ex-Zorba-Tent Grill. To the right, the weathered clapboard wall of an old general store had been crudely painted with the words, "Captain Jack's Casino & Saloon."

Suddenly Neil realized how hungry he was. He checked his phone for messages. Nothing. Susan wasn't expecting him until tomorrow. He sent her a quick text: *"I'm in Raja a day early. Will be in Zorbas at 7. Love, Dad."* That gave him a few hours. He locked his bike to the old gas station's SHELL sign. Then he considered the two eateries. He decided to explore Jack's first.

Neil had to squeeze through a crowd on the porch, past a man wearing chains and a holster. Inside, the noise and smoke hit him like a baseball bat. Blinking slot machines lit the murk. He pushed his way to a counter where a dark woman in some kind of feathered swimsuit shouted, "What'll it be, captain?"

"What have you got?"

"Canned Bud, pop, and hot dogs. Ten bucks each."

"Ten bucks? A hot dog, I guess."

She held up a hand, rubbing her thumb against her fingers.

Neil fished his wallet out of his torn Lycra pants and held out a ten. She traded the bill for a hot dog in a bun with a napkin and a packet of mustard.

Neil shouted, "Who's in charge in this town?"

"In Dawson?" The woman laughed.

"I want to bring a few thousand bicyclists to the hot springs next week. Who can I talk to about setting that up?"

"Jesus!"

"The swami?"

The woman shook her head. "Maybe Tom Shontin."

Neil remembered the quiet-spoken Modoc elder from the presentation at the Moda Center. "Where can I find him?"

She rubbed her fingers together again.

Neil fished out another ten.

She tucked the bill into her feathered bra. "Try the construction site across the road tomorrow. Friday's payday, so he should be around. But watch yourself, sugar buns."

"Thanks." Neil looked around at the crowd and decided it might be easier to fight his way out via a back door, if there was one. Hot dog in hand, he struggled past gaming tables in what must once have been a series of low-ceilinged sheds. The clamor dimmed and the number of red robes increased. The stacks of chips on the tables also grew taller, suggesting higher stakes. He was almost to the back when he noticed a brawny arm with a hook raking in a pile a colored chips.

"You?" Neil asked, surprised. He held up a hand in greeting.

The clerk from Belknap Hot Springs squinted at him. "Damn. You look like you got eaten by a truck even meaner than mine."

Neil hid his bloodied hand. "I guess you were serious about joining the Rajneeshees."

"Naw. I drove here last night for a look-see and wound up lightening some red pockets by a few grand. Quit my job, got a room at the motel."

"There's a motel?"

"Full at $500 a night." The clerk sized Neil up. "You and your biker friends will wind up camping with all the rest."

"Where's that?"

"Cow fields by the creek, out Modoc Avenue." He turned back to his game. "You boys know how to play Seven-Toed Pete?"

Neil wandered out the back and found himself in an alley against an impromptu Berlin Wall — Raja's barricade of chain-link, black plastic, and razor wire. He was a stone's throw from the East Gate, a Checkpoint Charlie with metal detectors and video cameras. Even at this distance he recognized one of the security staffers — the young woman who had taken the banners away from the "Trust Jesus" protesters at the Moda Center. Neil lowered his head, hoping to slip under her radar.

Back at the four-way stop sign he had time to eat his hot dog and think. In the 1980s, when the Rajneeshees' Portland hotel had been bombed, the sect had retreated to a desert complex with armed guards. This time, with two Rajneeshees dead, the group had withdrawn once more. But what was the point of their wall of fear? If a gunman was looking for red targets, he would find plenty in Dawson. The new Rajneeshees were evidently free to walk away from the rules of Raja, and obviously enjoyed gambling. The fact that no one had been shot in Dawson suggested to Neil that the killer really might be an infiltrator, on the other side of the fence.

Neil checked his phone, worrying again about Susan. There were no messages from his daughter, and it was too early to call Connie.

He unlocked his bike and wheeled it out Modoc Avenue toward the campground. A man at an abandoned gas station on the right was selling five-gallon jugs of water or gas — your choice — for thirty dollars. To the left, cranes and rebar pillars rose above the plywood fence that screened a huge construction site. A sign announced, COMING SOON! *Captain Jack's Resort / Casino / Hot Springs / Spa / Hotel / Saloon / Modoc Heritage Center.*

The Rajneeshees were obviously making good on their part of the bargain, helping the Modocs build a business.

The street's pavement gave way to gravel, with pallets and plastic pipe stacked on either hand. Beyond the construction site a boy sat at a card table under a canopy with the sign, "Camping $40."

Neil walked up and asked, "What do I get for forty bucks?"

"Hot tubs. Drinking water." The boy pointed to a line of people waiting to fill containers at a hose beside an old farm house. Behind them, other people had crowded into a dozen galvanized metal cattle troughs — apparently the hot tubs. Beyond that, cars and tents littered a grassy field.

"Bathrooms?" Neil asked.

"A load of Porta-Potties are supposed to come in tonight."

Neil took a couple of bills from his wallet. His cash was disappearing fast in Dawson.

The boy added the twenties to a wad in his pocket, briefly exposing the butt of a pistol. Then he took out a green felt marker. "Hold out your hand."

Neil held out his palm.

The boy wrinkled his nose. "Geez, you're all bloody. You can't go in the spa like that."

"I'll wash first."

The boy drew a green F on Neil's wrist. "Just don't wash off your receipt. There's a different code each day."

Neil looked at his F. "You've been in business six days?"

The boy's eyes widened. "How'd you know?"

"I'm a detective."

Neil took his bicycle out past a row of motorhomes and a yellow school bus marked TROUTDALE BAPTIST CHURCH. Wasn't that the church of the "Trust Jesus" protesters? He hadn't yet seen them or their signs in Dawson.

Neil set up his little tent in the emptiest spot he could find and un-rolled his sleeping bag inside. Then he took his only other set of clothes — the yellow-and-orange bicycling outfit — to the cattle troughs. He washed up in the warm water of an overflow pipe, dunking his head and scrubbing his torn outfit. The only place to change clothes was behind a patch of willow brush. Of course this was also the latrine, a smelly, shallow pit with a shovel and a plank where people squatted. He held his breath while he used the pit. Then he changed clothes.

He checked his watch: It was nearly six thirty. He hoped Susan had gotten his message to meet him a day early at Zorba's.

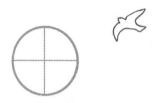

Chapter 19

But Susan hadn't gotten his message, or else she was too busy with her recycling work to get away. Surprisingly, the picnic tables in the rainbow-colored circus tent of the Zorba Grill were not crowded and the prices on the menu were reasonable. Neil guessed that vegan fare didn't interest Dawson's construction workers, and the Rajneeshees who ventured into the wild side of town were probably looking for more than fruit smoothies.

He ordered a Shiva enchilada and ate it alone, uncomfortably aware that he was being watched. His messy dismissal as security chief left him all too recognizable among Rajneeshees.

At seven o'clock a waitress in a skimpy red dress hit a gong with a mallet and turned on a flat-screen TV. Conversations stopped. Everyone but Neil placed their palms together and bowed toward the snowy screen.

After a minute the screen flickered to red, with the white dove symbol in the middle. A voice Neil didn't recognize — certainly not Harmony's — announced, "*Namaste,* and welcome to the Rajneesh World Service podcast, live from Raja. Tomorrow we anticipate the arrival of Swami Jesus, who achieved his awakening at the same moment that Swami Bhrater's spirit moved on to other lives. Tonight our host is the reborn Bhagwan, Rog Nash."

The screen cut to a wide-angle shot of a vast crowd, mostly in red, on either side of a gravel lane. The Rolls Royce that Neil had armored drove slowly through the throng to a stage. The car's door opened and Rog got out, smiling and holding his thumbs up. When the camera zoomed in to follow him up the stage's steps, Neil saw that the platform consisted of hundreds of wooden shipping pallets. Plywood sheets had been nailed on top as a floor. Even the stairs on either side were staggered stacks of pallets. The stage looked like an Aztec freight yard.

Rog took a microphone off a stand and shouted, "Hello, Raja! Hello, world! We can meditate later. First put your hands together and make some noise!"

Even from Zorba's, the applause seemed like the roar of a sea. Still, Neil couldn't help but notice that Rog was a lot less convincing without the older Swami Bhrater as an opening act. Rog's square black beard looked scruffy, and the red doo rag around his head seemed amateurish. Perhaps that was why the announcer had talked up the impending arrival of Swami Jesus.

Roger held up his hands to quiet the crowd. "Thanks to all of you our city of Raja is rising. The provisional greenhouses are up. Our first crops are being planted. Hot water is in short supply, but we're drilling for more. Food service, housing, security, fire crews, sanitation, coffee drinks — Raja is a work in progress, and together we're making it happen."

The applause after this speech was thinner, suggesting to Neil that there had been complaints, even here at the gates of Nirvana.

"Tomorrow," Rog went on, "Our new swami will lead us through ceremonies for the two we have lost — a vigil for Juan, and a farewell for Swami Bhrater. In the meantime, I want to try out this amazing new trick I've learned. I'm going to marry all of you beautiful people."

This time there was no applause. A few voices laughed nervously.

"You won't be marrying me! It's the other way. I'll be marrying you. To each other. If you want." After this struggle for words, Rog explained, "I've just been ordained as a justice of the peace. We've even got a few couples here so I can try it out. Come on up, guys."

Three couples climbed the steps, shyly holding hands. One couple wore cowboy hats. Another wore red robes. The third were two bearded men in tuxedos. Roger read an abbreviated wedding ceremony. Then he pronounced them spouse and spouse and asked them to kiss.

While the crowd cheered, Roman candles at each corner of the stage began shooting up red fireworks.

"That's it for tonight," Roger said, waving. "Think peace, do love, and find happiness, my friends. In the morning, prepare to meet Jesus. *Namaste* and good night."

The waitress at Zorba's turned off the TV. Apparently this was a signal that the restaurant was closing. Everyone began paying their bills, including Neil. He took out his phone: Still no messages, and no answer from Susan. He wanted to call Connie, but he didn't want to be overheard, so he left the tent and walked out Modoc Avenue until he found a quiet spot behind a stack of plastic pipe. To the south, the broken outline of the unfinished resort against the twilight sky looked more like a bombed-out ruin than a city under construction.

Connie answered with a disturbingly weary, "Hi, Neil."

"Hi, Connie. Everything OK?"

"Great." Same tired tone. "How about you?"

Neil was about to say, *I fell off my bike*, but even in his head this sounded petty. Instead he said, "I'm in Dawson."

"Dawson? Where's that?"

"It's what they're calling the Modoc side of Raja."

"I thought you were supposed to be at Toketee Hot Springs."

"I was, but Bear saw me while he was driving a truck through Oakridge. He stopped to offer me a lift to Raja, and I took it. I'm camping on the edge of town. Dawson's a rough place, and Raja's locked up tight. I haven't even been able to get in touch with Susan yet." He paused, then added, "I'm looking forward to seeing you on Saturday."

Connie didn't respond right away. The sky was starless. Half a dozen young men walked by with flashlights and beer bottles, laughing.

Neil asked, "Are you sure everything's all right?"

She sighed. "This morning Dickers called me in and took away half the investigation."

"What? Who else is he putting on the case?"

"Luis Espada."

"He's not even in homicide!"

"I know. But the captain says we need new ideas. He especially thinks I've been wasting time asking about the Rajneeshees' finances when I'm supposed to be finding their murderer. I'm starting to think so too."

"Really? What did you find out about their finances?"

Connie told him about the Singapore office that hid the details of the Rajneesh Commune's partnership. "Dickers couldn't care less. He said everyone knows the Rajneeshees are based in Asia."

"So you aren't going to follow up on the office's address?"

"I can't. Besides, more useful leads are turning up in the places you overlooked. Again."

That stung. Neil asked, "Such as?"

"Well, I went out to visit Patricia Holmes in that Buddhist retreat, like you said."

"What did you find?"

"Ms. Holmes isn't any older or more decrepit than you or me. She works there as a masseuse. When she heard I was a cop, she ratted out her sister for the murder of Juan Guerrero."

Neil whistled. "So she really is the crazy aunt."

"Maybe not so crazy."

"Huh? Roger's mother hardly matches the profile of an assassin."

"Patricia says her sister keeps a .22 pistol under the bed in her Airstream travel trailer."

Neil felt the blood drain from his face. A .22 pistol was the weapon used to kill Guerrero. And suddenly Neil saw how it could have been done. "Catherine would have had a motive — getting her husband off the hook for the first murder."

"Right," Connie said dryly. "How could John Nash possibly be guilty if he's locked in jail when the second Rajneeshee gets shot? We even make it easy for Catherine by holding her husband a full week, giving her time to come up with a plan. Finally she gets in her car and cruises past the Jupiter Hotel down Burnside, looking for people wearing red."

Neil slapped his forehead. "And Juan jumps into the car, but it's not because he knows the driver. He gets in at the point of a .22. Did your team search the Nash trailer for pistols?"

"They only searched the house. And now I'd look like an idiot, trying to get a judge to give me a second search warrant, especially after I've already released John and told the world he's innocent."

"No point, anyway," Neil said. "If Catherine shot a random Rajneeshee and dumped him at Wildcat Mountain, then she would have been smart enough to throw the weapon in a river on the way home."

"That route passes dozens of suitable bridges. I can't send divers to all of them."

"So unless you find a witness who's seen Catherine's car, the only evidence you have for a grand jury would be Patricia Holmes' say-so. The spiteful suspicion of a crazy aunt." Neil leaned against the pipes and looked up at the sky. An ivory glow suggested that a half moon was hiding behind clouds. "Still, I don't know. Roger's parents are pro-life. They protest at abortion clinics. I'm not sure they'd assassinate strangers, even to protect their son."

"Neil, protesters at abortion clinics sometimes assassinate strangers."

"That's not what I felt about Mrs. Nash."

"Lucky for you, there's another new suspect. Unfortunately, it's another one you'd written off."

"Who?"

"Roger's Sunday school teacher."

"Oh, come on," Neil groaned. "Now you're just teasing me."

But Connie didn't sound like she was teasing. "Remember how Espada has been assigned half the case? He calls Mrs. Lawrence 'Suspect X.' This afternoon when I got back to my office, his report was lying on my desk. Want me to read it to you?"

"All right," Neil said warily.

"'Mrs. Alma Lawrence, age 63, served as Roger Nash's teacher at the Hillsdale Baptist Bible Church from September 2001 to June 2002, when Roger was twelve. She has no police record, and no record of traffic violations. On June 29 of this year her husband Vernon, age 65, drove her to the Rajneeshee event at the Moda Center so that she could collect signatures for a petition to deny the Rajneesh group tax-free status. The petition — '"

Neil interrupted, "Connie, this is just proving my point. She's really not —"

"Shut up and listen for once."

Neil reeled back. Connie had never talked to him like this, even when she had refused to let him date her. "Sorry, Connie. Go on."

"'The petition is an initiative from the 1000 Friends of Oregon, a nonprofit group that confronted the Rajneeshees with similar complaints in the 1980s. Her husband Vernon is a retired lawyer who has been on the board of both that organization and the Oregon chapter of the National Rifle Association. On weekends he trains high school students in marksmanship at a rifle range in Hillsboro. In the three years since his retirement he has been convicted of selling high-powered rifles to a felon. Contacted by cell phone, Mr. Lawrence said that on the night of June 29 he did not accompany his wife into the Moda Center. Instead he said that he waited for her in the car outside. On July 6, the day Juan Guerrero died, Mr. Lawrence claims to have been hiking alone at Shellrock Lake in the Mt. Hood National Forest. When asked his current whereabouts, Mr. Lawrence terminated the conversation, but a check with his cellular coverage company reveals that his signal is coming from Fort Klamath, Oregon.'"

Connie stopped reading.

Neil's stomach had begun a sick churn. Could he screw things up any worse? Actually, he realized that he could.

"Neil?" A steely voiced asked from the phone. "Are you there?"

He took two deep breaths before answering. "Yeah, I'm still here. And there's something I saw today I didn't want to believe."

"Oh? What?"

"Mrs. Lawrence's face. The Sunday school teacher. In the glass door of a Dawson gun shop."

They were both silent for a long time. Somewhere in the darkness a car engine roared and voices shouted.

"Connie," Neil said at last. "I'm not perfect. I've made mistakes, and this case is a mess, but let's not let it come between us. We need to work together. We —"

"We! We?" Connie's voice jolted his ear. "When I was about to walk away from Patricia Holmes I asked her that same stupid question you'd used to make John Nash clam up on us. Remember? About the baby shower? And guess what? She clammed up exactly the same way. What aren't you telling me?"

Now Neil really did taste bile in his throat. "I had a box."

"A box? What kind of box?"

"A little wooden case sealed with the logo of the old Bhagwan."

"Not the one Roger waved around at the Moda Center?"

"Yes. Catherine Nash told me it had appeared mysteriously at his baby shower twenty-six years ago. She'd kept it ever since. Then she gave it to me."

"To you? Why?"

"I don't know. I had it in my apartment for two weeks, until there was a break-in. The burglar must have had a key or a pick-lock. All he took was the box."

"You had the case of the reborn Bhagwan? And you told me nothing? What an asshole."

The line went dead.

Neil bent forward as if he had been punched in the stomach. Why, if he loved Connie, had he failed to tell her about the box? He had led her away from two top suspects because he'd been fooled into thinking they were harmless church ladies. And Harmony — the whole thing had started because of his beguiling niece — instead of keeping her safe he had managed to drag his daughter Susan in the cult's vortex too.

Finally it all came up, with the sick taste of lentil enchilada, hot dog mustard, his whole damned involvement with the Rajneeshee mess. One horrible heave after another.

When his stomach emptied Neil staggered back toward the campground. His damaged knee shot pain up his leg with each step. He wanted a drink to wash the taste of failure from of his mouth. Just one shot of bourbon. Jack's would still be open. The craving for alcohol followed him like a cougar in the shadows. Normally he resisted the urge by bicycling, but now he was simply too weak. His best hope to dodge a relapse would be to crawl into his sleeping bag. To shut his mind to the demons. To sleep.

When he limped out past the motorhomes to his campsite he found a small crowd had gathered there with flashlights. His bivvy tent lay flattened, a crease across the middle.

"What happened?" he asked.

"A car drove right through the fucking tent," a man said. "We all thought the guy inside would be dead, but it looks like the sleeping bag was empty."

Neil's stomach clenched for another dry heave. He managed to ask, "Anyone recognize the car?"

"Sort of." The man tipped his head toward Raja. "It was a red Prius. One of theirs."

Chapter 20

Susan's journal

I worry about Dad.

He's supposed to bike here tomorrow. But I can't contact him. Tico trolls took away phones. No more blogs. They gave us little blue books instead. I will give this one to Dad tomorrow at Zorba's. If he is there. I worry that both of us may be in danger if we are seen together.

Strange. One of my new hires on Shiva Shift says she met him bicycling at a hot springs. Margaret. She said he was too tired for anything. She repeated "anything" in a strange voice, sung high-low. What do these things mean?

Most sannyasins think recycling is the worst assignment. So wrong! Margaret was inept at hauling trash cans. She hated sorting. But what a talker. I envy her. A social Einstein, compared to me.

I decided to transfer her to a waitress job at Zorba's. When I told her she jumped up and tried to hug me. I backed away. I don't hug.

Dregs lasted two hours on the drilling crew. Moving heavy pipe. Shoveling muck. Not his thing. Now he's running sound and video for the Plaza stage.

Gilberto arrives tomorrow, flight to K Falls, red shuttle bus. Just before the Harmony/Jesus show. Funny!

I don't see Dregs much. Separate dorm tents. Will H even notice G?

Green armbands everywhere. Each day the Tico Patrol makes a new rule. Some say their security makes Raja safe. No new attacks, see?

Something is wrong. Getting worse.
Curfew. Stay safe, Dad.

PS — Just had a brilliant idea for getting these journals to Dad. Use Margaret!

Chapter 21

In the dream a white raven and a black dove were flying in circles above a double ghost town. Neil was running atop the S-shaped wall that divided the derelict cities, a relay race without a team, searching for a lost child. Should he look west, in the tattered white tents that remained of Raja? Or east, in the charred black ruins of Dawson?

He heard a cry, turned, and fell — but on which side? Down and down he spun. Just before he hit, he awoke with a start.

Blue nylon fabric twisted around him, wet with cold dew. He was in a box, a wooden well.

Pallets. Now he remembered the tire tracks on his tent. He had stacked a fortress of castoff pallets around his broken tent before crawling in.

The rest of the campground was still asleep, but dawn had grayed the sky. Neil was wide awake so he got up, used the newly arrived Porta-Potties, and washed in the outflow of the cattle trough hot tubs. Then he sat by his bike, eating a cold breakfast of granola and water. His knee still ached, but his bloody scratches had scabbed over.

He decided to take a bike ride to clear his head and see the rest of the settlement.

He pedaled slowly to the crossroads in the middle of town. The lights were still on in the windows of the old general store, Captain Jack's Casino. Neil turned right toward Crater Lake, passing the construction site of the future casino. Beyond was a small motel named

The Palms, a few rundown houses, a farm, and another campground. Feathered flags and bumper stickers for Indian Pride suggested that this was where the Modocs stayed.

Beyond the Modoc camp the highway struck off across empty pastures, without the booths and trucks he had seen on the south side of Dawson. Apparently most traffic came from Klamath Falls, and not from the national park. When Neil looked back over his shoulder he could see a wisp of steam and a metal tower above Raja's north wall — the hot springs and the drilling rig.

Neil remembered from Susan's blog that her boyfriend Dregs planned to work there. He wondered if Dregs had really managed to get a visa for Gilberto, and if so, what would Harmony think?

Neil had a lot of questions for his daughter Susan. From her previous text, it sounded as if she had been accepted as a Rajneeshee. As a garbage collector she would have opportunities for snooping around — visiting remote parts of the city and sorting through the things people threw away. He wondered if the Rajneeshees realized she was the daughter of their former security chief. Perhaps they already suspected she was a spy. Certainly that would explain why Susan no longer answered her phone or posted blogs.

Of course, his infiltrator theory seemed weak after talking with Connie last night. The Sunday school teacher's husband, Vern Lawrence, was a dangerous outsider with a motive for murder. The memory made him angry with himself.

Neil pedaled harder up the empty highway, climbing from the valley fields into forested foothills. Never had he felt so wounded as when Connie had hung up. She had accused him of betraying her confidence — and she had been right. He hadn't told her everything he knew. Perhaps a part of him had still viewed her as a former colleague, the woman who had stolen his position as lieutenant. Even on the night when they had become lovers he hadn't shared everything with her.

This was not the sort of rift that could be mended by sending flowers. He doubted she would answer if he tried to call her. Would she come to Raja tomorrow as agreed? And if so, what new apology would he have to offer?

Neil stopped at a switchback. The view stretched across the valley to the silver sheet of Upper Klamath Lake. The best apology would be to solve the murders. The Rajneeshee case had already ruined his career, and now it threatened to destroy Connie's as well.

Despite all the evidence against Roger's mother, Neil could not believe that Catherine Nash would commit murder, even to free her husband from jail. Neil had sat in her living room, drinking her awful coffee. She had spoken about her respect for human life. She had made Neil swear to protect her son. And only then had she given him the mysterious box — as if to seal his oath. Perhaps she had been lying about something — yes, that now seemed likely — but Neil did not believe that she had been lying about the sanctity of life.

The Sunday school teacher, Mrs. Lawrence, was a different kind of suspect. Neil knew her only from the Rajneesh Revival. He should have interviewed her afterwards. Then he would have learned about her violent husband, Vernon. What were they doing in Raja? And now that he thought of it, why was the bus from the Troutdale Baptist Church in Dawson's campground? That group had brought the "Trust Jesus" signs to the Moda Center, but he hadn't seen them protesting here.

Neil turned his bike around for the downhill ride back to town — and in so doing, remembered that he still hadn't made arrangements for Cycle Oregon to end their tour at Raja's hot springs. He had a lot to do.

What troubled him most, however, was that he didn't have a clue about how to patch things up with Connie.

Chapter 22

Neil decided to start with the easiest task first — convincing the Modoc elder, Tom Shontin, to let Cycle Oregon camp in Dawson. But even this proved problematic.

A young Modoc woman with a hardhat and a clipboard stopped him at the gate to the casino construction site. She made him wait there an hour before telling him that Mr. Shontin was overseeing work on an airstrip in the southeast corner of the reservation.

At the airstrip the workers told Neil that Shontin had gone to lunch at Jack's. But Shontin wasn't at Jack's either — or at least Neil couldn't find him in that jammed, murky madhouse. Perhaps because Neil was still a little off balance from his bruises and a bad night's sleep, it took him half the day to realize he was being given the runaround. Shontin obviously didn't want to talk to him.

Neil switched his search to the Lawrences, but nobody seemed to have seen the Sunday school teacher or her husband either. And although the Troutdale church group was now marching with their "Trust Jesus" signs at the intersection of Modoc Avenue and Vishnu Way, they refused to talk to him as well.

While Neil stood there, unsure what to do next, the protesters formed a human chain across Vishnu Way, trying to stop two red buses from reaching the East Gate. The wide-eyed faces of new sannyasins peered out the bus windows. Within moments, Tico Patrol security people pushed the protesters to the side of the road — shoving more forcefully than Neil would have allowed when he was in charge of security.

By late afternoon Neil had worked up his nerve to call Connie — although he wasn't sure what to say. After four long rings the phone switched to an out-of-office recording and beeped for him to leave a message. Suddenly uncertain, he hung up. Neil waited two hours, until Connie would be off work, and tried again. Her home phone switched to an answering machine. Her cell phone didn't answer at all. Obviously he had screwed things up so badly that she wasn't picking up, and she definitely wasn't coming tomorrow. He was on his own in Dawson.

Now Neil pinned his hopes on Susan. He hadn't heard from his daughter for two days, but at last contact they had agreed to meet at Zorba's at seven o'clock. Everyone else might fail him, but surely not Susan.

Except that Susan was not at Zorba's. Neil searched the café three times. Susan could behave strangely, but she never broke a promise. She was in trouble, and it was all because of his stubbornness. He should have walked away from the Rajneeshee debacle long ago.

"Hey, bicycle cowboy."

The woman's voice sounded familiar. Neil looked up. An attractive middle-aged woman stood before him in a rainbow-colored smock. An amethyst crystal hung from a necklace in a cleft of pink skin. The Toaster Lady?

"You're looking glum, honey," she said, clucking her tongue. "Wake up on the wrong side of town?"

"You," Neil managed to say. "You're the one who danced at Breitenbush Hot Springs."

She reddened, obviously remembering her naked dance in the hot springs pool and her impetuous offer at breakfast the next morning. "Last time we met I didn't really understand the Rajneeshee way. Life here turns out to be less about sex and more about work. See?" She pointed to a 'Margaret' nametag on her breast. "How about a Shiva enchilada? Cheer you right up."

"You're a waitress."

"Here they call us 'food offerers.' They moved me to Zorba's because I stank at my first job." She leaned in and whispered, "Shiva Shift."

Neil looked up. "You were in recycling? Did you meet —" He stopped himself.

Margaret nodded. "Susan's fine. I'll tell you more after the show. Enchilada?"

"Anything but that. I threw one up last night."

"Maybe fried potatoes? I can have them hold the tofu."

He nodded gratefully.

Margaret stood there a moment, biting her lip as if debating what more to say. Finally she blurted, "Susan doesn't want you here. No one does. You should get back on your bicycle and leave." Then she turned and hurried away through the crowd.

Neil had some time to puzzle about Margaret. She had left her husband, fearing for her life, and that made sense. But she didn't seem as comfortable in her new Rajneeshee role as she wanted him to believe.

After fifteen minutes she brought him hash browns and ketchup. By then another of the food offerers had rung a gong and turned on the TV. The entire café focused on the screen's white dove, waiting for the seven o'clock presentation.

Bells tinkled as words slowly faded into view beneath the dove: "Jesus is coming."

It took Neil a moment to remember that the message was about the new swami.

A faint thump-thump-thump began echoing outside. A man drew back the café's tent flap and pointed to the sky. "A red helicopter!"

The aircraft slowly circled Raja, drawing cheers. Then the screen showed the chopper landing in a roped-off circle, surrounded by a vast throng of sannyasins. When the blades stopped, security staffers unrolled a red carpet from the stage to the helicopter. The door opened and out stepped — Harmony.

Neil's heart lurched at the sight of his beautiful niece. She looked tired. She stepped aside, holding out her bare arm to the man behind her.

Barrel-chested, bald, beardless, but with an enormous white mustache and fierce dark eyes, Swami Jesus strode out to meet the crowd. Neil couldn't help thinking that the man looked like a professional wrestler who had retired from the ring. Even the shimmering red cape he wore could have been part of a Chicano wrestler's *lucha libre* costume. The swami surveyed the crowd and held up his palms beside his head — a gesture Neil did not recognize, but which prompted louder cheers from the audience.

On stage, Roger Nash was welcoming the new guru and talking about what would happen next, although no one seemed to be paying much attention to him. Swami Jesus walked to the stage and took the microphone out of Rog's hands.

"*Namaste*, sannyasins of Raja," the swami said, holding the microphone close. A slight Spanish accent clipped his words. "As your new swami, it is my first task to honor our dead. Then we will celebrate the transcendence of my predecessor."

Tico Bob, the lanky, red-haired chief of security, pulled back a tarp at the end of the stage, revealing a red English telephone booth. With some shock, Neil realized that Juan Guerrero was still inside, but that his corpse now had been forced into a cross-legged yoga pose.

Security people with fire extinguishers encircled the booth. Tico Bob lit a torch and held it out.

Swami Jesus stepped forward, grabbed the torch, and declared, "Good bye to our comrade and sannyasin, Juan. The enemies of Raja have only succeeded in setting your spirit free." He tossed the torch at the base of the telephone booth.

Soon flames roared about the windows, lighting the ghostly corpse inside. Minutes passed before the booth burned down to a smoldering black frame. The heat had been so intense that the figure inside slumped into an unrecognizable black heap.

"Farewell, Juan. May you find peace," Swami Jesus said. "Two weeks ago, Swami Bhrater's spirit was released in just this manner. And at that moment I awakened, my heart suddenly open to the unity of being, on a plane beyond suffering. It is a dawn I hope to share with you, sannyasins." He bowed to the audience and then to Roger.

Neil marveled that the new swami had been in Raja less than an hour, and yet he had already taken command, relegating Roger to the position of an assistant. On whose authority, Neil wondered, had this *lucha libre* guru awakened? The crowd cheered him on as if there had been no coup. The television, however, zoomed in to show Roger open his mouth and then close it as though he didn't know what to say — and indeed he had no microphone with which to say it. Neil found this interesting as well. Who was directing the camera?

"In his transcendence," Jesus continued, "Swami Bhrater's spirit shared enlightenment with me. Now that his body has been gone for two weeks, it is time he passed on his possessions. Bring them out."

Tico Bob and a helper carried out a folding table. On it were a robe, a pair of sandals, and a small wooden box that Neil knew only too well.

"This was Swami Bhrater's robe," Jesus declared, holding high an old maroon sheet. "It is a cloth of humility, a shell he knew he would have to shed to achieve transcendence. And now it will belong to our young Bhagwan as he learns his way." Jesus draped the robe about Roger's shoulders. The audience applauded.

"The old Bhagwan's sealed box," Jesus continued, holding it aloft. "This the teacher will keep safe until the student is ready."

Even Neil couldn't see exactly what happened next, but the new swami swept his red cape and the box vanished. While the audience was still puzzling over this, Jesus held up Swami Bhrater's sandals. "To walk in holy shoes is to follow the path of a saint. How many paths do you think these sandals have seen?"

The camera closed in on the worn, braided leather of the shoes.

"The Bhagwan Shree Rajneesh, in his former life, believed that these were the sandals of Jesus of Nazareth. That sage did not die on a cross in Jerusalem, our Bhagwan told us, but rather escaped to India, where he lived to old age as a holy man. Since then his shoes have been resoled a hundred times, worn by a hundred sages. Now their path has brought them here to Raja, to another swami of that name."

Jesus took off his own shoes. He was about to slip the old sandals on his feet when Harmony stepped forward, speaking so loudly that her voice could be heard through his microphone.

"Stop! This isn't what Swami Bhrater wanted."

Jesus looked up at her from the side. "There's an objection from the escort?"

"Yes." She crossed her arms and spoke into the camera. "Swami Bhrater wanted his robe to go to Roger, but he didn't own the Bhagwan's box, and he didn't want his sandals to go to you."

Neil had stood up, electrified. His niece, a spokesperson for the Rajneeshees, was defying the new swami. Why?

Jesus seemed just as disconcerted. "And how, sannyasin Harmony, do you know these things?"

She gave a shrug with one shoulder. "Because he put it in his will."

Now it was the security chief, Tico Bob, who confronted Harmony. "Swami Bhrater left no will. We are his family."

"Maybe we're his family, but there is a will." Harmony took her cell phone out of a pocket. "I have a picture of it. I'll post it so everyone can see."

"No phones in Raja. Security rules." Tico Bob put his hand on her phone. A look of uncertainty crossed Harmony's face. Then she glanced out at the audience, as if for support. Suddenly she seemed so startled that she let go of the phone.

The camera shifted back to Swami Jesus. He quickly moved on to other matters, diverting attention from Harmony by introducing another group wedding.

Neil sat back, lost in thought. Did Swami Bhrater really leave a will? The guru hadn't had many possessions, but perhaps his sandals were more valuable than they seemed. If there was a will, how had Harmony managed to get a picture of it? Neil remembered last seeing Harmony at the Zorba restaurant in Portland, where she took a picture of the box's Sanskrit text. Apparently she liked to take pictures with her cell phone. She was close enough to the Rajneeshees' inner circle that she might have photographed Bhrater in private. Still, it seemed strange that a will would have been kept secret, and that she would wait to reveal it now, at a televised ceremony.

Another issue that troubled Neil was that Tico Bob's security squads had apparently confiscated all private telephones in Raja. No wonder Susan hadn't been answering his texts. This also explained why she would try to forward a message via the Toaster Lady. Susan might even have transferred Margaret to the café specifically to contact him.

Neil endured the last half hour of the TV presentation — a long meditation by Roger and the new swami — while he waited to see what else Margaret had to tell him about Susan. When fireworks concluded the Raja show and the café began emptying for the night, Margaret showed up with a thin blue booklet. She handed it to him, saying, "Greetings from the garbage brigade."

Neil recognized the booklet as the kind he had used for final exams years ago at the University of Oregon. He opened it and read:

Susan Ferguson — Journal
Thursday, July 12, Raja

I worry about Dad. He wants to bicycle here tomorrow. Big mistake! Dregs and I fit in at Raja, but Dad won't. Dregs is a tech at the Plaza stage. Perfect for him. For me, recycling is the best assignment of all.

Strange. One of my new hires on Shiva Shift says she met Dad bicycling at a hot springs. Margaret. What a talker! I envy her. A social Einstein, unlike me. When she admitted that she didn't like sorting garbage I transferred her to a food job at Zorba's. She was so happy she hugged me.

Gilberto arrives tomorrow, flight to K Falls, red shuttle bus. Just before the Harmony/Jesus show. Happy!

Dad was troubled when he worked for the Rajneeshees. Two people died. I don't want to see him here. I will ask Margaret to take this journal to him at Zorba's. I hope he understands and goes home. I will see him later in Portland. Stay happy, Dad.

Neil closed the journal, thinking. The journal's tone was cold and remote — but his daughter often sounded that way. She had always craved order. Raja's regimentation really might suit her. And yet something about the journal struck him as wrong. Would Susan really have allowed anyone to hug her? Even he wasn't permitted to do that.

He looked up to see Margaret wiping tables in the otherwise empty café. "Aren't the Rajneeshees still posting blogs?" he asked.

"Blogs? The Internet is off limits. We all write journals like this now." Margaret stopped, her brow wrinkling as if from a sudden headache. "There was another message for you. That is, if you insist on staying in town tonight."

"Another message from Susan?"

"No, from someone named Tom. One of the Indians, I think."

"Tom Shontin?"

"Yeah, that's him. He said you'd find him at the casino construction site tonight at nine."

Neil weighed this message, and Margaret's nervousness, and Susan's block-lettered handwriting. "How much do I owe you for the hash browns?"

"Oh, they got rid of the prices. Everything's by donation now. It's on me."

"You've earned something for your trouble." Neil took a twenty-dollar bill from his wallet. "I think what you've done is worth twenty pieces of silver."

From the way her face flushed red, Neil knew he'd struck a nerve.

Margaret fingered the crystal at her neck. "Don't go to the construction site. Leave town now. Right away."

Neil shook his head. "Not until I find out who moved the toaster, and why."

Margaret froze. The twenty-dollar bill blew off the table as Neil walked out of the tent into the dark streets of Dawson.

Chapter 23

Neil glanced at his watch: almost nine. Music and laughter still shook the clapboard walls of Captain Jack's temporary casino. The construction site across the street, however, was a graveyard of silhouetted steel skeletons and silent gravel mounds. The chain-link gate should have been locked, but it stood ajar, as if it were the entrance to a trap. And sure enough, the bait had been left in plain sight. The window of an office trailer framed Tom Shontin's dark head and broad shoulders, apparently crouched over a desk full of paperwork.

How many would there be, Neil wondered? Three? He scanned the yard for boards or chains that could be used as weapons, but of course it had been neatly cleared.

He was too old for this. But sometimes the only path is the one straight ahead.

Neil took a steadying breath and walked through the gate toward the window. "Tom! Tom Shontin!" If the Modoc elder had agreed to this meeting, at least he had better watch.

The shadows began closing in almost at once. There were half a dozen. They wouldn't be trained in this line of work, but it was still more than he was prepared to confront. He turned toward the gate, and found it blocked by tall, bearded Tico Bob.

"What happened to non-violence, Bob?" Neil could see police clubs in their hands. Then the light in the window went out, and he could see nothing. Gravel crunched as their footsteps neared.

"We do what works now, Ferguson. Anything but firearms."

Neil wondered if their new tactics included forging journals and threatening women. He wanted to ask how much it had taken to turn a waitress into their stooge. But that might put even more people at risk. Aloud he suggested, "Does it work to drive cars over campground tents in the dark?"

"We don't need outsiders, Ferguson. Especially not you."

The first blow hit Neil unawares, a painful crack to the same shoulder he had hurt in the bike accident. When the second club struck — also from behind — he swirled and caught a wrist. His attackers were working in the dark too. He wrenched the wrist 180 degrees until there was a scream and the club fell. While he searched for it in the gravel, a boot knocked the wind out of him from the side. Still on his hands and knees he found the club and swung hard, connecting with something solid that groaned.

But then the blows starting coming from all sides — to his neck, his eye, his legs — and all he could do was curl on his back, trying to protect his face with the club.

How long this went on he couldn't remember. Somehow the pain became a wall, and his memories retreated to the other side, to a Roseburg playground. He had tried to stop the fifth-grade boys from throwing bark dust chips at the new Vietnamese second grader, and they had turned on him instead. He had built his first wall that day, a barrier of pain and defiance. At the age of ten he had become a cop.

Only this time the blows wouldn't stop. The wall began to give way. Distantly he realized that they actually might kill him by mistake. Of course they merely wanted to frighten him away, not murder him in front of a witness. But amateurs wouldn't know when to stop.

He had lost everything on this dead-end trip to Raja, and for what? When a bright light suddenly surrounded him, he realized he'd lost the wall itself. He was on the far side, looking back into the blinding glare of his past life.

What he didn't expect from death was that it would include a voice shouting, "Freeze!"

What?

"Hands in the air!"

Neil managed to open an eye. There were two bright lights. Headlights through the chain-link gate. And a woman in a black turtleneck aiming a service revolver with both hands.

"This is the police! Step away with your hands in the air!"

Tico Bob squinted into the headlights. "Who the hell are you?"

"Lieutenant Wu. Portland police."

"Sorry, lady. This is a Modoc reservation. You don't have jurisdiction here."

"My Glock does." Connie steadied the gun at him. "Last I heard, real police don't beat people up, even on a reservation."

Tico Bob looked to the dark window. "Shontin? Why aren't you out here, man?"

Connie clicked off the safety on her Glock. "Get your goons out of here. Now. Before I start making mistakes too."

The Rajneeshee security chief looked from the gun to the dark trailer. Then he cursed and motioned for his staffers to follow him. As they walked past Connie he said, "You'll lose your job for this. Just like your boyfriend."

Even before they were out of the gate, Connie hurried to where Neil lay crumpled on the ground. "Neil?"

He managed to lift himself to an elbow. His face was covered in blood, one eye swollen shut. "I — I thought you —" He coughed.

Connie's eyes were damp. "You're hurt! How bad is it?"

"Tenderized. I'm a tough steak." He tried to smile, and coughed. "I thought — you —"

Now Connie was crying. "Yeah, I'm still mad, you asshole. You keep getting us both into the worst shit."

"But — but you came anyway?"

She was shaking her head. "I knew something was wrong. I wasn't going to be able to sleep, so I drove down after work."

"How —" Neil wheezed, " — find?"

"A waitress closing up the café said to go here. Are you sure nothing's broken?"

A mercury-vapor floodlight flickered on over the roof of the office trailer, casting them white with stark shadows.

"Shontin." Neil nodded toward the trailer. "Gotta talk."

A short, broad-shouldered man in a suit coat opened the office door, shading his eyes with his hand.

"Hey!" Connie called. "Get some help. This man needs a doctor."

Tom Shontin nodded. "My daughter-in-law is a healer." He took out his phone and made a short call. Then he walked closer, frowning. Neil struggled to sit up, wincing. "How'd you like the show?"

The Modoc elder shook his head. "Usually I see Indians beating each other up on reservations. Not as good as I thought, watching white people do it for a change."

Connie glared at him. "You let this happen? What about your tribal police?"

Shontin shrugged. "Our reservation is young. The county sheriff doesn't want to send patrols. We have been relying on the Rajneeshees."

Neil spat bloody saliva. "What did Bob tell you?"

"That you are dangerous. A rogue lawman, bringing white vigilantes to our reservation."

Connie laughed. "You mean Cycle Oregon? They're bicycle tourists, just the kind of publicity your resort needs. The only vigilantes here are the ones you saw beating up a retired cop."

"Yes, perhaps so."

"Last night," Neil said, wiping his face with his sleeve, "A red car ran over my tent."

"What!" Connie exclaimed.

"I think they knew I wasn't in it. Just another warning."

The Modoc leader asked, "Perhaps this woman has a safer place for you to stay?"

Connie reddened. "I reserved a room at Crater Lake Lodge, but it's a single, and I'm not sharing."

Shontin shielded his eyes, watching a new pair of headlights approach on the highway. "My daughter-in-law is the Modoc doctor. Your rogue lawman can stay with her. We will talk later about the bicyclists."

"And a tribal police force?" Neil suggested.

Connie added, "That would be a hell of a lot better than using the Tico Patrol."

Tom tilted his head. "It would also mean breaking a treaty."

"What treaty?" Neil asked.

"Our treaty with the Indian Indians."

A car door slammed. "Tom? Where's the wreckage?" A woman in her thirties with a long black hair and a white shirt shined a powerful flashlight across the construction site. The beam stopped on Neil. "Is he armed? On drugs? Any knife wounds?"

"None of the above." Shontin held out his broad hand. "Ferguson, meet Doc. Doc, meet your new house guest."

"Oh, God. Not another." The daughter-in-law knelt beside Neil, checking his pulse and examining his one open eye. "Where does it hurt?"

"All over. But you should have seen the other six guys."

The medic snorted. "Can you walk?"

"Dunno." With Doc and Connie helping on either side, Neil staggered up on wobbly legs. Through clenched teeth he said, "I'm OK."

"You're a mess, cowboy." Doc nodded to Connie. "Help me get him in the back seat."

Connie asked, "Where are you taking him? He needs X-rays."

"I'm the only medicine here in Triage City. They have to be worse than this before we helicopter them into K Falls."

Doc put a sheet of plastic on the back seat of her car before helping Neil slide in. Through the open window Connie could hear Neil mumbling. She leaned closer. "What?"

"I love you, Connie."

Connie rolled her eyes. "You're still an asshole." She asked Doc, "Are you a real doctor?"

Doc nodded. "I'll take care of him. Go get some rest. No visitors at the clinic until morning."

"I'll be there."

After the car was gone, Tom Shontin's voice came from the darkness behind Connie. "He has the spirit of Coyote, this one. Troublesome, but strong."

"Mostly troublesome," Connie replied.

"If he is knocked down nine times, I think he will get up ten."

Connie shook her head. She walked to her own car and opened the door.

"Be careful at Crater Lake," Shontin said.

She paused, her hand on the door. "At the national park? Why?"

"In our legends it is the battleground of spirits. Only the most powerful of shamans venture there."

"I'll keep that in mind."

Chapter 24

Gilberto Montale's journal
Tuesday, July 13, Raja

I came to show Harmony, my *Armonia*, that religion is not a barrier to love. Already on my first day in the Rajneeshee city, I can understand why she has joined with them.

We are all asked to write our thoughts in blue books. Harmony's cousin, Susan, says she has a way to deliver journals to her father, a detective. This may help, so I am telling what I have seen and felt.

My joy was great to see Harmony again, although I do not know if she saw me. I worry that she does not want to see me at all. How can I change that, if not by trying?

My trip has been full of surprises. The jet travel from Rome to Portland was as horrible as expected. But Air Rajneesh to Klamath Falls was beautiful: smiling people with guava nectar and incense above the clouds. By the time we had meditated, we were landing. A modern red bus took us along a lake full of white birds to a valley as scenic as any in the Alps. People with signs tried to stop our bus shouting, "Trust Jesus!" The people on the bus responded, "We do."

Beyond the gate we were welcomed like saints to Heaven, with kisses, scarves, and necklaces. Do we need cell phones or money in Heaven? They say we do not.

An attractive young woman named Sunshine took me and my baggage in an electric cart. We drove along dirt streets with white tents to a corner of the city. Here I met my colleagues on the hot springs drilling team. Chuck, Butch, Doug — these men with bare muscles and big stomachs are not like the other Rajneeshees. They live in large trailers and eat meat. They gave the name "Professor Plum" to Susan's friend Dregs. When I told them I am an astrophysicist from Italy, they said they will call me Professor Pizza. For Harmony, I tolerate even this.

Once I had unpacked, Sunshine took me in the cart along a hot water pipeline to the baths — a hundred steaming tanks full of nudes. Can I do this? I do.

Then she took me to a tent with vegetarian food, as I prefer. When I asked to see Harmony, the girl pointed to the sky. She said, "Harmony is coming soon." She smiled, but would not explain.

I asked if it would be easier to see my friend Susan Ferguson, who works in recycling.

Sunshine said, "You know a sannyasin? You can join the Plaza meditation together."

Her golf cart took us to a garbage pile, where Sunshine said good bye.

It is difficult to believe that Susan and my *Armonia* are related, although both are named Ferguson. Harmony: long blonde hair, chic dress, and the scent of blossoms. Susan: short black hair, overalls, and the smell of garbage. She does not smile. She does not look at me. She does not ask about my trip. She asks, "What have the drillers found?"

I do not know what to say.

Then she asks, "What is in the greenhouses?"

Again I shake my head.

Then she too points to the sky. "Ten minutes. Come."

As we walk together toward the center of Raja, a red helicopter circles the city. People cheer as if at a soccer match. We reach a big piazza with thousands of people in red. The helicopter lands beside a stage. We are far away, but I see the helicopter door open.

My heart nearly stops. It is Harmony. I push my way through the crowd. When at last I reach the front, I see a tall, angry man with a reddish beard trying to take a mobile telephone from Harmony's hand. She is in doubt, in fear. She looks to the audience for help. I jump up, but there are guards that keep me from the stage.

Raja is a young city, full of energy and hope. I understand why Harmony wants to be part of that excitement. Her eyes, however, tell me something is wrong. I need to do something.

Chuck is talking about moving pipe at dawn. It is nearly midnight. I am too tired to think.

Good night, *amore mia: Armonia.*

Chapter 25

It was nearly midnight when Connie arrived at Crater Lake Lodge. The few struggling pines around the parking lot had been bent into yoga poses by winter snows and mountain winds. The lake itself was a starless void at the edge of a black cliff behind the rambling old bunker of a hotel. Rows of dormers peered out from the shake roof like gun turrets.

Connie wheeled her suitcase into a lobby paneled with tree bark. She had managed to get a room because of a last-minute cancelation — the lodge was otherwise booked for months. She wound up in a third-floor garret facing away from the lake. The tiny room was ridiculously expensive, but she hadn't complained. The alternative was camping with Neil in Dawson. She hated camping and she had no intention of sharing a tent with Neil. Dawson itself had sounded like hell even before she learned that Rajneeshee cars run over tents there in the dark.

She climbed the stairs to her room, showered, and lay in the bed amidst a mountain of pillows. She pulled the thick comforter to her chin and stared at the black dormer window.

She remembered Neil's bloodied face with his eye swollen shut, and she shivered. How had she known he would be in trouble, and why did it always tear her up inside? He had lied to her for weeks about the case. All of his ideas had brought her nowhere. And then he had mumbled that he loved her — which made her even angrier.

She had spent the past two days investigating Roger Nash's mother,

Catherine, the likeliest suspect for the second Rajneeshee murder. The squad Connie had sent earlier to search the Nash house for weapons had stupidly overlooked their Airstream trailer, so the sniper rifle and Catherine's .22 really could have been there all the time. Catherine's neighbors had been at work or at school on the day Juan Guerrero was shot, so no one could say if she had opened the trailer, fetched the guns, and driven off to shoot a random Rajneeshee. Catherine's car had not been noticed by witnesses on Burnside or on Wildcat Mountain Road. Only a confession would convict Catherine Nash of murder now, and how was Connie to get that? Captain Dickers didn't want her bothering the Nash family anymore.

Meanwhile, Connie's rival investigator, Lieutenant Espada, was making surprising progress with his two suspects, X and Y. Not only could the Sunday school teacher's husband, Vernon Lawrence, have shot Swami Bhrater after the Moda Center show, but so could someone in the "Trust Jesus" entourage. Connie's team had interviewed Mr. Hamsby, the angry Baptist leader, and every passenger on the church bus. Their alibis had matched seamlessly. Espada, however, had discovered one person Connie had overlooked — the bus driver. While the protesters had been waving their "Trust Jesus" signs inside the hall, the bus driver had been left to wait in a parking lot below the freeway, close to the place where the sniper bullet had been fired.

So far all Espada knew about the bus driver was his first name — Erik — and the fact that he had also been the driver when the busload of protesters came to Raja. In short, two of the top murder suspects were now at the gates of the Rajneeshee city. Both Vernon Lawrence and the mysterious Erik were in a position where they could strike again.

Officially, Connie had been sent to Raja by the Portland Police Bureau to stop a serial murderer. But it was also true that she had hurried here because she worried about Neil. Now, remembering how her heart had lurched at the sight of him lying on the ground, she realized how frightened she was for him.

The old lodge shuddered, as if from a great gust of wind. The window rattled. A hanging lamp swayed. Connie pulled her covers tighter. Why, she wondered, if Neil's investigations in Raja were so far off the mark, did the Rajneeshees want to scare him away?

In the morning the sun was shining across the broken rim of the caldera. The lake seemed to glow blue from within. Connie ordered an omelet at a table on the patio, next to the cliff edge.

"Sleep well?" a young waiter with a fuzzy beard asked.

"Pretty good," Connie lied.

"Really? Everyone else has been complaining about the earthquakes."

"What earthquakes?"

"Didn't you notice? We had a whole swarm of tremors between one and two o'clock this morning."

Now Connie recalled the rattling window and the swaying lamp. "Is that common here?" She knew Crater Lake was in a volcano. It had blown up thousands of years ago.

"Not really." The waiter set out her silverware. "I guess the old spirits are restless."

Chapter 26

Morning for Neil was a confused, one-eyed hangover. A dull pain seemed to be everywhere, but especially in his shoulder and chest. There was an overpowering smell of sour milk. A throaty snore. Whitewashed stone walls. Where was he?

Gradually the nightmare came back, one ghastly scene at a time. Being beaten in the construction site. Connie still angry, but by his side. Then, when he couldn't stop groaning at each jolt in the car ride, the lady doctor had pulled over and stuck him with a needle.

Drugs made the morning misty, as if he were in someone else's damaged body. He raised a hand to his blank left eye and felt a bandage. Not a good sign.

Why the sour milk? With an effort he turned his head. Half a dozen other men lay in the white room, asleep on tables and cots. Some of them also wore bandages. One was snoring. Stainless steel pipes crisscrossed the ceiling. A shiny vat sat in a corner. The smell of cows.

He was on a farm. A drunk tank in a dairy?

A door opened, framing a long-haired woman in a blazing aura of sun. "You're awake? I gave you enough for a horse."

Neil's voice croaked, "What's with my eye?"

The doctor checked the pulse at his neck. "Another millimeter or two and you'd have lost it. As it is, you'll wear that bandage a few days. Oh, and you've broken a rib."

"You have X-ray vision?"

She smiled, exposing white teeth. "I photograph a lot of broken stuff here in Dawson. But this is the first time the perps were Rajneeshees. What the hell did you do to make them so mad?"

Neil looked aside, his mind clearing. The attack did seem to show he was right about something, but what? At least he had uncovered a new suspect. Tico Bob might not be as clueless as he seemed.

When Neil didn't answer, the doctor shrugged. "Anyway, you've made an impression on my father-in-law. He says you're trouble, but that didn't stop him from sending the tribal council an email about hosting a bicycle rally and starting a police force."

Neil raised an eyebrow.

"Now roll over for the bed pan."

"Wait." Neil forced himself up. He swung his legs to the floor, a maneuver that lanced a pain into his side.

"Don't move the rib!"

Neil stood up, his teeth clenched. "Where's the john?"

"You really are trouble, aren't you?" She gave him an arm and led him a few limping steps to a bathroom door. When he was done he returned to his bed, which he now realized was just a futon on a coffee table. He fell back onto it with a groan.

The doctor shook her head. "All right, cowboy. I'll have my son bring you some breakfast. Then there's a woman who's been waiting to see you."

Neil caught the doctor's sleeve. "Send her in now." Connie had come to see him! She had rescued him the night before, but she had been angry. "I need to talk to her."

"Visitors after breakfast."

"No. I'm not hungry. Let me talk to her. Please."

The doctor sighed and walked out.

Neil watched the door, his heart beating fast enough to blow the last of the fog from his mind. Last night he had blurted to Connie that he loved her. Now that she had had time to think about those words, how would she reply? Either she had come to tell him their relationship would return to a professional level — a retired cop and his former boss — or she had decided they could be a team.

Crows cawed angrily outside. A snoring man grunted and rolled on his side. Then the door opened a crack. Neil raised himself to an elbow. His breath stopped.

The sun shone through the crack so brightly that even when the door opened wider it took Neil a moment to realize that this woman did not look like Connie.

"Oh, Neil!" she cried. "I'm so sorry!"

The snoring man sat up and groaned at the light. "Shut the damn door."

"Oops!" The woman stepped inside, closed the door, and tiptoed to Neil. She wore blue eye shadow, tight blue jeans, and a low-cut pink blouse with a strategically dangling amethyst necklace. The "Margaret" nametag was gone, but this was definitely the Toaster Lady — the person who had served him a load of lies in the Ex-Zorba-Tent Grill.

"I heard what happened," she whispered. "I was mortified. Did they hurt you very bad?"

"Busted a rib. I won't even lose the eye."

"Oh!"

Neil narrowed his eye at her. "Is my daughter all right? Did you even see Susan before inventing that crappy journal?"

She nodded. "I went to see her early this morning, at yoga. She really is worried about you, but she's worried about a lot of other things too. Here's her real journal. I didn't make everything up."

Neil held open the blue booklet with his left hand and read through it skeptically. It started the same, "I worry about Dad," but ended differently, with the words, "Something is wrong. Getting worse."

"I'm no good at lying," Margaret admitted, "But people don't believe me when I tell the truth either. So I brought a second journal for proof. Susan says it's from some Italian guy."

Neil examined the second booklet, by Gilberto Montale. It began, "I came to show Harmony, my *Armonia*, that religion is not a barrier to love." This did seem difficult to fabricate. Few people would know the Italian boyfriend's name for Harmony, or his true reason for joining the Rajneeshees. But even after reading the entire journal Neil still didn't trust the Toaster Lady's sudden change of heart.

"What did Tico Bob offer you?"

She lowered her head. "Nothing, at first. I'd only been in Raja a day. I wanted to believe everything they said."

"And afterwards? No reward?"

Her cheeks reddened. "He told me to wait at the café after closing last night. When he finally showed up he gave me my cell phone and a gate pass."

Neil perked up his ears. "Don't all Rajneeshees have permission to come and go? I've seen a lot of them in Dawson."

Margaret shook her head. "Only the ones who joined before the new Bhagwan. And the ones with money."

"Now that you've seen Raja, will you go back to Molalla?"

"The next time my ex-husband breaks into my house in Molalla, he'll do more than move my toaster."

Neil said nothing.

Margaret bit her lip. "Why did you go to the construction site last night? You seemed to know it was a trap."

Neil lay back and closed his eye. "Cops are idiots. They go to the worst places on purpose. That's where the answers are."

Margaret ran a finger up his arm, along a seam of his Lycra bicycling suit. "You let Tico Bob believe I'd fooled you about the fake journal. You could have turned me in. Why didn't you?"

Neil had wondered about this himself. "Just trying to reduce collateral damage, I guess."

"That's what I thought." She sat on the edge of the mattress beside him. "Well, I can be brave too."

Neil opened his eye, alarmed. "What do you mean?"

"This time I won't run away either." She leaned forward, her lips parted. The amethyst swung out from the between the curves in her pink blouse.

"Margaret —" Neil began.

She silenced him with a fingertip on his lips. "Let me be your messenger. I'll tell Tico Bob that I'm changing the journals like he wants. Instead I'll give you the originals."

Neil started to speak but she tapped his lips. "No objections! Meet me at Zorba's each evening at seven. If you can't come, send someone. In the meantime let me know if there's anything you want to tell your daughter."

This was indeed a brave offer, as welcome as it was practical. Neil had been wondering how he could communicate with his Raja insiders. Now that he had the chance, however, he wasn't sure what to tell his daughter.

"Ask Susan why she's interested in the greenhouses and the drilling rig. Find out if she can talk to her cousin Harmony. And tell her not to take risks. I never wanted her to be a cop."

Margaret smiled and nodded. Then she bent over him and kissed him on the forehead.

Enveloped by the perfume of the Toaster Lady, face to face with the amethyst in her cleavage, powerless to escape this embrace, Neil closed his eye. But he opened it again quickly when a bright light shone across the room.

This time the doorway framed a smaller woman, with her fists propped angrily on her hips.

Connie.

Chapter 27

Susan heard Margaret fading in and out against the background static as if the rapid words were coming from a distant radio station. Eventually Susan lost the signal altogether. She put her hands over her ears and fled the dining tent. Mealtimes were painful in Raja. Lunch was the worst, with everyone talking at once. Susan had long ago decided that autism is like being born with a hearing aid turned on high. When the noise becomes intolerable, her brain simply shuts it all off, leaving her temporarily deaf.

Outside, Susan sat on a bench made of pallets — everywhere, there were pallets. And a faint, jittery red dot. All that morning she had been chased. At first she had been puzzled, then scared. Now she quickly moved to a bench on the far side of the dining tent, closed her eyes, and practiced the meditation breathing exercises that helped.

Gradually the distant radio channel began tuning back in.

"Did I frighten you? I'm so sorry," Margaret's voice returned. "It must be upsetting to hear someone describe your father as attractive, especially since he's been hurt. But he's in good hands now with the doctor lady. She says he's going to recover just fine if we can make him rest. I just don't understand what he sees in that policewoman, such a snippy little gnome. She yelled at him and stomped out before —"

"Stop," Susan said. "Stop turning."

"Turning?"

Susan knew she had trouble reading other people. She had learned to visualize relationships as doors. Her father was the steel door of a vault with a tricky combination. Her boyfriend Dregs was a sliding door, able to disappear into a wall. Her cousin Harmony was a swinging glass door, fragile, coming and going at the same time. And Margaret was a revolving door.

"Stop turning," Susan repeated, staring at the ground. "First you say you lied to me. Now you say you are telling the truth."

"Don't you believe me?"

Yes no yes no. What words can answer a contradictory question like this? When Susan was young she had sometimes chosen to scream rather than speak. Occasionally it still seemed that screaming would be easier than using words.

Margaret went on, "You don't have a phone, and you can't leave Raja. Your father isn't allowed inside the city. But I can take your journals to him and bring messages back to you. Just think of me as your telephone."

Susan hugged her knees, imagining Margaret as a cell phone in a revolving door. "What is the message?"

"Oh! Well, let me see. Your father wanted to know more about the greenhouses and the drilling operation."

"Those are the same questions I wrote in my journal."

Margaret gave a little laugh. "I guess that's why he asked. To find out if you've started your investigation. Oh, and he said not to do anything risky. He didn't want you to be a cop."

Yes no yes no.

Margaret's voice said something about picking up Susan's journal before the words once again faded into static.

Susan got a pita wrap from the dining tent and took it with her on Shiva Shift, the afternoon garbage pickup. She preferred to eat in the truck anyway, because of its metal plating. A bullet would travel far in a city made of tents. She could feel the eye of a scope watching from the pine hills to the west. Was it possible that she was the only one in Raja aware of the red laser dot? Other people seemed oblivious to details of the world around them.

Fuming with outrage, Connie had driven as far Dawson's main intersection before her cell phone rang.

She knew from the ring tone that it was Neil. She'd assigned Ferguson the theme from the old *Dragnet* TV series.

Connie pulled into a gas station parking lot where some idiot was selling water for thirty dollars, and let the theme play out: *Dumb-de-dumb-dumb.* Less than a week ago, on the night Neil set out on his bicycle ride to Raja, he had let her first call die. Now, after he'd been kissed by a waitress, she was willing to let him stew a while. Would he be desperate enough to call twice?

Dumb-de-dumb-dumb. Connie sighed and pressed the green button.

Neil's voice was hard to understand amid what sounded like a bunch of growling men. Evidently her brief, tumultuous visit in the dairy clinic had roused the drunks. Connie said nothing, but gradually began piecing together a long, confused story about a Toaster Lady at a hot springs.

"She's the one who sent me to the construction site last night, knowing I'd get beat up," Neil said.

"Wait." Connie broke her silence. "Are you saying the waitress at Zorba's was also the 'Toaster Lady' at the hot springs?"

"Yes! The woman's a messed-up wreck, like half the people at Raja. But she's the only way we can contact Susan and the others behind the wall. I don't care about the damned Toaster Lady, Connie. You're the one I love."

Voices in the background hooted, "Me too, Connie!" and "You tell 'er, Jack!"

Neil started to shout, but the sound turned into a moan.

By now Connie was holding the phone pressed to her ear. "Neil?" Were the drunks attacking him? Had he fallen and hurt himself? And how on earth was this man able to yank her emotions about so quickly? A moment ago she had been ready to strangle him.

Eventually Neil said, "The broken rib. Doc was right."

"I'll bet she told you not to raise your voice."

Neil's breath came as a series of wheezes. "Could you — get my bike?"

"Where is it?"

"In the campground. On Modoc Avenue. By a smashed blue tent."

"Don't worry," Connie said. "I'll get your stuff."

"And you?"

Connie sighed, remembering her actual assignment in Dawson. "I'm supposed to track down X and Y before they shoot more Rajneeshees."

"Seven o'clock," Neil muttered, as if he were already falling back asleep.

"Seven o'clock tonight? What's happening then?"

"Get Susan's journal."

"Where? How?"

"At Zorba's. From the Toaster Lady."

Connie felt her anger surge back. Why did Neil keep bringing up the Toaster Lady? She looked at her phone and pushed the red "disconnect" button as if she were poking someone in the eye.

Susan poked her finger into the broken husk. She was puzzled to find a dozen smashed maracas and several ruined rain sticks in the garbage bins behind the new greenhouses.

Susan disliked percussion instruments, especially noisy ones that added nothing to a melody. The rattles had been as unnerving as jet engines when they had been used as a rhythm accompaniment at Swami Jesus' meditation session the night before. But she would not have destroyed them like this.

Could the remains be composted? Probably, yes. The maracas were just painted gourds, and the rain sticks were made of some sort of dried cactus stalk. They could go into the compost container. But she kept a sample to share with Dregs during yoga.

Yoga was the most popular activity in Raja, although it had a different meaning at the commune than most new arrivals suspected. While crowds of sannyasins stretched and swayed together — in the plaza during nice weather, or in the dining tents if it rained — couples were encouraged to use the occasion to practice their own kind of intimate "yoga" in privately screened sections of the sleeping tents. The rules for here were looser, so people could experiment with different yoga partners and more interesting yoga positions.

Susan was not an experimenter. What she wanted most was to be squeezed while in complete control. Even as a child she had wanted and feared hugs. When someone — even her mother — had tried to hug her she had struggled like a wild animal. But she needed that contact. Eventually she had invented a "hug dispenser." She had piled books on the living room sofa and then crawled under the cushions. The comforting pressure had slowed her heart rate and soothed the anxious animal within.

As an adult, her craving for sex had led to some terrifying encounters. Boyfriends had tried to grab her, press her, control her. No one had understood until she met Dregs, an unemployed physicist who had spent three years sleeping under Portland bridges. Like autism, Skid Road was a strange world with a powerful code of respect.

After her garbage collection shift Susan quickly bathed and hurried back to her dorm. There she took off her clothes and lay on her mattress. Then she closed her eyes and slowly counted down from one hundred and twenty-seven, the only correct number. She could hear him breathing in the room, taking off his clothes. At twenty-three she could sense him poised above her, holding himself in a push-up with the strength of his arms.

Instead of zero, she said, "Now, Dregs."

When they were done he lay there on top of her, immobile, more soothing even than the hug machine she had invented as a child.

"I have a broken rain stick," Susan said.

Dregs didn't move.

"Enough, Dregs." She opened her eyes. He had a red scar down his face that made his right eye sag. He had unkempt shoulder-length hair and perfect white teeth. She had gotten used to it.

Dregs lifted himself, moved to one side, and lay there without touching her. "What the hell is a rain stick?"

She got up, handed him the broken cactus stalk, and began putting on her clothes.

"Whoa, somebody seriously hates rattles." Dregs looked at her from the side. "Did you do this?"

"I found a dozen like that in the trash outside the new greenhouses."

"So what's in the greenhouses anyway? Fruits and vegetables?"

"I don't know. What I saw were trays with 96,240 identical dirt-filled planting pots."

"Sure it wasn't 100,000?"

She was sure, but didn't bother to say so. Instead she pointed to a crack on the inside of the rain stick where several small round grains had lodged. "What kind of seeds do they use in Latin American rattles?"

Dregs pried loose a few of the grains. He examined them closely with his scar-sagged eye. Then he put one on his tongue and chewed it thoughtfully. "Not sure. But these seem a lot like marijuana seeds to me."

"Is it illegal to import marijuana seeds?" she asked.

"Not if they're declared and taxed. And maybe not on an Indian reservation anyway. Still, it's strange." He sat there a long time thinking, naked on the edge of the bed.

When a gong resounded over a loudspeaker outside, Dregs suddenly jumped up. "Whoa! I'm supposed to be at the Plaza Stage getting ready for the show." He began pulling on his pants, hopping on one leg. "Oh, and by the way, Harmony wants you to sneak into the central compound so the two of you can have a talk."

"Why doesn't she come here?"

"The Tico trolls are keeping close tabs on all the VIPs. You know, for safety's sake?" He pulled on a hooded sweatshirt as he turned toward the tent entrance.

"What have you heard from Gilberto?" Susan asked.

"Nothing. His fracking crew is working around the clock. They've hit hot water big time." Dregs blew her a kiss from the tent flap. "See you, babe."

Susan took a blue booklet from a stack on a desk. Yoga had relaxed her enough that she felt ready to write in her journal. Would she tell her father about the faint red dot? No one else had seen it. Perhaps she had imagined the whole thing?

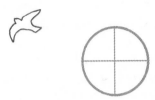

Chapter 28

Connie drove her unmarked Buick out Modoc Avenue to the jumble of motorhomes and tents in Dawson's campground. It took a while to spot Neil's blue tent, partly because it was flat, but mostly because it had been barricaded behind a wall of wooden pallets. She was appalled by how little gear Neil had brought: a single change of clothes, a rain parka, an empty granola box, a sleeping bag, and a pad.

She stowed his gear in her car's trunk and was puzzling over how to take his bicycle — which had been chained to a pallet — when an older woman in a wool coat approached.

"Excuse me," the woman said. She wore her hair in a gray bun that matched her coat. "I couldn't help noticing. You must be with that nice policeman. Is he all right?"

Connie frowned. "Actually, he's pretty beat up."

"Oh my."

Connie pointed to the chain. "He asked me to get his bicycle."

The woman also frowned, examining the pallet. "Would you like to borrow a chainsaw, a bolt cutter, or a crowbar?"

Connie looked at the woman more closely. She was frail, in her late 60s, with a high-cheekboned face that had not seen much sun. "You have tools like that?"

"Let's try the crowbar first." The woman walked to a nearby motorhome and returned with a three-foot-long iron rod. Without a word she jammed the bar between the boards and yanked downward, prying nails loose as if they were clothespins. "There."

Dumbfounded, Connie lifted the bicycle free. "Thanks." She held out her hand. "My name's Connie."

"I know. You're the Portland lieutenant everyone's talking about. I'm Vera. Vera Lawrence."

"You're X?" Connie was so startled that she said it out loud.

Vera laughed. "No, my husband and I have never divorced. Would you like to come in for some coffee?"

"Oh yes, very much so. Thank you." Connie stumbled over her words. Her assignment had been to find X. Instead, Espada's top suspect had found her.

Connie tried to put Neil's bicycle in the Buick's trunk, and when that didn't work, she crammed it into the car's back seat. Then she locked the car and followed Mrs. Lawrence.

The motorhome was spacious, with an awning on one side, a pop-out extension on the other, and a solar panel on top. Vera led the way to a pair of plush swivel chairs in a multi-purpose living area with a dining table, a flat-screen TV, and a kitchen.

"I just brewed a fresh pot, hoping for company," Vera said. "Cream?"

"Please." Connie wasn't sure how to bring up the subject she was supposed to be researching. It wouldn't do to ask this pleasant hostess if her husband was a rifle-toting murderer. She would have to start the conversation further afield, with something safe.

"Your motorhome is certainly comfortable."

"Thanks." Vera set out coffee cups. "We bought it four years ago when Vernon gave up his law practice. Now we winter down in Arizona and drive back when it gets too hot."

"So, Mrs. Lawrence —"

"Call me Vera."

"Vera," Connie said. "I understand you were collecting signatures for a petition at the Rajneeshee event in Portland. Is that why you're here in Dawson too?"

A shadow crossed Vera's face as she poured coffee. "Yes, mostly. I've been having second thoughts about the whole idea of petitioning, though."

"Why?"

"Well, the petition is about the Rajneeshees' tax-free status, and that's something the attorney general decides, not people on the street.

Besides, my former Sunday school student seems to agree with us. Roger Nash says the Rajneeshees aren't a religious group. It's also true that part of what they do could be considered charity, so there's probably some middle ground."

Connie had expected this elderly church lady to be an intractable zealot, but she actually seemed both reasonable and moderate. "Then you're dropping your petition?"

"Not entirely." Vera set the coffee cups and the creamer on the table. Then she sat in the other swivel chair. "It's important to raise questions about a faddish group like this. But you don't want to frighten them either. That's what we did wrong last time."

Connie stirred cream into her coffee. Casually she asked, "You were involved with the 1000 Friends of Oregon in the 1980s?"

"Yes, but the one who secretly led the fight against the Rajneeshees back then wasn't part of our group. Personally, I think it was Bill Bowerman."

"The track coach who founded Nike? Are you sure?"

Vera cocked her head. "Aren't you detectives told to follow the money?"

Connie nodded. Neil had told her this too, and it didn't always work.

"Bowerman had earned millions of dollars selling shoes," Vera explained. "So he and one of his sons decided to retire to a piece of paradise — a ranch on the east bank of the John Day River. He'd grown up in Fossil, a town twenty miles away. The family he bought the ranch from were named the Goons. Locals thought they were nuts. Maybe they were. Ranching certainly didn't work there. After they sold the place they tried to move their house, but it was too big, so they chainsawed it in half, right down the middle of the roof and walls. Of course it fell apart."

Connie sipped her coffee. "A millionaire would want to build a new house anyway."

Vera nodded. "Bowerman had just gotten the Goons out of his paradise when a new set of unwelcome neighbors moved in. A cult from India bought the Muddy Creek Ranch, directly across from him on the west side of the John Day River. He wanted to get rid of them too. He called on some friends — attorney general Dave Frohnmayer and my husband's environmental group — and asked what they could do."

"Are you suggesting that Bowerman bribed people to get rid of his neighbors?"

"No, no." Vera shook her head. "It's just that people listen when a man like him complains. The 1000 Friends of Oregon decided the Rajneeshees were violating land use laws by building a city on ranch land. The Rajneeshees responded by incorporating their development as the City of Rajneeshpuram. Then the attorney general said the city wasn't legal because it was owned by a religious group, violating the separation of church and state."

Connie thought about this. "Didn't the Rajneeshees take over another town nearby?"

"Yes, they bought up land in Antelope and elected their own city council. I think that was their backup plan, in case Rajneeshpuram couldn't be a city. But the county has the final say over city incorporation. So the next thing the Rajneeshees did was try to elect their own county commissioners."

"They'd have to outvote an entire county."

"They tried. They bused in thousands of homeless people to register as voters. But guess what? The state suddenly changed the voter registration rules. Instead of signing up by mail, people in Wasco County had to go to The Dalles to apply in person, and the state was rejecting most of the applications. The Rajneeshees could tell they were going to lose."

"What did they do then?" Connie knew most of this story, but wanted to hear Mrs. Lawrence's version.

"The Bhagwan's lieutenant went crazy. Ma Anand Sheila poured salmonella poison on salad bars in The Dalles to see if she could keep voters away from the polls. Finally she tried to murder the attorney general."

"Serious crimes," Connie said.

"You see how things escalate if you push people too hard?" Suddenly Vera set down her coffee, her eyes wide. "Oh my Lord, what have I done?"

"What?"

"I've left you sitting here without any cookies." Vera stood up, opened a cupboard, and poured a box of Vanilla Wafers onto a plate. "Here, these are good dunkers. Once I start lecturing, I lose my head."

Connie dipped one of the cookies in her coffee. "You weren't lecturing. I think you were making a point about your petition."

"That's right. You see, I've learned not to twist the knife." Vera smiled wryly. "I don't think that's in the Bible, but the idea is there. I want to fix the Rajneeshees' tax status without driving them to desperation."

"And yet somebody really is trying to drive them to desperation," Connie pointed out. "Two Rajneeshees have been shot."

"Yes." Vera's face clouded once more.

"Is that the other reason you and your husband are here?"

Vera nodded without looking up.

With this encouragement, Connie felt it was time to take a bigger gamble. "You were in the gun shop here in Dawson, weren't you?"

Vera nodded again, her lips tight.

"Your husband teaches at a rifle range. He's been convicted of selling automatic weapons to a felon." Connie let that sink in a moment. "Where is Vernon right now?"

Vera turned away, covering her face with her hands. "I'm worried sick. And I can't help but think that this has all been my fault."

Connie took a deep breath, giving Vera plenty of time. It seemed surprising that the Sunday school teacher who had just been arguing for moderation would now be on the verge of confessing that she was an accomplice to murder. But Connie had seen criminals justify even stranger contradictions.

Connie folded her hands on the table and said gently, "While you were inside the Moda Center that night in Portland, someone was waiting outside with a sniper rifle."

Vera nodded fearfully.

"You never wanted Vernon to shoot the swami, did you?"

"What! Vernon wouldn't shoot anybody! That's —" Vera jerked the plate of cookies away, spilling them across the table. She fumed a minute, glaring as if her guest had slapped her.

Then Vera's shoulders sagged. She pushed the nearly empty plate back. "But Vernon and I are afraid Hamsby might have done it."

Connie reeled, caught off balance by this sudden shift in the conversation's direction. "Hamsby? The minister of the Troutdale church? You think he was the one who shot the Rajneeshee guru?"

"No, his son Erik."

Now Connie began to see a dim light. Erik had been the name of

Espada's mysterious Suspect Y, the driver of the Trust Jesus bus. "So it was Hamsby's own son who drove the church bus?"

Vera sighed. "He was in my class of sixth graders the same year as Roger. They didn't get along. I suppose Erik was a bit of a bully. I tried to stop him, but sometimes — well, he was pretty harsh the day Roger showed up with a tattoo of an elf on his face."

Connie remembered hearing about the henna tattoo from Patricia. Roger's liberal aunt had apparently enjoyed letting the boy run wild while she worked her Saturday Market massage booth. But the tattoo must have crossed a line. The next day Roger had been bullied about it in Sunday school. And then his mother had forbidden him to visit Patricia altogether.

"Did you keep in touch with Erik?" Connie asked.

Vera gave the slightest of shrugs. "When Erik was in middle school he took my husband's gun safety course at the Troutdale range. The boy turned out to be a naturally gifted marksman. Everyone was proud when he joined the Army and was promoted as a sniper in Iraq."

"A sniper," Connie said.

Vera began gathering the spilled cookies from the table. Instead of putting them back on the plate she dropped them one by one into a garbage pail. "I don't know how long Erik was over there, but last year he showed up at the range and asked Vernon if he could buy some rifles. Of course he agreed. I mean, why not? Erik Hamsby had been one of his star students."

Connie suggested, "But by then Erik was also a felon?"

Vera looked up sharply. "How was Vernon supposed to know that?"

"He could have run a background check."

"Not on a boy you think you know!" Vera threw a cookie into the pail with a clang. "It turns out the only job Erik could get was with his father's church, driving a bus."

"Did your husband see Erik with a rifle at the Moda Center?"

"It was too dark to tell what Erik was doing. But that boy had never liked Roger, and he'd been pumped full of suspicion by the 'Trust Jesus' crowd. Sometimes I think they don't know the first thing about religion."

Connie finished her coffee. Vera Lawrence was obviously a woman with a conscience. She held herself responsible for the bullying of a sixth grader. Her husband was in fact responsible for supplying rifles to a felon. But they had made a bigger mistake.

"If you thought Erik Hamsby might have shot the Rajneeshees, why didn't you report it to the police?"

Vera stared at the garbage pail. "I suppose we should have. But there was no proof. All we had was an uneasy feeling."

"Is that why you were in the gun shop? To see if Erik had been there?"

Vera nodded. "They hadn't let him buy a rifle, but he got three scopes, one with night vision."

"Where is your husband now?"

"On a pine hill." Vera wiped her eyes with her apron. Then she stood up and began collecting the dishes, a signal that their kaffee klatsch was over. "It's a slope that overlooks the Rajneeshee city from the west. Erik camps out there with his spotting scopes, watching."

"And now Vernon has gone there too? To watch?"

"Yes. Before things escalate any further."

Chapter 29

Susan wanted to sneak into Raja's central Nirvana complex, but the VIP compound was a fortress. Twelve mobile homes had been placed in a square, with three on each side. They were so close together that it was impossible to see whatever might be in the middle. The only gaps were a locked door on the east that led directly onto the Plaza's stage and a ten-foot-tall plank gate that faced the greenhouse farms to the west. Guards with the green armbands of the Tico Patrol stood at both entrances. Sneaking did not seem possible, even if that is what Harmony had suggested she do.

Susan returned the following morning, on Monday, to check again. This time a dozen sannyasins stood waiting by the west gate. They were mostly women in their twenties. Susan joined the group without speaking, and without looking at anyone in particular. From their conversation she concluded that they were training for positions as day care providers.

"Harmony's just a pretty face," a young man said. "Is she even qualified to be an instructor?" Others replied, "She taught kindergarten for years." "And she says we'll get to meet Rog himself." "In Nirvana!" They laughed.

The gate opened at exactly seven thirty. A guard let them in one at a time, checking their names on a clipboard. He stopped Susan. "You're not on the list."

Susan looked down. "There may be a different list for autism counselors. Ask Harmony."

The guard grumbled, but he came back a minute later, nodding. "Sorry about the mixup. Harmony's with the others by the pool."

The courtyard had been hastily landscaped with plants that were still in their pots, some still on pallets. Ten-foot palm trees and giant ferns gave the makeshift garden a tropical look. A gravel path curved toward a fifteen-foot-diameter above-ground plastic swimming pool, of the temporary sort that sometimes appear in suburban backyards during summer. This pool steamed, apparently because it had been filled from Raja's hot springs.

Harmony and the other sannyasins stood in a cluster nearby, in front of a fiberglass shelter that looked as though it might have been originally designed to serve as a bus stop. Inside, Rog Nash was setting aside a book and smiling. "Before you start your studies, clear your hearts of trouble." He was wearing the maroon robe of Swami Bhrater, but his sandals were Keens. His black beard made his face look pale and gaunt. He held out his hand toward a large carpet. "Please, join me here, meditating on the peace of the unrippled pool."

While the dozen sannyasins sat down cross-legged on the carpet, Harmony caught sight of Susan and pulled her aside. "Thank God. Quick, this way."

Harmony led her cousin into a dark, sparsely furnished mobile home. The windows in back had been bolted closed with plywood, and the windows on either end faced the metal sheeting of adjacent trailers.

Harmony closed the door. "I saw Gilberto in the crowd at the Plaza stage the other day. Why is he here?"

Susan liked this direct sort of approach. "Your former fiancé says he has come from Italy to rescue you."

Harmony laughed. "No, really. Why is he here?"

Susan frowned, thinking of something else to say that would be true. "I think he has also come in the hope that you will rescue him."

"Yes, OK. That makes sense. If ever there was a religion that dwells on suffering, it's Roman Catholicism. The Rajneeshees might really be able to help set him free."

"Do you feel free?" Susan asked.

"Of course. Why wouldn't I?"

Susan looked around at the dim, bare room. "I think you are under house arrest."

"What? I'm in Nirvana. It's the safest, most sacred place in Raja."

"You were the Rajneeshees' public relations person. Now you can't speak to outsiders at all."

Harmony rolled her eyes. "That part of Raja's development is over. We don't need more public outreach. There are plenty of sannyasins here already. Now they need my skills as a teacher."

Susan looked out the window. Through the tropical leaves of the garden she could see the shelter by the pool. "Roger has been cut off from outsiders too. I think someone is afraid of him." She turned to Harmony, but looked past her to the wall beyond. "I wonder if you know why. You are close to him."

"I am not close to Rog!" Harmony shook her head, as if this might rattle out the correct words. "I mean, I am, or I used to be, but not in that sort of way! Can't you see? His whole being is turning inward, studying and thinking. One of these days he's going to blossom."

"Blossom?" As far as Susan could tell, Roger had lost weight and gone pale. Harmony too, seemed suspiciously wan.

"Like a lotus." Harmony wrenched her head to one side, groaning. "Talking with you is so maddening! I used to rely on you for help. Somehow I thought if we could just get together you could help me explain the problems."

Susan let this settle a minute, waiting for Harmony to calm. Nonetheless, she felt a tiny tremor. "There are problems? Ripples?"

Harmony rubbed her eyes. "They keep asking me about Swami Bhrater's will."

"Problems need detectives." Susan walked to the door. "How often does your teacher training class meet?"

"Every other day, for an hour."

Susan opened the door. "I want to study special education with you. To understand the problems."

Harmony managed a smile. "OK."

When they returned to the center of the garden the sannyasins were standing around the pool.

"Look, Rog!" a young man said. "There's another."

"Another what?" Harmony asked.

Rog pointed to the pool.

Although no one had touched the water, a small circular wave was converging on the center of the pool. The ring met in the middle, splashing a drop of water an inch into the air. When the droplet fell it sent a confusion of smaller ripples toward the rim.

Chapter 30

Connie Wu didn't like the idea of confronting a sniper. To be sure, the Portland Police Bureau had sent her to Raja to prevent another Rajneeshee murder by tracking down suspects X and Y. Apparently Vernon Lawrence and Erik Hamsby, the Trust Jesus bus driver, were both on a hill overlooking the tent city. Lawrence might not be dangerous, but Erik was wanted for two murders and was almost certainly armed. You don't walk up to someone like that with handcuffs and a smile.

She couldn't ask Neil to join her on this venture. Although she had partnered on patrols with him for years, he was a private citizen now. He had a broken rib. And she was having trouble shaking the memory of him together with the Toaster Lady.

What other choices did she have? The county sheriff wouldn't want to venture onto the Modoc Reservation. She couldn't ask the tribe for help because it had no police force. And the Rajneeshees' security patrol seemed to be made up of paramilitary thugs. She considered calling Captain Dickers for backup, but Portland was five hours away.

In the end Connie simply drove her Buick on a gravel road around the south edge of Raja's wall to size up the situation on her own. Red flags with white doves fluttered from the razor wire of the South Gate. Tractor-trailer rigs idled in a queue. Black tarps had been tied to the chain-link fence with zip-fasteners to block the view, but through the gate itself she could see piles of what looked like garbage.

She drove on around the city, although the road soon became a rutted dirt track across a cow pasture with grass and sagebrush. At the fence corner, nearly a mile before the pine slope, the road ended altogether at an irrigation ditch.

Connie got out for a better look at the murky water. There was no bridge, and the ditch was too wide for her to jump across. The water was muddy, so she couldn't tell if it was deep. It occurred to her that this was probably runoff from Raja's greenhouses. The Modoc Reservation protected the new city from the state's land-use laws, but water-quality regulations might yet trip them up.

Then she noticed a plank lying on the far side of the ditch. The wood was wet. Someone had crossed the ditch on the board and pulled it up after them. She scanned the distant hill for signs of life. All she could see were big ponderosa pines. If anyone was there they would have no trouble hiding behind the pine branches.

Just then she saw the tiniest red flash — the sort of spark you might imagine if you were straining your eyes too hard. Fear suddenly made her look around. A faint red dot was jiggling in the grass. She bolted for the car just as a shot cracked from the hill.

There was no time to get into the car — and she'd be an easy target through the windshield anyway. Connie dived into the grass behind the bumper. She cowered there, panting. What an idiot she had been, standing in the range of a sniper with a high-powered scope. Now she was trapped on the ground behind her own Buick. She had gotten into trouble the same way during the D.B. Cooper case, walking out toward the suspect's SUV just before it lunged at her. Neil had been safe somewhere else that time too.

She pulled out her cell phone. Not Neil. Not Dickers. She didn't know the Klamath County Sheriff's number. She punched in 911.

"What is your emergency?" The pleasant voice on the phone was calm.

"This is Lieutenant Connie Wu of the Portland Police Bureau. I'm being shot at by a sniper just outside of Raja."

"Raja?"

"You've got to know about the Rajneeshee city at Fort Klamath. Connect me to the county sheriff. I need backup out here, and fast."

"The sheriff's office. OK."

The telephone clicked and rang for what seemed like an eternity. A faint voice shouted indistinctly somewhere in the distance. Either on the hill or in Raja — Connie couldn't tell which.

Then the phone said, "Klamath County Sheriff's office. How may I direct your call?"

Connie repeated what she had said about the sniper.

"You're with the Portland police?" the voice asked.

"I'm investigating the Rajneeshee murders. I've tracked a suspect here, and I'm under fire."

"Are you on tribal land?"

"I'm at the southwest corner of Raja, just outside the perimeter fence. I don't think the sniper's on the reservation either. He's on Forest Service land or something, to the west."

"Copy that." There was a pause, and then, "Sheriff Tolufsen's car is in Chiloquin. He can be there in ten minutes. I've got a second car at Rocky Point that can get there almost as fast. I'm redirecting both your way."

Connie let out a breath and sagged her head against the Buick's bumper. "Thanks."

"Are you exchanging fire, Lieutenant?"

"No, I'm hiding behind my car."

"Copy that. Behind your car. The sheriff will be there soon."

For the next ten minutes, sitting there in the grass, Connie had time to think about the sniper on the hill. Erik Hamsby's experience with rifles and night scopes in Iraq would have made it easy for him to pick off Swami Bhrater after the Rajneesh Revival show at the Moda Center. Then Erik could simply have packed up the weapon in a case, loaded it on the bus, and driven the bus back to the Baptist church in Troutdale. His motive was clear: Erik's father had announced that the Rajneeshees were an evil cult, bent on killing everyone in their path. Erik would have wanted to pick off a prominent Rajneeshee to scare them away.

Connie had a harder time imagining Erik killing the second Rajneeshee victim, Juan Guerrero. Evidence suggested that Guerrero had been shot at close range with a .22 pistol. Then the killer had driven to a remote quarry on Wildcat Mountain and shot Guerrero again with a sniper rifle. Certainly a .22 would be less conspicuous in broad daylight on Portland street, but a pistol seemed more like a weapon Catherine Nash would choose.

As soon as Connie thought of this, she wondered if Erik and Mrs.

Nash might have been working together on the second murder. If Catherine had shot Guerrero with the pistol, Erik might have been tasked with disposing of the body. After dumping Guerrero at the quarry, Erik might have shot him again with his rifle, just for good measure.

Connie made a note to find out how well Erik and Catherine Nash knew each other. They were both connected to Baptist churches. She would also want to check all of the vehicles Erik Hamsby had driven. If they had been used to transport a dead man, some trace of blood, hair, or clothing might remain.

What puzzled Connie most was that Erik had evidently been camped on a hill overlooking Raja for several days, with a clear view of thousands of Rajneeshees, and yet had not used the opportunity to strike again. The only shot he had fired had been at her, a plainclothes detective in an unmarked car. She wasn't wearing red. She wasn't inside the city. She obviously wasn't a Rajneeshee. Had someone warned Erik that she was with the police?

Then Connie spotted a man walking toward her from the hill, and her fears multiplied. Why hadn't the sheriff shown up yet? She needed backup, and fast. The man was already more than halfway to her, striding purposefully.

Connie scrambled to her knees and drew her Glock, peering out from the cover of the fender. In a shootout, even with the car for protection, she would not be much of a match for a naturally gifted marksman. She sighted down the barrel of her semi-automatic at the approaching man.

She didn't know what Erik Hamsby looked like, but somehow this man looked wrong. He was tall, unhurried, and surprisingly well dressed. A sport jacket? White hair?

She lowered the Glock. This wasn't Hamsby at all. It must be Vernon Lawrence, the retired lawyer. He waved at her, showing that he held no weapon. Then he stooped to pick up the wet plank.

While Lawrence was positioning the board as a bridge across the irrigation ditch, flashing lights and sirens began wailing up from behind Connie.

Two patrol cars fishtailed up on either hand. The doors flew open and men jumped out behind them, bracing pistols in two hands.

"Wait!" Connie shouted. "Don't shoot!"

Lawrence stood up beside the ditch, hands over his head.

"Lieutenant?" the sheriff shouted. "Is that your sniper?"

"No! He's a lawyer."

"You brought a lawyer from Portland? It figures." Connie walked clear of the car, forgetting in her exasperation that she was hiding from a scope's laser. "This is Vernon Lawrence. He's here on his own. The sniper's name is Erik Hamsby. He's camped out on that hill over there."

"Actually, he's not." Lawrence lowered his arms and walked across the bridge. "When you pulled up in that black car you spooked him. Erik's already packed up and taken off into the woods."

"But he fired a shot," Connie objected.

"That was me, I'm afraid," Lawrence said.

"You?" Now Connie was truly confused.

Lawrence nodded. "I've been worried about Erik. He's a felon, so he's not supposed to have firearms, but he set up some kind of sniper blind with a view of the Rajneeshees. I knew him as a kid, so I wanted to make sure he wasn't getting into more trouble."

The sheriff looked from Lawrence to the hill. Then he asked, "Is there a sniper here or not?"

Lawrence sighed. "Erik's a sniper all right. He served in Iraq. But I don't know if he actually has a rifle. He wouldn't let me within a hundred yards of his camp. I staked out a spot behind a tree to watch. I saw him aiming a scope at the lady here. So I fired a shot in the air to warn her."

"Then you're armed?" the sheriff asked.

Lawrence tapped the side of his sport coat. "I have a concealed carry permit."

Sheriff Tolufsen was a heavyset man with a crewcut and a square chin. He holstered his gun, and the three officers with him followed suit. "Let me get this straight. You fired into the air. Nobody's shot at anyone. No one's seen illegal weapons. A kid's been camping with a telescope. Why are we here?"

Connie answered, "Because Erik Hamsby is the top suspect in the murders of two Rajneeshees in Portland. I'm Lieutenant Wu, in charge of the investigation for the Portland police. We don't yet have evidence, but we want Hamsby for questioning. And we don't want him killing anybody in the meantime."

"Except Rajneeshees, if they're in season, right?"

"What?" Connie looked at the sheriff, startled. Did he really believe Rajneeshees should be fair game for shooters?

The sheriff grunted. "I'm just saying, a lot of people in this county would be on Hamsby's side." He looked to Lawrence. "What about you? If you've known this kid for so long, do you think he's dangerous?"

Lawrence tilted his head one away and then another. "Erik was always a bit of a bully, but I've never known him to hurt anybody. After he got back from the Army, I don't know. And I really don't understand why he's been watching the Rajneeshees with his scopes."

Connie noted, "He's part of a Baptist protest group."

"That's true," Lawrence admitted.

"He couldn't have gone far. We can track him down," Connie said.

"Actually, Erik trained in survival with the Army. He could move fast and get by for weeks if he wanted."

The sheriff asked, "Which direction did he go?"

Lawrence pointed west.

The sheriff squinted at the mountains. "The Sky Lakes Wilderness? That's next to the national park. Sixty miles with no roads. I don't have enough men to search an area like that."

"Can't you follow him with dogs?" Connie suggested.

"Maybe, if they don't get eaten."

Connie looked at the sheriff questioningly.

"Wolves," the sheriff explained. "There's a pack in that wilderness now. Wolves don't like dogs."

"What about people?" Connie asked.

"Oh, wolves love people. No, I'm sure your murderer will do just fine out there."

That afternoon when Connie drove back to her room at Crater Lake Lodge, she was still feeling shaky from her confrontation. Erik remained at large, possibly with a rifle, and certainly with a laser scope. Sheriff Tolufsen had reluctantly agreed to send out half a dozen searchers, but only after a call to Captain Dickers convinced him that Portland would pay most of the bill.

Connie had showered and gotten a table by the window of the lodge's dining room before she remembered her promise to Neil. She had picked up his camping gear, and she still had his bicycle in her car, but she had forgotten to meet the Toaster Lady at the Rajneeshee café at seven. She decided to let it go until tomorrow. She didn't like playing messenger for Neil and his Toaster Lady. And besides, Neil had kept her in the dark about the Bhagwan's case for weeks. Now it was his turn to sweat a while.

She ordered salmon with herb potatoes. The waiter was the same young man who had brought her an omelet on the patio that morning. She asked, "Any more earthquakes?"

"Just aftershocks. So small no one can feel them." He looked out the window and tapped the side of his beard with his pencil, as if he were thinking. Then he said, "I'll get that order in for you."

After her long day Connie was so thirsty she drank most of the water in her glass. When the waiter returned with a pitcher to fill it, she asked, "What was it you were you thinking when you mentioned the aftershocks?"

"Oh, nothing really." He reddened. "It's just we were joking this morning about the spirits being restless."

"I talked to a Modoc elder the other day who believes there really are spirits in Crater Lake. Do you?"

"No. I'm not into religious stuff. But I think there's only so much you can do to a national park before it starts to bite you back."

The restaurant hadn't yet begun to fill with the dinner crowd and the waiter seemed to have time to talk, so Connie asked him to explain.

"Well," he said, waving his hand at the restaurant. "Look around. We built a hotel on the rim. We run diesel powerboats with tourists all over the lake. One guy drove his car into it."

"Really? How did he manage that?"

"He forgot to set his parking brake at the Devils Backbone viewpoint. When he walked over to look at the lake his car rolled past the end of the wall and over the edge. With his dog inside."

Connie gasped.

"Oh, the dog got thrown out the sunroof right away. It walked back to the viewpoint just fine. But by the time the car hit the lake it was spinning so fast it threw out the engine too."

"Did they get the car out of the lake?"

"I don't know. They sure left the helicopter in."

"What helicopter?"

He swirled the pitcher, tinkling ice. "A brand new one, built in Seattle for a client in Arizona. The pilot who was delivering it took a friend along for the ride. The guy dipped down low to show them Crater Lake. He hit an air current. Hundreds of people in Rim Village saw it go in. Sank within seconds. It's still down there, under a quarter mile of water. With the bodies inside."

"That's horrible!" Connie said. "But it wouldn't cause earthquakes."

"No, I figure that's the drilling."

"Drilling?"

"Frackers, you know? They've been blasting for hot water beneath that new Rajneeshee commune, just outside the park. Think about it."

A diner tapped a glass across the room, an impatient signal. The waiter glanced at him with a nod. But before leaving Connie he said, "Maybe not such a good idea, setting off explosives next to a volcano."

Chapter 31

Neil had moved from the milk room of the old Fort Klamath dairy to the neighboring hay barn, partly to escape the snores of Doc's other patients, and partly because the cellular signal was better. His broken rib still hurt whenever he stood, walked, shouted, or laughed, so he spent the day lying on straw bales, placing a series of expensive phone calls to Singapore. He hadn't yet discovered much about the inner workings of the Rajneeshee commune.

He was delighted when his phone registered an incoming message. Caller ID revealed that it was his older brother Mark, and not from Singapore or Connie, but it was better than nothing.

"Hey, little bro," the familiar voice bellowed, "You lucky dog. How are you loving it at the red gates of Nirvana?"

Neil had to remind himself that laughing would hurt his rib. "Do you really want to know, Mark?"

"Sort of, yeah."

"Well," Neil swatted a fly away from his face. "I seem to have lost my girlfriend, my job, and pretty much everything else. Somebody drove over my tent trying to scare me. Then six guys from Raja beat me up and broke my rib. Right now I'm in a cowboys-and-Indians clinic, lying on a hay bale in a ripped bicycle suit. How are you?"

"Good, good, thanks for asking. Say, have you heard anything lately from my daughter?"

"No, Harmony's been out of touch since she arrived down here. I suppose you saw her that night on the podcast with Jesus?"

"We did."

"What was she talking about with Swami Bhrater's will?"

Mark cleared his throat. "You see, that's why I'm calling. Someone broke into our house last evening while Melanie and I were at a toy fair in Corvallis. They turned the place upside down. Didn't seem to take anything. The security camera hidden in my shop shows two guys with beards and armbands."

"Tico trolls," Neil said.

"Come again?"

"That's what they're calling the Rajneeshee security staff now, because they're mostly from Costa Rica. Did they find the will?" Neil had already figured out that Harmony's parents must have been involved. A valid will needed two witnesses, and Harmony's mother was a notary public.

"I can't figure out why they'd care. The old swami had nothing. He gave his robe to Roger and his shoes to Harmony. So what?"

"Is that all the will mentioned? Just the robe and the shoes?"

Mark grumbled. "I forget exactly. And no, they didn't find the will. But now I'm worried about Harmony. Do you think Susan could get us in touch? Your daughter's doing her garbage thing at Raja, isn't she?"

Neil sighed. "The Tico Patrol has confiscated cell phones, and they won't even give most people gate passes. But I've got a contact who can get messages in and out."

"Could you let me know as soon as you hear anything about Harmony?"

"Sure, Mark. I promise."

Mark was silent for a long time. Neil knew his brother didn't like to talk about bad news. And he didn't believe in apologies. Neil gave the silence plenty of time.

"Little bro?" Mark's voice was uncharacteristically quiet. "The Rajneeshees are fucking up again, aren't they?"

"Maybe some of them, Mark."

"You know we were pushed into it last time, in the '80s? We didn't have security patrols until terrorists blew up our Portland hotel." Mark's tone was strident now, and a little angry. "The old Bhagwan had hundreds of ashrams and hotels all over the world, and none of them had problems. Only in Oregon. Here some assholes dynamite the

Hotel Rajneesh and the police just shrug. They say it must be some secret Muslim group. Couldn't possibly be local bigots. Portland doesn't
have armed white Christian supremacists. You know what? If terrorists had blown up the Benson Hotel instead, the FBI would have torn
the state apart to find out who did it. So what were the Rajneeshees
supposed to do? If the police aren't protecting you from wingnuts
with bombs, you have to form your own security force, right?"

"Mark?" Neil interrupted his rant. "I know you want to defend the
old Rajneeshees, but they broke the law. They tried to take over the
government. They armed themselves with automatic weapons. They
weren't good neighbors."

"Good neighbors? You sound like a TV documentary. The media
jumped all over us back then, showing videos of guys in red robes
training with machine guns at Rajneeshpuram. Jesus tap dancing
Christ! Every ranch in Eastern Oregon is protected with automatic
weapons. Why didn't they put redneck militiamen on the news instead? Tell me that, OK?"

Neil waited a while before asking, "Are you through?"

Mark didn't answer.

"It's different this time, Mark. The police are on your side. We're
trying to find out who's killing Rajneeshees. But there's something going on in Raja we don't understand. Whatever it is, it's putting both of
our daughters at risk."

"I —" Mark cleared his throat again. "I want to help."

This was as close to an apology as Neil had ever heard from his
brother. From the first, Mark had encouraged Harmony to trust the
new Rajneeshees. If Mark was now having second thoughts, perhaps it
was because Mark himself had once broken ties with the old Bhagwan.

"Would you be willing to take a vacation?" Neil asked.

"A vacation?"

"Some of the Rajneeshees spent thirty years on a farm in Costa Rica.
I need to find out what happened down there, but I can't send a cop. It
has to be someone with red cred. Wasn't your Rajneesh name Swami
Deva?"

"Yeah. The god master."

"That's exactly what the investigation in Costa Rica needs. Want to
go to the tropics?"

Mark answered with a noncommittal grunt.

Chapter 32

Connie was running short of time on her weekend investigation. But when Tom Shontin, the Modoc elder, called Sunday morning to say he wanted to meet her at Dawson's airport site, she dropped everything and went. The Modoc reservation needed a tribal police force, and Shontin seemed like the man who could make it happen. Anything would be better than trying to work with the Rajneeshee security people.

When Connie drove to the airport site in the southeast corner of the reservation, earth-moving machines were crawling about like dinosaurs, ripping up sagebrush. She found Shontin in a pickup truck by a stack of picnic tables where two rough dirt runways converged.

"Lieutenant Wu," Shontin greeted her, opening the truck's door and climbing out. He wore a bolo tie, as always, but he had traded his suit jacket for a work coat with reflective yellow stripes. "How do you like our new campground?"

"I thought it was an airport."

"That too. I got permission from the tribal council to bring Cycle Oregon here next weekend. They need a campground for a few thousand bicyclists, so we're converting the airport."

"You move fast." She looked at the stacked picnic tables. How could he have collected hundreds of tables so quickly?

"Your argument about publicity helped me convince the council. We want to show that Captain Jack's resort will be open to everyone, not just Indians."

"What does Cycle Oregon think about this? Have you asked Neil?"

Shontin shook his head. "Ferguson is recovering at Doc's. We talked directly with the Cycle Oregon people in Portland." He lowered his voice, although the two of them were standing there alone. "They like that we have a hot springs. Their tour is about hot springs, and the alternative endpoint at Prospect doesn't have any. The problem here is bad spirits."

"Dawson has a rough reputation," Connie agreed. "I bet Cycle Oregon wants you to provide police protection."

"They do, but that's not what I meant." Shontin looked about suspiciously. "Can I take you for a ride?"

Connie studied the man. What was he after? He looked out of shape but might be stronger than he seemed. If he tried to make a pass at her, she could handle herself. She had worn a loose jacket that hid her service Glock.

"Where are we going?" She asked.

He shook his head. "Doesn't really matter." He got in the driver's side of his pickup and waited, looking straight ahead.

Shontin's old Toyota truck had seen better days. The sides were dinged. A spidery crack crossed the windshield. Years of sun had reduced the hood's blue paint to the gray of a mangy beast.

Connie opened the passenger door and shoved magazines off the seat. Only after she had gotten in and closed the door behind her did Shontin seem to relax. He started the engine, a grumble that pinged, and shifted to first gear. As they bumped down the dirt airport runway, he said, "They can't hear you when you're driving."

"Who can't hear you?" Connie hesitated, about to latch her seat belt.

"The spirits." He chuckled. "Hell of a thing, isn't it? They're even slower at adapting to new stuff than guys like me."

"So you and these spirits talk to each other?" Apparently the Modoc elder wasn't going to hit on her. Connie found it only slightly less troubling that she was riding in a truck with a man who heard voices in his head.

"Spirits aren't omnipotent, you know? Sometimes you can trick them for a while. And sometimes they get pissed off." He glanced at her meaningfully.

"You're trying to tell me that the spirits are angry."

"Sounds stupid, when you put it that way. To you, other people's religions are probably just a bunch of crap."

"That's not true." Connie felt her face flush. She wasn't a religious person, but she thought of herself as tolerant. "I'm here to defend the Rajneeshees, aren't I?"

"The Rajneeshees' beliefs go back decades. Maybe a couple of millennia if you count Jesus and Buddha. Ours go back 14,000 years." He stopped at the highway crossing at the south end of Dawson. Traffic on the road was so heavy there were no openings in sight.

Connie filled the wait by saying, "I'd like to know more about your beliefs."

"Beliefs." He frowned at the traffic. "There's proof, too, if you prefer that."

"What kind of proof?"

"Archeologists from the U of O dug up coprolites at Paisley Cave, just east of here. Know what coprolites are?"

Connie shook her head.

"Dried human feces. And right now you're thinking: Big deal. They found some old turds. But according to radiocarbon dating, these were 14,300 years old. The oldest evidence of humans in the Americas. DNA showed that the descendants of those people are the Indians of North and South America. We spread out from Oregon to populate two continents."

Shontin didn't exactly smile, but his eyebrow lifted a little. "Some of us didn't wander too far afield."

Finally there was a gap in the traffic. He gunned the motor, crossed the highway, and steered west on the same road Connie had taken the day before.

"Where are we going?" It was the second time Connie had asked the question. She had an uneasy feeling that Shontin was taking her to the pine hill with the sniper blind. What did he know about Erik Hamsby?

"We're taking a little tour of the spirit world." Instead of driving past Raja's South Gate he turned right, toward the city. To Connie's amazement he bypassed the line of trucks waiting to enter the gate, waved at the Tico Patrol guard by the razor-wire fence, and drove on in.

Suddenly they were inside Raja. The garbage Connie had glimpsed through the gate the day before was still there, but now she realized that it consisted of piles sorted for recycling. Susan must be here somewhere, although there were so many people that it was hard to tell. Tents, pallets, and trucks were everywhere.

Tom Shontin drove at a walking pace along Raja's gravel streets as if he owned the place. It occurred to Connie that this was in fact Modoc Reservation land. Evidently tribal members, or perhaps just tribal council members, could drive wherever they liked.

"Our legends say Crater Lake used to be a mountain," Shontin said. "A big mountain, like Mt. Shasta."

"That part sounds true." Connie was busy looking out the window. Crowds of red-robed people stood in formation in a field, slowly moving their arms.

"Yes, but the mountain was the home of a spirit. A bad spirit named Llao. There was also a good spirit, Skell, who lived in a different mountain, the Home of the North Wind. Back then the Klamath and the Modocs were a single tribe, not like now. And one day the most beautiful girl in that tribe got a message from Llao, asking her to be his wife."

"Did she marry him?" Outside the window, rows of fiberglass greenhouses extended into the distance.

"Are you kidding?" Shontin looked at her from the side. "Marry an evil spirit? The girl said no."

"I guess that makes sense."

"Yes, but it made Llao blow his top. He decided to kill the entire tribe by destroying his mountain. Fiery rock fell from the sky. Almost everyone died. Only a few of us survived by diving into Klamath Lake and breathing through reeds."

This caught Connie's attention. "Wait a minute. The mountain really did blow up. At the park they were telling me that hot pumice rained all around. That really might have killed anybody who wasn't underwater."

"That's why we remember Llao. For years he sat up in his broken mountain, fuming while the crater filled with water. After a while a mysterious marten came from the Home of the North Wind. The marten turned out to be Skell in disguise — a good spirit, a hero god. Skell wrestled with Llao at the top of Llao Rock, the cliff beside Crater Lake. The battle was terrible. It lasted for days. Finally Skell threw the demon into the lake to end his troublemaking."

Now Connie was watching Shontin instead of the Rajneeshee city. "Was that really the end of trouble?"

"Spirits are tough. You can kill them for a while. But not forever."

"Your tribe believes in reincarnation?"

The Modoc elder nodded slowly. "That's why we're talking in my truck, where Llao can't hear. He is coming back."

Chapter 33

On Sunday evening, just before Connie had to drive back to Portland, she finally stopped by Doc's clinic to see Neil again. She pulled Neil's bicycle out of the back seat of her car. She loaded the bike with a precarious pile of gear and clothes. Then she wheeled the bike to the old milk room. The men in the Modoc doctor's makeshift clinic explained that the beat-up cop had moved next door.

She found Neil in the dairy barn, trying to arrange a sheet over hay bales as a bed. He wore a bandage on his head and a brace on his chest. Is that why she didn't rush up to hug him?

"I brought your stuff," Connie ventured.

"And Susan's journal?" Neil wasn't greeting her with open arms either. "Did you meet the Toaster Lady at the cafe?"

"She gave me two days' worth of your daughter's notebooks."

"Any important news?"

"Margaret didn't seem worried, and I didn't want to pry, so I haven't read them. Here." Connie balanced the overloaded bike on its kickstand. When she tried to pull the blue booklets out from the stack of gear, however, the whole thing started tipping over.

Neil lunged to catch the bike. The sudden movement strained his broken rib, and a shot of pain left him so dizzy he lost his balance too.

He didn't quite black out, but the world was pretty dim for a while. When his head cleared, Connie was fanning his face with a black cowboy hat.

"Neil? Oh, thank God. I thought — I don't know what, I just —"

The pain in his side had been replaced by a lovely, tingling sensation. What magic was this? "Where —?" All he could think to say was, "Where'd you get the hat?"

Connie laughed. "You don't have any clothes."

"I don't?" He lifted his head to look.

She rolled her eyes. "You've been wearing the same Lycra outfit for a week. The booths in Dawson only sell red, so I went to a thrift store in Chiloquin."

He struggled to get up.

"Take it easy, Neil!"

For some reason the rib wasn't hurting. He sat on the edge of a hay bale. "Let me get this straight. You drove to Chiloquin to buy me a black cowboy hat?"

"I got you a whole wardrobe for thirty bucks. Levi's, two sizes of boots. Here, try on the coat." She brushed some straw from a sheepskin jacket with a suede collar.

"Thanks." He put on the coat. It was warm and Western. Then he picked up a boot. It had a pointy toe, a big heel, and fancy stitchery. "Do you have a thing about cowboys?"

"Maybe a little." She bit her lip. "But this isn't like the handcuffs. It's not really a thing. It's just, if you're going to stay in Dawson, you might get beat up less by fitting in. That bicycle suit makes you look like Spiderman."

Neil remembered hearing the same thing last week, from the firefighters in McKenzie Bridge. "If Cycle Oregon came here we'd have two thousand superheroes in town."

"Actually, they're on the way," Connie said. "I talked with Tom Shontin today. He's making all the arrangements. The Modocs are turning the airport site into a huge campground with hot tubs and tables."

"That's good news."

"And he wants us to help organize a tribal police force."

"Better and better."

"There's bad news too." Connie sighed. "Remember Suspect Y?"

"The Sunday school teacher's husband?"

"No, he was Suspect X. And I doubt he's the murderer." She described the whole day's discoveries from the start — about her meeting with Vera Lawrence in the campground motorhome, her attempt to visit Erik Hamsby's sniper blind by herself, the shot she thought had come from Erik, her call to the Klamath County Sheriff, and the armed confrontation that followed.

"Hold on," Neil interrupted her. "You've obviously done a lot of good work, and I've just been sitting in a barn. But it sounds like this Erik guy is on the loose and the sheriff's not trying very hard to catch him."

"I'm afraid that's right. Erik trained with the Army so he's hard to track, and the search area is huge."

"He could pick off someone in Raja whenever he wants."

She shook her head. "If he's really got a rifle, he could have done that long ago. I don't know what he's thinking."

"Maybe his father knows." Neil remembered the elder Hamsby from the protest at the Rajneesh Revival. "I know you interviewed the Trust Jesus people when they were in Portland. Now that they're here in Dawson, I think we need to talk to them again. Erik's father may be a loudmouth wingnut, but he's still a father. He's got to be worried about his son. "

"Good idea. I wish I could go with you."

"You really have to go back to Portland tonight?" Neil caught her eye.

Connie reddened and looked down. "Dickers wants my report tomorrow morning. He says we don't have much of a budget for travel."

"I can't leave Dawson until this is over," Neil said.

"I know." Connie managed half a smile. "You always say you don't quit easy."

"I'll miss you, Connie." He scooted closer and started to put his arm around her shoulder, but was stopped short by a sudden pain in his side. "Ooh, that hurts!"

"Here, let me try." Connie leaned gently against him and kissed him on the lips. Then she sat back. "Better?"

"Yowza. I mean, yes." Neil caught his breath. "When are you coming back?"

"I can take next weekend off, no matter what Dickers says."

"That would be when Cycle Oregon shows up here."

Connie stood up. "Wouldn't miss it for the world."

"I'll call every evening," Neil promised.

"After canoodling with the Toaster Lady?"

"There's nothing between me and that —" Neil ran out of words, exasperated.

Connie checked the time on her cell phone. "I've got a long drive. Oh, there's one thing I wanted to check. Have you felt any tremors?"

"Tremors?" Was she talking about their kiss?

"I haven't felt anything either," Connie admitted. "But apparently there's been a string of little earthquakes at the national park. Some people there think it's the frackers, drilling for hot water at Raja."

"Oh." Neil readjusted his line of thought to geology. "I suppose that's possible. People back East have been blaming earthquakes on fracking for years." He paused. "You don't think it's the volcano?"

"No. Not exactly."

"Not exactly?" Neil wondered why he could never guess what she was going to say next. He was supposed to be a detective, after all.

"The Modocs think the Rajneeshees have woken up something ancient under Crater Lake. An evil spirit named Llao."

"Really. An evil spirit."

"Really." Connie blew him a kiss on her way out. Over her shoulder she said, "Watch out, cowboy."

Chapter 34

The next morning, when Doc's son woke Neil up with a bowl of cereal and a cup of coffee, Neil dug the blue booklets of Susan's journals out from his pile of gear and examined his daughter's disjointed, looping notes.

Susan could have skipped the long, analytical account of sex with her boyfriend Dregs. Far more interesting was the news that the Rajneeshees had been importing marijuana seeds inside musical rattles. If the commune was supposed to be a self-supporting organic farm, why plant so much marijuana? Pot was legal, but the state had a permitting process for authorized growers. Perhaps a farm on an Indian reservation was exempt.

Almost as disturbing was the report that Harmony had become isolated in the central "Nirvana" compound, apparently as a willing captive. Under Swami Bhrater, Harmony had risen to prominence in the first weeks of the new Rajneeshee movement. As a spokesperson she had been so easy on the eyes that she had won hearts as well as minds. The arrival of Swami Jesus had apparently changed her position. The Tico patrols had begun acting like a Buddhist Gestapo. Harmony was incommunicado in their inner sanctum. And even Roger Nash, their putative reincarnated leader, had drifted into the role of a dreamy recluse. Neither Harmony nor Roger seemed willing to stand up to the security guards, perhaps because the guards did most of their dirty work on the sly.

What made Neil spill his coffee, however, was reading that a red dot had begun following Susan on her rounds through Raja. Erik Hamsby! A sudden terror tripled Neil's pulse. His daughter was being targeted by a sniper.

Neil pulled on his cowboy boots — they were tight, but fit well enough. Then he stumped out of the barn, thinking that if he could find Margaret at the Zorba cafe, he could get word through to his daughter about her danger.

Almost at once he began limping. His damaged knee still hurt. In front of the old dairy's milk room he wrenched his broken rib. He gasped, staggered back to the door, and clutched it for support. The hinges squealed as if he had set off an alarm.

A moment later the Modoc doctor was helping him to a cot inside. "Decided to go for a hike, did we?"

"My daughter —"

"The Raja recycler? You put on a cowboy outfit to check on garbage?"

"No. To warn her. To tell the waitress. At the Zorba cafe."

"Oh, you mean Margaret. Connie told me about her. I'm sending my son to pick up the messages every evening at seven."

"You are?"

"Well, you obviously can't go."

"But. I have to. To warn Susan."

"Don't you have Margaret's number? Connie gave it to me." She ran her hands over his jacket, and then his pants, until she found his cell phone. "Your power's down to thirty percent. Have to get it recharged." Then she typed in a few numbers. "There you go. It's probably tapped."

Dizzily, Neil held the phone to his ear. A woman's worried voice said, "Hello?"

"Hi, this is —"

"I know," the voice cut him short. "A wrong number. Is your toaster broken?"

It had to be the Toaster Lady, and she obviously did believe someone might be listening.

"The red dots," Neil said. "I'm worried about them. I need to tell somebody what they mean."

"Oh, we know what the red dots mean. The sheriff told us. Everyone is scared. Raja is in lockdown. It's been a while since anyone saw a laser, but people are building barricades around tents with pallets and shipping containers — anything that could stop a bullet. You'll hear more about it later, OK?"

"OK," Neil said uncertainly. The line went dead. He tried to raise himself up on an elbow. "I need to — "

"You need to rest," the doctor interrupted.

"No, I need — "

"Sorry.

Neil felt a pinprick through the jeans on his thigh. As the drug slowly took hold, a voice came from a distant place.

"Doctor's orders."

Even when the sedative wore off and Neil moved back to his hay bale bunk in the barn, he was so groggy that he forgot to call Connie that night, despite his promise. Tuesday morning he charged his phone in the milk room and left three messages on Connie's voice mail, one after the other.

When his cell finally rang he grabbed it greedily. "Hello?"

A gruff male voice demanded, "Who the hell is this?"

Disappointed, Neil replied, "That's what I'm supposed to ask."

"So why am I wasting my time calling you?"

"Tell me and we'll both know."

The voice grunted. "Who gave me your number."

"How should I know?"

"It figures." The voice let out a long sigh. "A cop like her would ask me to call either an idiot or a wise guy."

"Wait," Neil said. "Are you talking about Wu? Lieutenant Connie Wu?"

"Wu, who, whatever. The Chinese detective from Portland. You work for her?"

"I work *with* her. My name's Ferguson, Neil Ferguson, retired from the Portland Police Bureau. I'm in Fort Klamath as a private investigator."

"Are you an India lover too? That lady cop seems to think Rajneeshees are God's gift to Klamath County."

Neil felt a flush of anger. "I respect the law, no matter who's involved. Now I'm going to take a wild guess and say you're Tolufsen, the sheriff she told me about."

"Yessir, upholder of the county peace. Which is why I don't appreciate having a city cop send me on a wild goose chase where I end up with a deputy hanging in a tree by his ankle."

"What! Is he OK?"

"Just out of sorts, the way you are after waiting upside down for half an hour."

"What happened?"

"I don't think Erik Hamsby likes being followed. Before I waste any more time chasing this kid, I'd like to find out what he's done wrong. Do you know?"

"Well, he's a felon —"

"I know a lot of those. Being a felon is not a crime."

"He's a vet who hates Rajneeshees —"

"I know a lot of those too," the sheriff said, interrupting again. "If you brought them all in for questioning you'd empty half the bars in Klamath County."

When Neil didn't respond to this, the sheriff said, "So you don't know any more about this Hamsby kid than Lieutenant Woohoo?"

"No," Neil admitted. "But I bet his father does."

"Hamsby's father? Where's he?"

"Here in Dawson. I'll show you if you give me a ride."

"Where are you at?"

"The old dairy north of town."

The sheriff laughed. "The witch doctor's drunk tank. It figures."

When the police cruiser pulled up in front of the milk room the sheriff powered down his window. He sized up Neil's bandages and his cowboy outfit. "You Ferguson?"

Neil asked, "Does everybody in the sheriff's department go by last names?"

"Yeah, we kind of do." Tolufsen tipped his head to the left, an indication that Neil could walk around the car and get in.

When Neil got in, the sheriff asked, "What happened to you?"

"I fell off my bicycle."

"That figures too. Where are we going?"

"Downtown. Hamsby's father is the pastor of a Baptist church from Troutdale. They don't like the Rajneeshees either. They brought a busload of people down here with 'Trust Jesus' signs."

"Do they know the new Rajneeshee guru is named Jesus?"

"That hasn't stopped them."

"No, I don't imagine."

They drove on into Dawson. Neil had spent years on beats in similar patrol cars, with a wire screen behind his head, a dashboard full of gadgets, and a radio squawking like a bored electric parrot. Cars like that were islands of safety. Trouble always came when you stepped outside.

At length the sheriff said, "All I know about Erik Hamsby is that he trained as a sniper in Iraq."

"Lately he's been aiming his laser sights at Raja. Where did you find him?"

"We didn't. He left a trail of live 51 millimeter cartridges — little bread crumbs for my dumbass deputy. They led him north to the national park line. There my guy stepped in a brown nylon loop tied to a bent fir sapling. More like 'Nam than Iraq, if you ask me. Still, not a crime. Just a hint that the boy wants to be left alone."

"Alone and armed," Neil said. "For a felon, that's a crime."

"Firearms would be. Ammunition, not so much. No proof he's got a rifle. He can drop bullets all day, and it's just littering."

Traffic stalled them a dozen cars before the crossing of Modoc Avenue and Vishnu Way.

"Never again!" The protesters at the intersection ahead shouted. "Never again!"

"Damn," Neil muttered. The protesters were using the same slogan that had appeared on Portland streetcars before the murders. Had Baptists paid for that divisive ad campaign after all? One protester's sign had a big picture of the old Bhagwan with a Christian cross superimposed over his bearded face.

"Are these the guys you were talking about?" Tolufsen asked.

"I think so." When they drove closer Neil powered down his window and waved to a woman with a sign. "Excuse me. Didn't your signs used to say, 'Trust Jesus'?"

"The Rajneeshees got themselves a fake Jesus, so we're keeping up with the times. It's our pastor's idea."

"Reverend Hamsby? Is he here?"

"No."

"We'd like to talk with him."

The woman eyed Neil skeptically. His car door was painted with the blue logo of the Klamath County Sheriff.

"If this is about Erik, no one knows anything more than you."

The sheriff leaned over and demanded, "Where's Reverend Hamsby?"

"At the campground. I think he's cooking stew."

Neil powered up his window and said, "Turn left."

The yellow school bus from the Troutdale church was still parked on a bank near the creek. Beyond it was a scene that could have been from a Civil War photograph. Between two rows of canvas tents a man in a gray overcoat was stirring a kettle suspended from a tripod over a smoky fire. He turned when the patrol car doors slammed nearly in unison, *clunk-clunk*.

"It ain't soup yet. Go away."

"Reverend Hamsby? My name's Tolufsen, Klamath County Sheriff. And this here is — " he faltered, obviously blanking on Neil's name.

"Sergeant Ferguson," Hamsby replied. "I know. The Rajneeshee security chief." Hamsby left the fire, stooping under the flap of the nearest tent.

Tolufsen squinted sideways at Neil, his look an unasked question.

"Well, I was," Neil admitted. "For a month, until they fired me."

"You were on the red payroll?"

"I'm private now, trying to find out the truth about them."

Hamsby returned from the tent with a sack of potatoes. He dumped them on a picnic table, thumping the planks like a marimba. "So what have you done to my boy this time?"

"Nothing," the sheriff said. "Before he took off into the national park he left a snare that had my deputy dangling in a tree by his leg."

The reverend did a poor job of hiding his smile. He stabbed three Bowie knives into the tabletop. "Gonna help me peel or not?"

Silently, Neil and the sheriff pulled the knives loose. The blades were keen.

Hamsby rolled potatoes at them. "Peel thin."

Neil caught a spud one-handed as it fell off the edge. He sat down and started to peel.

"Tell me about Erik," the sheriff said.

Hamsby shrugged. "The boy's a good shot."

The sheriff sat down. "I know about his marksmanship. I want to know what he was like when he came back from the Army."

The reverend kept peeling. "Erik told me he'd killed eight Muslims over there. Six of them were verified insurgents."

Neil asked, "And the other two?"

"Targets of opportunity. Judgment calls." The reverend frowned. "He came home changed. He'd always been quiet, but after that he'd sit at the breakfast table doodling on the front page of the newspaper. He wouldn't talk. Sometimes he'd go into his room at night and shout. After a few weeks he said he had to rejoin his unit."

"In Iraq?"

"In Portland. Five of them had mustered out there at the same time. Couldn't keep jobs. Wound up smoking marijuana on the streets of Chinatown. Slept in doorways. They didn't exactly turn to God for help. Or anyone else, for that matter. Finally they gave him a cheap gun and told him to rob a cannabis store."

"The felony." Neil held out a peeled potato as if it were an egg.

"Cut them in quarters," Hamsby said.

Neil handed the potato to the sheriff. Tolufsen grumbled, but began cutting it as instructed.

"So Erik served six months in Pendleton. Then he came home, changed again. He sang hymns with the rest of us. Read the Bible. I got him a job driving the church bus. He was always on time."

Hamsby stopped, with a potato half peeled, and looked aside. Neil noticed that his gaze was directed above the fire, into the distance beyond the smoke.

"What made you worry about him?" Neil asked.

"What?" The reverend returned from his thoughts.

"About Erik. You could tell something was wrong."

"Little things. Strange things." Hamsby took another potato and began roughly cutting off thick chunks of peel. "He built a sculpture in his room out of mill ends — scraps of two-by-four lumber. He nailed them all together at right angles until they filled the place. He called it his mathematical theorem."

"Why?" the sheriff asked.

Hamsby shrugged. "He wouldn't talk to me about it. He told my wife it was a time machine. To take him back to when everything was right."

"PTSD," Neil said quietly.

Hamsby looked at him fiercely. "Of course I could see it was delayed stress from the war. I prayed for him, tried to keep him focused on his work, on the church. Still he went out and asked his old gun safety instructor for rifles."

"Does he still have them?" the sheriff asked.

"He had to give them back. But then he started collecting binoculars and scopes, saying maybe he could see into the past. And he thought if he could just somehow get there — "

Angrily, the reverend swept half a dozen potatoes off the table. Then he lowered his head.

The sheriff gave him a minute before asking, "Do you think Erik hates Rajneeshees enough to kill them?"

"We just want them to go away!" Hamsby looked up, red-eyed, furious. "They don't belong here. Their religion, their stupid red clothes, their everything. Can't you see? They need to go back where they came from."

The sheriff laid his knife on the table. "I agree with you."

"You do?"

"Yes, I do. I think a lot of them are illegal aliens anyway, without proper visas."

Neil objected, "But that doesn't mean we can sit by while snipers pick them off. They're people, and a lot of them are locals, not from out of state. In fact, my daughter's in there."

The sheriff and the reverend turned toward him in unison. "Your daughter is a Rajneeshee?"

"No! I mean, not exactly." Neil lowered his voice. If he told this story right, he might convince them both to help. "The Rajneeshees think she's one of them."

The sheriff asked, "Well is she or not?"

"She's an infiltrator. She smuggles out written reports every evening about what's happening inside Raja."

"Damn." The sheriff whistled. "That actually is a good idea."

Hamsby leaned forward. "What have you found out?"

Neil glanced both ways. "Their security force didn't have illegal aliens when I worked there, but it does now. They call themselves the Tico Patrol. At least half of them are from Costa Rica or Mexico without papers."

"I knew it," Hamsby said.

Tolufsen shook his head. "We can't touch them on reservation land. A raid like that would have to come from the feds, and they've got other fish to fry."

"But the Modocs could lead a raid," Neil said. "Tom Shontin, the Modoc elder, has got the tribal council interested in setting up their own police force." He looked to the sheriff. "They'd need help."

"By God, that's right up my alley." Sheriff Tolufsen thumped the table with the flat of his hand.

Neil turned to the pastor. "You know what else I've found?"

"What?"

"A lot of the Rajneeshees' new recruits signed up because they weren't being helped by their communities back home."

"You mean in India?" Hamsby asked.

"No, here in Oregon. I'm talking about battered wives, disabled men, single mothers. Desperate people with nowhere else to turn. Quite a few of these lost people are on this side of the wall, in Dawson. They're drinking, gambling, homeless, broke. Every night volunteers patch them up at a makeshift clinic north of town. But they're just treating the symptoms, not the disease."

"Exactly!" Hamsby balled his hand into a fist. "That's why we're marching."

Neil shook his head. "Waving a bunch of signs isn't helping these people. If you want to save souls, open a safe house."

"A what?"

"A place with free beds and food. You can pitch a tent across the street from Raja's gate if you want. You can make people sing hymns or pray for all I care. Just make them feel welcome. Give them a place to call home."

"You want us to compete with the Rajneeshees?"

"That's right." Neil's voice was low and conspiratorial. "To stop the Rajneeshees, you've got to beat them at their own game. When people are hurting they can turn to the wrong Jesus. You've got to prove that the real one is better than a red-robed fake."

Chapter 35

Connie didn't answer her cell phone until six o'clock that evening, and then it was with a perfunctory, "Hi, Neil."

"You're angry," Neil said.

"No, I'm tired. Don't leave voice mails all day. You know I can't talk until after work."

"You're still angry. I promised to call every night, and yesterday — "

"Forget it." Connie really did sound tired. "I figured you were on drugs."

"Actually, the doc did give me a sedative."

"You see? Anyway, I didn't have news yesterday, and now I do."

"So do I," Neil said. "Who's first?"

"Age before beauty. Shoot."

"Don't say that. Your sniper, Erik Hamsby, is still on the loose." Neil told her about the trail of bullets, the snare, and the red laser dots that suggested Erik had been sighting in on Susan.

"That's cute," Connie said.

"Cute?"

"The doting Dad hears that his daughter has noticed red dots, and he thinks, out of the thousands of people in Raja, she's the target."

"But — "

"Those dots are hard to see in daylight, especially at a distance. Your daughter is just hyper aware of anything weird."

Neil realized this was true. Had his reasoning been swayed by emotion? "Nonetheless, Erik's still out there, and the whole city's on alert. The Rajneeshees are worried that the county sheriff has given up the chase."

"Has he?"

"Yes, he has. I think Sheriff Tolufsen likes traumatized veterans more than he likes Rajneeshees."

"This is frustrating, being stuck here in Portland."

"Actually, Portland's a good place to start a little research."

"Like what?"

"Erik spent six months in the Pendleton penitentiary for robbing a cannabis store at gunpoint. The prison psychiatrist's report would be interesting reading."

"I'll get on it." Connie's quick reply gave away her eagerness. She loved this kind of research.

"Meanwhile, I talked to Erik's father today at the Dawson campground. Even he admits his son is suffering from post-traumatic stress syndrome."

"Because of Iraq?"

"Erik shot eight people there, two of them possibly random civilians."

Connie was silent for a while. "Sounds like a guy who could decide to shoot Rajneeshees."

"When he came home from the penitentiary he built a giant wooden sculpture in his bedroom. He called it his mathematical theorem. He said it was a time machine to take him back before things went bad."

"Before foreign gurus came to Oregon?"

"Maybe. You might take a look at his home in Troutdale. See if his theorem is in working order."

"Will do." Connie paused, evidently taking notes. At length she said, "My turn. I've got a bombshell. Ready?"

"I think so."

"The DNA test you requested for Roger Nash came back from the lab."

"And?"

"You didn't get a very good sample of Roger's DNA, but the preliminary results show it's a match."

"A match? For what?"

"You know. For the old Bhagwan. Apparently Roger Nash and the

Bhagwan Shree Rajneesh share the same DNA."

Neil lay back on his hay bale, stunned. Then he laughed. "That's impossible! Nash was born three days after the Bhagwan died, on the other side of the planet. Dead people don't really come back to life somewhere else."

"The lab admitted it could be a false positive. The sample you provided of the old Bhagwan's hair was pretty good. I guess it had been sealed up in a bead or something. But the hair Harmony got from Roger could have been contaminated, or even switched. Your niece isn't exactly a forensics expert."

"No, she's not. We need a better sample. In the meantime — " Neil's voice trailed off.

Connie finished his sentence. "In the meantime we've got to keep these results absolutely secret."

"No," Neil said. "We need to shout the news from the rooftops. Hold a press conference and put it on page one that Roger may really be the reborn Bhagwan."

"Are you kidding? People would think the Portland police are nuts."

"Not if you tell the truth, just like you told me. Say that it's a preliminary lab report, and we need a better sample of Roger's DNA."

Connie sighed. "What do you have up your sleeve?"

"I bet we'll get a fresh DNA sample, and fast."

"Oh, come on. What are you really after?"

"I think Roger could use some good publicity," Neil said. "He's being sidelined down here in Raja. They've got him meditating in a hidden trailer while Tico Bob and Swami Jesus run the show. It wouldn't hurt to boost the barista a bit."

"I think you like him."

"Other than my daughter, he might be the clearest-headed person in Raja."

Neil's phone gave a warning hum. He looked at the screen and swore. "I just recharged the battery this morning and already it's down to twenty percent. Listen Connie, it's important that you find out everything you can about Erik Hamsby. The Klamath County Sheriff is letting him run wild."

"Why exactly did he call off the search so quickly?"

"A deputy stepped in a snare and wound up in the treetops.

Anyway, Tolufsen is shifting the department's resources elsewhere. I've convinced him to help the Modocs set up a tribal police force."

"At least that part's good," Connie said. "I asked the state police about it, but they're slowed down by bureaucracy."

"And by the way, could you dig up some information on marijuana for me?"

"Are you in that much pain?"

"No. I mean sometimes, but that's not why. The Rajneeshees are planting most of their greenhouses with marijuana seeds that they smuggled in, probably from Costa Rica. I want to know why they're dodging the rules by growing pot on a reservation. Maybe it's a tax thing."

The phone blanked out for a moment.

"Connie? Connie?"

"I'm still here.""

"I love you."

"Keep it up. Any more tremors?"

"You mean earthquakes? Not that I've noticed."

"Good, because Cycle Oregon left Portland this morning. You'll have two thousand bicyclists going around the rim of Crater Lake by Saturday."

Chapter 36

Raja had the desperate air of a city under siege. Susan drove the recycling truck with only one helper on Tuesday because most of her staff hadn't shown up for work. Carpentry crews were building watchtowers along the city's west wall, facing the pine hill where a shot had been heard. The farm fields were empty, and even the greenhouse staff had been reduced to the minimum required to keep irrigation lines open.

Nirvana, the central complex surrounded by metal trailers, was obviously the safest place in the city. When Susan showed up for Harmony's second training session on Wednesday morning, she joined a dozen young day care providers filing in the gate.

Inside the compound, the garden paths were crowded with Rajneeshees Susan did not recognize — older, serious people in business suits and red shirts. They talked in low tones, walking from one trailer to another. Harmony herded the day care teachers to Roger's meditation shelter.

Since their last visit the young Bhagwan had rigged up a sort of tea bar, with hot water piped to a steaming spigot.

"Welcome back, sannyasins," Roger said, filling a row of insulated paper cups. "I only have tea bags, but you can choose your own." Despite his lengthening black beard, Susan thought he looked pale, and his cheeks hollow. For that matter, Harmony wasn't exactly glowing from within either. For the first time, Susan realized that her cousin was no longer young. Susan held her cup of hot water, thought a moment, and then set it aside. Something had always been wrong here. But it was worse now.

"I'm afraid my trailer is being used for other meetings," Harmony told the group. "Today we'll have to hold our class out here by the pool."

As soon as they had sat down on a circle of benches, Harmony said, "The first rule of any school is to keep the children safe. I'm told the day care centers were the first to get armor. How have you been managing?"

The teachers looked at each other. A young woman with purple streaks in her blonde hair said, "They parked a couple of delivery vans in front of our tent to stop stray bullets. I guess that works for now."

"We got plywood stapled to our wall." The only man in the group hunched forward as if for a football huddle. "But that's not my biggest problem."

"Then what is?"

He looked down, his voice weary. "Everything."

Harmony nodded. "I think I understand."

"You do?"

"It's not about the sniper, is it? This is your first week of teaching. You've got twenty half-wild kids for six hours a day. I've been in that situation before, so I know. If you don't get help soon, you'll burn out. It's hard to admit you need help."

The young teachers looked at Harmony uncertainly. Susan could sense that Harmony had read their minds.

"Go ahead," Harmony said, shrugging with one shoulder. "Tell me the worst behavioral problems you've got."

"The kids won't sit still!" The young man complained, roughing up his short hair with his hands. "They're flying all over the place. I'm afraid they'll run out into the street."

"Start with a circle," Harmony said. "Get mats with each child's name, so they know where to sit. Then do something fun, so they pay attention. Bring a surprise bag. Declare that it's shark week. Take a toy shark out of the surprise bag. Then read a book about sharks. Teach them a song about sharks. Next week tell them it's dinosaur week."

"But they don't listen," he objected. "I'm shouting all the time."

"Children ignore people who shout all the time. Even dogs learn that. To be in charge you need a different signal. If you're indoors, turn out the lights. If you're outside, clap your hands. Then point to the circle and wait there with your surprise bag. No one gets to see what's in it until they're all quiet, sitting on their mats."

"In my class the children are always fighting," the woman with purple-streaked hair admitted. "They won't share toys. The boys use sticks as guns. When I take them away, they pretend their fingers are guns."

Harmony sighed. "I grew up without a lot of rules. But children need rules. Children want rules."

"Like no weapons? Real or pretend?"

"You could use that one. One school I worked at had the rule, 'You get what you get, and you don't throw a fit.'"

Several of the young teachers laughed.

"Or you could make it even simpler," Harmony went on. "Just have one rule: Respect others. That means you don't hurt other people. You don't touch people without permission, and you don't grab their toys. You take turns. You listen when the teacher needs to talk."

"What about the ones who just cry?" a woman asked quietly. "I've got a couple of three-year-old twins who cry all day. If one stops, the other sets him off again. It's breaking their mother's heart. She hangs around, trying to comfort them."

"Tell her to go away," Harmony said firmly. "The twins are putting on a show for her sake, to get her attention. After she leaves they'll cry for a while, but then they'll get distracted by kids, toys, and games. Preschool is more fun than Mom."

"Shouldn't we be teaching them about Raja?" the woman with streaked hair asked. "The communal spirit? The path to enlightenment?"

"Yes, but they're young, so you do it a different way. Three year olds need to burn off energy. Start the day with a Raja parade. Give them red scarves and tabla drums. Let them dance and make noise for a while. With four and five year olds you could try starting with a quiet meditation circle. Call it 'mindfulness' if you like. Give their thoughts some focus by talking about nature — bugs, plants, birds — something physical and new each day. The spiritual insight will come later."

Most of the young teachers were taking notes. But one of them, a woman with a red scarf on her head, was biting her lip.

Harmony caught her eye. "You have a different worry, don't you?"

The woman nodded. "One of my five-year-old girls sits in a corner and screams. Her Dad says she's smart, but I don't see it. When I put my arm around her she jerks away, shaking."

Harmony held out her hand to Susan. "I think you should meet my cousin. Susan is our specialist in the remarkable world of autism."

Susan stared at the ground. This was not why she had come to the class, and yet it was. "Imagine that you are a wild animal suddenly transported to a street in New York City," she said. "Taxis are honking, people are shouting, noise is everywhere. This is the way the five-year-old girl in your class feels. There's too much input. She can't filter out the noise."

The woman with the scarf frowned. "I'm not so sure. My class is quiet, but the girl still screams."

Susan shook her head. "She doesn't think in words like other people. She thinks in pictures. There are too many pictures, and she doesn't have words. So she screams. If you touch a wild animal like that, she's terrified."

"Are you saying she's feral?"

Susan didn't respond. After a moment Harmony explained. "Not feral, just wired differently. Autism is a spectrum. Some people function better in groups than others. A boy in one of my classes crawled into our pet rabbit's cage — not because he thought he was a rabbit, but to shut out the extra stimulation. Another boy fixated on vacuum cleaners. He didn't play with the other children. He just drew diagrams of vacuum cleaners all day. You need to give these children space, and let them focus. Autism can be a gift."

"A gift?" The woman looked skeptical.

"You've spoken one hundred and thirty-seven words in the past forty-nine minutes," Susan said, looking down. "Knowing things like that is a gift. Does she tell time?"

"Who?" The woman with the scarf blinked.

"The girl in your class is five years old," Susan continued. "Children with autism learn to tell time at a young age. Routine is important. Anything out of the ordinary upsets them. If your preschool starts at eight thirty, and I'm guessing it does, then you have ten and a half minutes before it starts. If you aren't there on time, that girl will rock in the corner and scream all day."

Harmony took a watch out of her jeans pocket. "We really are about

out of time. Stay safe, think good thoughts, and we'll meet again here at seven thirty on Saturday morning."

The group stood up and put away their notes. The woman with the purple-streaked hair walked around the pool to thank Roger for the tea, but he was sitting cross-legged, reading a book so intently that he didn't seem to notice.

When the others had left, Harmony thanked Susan for speaking out about autism.

"They are poisoning you," Susan replied, looking across the pool.

"What do you mean?"

"You and Roger both," Susan went on. "You're pale, losing weight. You are being poisoned."

"That's ridiculous. We eat well. We're protected here. Why would anyone poison us?"

"Why did they break into your parents' house?" Susan asked.

"What?"

"Tico trolls ransacked your parents' house in Eugene. Another group of Rajneeshees beat up my father so badly he's still in a clinic."

"These things aren't true."

"Do I ever lie?"

Harmony opened her mouth but then stopped, as if she didn't have an answer.

Susan picked up her cup of long-cold tea and sniffed it. "I think this is Gilberto's other discovery. The thing he says he can tell only you."

"Not Gilberto again." Harmony rolled her eyes. "If all he's doing is trying to get my attention, it was a waste of time for him to come from Italy."

"You still love him."

"I do not."

"Gilberto came to save you, and now he's in trouble," Susan continued. "He says the drilling rig is crooked. The new hot water well angles under the national park. But there's something else. It's getting harder to meet him. He spends all day in the lab where they store the fracking chemicals."

Harmony sighed. "Susan, I love you dearly. But you sometimes make me want to crawl in a corner and scream. Look around you. Raja is a community of peace, or at least it's trying to be."

Susan poured out her tea onto the gravel path. "What does 'Nirvana' mean?"

"Nirvana? It's paradise."

"No, that's a metaphor. What does it mean in Sanskrit?"

"I don't know. Enlightenment? Did you look it up?"

Susan nodded. "Nirvana means extinguished, like a flame. Snuffed out. Dead."

Harmony opened her mouth again, wordlessly.

Susan dared to look her in the eyes. Susan had trouble reading most emotions, but she had always been able to sense fear. Doubt had finally begun to flicker in her cousin's eyes.

Susan crumpled the paper cup. "Saturday morning at seven thirty. Be ready." Then she turned and left.

Chapter 37

By Thursday Neil had become so frustrated by his confinement in a hay barn that he tried out his bicycle. He couldn't walk more than a few blocks without aggravating the broken rib, but if he balanced on the bicycle seat without pedaling too hard, he found he could coast all the way to downtown Dawson. He wove past traffic, veered left on Modoc Avenue, and rolled into the campground, hoping to find out more about the missing sniper, Erik Hamsby.

The Baptist school bus was gone, but the Lawrence motorhome was still there. Connie had told him about her conversation with Vera Lawrence, the retired Sunday school teacher. He didn't have more questions for her, but he was curious about her husband Vernon, the lawyer who had trained Erik in marksmanship.

A blue plastic parrot on the porch awning held a "Welcome" sign in its beak. Neil tapped on the glass of the screen door.

A few seconds later a grandmotherly face appeared behind the glass, wisps of white hair dangling loose. Her eyes wrinkled into a smile. "Well if it isn't that nice Portland policeman. Come on in, I've just made cookies."

She pushed open the door, releasing the aroma of fresh baking.

"I didn't want to bother you, Mrs. Lawrence, but I wondered —"

"Look at you," she interrupted, clucking her tongue. "They said you'd been hurt, and now you're dressed like a cowboy. Is that to hide the bandages?"

"Is your husband at home?" Neil asked. "I wondered if I could ask a few more questions about Erik Hamsby."

"Not until you try my ginger snaps." She pointed him to a chair. "Now you sit on the swivel while I fetch a plate from the kitchen." The swivel was a plush pilot's chair mounted by the dining table. The kitchen in this compact house was a row of half-size appliances on the opposite wall. Neil sat down.

"Did you hear the news?" Mrs. Lawrence asked, scooping cookies from a baking sheet to a plate with a spatula. "On TV last night they were saying that Roger Nash — little Roger, the boy from my Sunday school class — really might be the Bhagwan Rajneesh."

"That's a preliminary report. The police want to recheck the DNA." Neil raised an eyebrow at her. "Or do you believe in reincarnation?"

"No." She paused, spatula in the air. "And yet there was something about Roger. He was such a spiritual child. I think that's why Erik bullied him so badly. People do that, you know. They ridicule things they don't understand."

Neil recalled hearing that Roger and Erik had been in the same Sunday school class. Roger had suffered the day he showed up with a temporary tattoo of a warrior elf. "Do you think Erik is still trying to bully Roger? Perhaps by shooting Rajneeshees?"

She set the plate of cookies on the table between them. "Erik certainly has the skill to shoot anything he wants. It's harder to know what he's thinking. Hate, jealousy, confusion, even love — these emotions are closer to each other than we'd like to believe. Young people flip from one to another so easily. Especially Erik, who came back from the war with a troubled mind."

"I talked to Erik's father, Reverend Hamsby. He said his son built a time machine in his bedroom in Troutdale."

"A time machine? Does he think it works?"

"It's just scrap lumber, nailed together. But it suggests that Erik wants to go back to an earlier, less troubled time."

"Or that he wants to undo something he's done," Mrs. Lawrence said. "You should talk to my husband. I haven't seen Erik for years, but Vern kept in touch."

"Where can I find your husband?"

"He's a legal advisor in the refugee center."

"What refugee center?"

"You don't know?" She raised her white eyebrows. "I was told the whole thing was your idea."

Neil thought back. "I may have suggested that the Baptists open a safe house."

"Well, it's up and running. They set up tents on the gas station lot on the corner. You must have gone right by it on your way here."

Neil stood up to leave.

"No, you don't!" Mrs. Lawrence stopped him with a pointed finger. "You haven't even tasted my ginger snaps."

Neil sat back down. The cookies, as it turned out, were quite good.

Back at the corner of Modoc Avenue and Vishnu Way, Neil was surprised that he had overlooked the new tents on the derelict gas station's parking lot. The giant "SHELL" sign still towered over the intersection, but the S had been replaced by smaller lettering that read, "Escape From." Below it, the sign that had once advertised gas prices now announced, "The Real Jesus Refugee Center." The message was positioned so it aimed across the intersection to confront both the Ex-Zorba-Tent Grill and Captain Jack's Casino.

Neil chained his bicycle to the signpost. He reached up to take off his bike helmet, but realized he was wearing a cowboy hat — part of Connie's plan to help him fit in. He sighed and walked through a tent flap marked "Enter Here."

A girl at a card table greeted him, "Welcome to the Real Jesus. How can we help you?"

Protest signs covered the walls of the six-by-nine-foot tent: "Trust Jesus" and "Never Again." What caught Neil's attention, however, was the receptionist herself, a girl with a blonde hairdo that curled up at the shoulders — a style that had been popular in the 1960s. Her pleated, pale yellow blouse puckered out over breasts as pointed and protruding as 1960s car bumpers. A white belt cinched her narrow waist. If ever there were a rival to the red-wrapped Twinkies of the Rajneeshees, it was this wholesomely sexy Christian girl dressed as an Easter treat.

"I'm looking for Vernon Lawrence," Neil said.

"Our lawyer? Everyone wants to talk with him. He's been so busy, seeing clients all day."

"Pro bono?" Neil asked.

She wagged her finger. "I'm not allowed to give out client names." In a confidential whisper she added, "But you're right, a lot of them are Hispanic."

"Actually I meant to ask if Mr. Lawrence is being paid for his legal advice."

"Oh. We're all volunteers, doing God's work. Are you a refugee from Raja?"

"Not exactly. I'm a private investigator from Portland." She drew in her breath. "When do you think Mr. Lawrence will have time to answer a few questions?"

"I'll go check." She squirmed out of her folding chair, dangerously wobbling the projectiles in her blouse. Then she leaned through a flap door at the back of the tent, pulling the canvas together behind her back. Her purpose was obviously to block Neil's view of whatever might be in the adjoining room, but in fact it left him watching her tight-skirted bottom as if it were the star of a puppet play.

"You're in luck." She turned, drawing the curtain on her act. "Mr. Lawrence has just finished with the previous clients. He'll be with you shortly."

A moment later a young boy in a pink T-shirt opened the flap door behind her. The boy stopped, looked at Neil, and said, "Moo."

The boy's older sister pushed past him. "Paul! You're always blocking doors." But then she too stopped. "Oh! You're a cowboy now. And your head's bandaged. Did you escape in disguise?"

"Come, children," their mother said, herding them past the reception table.

"But Mother!" the girl objected. "It's the bicycle man from the hotel."

The mother paused. She still tied her brown hair back with a beige scarf, as Neil remembered from the Oakridge bed & breakfast, but her ankle-length dress was now red. Her name sprang to mind: Mary Landenburger.

"Mr. Ferguson," she said. "Once again you have caught me at an embarrassing moment, running away."

The lawyer stepped into the room and sized up the scene. "I see you already know each other."

"We crossed paths in Oakridge a lifetime ago." Neil touched the brim of his hat toward Mary. "That's a little over a week in local time. Did you find rapture in Raja?"

"No, on the contrary. They assigned me to plant marijuana in fiberglass greenhouses. The children were abandoned in a one-tent school with unqualified staff."

"But they let you drive away?"

"I'm afraid I donated our car to the commune when we arrived. When I later decided that I prefer a traditional Christian community, I asked that they return the automobile. I plead my case all the way to their operations manager."

"Vijay Collins. What did he say?"

"He said our gift was irrevocable. So my children and I walked out of his office and through the East Gate." Mary Landenburger held her head high. "It turns out that there are miracles on the Indian reservation, but they are all on this side of the street."

"You found a miracle after all?" Neil asked.

"Yes. Mr. Lawrence has located my truant husband."

The lawyer held up his hands in objection. "These are confidential matters."

"Not at all," she said. "After a surprisingly brief search on his pocket computer, Mr. Lawrence determined that my husband, Jason Landenburger, has spent the past two years living under his own name as pastor of the New Life Church of Revelations in Redmond."

"Moo!" the boy said fiercely.

His mother shot him an equally fierce glare. Then she turned back to Neil. "Mr. Lawrence says he will see to it that my husband starts sending monthly child support payments. In the meantime the children and I are riding a church bus to a hotel in Klamath Falls, courtesy of the Real Jesus."

She swept out of the tent, followed by her daughter. The boy, however, hung back.

"Moo?"

Neil lowered himself to one knee so he could look the boy in the eye. "You're not a beast anymore, Paul. That phase of your life is over. It looks like your father is not coming back, no matter what you do."

The boy's lip quivered.

"That means you have to be the man of the family now," Neil told him. "Your mother is a proud woman, but she and your sister need your help. They need you to be strong."

Paul swallowed, but lifted his chin.

"Do you understand?" Neil asked.

The boy nodded. "Yes, sir."

"Then go out there and take care of your family."

Without another word the boy turned and walked out, a soldier on a mission.

The receptionist had tears in her eyes. "My God. You're not just a private investigator. You sound like a preacher."

"I'm a retired cop. We save souls a different way."

"You wanted to see me?" Mr. Lawrence held open the door flap. "Alone, I assume?"

Neil followed him in. The adjacent tent had a yellow canvas roof that gave everything a stuffy, jaundiced look.

"Thanks for helping the Landenburgers," Neil said. "When I met them in Oakridge I knew they were in trouble, but I was having too much trouble of my own to do anything."

"Trouble seems to follow you and your colleagues, Mr. Ferguson." He held out his hand toward a folding chair. "Have a seat."

"Which colleagues?" Neil sait down.

"Recently I had the pleasure of being threatened at gunpoint by your Lieutenant Wu. And now I hear she's done a DNA test on the Bhagwan."

"Yes, I wanted to ask you about that. You're a lawyer. What do you think about reincarnation?"

Lawrence leaned back, touching his fingertips together to form a little cage in the air. "There are precedents — examples of people who have been declared legally dead coming back to life."

"Such as Jesus?"

The lawyer spread his hands, opening the cage. "The cases I'm referring to have involved a few minutes or at most a few hours of suspended animation. To recover after three days, as Jesus did, requires divine intervention."

"Roger was born exactly three days after the Bhagwan died in India."

"To achieve legal status as the same person, you have to reanimate the same body."

"Clones don't count?"

"I have known Roger and his parents for twenty years. He is not a clone. He is not the Bhagwan. If you are a diligent investigator, I'm sure you will discover that the Rajneeshees are perpetrating a hoax in order to reestablish a foothold here in Oregon."

"I'm working on that," Neil said. "But I'm also investigating the people who want to drive them out. Are you a member of the Baptist church in Troutdale?"

"No, I'm non-denominational, and my wife is a Baptist of a different affiliation. I've only become interested in Reverend Hamsby's group since they shifted their efforts from protest marches to charitable work. I'm retired, so I can donate my time to a number of worthwhile causes."

"It surprises me that a small Troutdale church would have the money to open a center like this so quickly. They're even able to rent hotel rooms for Raja refugees."

The lawyer shrugged. "All evangelical denominations have funds for missionary work."

"Could their church also have paid for the Portland advertising campaign that showed the Bhagwan in a gun's crosshairs? They've started using the same slogans."

"I really don't know anything more about their finances."

The lawyer had sidestepped Neil's questions —a sign that these were issues he would never address. Vernon Lawrence had ties to all three groups that had announced their opposition to the Rajneeshees — the Baptists, the Oregon chapter of the NRA, and the 1000 Friends of Oregon. He hadn't denounced the ad campaign or its incendiary slogans. In fact, he was still a suspect in two murder cases, having had both the motive and the opportunity to kill Swami Bhrater and Juan Guerrero. The kindness he had shown toward the Landenburger family might not extend to non-Christians.

"Let's talk about Reverend Hamsby's son Erik," Neil suggested. "You were the last person to see him before he retreated into the woods. Have you been in contact with him since?"

"No."

Neil decided to throw the lawyer off guard. "Did you know that Erik has built a time machine?"

Mr. Lawrence knit his brow. "Yes. He told me about the sculpture in his bedroom. He understood that it wasn't really a time machine."

"Then why did he call it that?"

Lawrence looked aside, his gaze distant, his features yellow in the tent's filtered light. "Only people like him who have suffered would understand. Dreams can take you back in time to your childhood room, your house, your street. It always seems to be a better, purer world. Then you wake up and realize they're just —" His voice drifted off.

"Ghost towns," Neil said.

"That's right." He looked to Neil, and for the first time his eyes seemed to share a sadness.

Neil decided to ask the same question he had asked Vera. "Do you think Erik could have shot the Rajneeshees in Portland? He'd bullied Roger as a child. Could he still be doing that?"

Lawrence sighed. "Bullying is usually about jealousy — trying to put down someone who is smarter or better than you. In Erik's case, it was about someone happier than him. Roger lived a charmed life. He never seemed to worry. He even shook off the bullying, like water off a duck."

"Jealousy is a powerful motive."

"Is jealousy still Erik's motive? Now that he's older, I'm not so sure. I trained him as a marksman. The Army trained him as a killer. But a sniper is really a voyeur. I think Erik is being driven by curiosity."

"Curiosity about what?"

Lawrence tightened his lips. "About someone who's happy. Someone who seems able to bring ghosts back to life."

Chapter 38

"Sorry, bro, I've got drunken monkeys screeching at me here, too many rotten pineapples. Lemme try from the beach."

It was Thursday evening, and Neil had been in his dairy barn waiting for word from Susan when his brother Mark called. A scrawny white cat prowled behind the barn's hay bales.

"Mark? Where are you?"

"Place called Puerto Viejo. What a brainstorm, asking us to check up on the Rajneeshee Commune. Melanie and I are loving it."

Neil had to think a minute. His brother had last called him four or five days ago, trying to find out what was happening inside Raja. Neil had suggested Mark undertake a research trip farther afield. "So you're actually in Costa Rica?"

"Yeah, you know there aren't very good flight connections from Eugene? We had to spend Monday night in a Houston airport hotel. The next day our plane drops out of the clouds beside one of those prehistoric volcanos you see in the Flintstones. We rent a Land Rover and drive all day on unmarked roads. There's tin shacks and banana trucks everywhere. Turns out the Rajneeshees sold their farm to a Dutch yoga resort for a couple million last year, and they're hiring."

"Do you think the Rajneeshees were farming marijuana?" Neil asked. The white cat had stopped hunting for mice and was watching him with shiny red eyes.

"That's for sure. Some coffee and tobacco, mostly as a screen. When the States started legalizing pot, the bottom fell out of the export market. Rather than adapt, the commune cashed out and moved back to their old stomping grounds in Oregon. No! I don't want one, and not pink!"

"Mark?" Neil had always struggled to understand his brother, especially on the phone.

"Some guy's selling hammocks, but they're nylon crap. Anyway, the new Dutch owners love the Rajneeshee angle. The people who sign up for yoga retreats are nuts for that mystic stuff, but all the real Rajneeshees vanished. They hired Melanie just like that. She's teaching a class right now on paddle boards in a pool with fake waterfalls and real lizards. Harmony would love it here. You got surfing, coconuts, toucans, and an easy gig with the Dutch guys. You heard from her?"

"Your daughter? She's in Nirvana."

"No! Already?"

"That's what they call the central complex in Raja," Neil explained. The cat was advancing toward him warily, its tail up. "Harmony is training kindergarten teachers there. It's safe, but kind of out of touch."

"Tell her to get her ass down here. They've got these beautiful hardwoods, and local workers will carve it for pennies. I'm staying."

"You're staying in Costa Rica?"

"Thinking of it, yeah. I might open a toy factory down here, export better stuff at a quarter the cost."

"What else have you found out about the Rajneeshees?" The scrawny cat bumped Neil's leg. It had a watery eye and clumped fur that suggested fleas, but Neil scratched the top of its head anyway. It blinked and purred.

"People here don't know much, or at least they won't say much. When they do talk, they mention three names: El Hermano, El Guerrero, and El Viejo."

"My Spanish is rusty," Neil admitted.

"The Brother, the Warrior, and the Old Man," Mark said. "Hermano means brother. He was the one who ran the spiritual side of the commune, doing meditations and readings."

"That would be Swami Bhrater. He claimed to be the Bhagwan's brother."

"Or brother-in-law or something. But yeah, he must have been El Hermano."

"I can figure out El Guerrero," Neil said. "That would be Juan

Guerrero, the other Rajneeshee who was shot. What role did he play in the commune?"

"Mule," Mark said, his voice obscured by the crash of a wave.

"What?"

"El Guerrero wasn't a Rajneeshee at all. People here say he was a Mexican gangster."

Neil thought a moment. "That matches what we found out about Guerrero. He grew up in a Guadalajara slum. He liked marijuana, telenovelas, and cash. Why was he working for the Rajneeshees?"

"Simple. The Costa Ricans learned how to grow world-class weed, but only The Warrior knew how to smuggle it through Mexico to the U.S."

"Oh, that kind of mule." The cat suddenly turned its head, its ears pricked. Even Neil could see a mouse running along the feed trough that fronted the cows' old stanchions. The cat leapt forward, but the mouse darted into a hole.

Neil asked, "What about the other 'El'? Who was he?"

"El Viejo, the Old Man. No one talks about him. It's like they're scared."

"Of someone in Oregon? Maybe he's still down there in Costa Rica."

"Or maybe he's just really old and scary. I've got this idea. If the old Bhagwan faked his death in India, he'd be in his eighties now."

"Why fake your death when you can be reincarnated? Did you hear about the DNA test?"

"Yeah, we heard the police announced something, but who believes cops? No, I've got this weird feeling the Old Man is still among us. Any day now he's gonna blow your case wide open."

The cat couldn't quite reach the mouse with its paw, but time was on the cat's side. Sooner or later the mouse would have to come out. Neil couldn't help thinking that the toughest cases come down to a similar game. Was the answer just out of his reach, waiting to be revealed? Or was he the one who was trapped?

"What about Tico Bob and Swami Jesus?" Neil asked. "They were both in Costa Rica, and now they seem to be in charge."

"Are they old?"

"Not particularly. Still, I'd like you to ask around about them. Oh, and about Swami Bhrater's will. Are you keeping it in a safe place?"

"Sure."

"Can you get me a copy?"

"I've got a picture of it here on my phone. I'll email it to you."

"Do that. And Mark? Thanks for checking on things in Costa Rica."

"No problemo, bro. Thanks for keeping an eye on my daughter."

After Neil ended the call he sat there watching the dairy barn cat. Dim light fell from the barn's broken, fly-specked windows, and as the long summer evening slipped away, the light was fading.

Suddenly the cat twisted about, its wide eyes scanning the loft. Then it sprinted out a gap in the barn door into the night.

A moment later a huge, silent shape in the shadows over Neil's head sent him crouching. Wings as wide as a dark angel's glided among the rafters. Then the great horned owl perched, folded its wings, and swiveled its head, aiming its big black eyes where the mouse had hidden. Now that the cat was gone, the mouse would venture out. And it would find itself in the talons of an even larger, stealthier killer.

Captain Dickers pointed to the long-range M40 rifle on the conference table. Mounted on the barrel were two flared scopes and a V-shaped brace. "This is police work, Lieutenant Wu. While you've been making us look like fools, Espada went out and found the murder weapon."

Connie bit her lip. This time Dickers was right.

The captain turned to the mustachioed forensics lieutenant. "I've read your report, Espada, and it's brilliant. Sum it up quickly for the woman who used to be in charge of this investigation."

"The rifle was right there, in the ditch by the entrance to the quarry where we found Guerrero." Luis Espada was new to the homicide department, and his nervous excitement showed.

"Any fingerprints?" Connie asked.

"Of course not," Dickers said. "We're dealing with a professional."

Espada added, "Ballistics shows it's the weapon that shot both Guerrero and the Rajneesh swami. I'm still tracing the serial number. But get this —" he paused for effect. "It's the same model that Erik Hamsby bought from his marksmanship instructor, Vernon Lawrence. Of course that weapon was turned in when word got out about his felony, but it shows his taste in rifles."

"Hamsby's our man, and he's still at large." Dickers squinted at Connie. "I don't know what you did down there to alienate the Klamath

County Sheriff, but he refuses to lead the manhunt. Fortunately, Espada has done better with the National Park Service."

"Crater Lake doesn't have enough staff to launch a search," Espada admitted, "But they've sealed off the backcountry and alerted visitors to report sightings. Pacific Crest Trail hikers have been instructed to bypass the whole area. Eventually Hamsby will have to come out for supplies. The question is whether he'll strike again first."

Dickers nodded. "The Rajneesh city is like a college campus with a gunman on the loose. Their security people have got the place in lockdown mode. We're supposed to be helping them, Wu, not leaking distractions to the press."

Connie sighed. She had known this was coming. "I'm sorry, Captain. I should have checked with you first before releasing anything. It's just that the DNA test was authorized and paid for by private individuals, not the department."

"No one," Dickers raised his voice and his index finger. "No one involved with this investigation talks to the media except me. Understood?"

"Yes, sir."

"Especially not with a preliminary report, based on samples collected by amateurs. Roger Nash's mother is threatening to sue for libel. Dead gurus are dead. Their decaying bodies do not come back to life somewhere else. A reprimand is going in your file, and we're considering a demotion."

Connie felt like she had been slugged in the stomach.

The captain paused, eyeing her uncertainly. "I read your report about Hamsby's home in Troutdale. At least there you're on the right track. That contraption he built in his bedroom shows how messed up he really is. A time machine?"

"He is a disturbed young man," Connie admitted. "I have an appointment to meet with his prison psychiatrist. Erik spent six months at the penitentiary in Pendleton. It's a four-and-a-half-hour drive, sir."

"All right. But this time, keep on task. You're either with the team, Lieutenant, or you're not."

Connie had plenty of time to fume as she drove out Interstate 84, first through the forested chasm of the Columbia Gorge, and then beside walls of desert rimrock. She had been through a lot with Neil

Ferguson, but he wasn't her boss. Why was she still listening to him instead of to her own captain? She had put her job at risk by leaking the DNA report to the media, and for what? No one in the real world believed that Roger Nash was reincarnated. Rationally, she knew it was time to shut Neil out of her decisions. Her brain told her to do her work and keep her job. But her body was speaking too. She remembered how her heart had clenched when she'd seen him being beaten in the Dawson construction site. How he'd believed her in the Cooper case when everyone else had shaken their heads. Even now she could picture him, unshaven, in the worn cowboy jeans she had bought. Damn him!

Isolated on a sagebrush plain amidst forbidding mountains, the gray block buildings of the Pendleton high-security prison looked like a Tibetan monastery. But while Himalayan monks might be seeking to escape from the world, penitents had been brought here so that there would be no escape.

With just twenty minutes until her appointment, Connie barely had time for a bathroom break and a bite of her sack lunch. Then an armed male guard accompanied her to the consultation room of Dr. Filip Varanyi, the prison psychiatrist.

The room proved to be a large, stark cell with curtainless windows, a shiny tile floor, and the sort of angular metal furniture that you might find at an office liquidation sale. No magazines, no carpets. For a psychiatrist's office, Connie found it intimidatingly stark.

"The doctor will be right with you," the guard said, closing the door behind him. A few seconds later a door at the opposite end of the room opened and a forty-something man came out, studying a clipboard. His white linen suit accented the light brown of his hands and face. He adjusted the thick black frames of his glasses without looking up.

"A homicide lieutenant from Portland," he said, enunciating the consonants with a precision that suggested he had been educated in Asia. "We cherish client confidentiality, even in the penal system, so I trust you have a warrant?" He looked up for the first time, baring very white teeth at her.

Connie took the warrant out of her jacket pocket. "A former inmate of yours, Erik Hamsby, is a suspect in two of our homicide cases. Perhaps you've heard of the Rajneeshee murders?"

"This sort of news spreads quickly through a penitentiary. What can I do for you, Lieutenant?"

"Hamsby is still at large. I'd like to see any reports or studies you might have about him. We want some insight into his frame of mind."

"Mr. Hamsby has an unusually artistic mind."

"Artistic?"

"Yes. Should I bring examples?"

They were still standing in the middle of the room. "Could we sit down to discuss this? Perhaps someplace more comfortable?" She nodded toward the door of his inner office.

Dr. Varanyi frowned. "Very well. You are not a patient. Still, I would ask you to remove your shoes."

Connie followed him to the door and slipped off her shoes.

The doctor stopped beside the door and opened a metal cabinet that contained boxes of what looked like hospital supplies. "Prisons are breeding grounds for bacteria, Lieutenant. I maintain a level of microbial defense in my private office. You will need to wear disposable slippers, latex gloves, and a hair net."

Connie nearly laughed out loud. "I'm not going to wear a hair net."

"Very well. Then you may wait for me here in the patient consultation room while I retrieve the documents you wish."

The man's expression was earnest. Why was it, Connie wondered, that psychiatrists had the strangest quirks? Perhaps their fascination with phobias led them to the profession in the first place. Still, she couldn't help feeling a flush of resentment as she put on the hospital supplies. "Satisfied?"

"Sufficiently." He opened the door to a room that was smaller and better lit, but every bit as sterile as the first.

Connie sat in a metal chair beside an empty metal desk. She crossed her arms and waited while the doctor retrieved manila folders from a bank of metal filing cabinets.

"You asked about Mr. Hamsby's frame of mind," the doctor said, tapping the folders on the desk to straighten them. "I assume you realize that he suffers from post-traumatic stress as a result of his military deployment?"

"Yes. Could that make him violent?"

"I've seen violent behavior in other PTSD patients. Mr. Hamsby, however, seems to have subsumed violent urges through his art." Dr.

Varanyi spread an array of circular pen-and-ink drawings on the table. "He is, quite honestly, one of the most gifted portrait artists I have ever known. Someday I would like to frame the sketch he did of me. Masterful, yet it took him only ten minutes."

Connie had to admit that the portrait had caught the doctor astonishingly well: the broad lips, the haughty eyebrows. A glint drawn into the corner of his glasses gave the portrait a slightly cartoonish feel. In fact, the bold, black-and-white style reminded her of Japanese manga. She glanced through the other portraits. Some had been carefully finished with watercolors. A few of the circular portraits had a red or a green wash. Most of the subjects were foreign-looking men. Suddenly Connie realized what was wrong.

"These are gunsights," she said.

"I beg your pardon?"

"Erik is a marksman. He served as a sniper in Iraq. These are portraits of people in gunsights."

The doctor drew back. He looked from the portraits to Connie. "Are you suggesting — "

"I'm suggesting that Erik subsumed his anger by drawing pictures of the people he's killed." She pushed the doctor's portrait forward. "Or the people he wants to kill."

"I — " The doctor shook his head. "I think you must be mistaken. He was doing well. He seemed ready for an early release."

"And now he's aiming a laser rifle scope at Rajneeshees in Klamath County. Tell me, doctor. Do you think he targeted you because you're from India?"

"I am from Pakistan." The doctor took off his glasses and waved them back and forth, as if to erase something in the air. "I developed a very good relationship with Mr. Hamsby."

"Then you don't think it's possible that he shot Swami Bhrater, a Rajneeshee guru from India?"

"This I do not know. India is a land of more than a billion people. They are all different. They have many religions. Asia is awash in fakirs. I myself am a man of science. This is one reason I choose to practice in Oregon, a state where the number one religion is 'none of the above.'"

Connie tried a different angle. "After Erik was released from prison he built a sculpture out of wood scraps. It fills most of the bedroom in his parents' house. He called it his 'time machine' Do you have any idea why he might have done that?"

"This is interesting." The psychiatrist put his glasses back on. "Mr. Hamsby used the expression with me, 'I wish I could turn back the clock.' It is not uncommon to hear this phrase among a prison population. Mr. Hamsby's sculpture, it would seem, is a manifestation of that same wish fulfillment."

The doctor frowned, thinking. "A desire to recreate the past indicates remorse. And remorse is a crucial step in rehabilitation. This is why I reject your interpretation of the portraits. Yes, they are circular, because he is familiar with this kind of frame. But no, I do not see violence in them. They exhibit remorse. Even affection."

Connie spun the doctor's portrait on the metal tabletop. "You think he liked you?"

"This I do not know. But an entire series of his portraits are of a girl he described with affection." The doctor took a few drawings from a separate folder and arranged them on top of the others.

The beautiful, black-haired woman in these circular drawings had indeed been lovingly sketched. Connie thought she had seen this winsome face before, perhaps in a movie or a comic strip. "Is this an imaginary person?"

The doctor smiled. "In a male penitentiary there is no shortage of fantasy women. But Mr. Hamsby assured me that this one is real, a girl he had watched, but had never spoken to. He said he had had his sights on her for quite some time."

"He said that?" Connie asked, alarmed. "He said he'd 'had his sights on her'? Where was this woman?"

The doctor looked flustered. "In downtown Portland, I believe. After his release from the military Mr. Hamsby had trouble finding employment. He lived among the homeless in Old Town."

"Shit!"

"I beg your pardon, Lieutenant?"

Connie recognized the backgrounds of the sketches. One was set in a dragon boat on Portland's waterfront. Another was at a thrift store. The rest were in a recycling center. And the black-haired girl in the foreground — the beautiful young woman who wore overalls, and who never looked anyone in the eye — the girl in the gunsight was Neil's daughter Susan.

Chapter 39

The owl flew away when Neil's phone rang. He fumbled the phone onto the barn's wooden floor, nervous in the expectation that it would be Connie.

"Hi, Love," he answered.

There was a moment's silence as the great wings beat the shadows, gaining altitude toward an open loft window.

"Um, Neil?" A man's voice.

Neil should have been embarrassed, but disappointment made him angry. "Who is this?"

"Dennis."

"Who?"

"Dennis Milovic. From Cycle Oregon."

"Oh, right." Now Neil remembered. He had been scouting the route for the bicycle tour, but his emailed reports had gotten shorter, and had stopped altogether when he reached Dawson. "Sorry. I was expecting a different call."

"Are you all right? I heard you fell off your bike." The concern in his voice sounded genuine. At the age of sixty, falling from a bicycle is no joke.

"I'm recovering. Where are you calling from?"

"Oakridge. We've taken over the whole town. Thanks to your tip, I got a private room in the B & B. Everybody else is trying to jam into a pool at McCredie Hot Springs, and I've got my own Jacuzzi."

Neil looked at his watch. Connie might be trying to call, and his line would be busy. "So what's up, Dennis?"

"People here are asking whether it's safe in Raja, or Dawson, or whatever you call it. The Modoc chief, Shontin, tells us the campground's all set up with tables and hot tubs, but the news reports say there's a gunman loose in the woods."

"And wolves," Neil added. "And earthquakes. Come on down. What this place needs is two thousand bicyclists."

"Are you serious?"

"You don't see me leaving. It's just getting interesting. Oops, there go the sirens again. See you Saturday."

Neil ended the call. There really was a siren outside. From the barn door he could see the doctor and her son Robbie unloading a man from the back seat of a county patrol car. Neil couldn't tell, but he looked like a knife fight casualty from the casino.

A few minutes later, when Robbie brought Susan's daily journal, the boy apologized for getting bloody smudges on the blue cover.

The twilight was deep enough that Neil sat on a bale by the barn door in order to read by the mercury vapor light mounted on the front of the barn. Susan wrote with a stream-of-consciousness style that churned out of her brain's mental whitewater. The text could have been made of telegrams, chopped up and spliced back together randomly. Still, Neil was able to decode some news.

The Tico Patrol was evidently using fear to turn Raja into a fortress, even though the red dots of Erik's laser scope had not been seen for two days. Harmony was still shut away in the central "Nirvana" complex, training preschool teachers, but for the first time, cracks of doubt might be weakening Harmony's allegiance to the Rajneeshees. The other interesting news was that the Rajneeshees' drilling operation really might have been angled under the national park. No wonder Gilberto was being kept isolated. Perhaps he —

Neil's phone rang, and he set down the journal. "Hello?"

"What happened to 'Hello Love'?"

"Connie, I —"

"That's OK." She sounded tired. "I've been debating all day whether to call at all."

"You can't mean that." Neil's heart sank. "I'm really looking forward to seeing you Saturday."

"I am too," she said, but the falling tone of her voice suggested this was an admission of guilt rather than a declaration of love.

"What is it, Connie?"

She sighed. "Oh, I'm breaking all kinds of rules by talking with you about the case. And now I've been arguing with myself about whether to violate client confidentiality too."

"Work up to it slowly," Neil suggested.

"Here's a start. I've found out that the INS wants to deport a Rajneeshee. "

"I guess that's good news. Which one?"

"Gilberto Montale."

Neil groaned. "For God's sake, why pick on Harmony's fiancé? There are dozens of worse visa violations out here."

"Someone reported the Italian guy. I'm betting the sheriff was involved. Now it's your turn. Break a rule by telling me something I don't know."

"OK. You were right about the tremors at Crater Lake. They really might have been caused by fracking. Susan says the drilling rig in Raja might have been angled under the national park to hit hotter water."

"You know, I wondered when I saw the creek below Raja. The runoff was muddy. Even on an Indian reservation, people have to follow some laws."

Neil thought a moment. "Maybe you should tell that to the press."

"No way. You've already gotten me one official reprimand. Dickers doesn't want anyone talking to the press except him. Why did you want me to tell people about Roger's DNA anyway?"

Neil winced. He hadn't meant to hurt Connie. "I hoped the Rajneeshees would send a better DNA sample. Did they?"

"Yes. But Roger Nash is not the dead Bhagwan."

"Did you get final results from the lab?"

"Not. Quite. Yet." She accented each sullen word.

"This time have them email the results straight to my phone."

"Aye aye. Sir."

Even Neil, who wasn't much of a romantic, realized that their conversation had taken a wrong turn. He tried something completely different. "Did you know that tonight is the honey moon?"

"Whose?"

"Everyone's I guess." He walked outside and looked around the corner of the barn at the eastern horizon. "There it is. A big orange ball glowing above a ridge of pine trees."

"Is your head injury acting up?"

"No. The full moon just came up. I think they call it a honey moon because it's rising at the lowest point of the year. Anyway, it's beautiful."

Connie sighed. "Neil, I know you're trying. I'm trying too. I want it to work out between us, but I don't know."

Neil had a lump in his throat. "I miss you Connie. Will you come tomorrow night?"

"No. But I'll get there Saturday morning. In the meantime, I can tell you what I found out from the prison psychiatrist."

"You went to Pendleton?"

"Yeah. It turns out Erik is quite the artist."

"If you count wood scraps as sculpture."

"He's got a talent for portraits too. The psychiatrist showed me a few dozen."

"Paintings?"

"Circular pen-and-ink drawings of faces, like you'd see in a rifle's scope. Mostly Arab-looking men — presumably the people he shot in Iraq. But there's also a portrait of the prison psychiatrist in a gunsight."

"No surprise there."

"And a whole series about a girl he saw when he was hanging out with the bums in downtown Portland."

"A girl?"

"Not just any girl, Neil. The same girl he's been watching in Raja. Your daughter Susan."

A chill swept through Neil, as if a night wind had blown in from the mountains. "Are you sure? Erik Hamsby drew Susan in a gunsight?"

"It's her, all right. But listen, Neil. There's something sweet about the way he's drawn her. At the dragon boat races, in the recycling center. She's looking to one side with a distant, longing, beautiful expression."

"That's how she always looks."

"Erik's captured that. The prison psychiatrist said Erik had never talked to Susan, but he talked about her a lot. I think he just liked to watch her."

Neil shivered at the thought. "A sniper is a kind of voyeur. Vernon

Lawrence told me that. He thought Erik might be watching Raja because he was curious about his boyhood friend, Roger Nash."

"That's possible too. But I'm wondering if Erik knows Susan's boyfriend, Dregs. A year ago they were both hanging out in Old Town Portland with the bums. They both took a liking to a pretty girl at the recycling center."

Now Neil's chill had turn to a cold sweat. Why did his daughter attract such dangerous people? He had never liked Dregs, even after the scarred man had repeatedly proven his loyalty to Susan. "You're suggesting that Erik came here out of jealousy? That his real goal is to get rid of his rival, Dregs?"

"Erik Hamsby is a lonely and confused young man. He's stressed because of what the Army did to him. I'm beginning to doubt that he's targeting the Rajneeshees. I don't even think he has a rifle. The only things he bought at the Dawson gun shop were scopes. I think he's just watching."

"I hope you're right. I just wish there was some way to get Susan out of there." The low moon cast an orange glow across the tent roofs of Raja, as if the vast plain of tents were a city in the sky, and not on the earth at all.

After a minute Connie said, "Meanwhile, I've still got a case to solve. If Erik didn't kill Swami Bhrater or Juan Guerrero, then someone else did. And that brings us back to Suspect Z. A mystery killer who left no clues."

"No, it's a mystery with too many clues. There was the ad campaign on Portland streetcars. Then the Bhagwan's box that turned up at Roger Nash's baby shower. The money from Singapore. The .22 that killed Juan Guerrero. What we need is a scenario that makes sense out of all of them."

"We're running out of time, Neil. Captain Dickers gave me an official reprimand. He's talking about a demotion." She paused before repeating, "We're running out of time."

The second time she said it, Neil heard a different meaning. The case had ruined his career, and now it was ruining hers. Their relationship was hanging by the same thin thread. He had gambled everything to find the Rajneeshee murderer, and now he was at risk of losing it all.

"I miss you, Connie," he said, but it didn't work.

"Saturday morning, Neil."

The little green telephone symbol on his cell screen turned red: CALL ENDED.

The moon had climbed higher, colder, and whiter. Neil pressed his eyes with his fingers. When he finally went inside the barn and crawled into his sleeping bag on the straw, he could hear the great horned owl calling from the cottonwood trees by the highway, asking the same question over and over.

Neil's dream that night taught him nothing. Once again he was balancing on the wall between two ghost towns, Raja and Dawson. This time he jumped, hoping that he would be able to fly, as he sometimes could in dreams. He fell onto a tent roof on the Raja side and bounced down toward a street. By concentrating he managed to fly a little, just enough to keep from hitting the ground. Then he hovered along like a ghost, a few feet above the street.

He floated through the empty town, steering hard with his mind at corners, looking for the central Nirvana complex. Finally the maze of alleyways opened onto a vast, empty plaza. Giant red gates stood at the far end of the square where the stage should have been. When he floated closer he could see that the wooden portal was carved with intricate patterns and Sanskrit texts, inlaid with rubies. The Red Gates of Nirvana! Incredibly, they opened inward with a push of his finger. He held his breath. What mysteries, what godhead would be revealed? Why couldn't he see?

Even when the gates had swung wide, the void beyond was not even a void. There was no brilliant light, nor even the blackness of empty space. Not even nothing. Less than that! The absence of absence.

Neil awoke, discouraged, to the same old barn. Dust motes drifted in long, raking sunbeams from broken windows. Evidently he had overslept. Robbie, the doctor's son, had already left his breakfast on a hay bale. A mug of coffee, a box of cereal, a little carton of milk, and a bowl. The same as always.

Except this time Neil did not hear birds. Usually swallows bickered from the rafters in the morning. No sound at all. And why couldn't he smell the coffee? Neil sat up very carefully, studying this silent world around him, devoid of smell. Was he really awake?

The test, of course, would be to pinch himself, or to shout, or to force his eyes wide open. But then he would lose what might be a gift. Only rarely did Neil have lucid dreams, but they were often like this, where he dreamed he was awake in bed. The brain is not always imaginative at night. Even the most mundane dream, if you are able to guide it, can open a gate to the subconscious.

Neil swung his feet to the barn floor. He lifted his arm and looked at his watch. The dial's hands were creeping backwards. The numbers were unreadable glyphs. Yes, this was the way of dreams.

What else had changed? The breakfast, of course. If he was asleep, it might not really be there. And sure enough, when he looked more closely at the box of Wheaties, he saw that the athlete featured on the front was a purple-faced man with bulging eyes, stringy black hair, and a noose around his neck. He was labeled "Captain Jack — American terrorist and Modoc hero." Without thinking, Neil leaned forward and loosened the noose. The Indian gasped and straightened his head proudly. The old Modoc warrior had killed an Army general. The military had hanged him. But the tribe called him a hero, the reincarnation of their defiance.

Two sides.

Neil thought: Every story has two sides. He turned the box around. The back looked a lot like the front, but this time the featured athlete was an unrecognizable silhouette. The label identified him "El Viejo — American terrorist and Rajneeshee hero."

Would he remember this when he woke up? Neil closed his eyes and repeated the name: Viejo, Viejo, Viejo, until he heard the chattering of the swallows in the rafters.

When Neil opened his eyes a second time the breakfast was gone, but dust motes still hung in morning sunbeams.

Could Viejo be the killer?

And who was he?

Neil thought back to the silhouette in the dream. Suddenly it matched a memory. And then a face. And finally, a name.

In the cold light of day, the name hardly seemed possible. How could someone be in two places at once?

Worse, if Neil was right, he would have no choice but to wait for Viejo to make the next move.

Chapter 40

The Old Man closed his eyes and sighed. He had only sought peace. Murder was a disruption in the cycle of being. He had disliked the first killings, and was even less serene in the knowledge that he would now need to plan a third.

A suicide. This time it would be a suicide, and he would be the one who tried to stop it. The Old Man placed his upturned palms on his knees. He could hold that pose for ages without needing to draw a breath.

With no other evidence than a Wheaties box in a dream, and no way to contact Susan until that evening, Neil spent most of Friday phoning Singapore. He didn't learn much, but between calls he had time to reread Susan's daily journals from the past week. How could he have missed something so obvious? He penned half a dozen replies, trying out different ways of telling his daughter what he had surmised. Was there nothing they could do but wait?

At five o'clock Neil got on his bicycle and pedaled down to the Ex-Zorba-Tent Grill.

Margaret glowered at him as she brought him a menu. "That's it. I'm quitting." She was wearing a red skirt, a little white apron, a pink blouse, and the amethyst amulet.

"Quitting?" Neil asked.

She whispered, "You're not supposed to come here in person. It's getting dangerous. The Ticos already suspect."

"Did you bring Susan's journal?"

"She didn't write one today. She just said they'd moved the Italian guy to one of those big metal shipping containers. It's locked like a prison."

"He must have discovered something even worse about the drilling. I'll change my message for Susan."

Margaret shook her head. "I'm finished with the messenger business. I felt bad about letting you get beat up, but now you're recovering. After this shift I'm taking the Real Jesus bus to Klamath Falls. Then it's home to Molalla."

"What about your ex-husband?"

"I'll change the locks and get an injunction against him. It'll be safer than staying here." She raised her pencil and her voice. "So what can I bring you? Another fucking Shiva enchilada?"

"Just take Susan one last message."

"With extra fucking jalapeños. Coming right up." As she turned she poked the order pad so hard her pencil point broke.

The café never became crowded, even for the dinner hour. Neil sat alone at a picnic table, pushing his enchilada around the plate, until a gong from the flat-screen TV announced that the Rajneesh World Service would once again be streaming live from the Plaza Stage in downtown Raja.

As the gong faded, a low tone rose from the dark screen. Then a second and a third note, a growing chord like the ringing of bells from beyond the grave. The television slowly shifted to a deep maroon of fuzzy lights, and finally resolved to pink stage lights reflecting from three brass bowls. White-bearded men, their eyes closed, ran their fingers around the bowls' rims to make the metal sing.

The camera zoomed out, revealing a dozen children in red outfits. The children danced in a circle, holding the edges of a red silk parachute. When they raised their arms the cloth mushroomed upward. The children's teachers stood outside their circle, directing the dance. Neil leaned closer, but none of the teachers was Harmony. Then he noticed a figure seated in an unlit chair at the back of the stage. As the camera panned across the dancing children he could make out the chair well enough to see that it was the same carved wooden throne that had been used in the ceremony at Portland's Moda Center. Could the man sitting in the throne really be Roger Nash? He seemed so old and frail, his face pale, his beard scraggly. His eyes were closed. The red cloth wrapping the top of his head looked more like a bloody bandage than a turban. For a moment Neil wondered if he was even alive. But then Roger lifted his hands from the chair's armrests and turned them so his palms were up. What had happened, Neil wondered, to turn the vivacious young barista into an otherworldly wraith? Susan's last journal had suggested poison. Now Neil wondered if it might be true.

Eventually the dancing children encircled the men with the ringing bowls. Gauzy silk billowed above the men in a glowing red dome. Then the children lowered their hands to the floor. White smoke puffed from the edges of the stage. When the silk slowly settled over the men, the cloth lay flat. Somehow the three men had vanished, although the faint ringing of their bowls remained.

Swami Jesus strode to the front of the stage, applauding. He wore a striped red-and-gold toga that revealed muscular, tattooed arms. Neil noticed that he was wearing the ancient leather sandals of Swami Bhrater.

"*Namaste,* seekers of peace throughout the world. Let us all applaud the Musicos of Tibet and the kindergarten dancers of Raja." Swami Jesus flashed gold teeth in the stage lights. "Today we celebrate in defiance of the threats that surround us. It is true that a rifleman has set his sights on Raja, hoping to scare us from our new home. Yes, we have already lost two of our number to bullets. And no, we cannot rely on the police for help. They have called off their search for the gunman outside our gates."

The crowd booed, but Jesus held up his hands. "We will not give in to fear. Our journey takes us beyond suffering, beyond the emotions that cloud our view of the infinite. Tonight we will meditate on peace, and later we will be visited by an elder whose wisdom has brought us together here at Raja."

An old man? Neil sat on the edge of his bench. Who did the swami mean? Had Neil's dream taken him in the wrong direction after all?

Neil waited impatiently while the swami led the audience through a series of breathing exercises and chants.

Finally a drum began beating and the lights went up. Swami Jesus held out his hand. "And now, once again, I put you in the hands of

Tom Shontin, an elder of our Modoc friends."

White smoke puffed up from the stage, turning the spotlights into frenzied pillars. When the smoke gradually cleared, a stocky, dark-haired man in a business suit and a bolo tie was standing in the middle of the stage.

He shielded his eyes from the glare of the lights. "In my tribe we tell stories to teach lessons and warn of dangers, so that is what I will do again tonight."

Shontin cleared his throat and squinted out past the camera. "Can you hear me?"

A murmur from the crowd seemed to satisfy him. "Yes. Well, then. I have begun to learn about the gods of India. I find that they are not so different from the gods of Indians over here. Gods are dangerous, powerful, immortal, and often two-faced. As a result, each of their stories has two sides."

Neil raised an eyebrow, recalling a similar thought from his own dreams.

"Earlier this week," Shontin said, "I told you about the gods named Llao and Skell. I described how Llao blew up his mountain when he was denied the hand of a beautiful Modoc princess. From that you might think that Llao is evil and Skell is good. Now you will discover that even the gods you trust are capable of deceit."

The Modoc elder looked up into the night sky, as if to draw inspiration from the stars. "Llao walked on two legs and spoke as we do, but he had the form of a badger. Among his many animal spirit allies were toads, snakes, and even Cougar. Skell, who lived on Yamsay Mountain, usually had the form of a pine marten. His allies included mule deer and Clark's nutcrackers. After Llao had blown up his mountain, he devised a new plan to win the Modoc girl. He changed himself to look like a marten, and he turned a dozen Cascade toads into deer. Then they all went down to the Modoc village, knowing that people would think he was Skell. And in fact they did. They invited Llao and his disguised friends to a feast in the village that night. After Llao had eaten his fill he told humorous stories by the campfire until the princess laughed out loud. As soon as she opened her mouth he jumped inside, tore out her heart, and ran with it back up to his den on Llao Rock. Without her heart, the princess lay as if dead. The people of the tribe were devastated. Not only had they lost their princess, but they had been tricked."

Shontin stopped to cough. Tico Bob, the lanky security chief, came out of the shadows with a bottle of water. The Modoc elder took a drink, thanked him, and then continued.

"Llao had two faces, you see? But others can play that game too. When Skell heard what had happened he positioned his deer at intervals along the trail from Crater Lake to the village. Then he turned himself into a snake and slithered toward Llao Rock. He found Llao, Cougar, and a group of toads playing ball with the princess's heart in the Pumice Desert, at the foot of Llao Rock. 'Let a snake join your game,' Skell said. But the toads just laughed. Even Llao scoffed, 'How can you play ball if you don't have arms?' 'Try me,' Skell replied. 'Or are you afraid I'd win?'

"Llao threw the heart at the snake as hard as he could. Instead of trying to catch the heart, Skell used his tail to flip it to the first of his deer, waiting at the edge of the desert. The deer caught the heart with its antlers and raced off into the forest. Llao shouted, 'After him, Cougar! Chase him down!' Cougar sprinted after the deer, but just as he was about to catch up, the deer tossed the heart to the next deer in line. In this way the deer kept ahead of Cougar, passing the heart from one to the next all the way to the Modoc village, where the last deer tossed the heart into the princess's open mouth. Right away she blinked her eyes and came back to life.

"Cougar limped back to the Pumice Desert, exhausted and discouraged. When he told what had happened, Llao realized the snake must have been his enemy, Skell, all along. 'Treacherous snake!' he cried. 'Do you dare to fight with me now, one on one? Or are you afraid I'd win?' In response Skell resumed his own form, rising up on his hind legs as a marten. The two gods roared so loud that the ground shook and trees around the desert bent backwards. Cougar ran away. The toads all jumped into Crater Lake to hide. For two days and two nights the gods battled, wrestling and roaring. Finally the toads in the lake saw their master standing victorious atop Llao Rock, the shore's tallest cliff. 'I have torn apart the marten, Skell,' the badger shouted, 'And now I will give you the pieces to eat.' He began throwing dismembered legs and arms off the cliff. As soon as they hit the water the toads gobbled them up. Finally all that was left was the head. When the badger threw this into the lake, the toads realized they had been tricked again. It was a badger's head. It belonged to their master, Llao. Skell had won the battle. Then he had transformed himself into a badger to fool the toads into eating their own leader."

The Modoc elder scanned the Rajneeshees in the plaza. "Gods are immortal. Llao is not dead. Good and evil are often disguised. It is easy to be fooled, especially if you want to believe that something is true." He paused, frowning. "Much has happened in the weeks since the Modocs invited the Rajneeshees to share our reservation. I have seen great courage and hope. We have built two cities. But there are signs that Llao is coming back. Perhaps you too have heard that Raja's drilling operation, in its search for more hot water, has angled underneath the national park. If this is true, it is illegal, and we will all answer for it."

The crowd began murmuring. Tico Bob stepped forward, but Shontin held up the flat of his hand to stop him. "More importantly, we of the tribe fear that you have angered a dangerous and duplicitous god. The ground is shaking. There are ripples in Crater Lake. We must either make amends with Llao, or we must battle him."

Swami Jesus and Tico Bob exchanged a worried glance.

Shontin saw their expression and nodded. "Someone must confront Llao. For thousands of years the Modocs have avoided Crater Lake. The land above timberline is taboo. The badger's den atop Llao Rock is the most dangerous place of all. Once our tribe had powerful shamans who might have met this challenge. Now our shamans are doctors and dancers and storytellers." He shook his head. "I am afraid we have awakened an evil we cannot meet."

In the pause that followed, a cold wind swept through Raja, luffing the tents. Even Neil, in the sheepskin coat Connie had bought, felt the chill of goosebumps on his arms. On stage, Swami Jesus seemed frozen in place. The camera zoomed back in silence.

"I will go."

The voice was so quiet it would have been easy to mishear.

Roger Nash stepped down from the dark throne into the stage lights. "I will go. This is my fault."

Shontin looked at him from the side. "Perhaps you think the danger of Llao is imaginary?"

Roger shook his head. "Beliefs are real. You welcomed us here, respecting our beliefs, and we have violated yours. I will go to Llao Rock and meditate until I find an answer."

Shontin pressed his lips together — to suppress a response? To show his skepticism? But then he gave Roger a slight bow and retreated from the stage without another word.

At this point Swami Jesus began clapping his hands. "Applause, please, for Tom Shontin, with his second installment of Modoc lore." The crowd applauded half-heartedly. Jesus strode about the stage with his hands in the air, as if the response had been an ovation. "That's our presentation for the evening, sannyasins. Enjoy the fireworks."

Every other evening, Roman candles had surrounded the stage with a curtain of colored fire while skyrockets burst overhead. This time, however, only a few feeble fountains sputtered beside the throne. A voice in the crowd actually laughed before the flat-screen television faded to black.

Margaret threw her nametag aside and walked out the café's entrance. From her look, Neil knew there was no point hurrying after her. The Toaster Lady would not be taking a message to Susan tonight. Raja was a fortress, and he was outside. His daughter would be on her own.

The Old Man slouched in his chair, chuckling at the black screen. He lit a cigar. Yes. Even he couldn't have planned things so well. Roger was going to Llao Rock. The time was right for the Bhagwan to be reborn.

Chapter 41

The next morning Erik Hamsby was puzzled by the turkey vultures. Had they found food? He was almost hungry enough to chase them away, if the meat wasn't too old. He had been hiking north on the Pacific Crest Trail, on his way to Diamond Lake. There he knew he would find a store, and a campground, and a telephone. He wanted to call his father to find out if he was still being chased, or if he could return to his job as a bus driver. Now a dozen of the big black birds were circling a high point on the Crater Lake rim. He took out his spotting scope for a better look.

Ugly, naked red heads. Flashes of silver from the undersides of the curving wings, the black tip feathers splayed like grasping hands. Erik liked to watch birds, even more than he liked watching people. Birds were never mean. You didn't hurt birds and they didn't hurt you. He had read that turkey vultures wintered in Costa Rica, like the Rajneeshees. Then they flew to Oregon to eat the things that died here in summer. They weren't vicious. They couldn't even kill a mouse. Sometimes they were just curious.

Now Erik was curious. Why were they circling a lonely cliff?

A speck of red caught his eye. Just a flash in the trees below. There it was again, on the park road. A little red car. He focused the scope, steadying it against a tree trunk. The red Prius pulled off into a viewpoint parking lot. Its brake lights flashed. Why were there no other cars this morning? Was it too early in the morning for tourists? Had they closed the roads because of him — the sniper?

The car's door opened. Erik focused and refocused on the head that emerged, hardly able to believe what he was seeing. A red turban. A black beard. It was him! It was the boy who had puzzled Erik all his life. For once, Roger Nash seemed worried. He was looking up at the gyre of birds in the sky. Incredibly, he closed the car door and began hiking up through the open woods toward the cliff.

Hungry and curious, Erik decided to creep closer.

Susan was so nervous her teeth chattered. It was 7:28 on Saturday morning. Where was Dregs? In two minutes a Tico troll would open the gates of Nirvana for the preschool teachers in Harmony's class. Susan wouldn't have another chance to get inside for three days, and by then it might be too late.

Last night, when the Toaster Lady hadn't returned from Dawson, Susan had convinced Dregs that they had to act on their own. They couldn't solve all of Raja's problems. They couldn't solve the murders — that was Neil's job. Instead they had to focus on rescuing Harmony and Gilberto. Harmony had fallen hard for the Rajneeshees, and although her devotion appeared to be wavering, she needed more persuasion. Harmony's former fiancé Gilberto had come to help, but he had angered the Rajneeshees by leaking word about their drilling operation. Even that didn't seem like a sufficient reason to lock him in a shipping container.

"We need to talk to Gilberto," Susan had said, cupping her hands beside her eyes like blinders to help her focus. "We can't get near enough to him to find out what's going on."

Dregs had raised his eyebrows, which made the scar on his cheek expose yet more of his sagging eye. "Let me see what I can do. Tomorrow I'm supposed to be installing loudspeakers for a public address system. I'll mount one by the shipping containers. Maybe I can talk to Gilberto."

"The Tico trolls have posted guards there."

"Big, dumb guards." Dregs had smiled.

Precisely at seven thirty the gate to the central Nirvana complex opened. A guard began checking preschool teachers off a list. Susan noticed he was new, a boy with a red security jacket that seemed a size too large. Susan stood last in line, hoping Dregs would show up. And sure enough, just as the guard was checking her off, Dregs came jogging up, out of breath, his sandy hair even wilder than usual. Instead of stopping to give her a message from Gilberto, however, Dregs simply barged on through, bowling both Susan and the guard aside.

"Hey! You can't —" the guard objected, scrambling to his feet.

"I'm installing loudspeakers," Dregs shouted back. He darted down a garden path. When he saw Harmony serving hot tea by the pool, he held up his hands. "Stop! Don't drink it!"

"What?" Harmony looked up, startled. "How did you get in here, Dregs?"

"I've been to see Gilberto," he gasped, out of breath. "He says the new hot water has arsenic. Inorganic arsenic, from the ground under Crater Lake."

One of the preschool teachers dropped her cup. "And we've been drinking this?"

"Only here," Dregs explained. "Everywhere else it's used for heating. Here they've piped it in to make Harmony and Roger sick."

"But why?" Harmony asked.

"Ask your fiancé. Gilberto's crazy in love with you. He came here trying to save your life. The Rajneeshees responded by locking him up in a metal cage like an animal."

"Nobody move!" The gate guard stood before them. He held a police baton in his right hand and a walkie talkie in his left. "I'm calling for backup."

"Good luck with that," Dregs said. "Most of the Tico trolls just took off in a motorcade of red cars from the North Gate. I don't know what they're planning. But I'll tell you one thing. This is our chance to break out of Raja and take Gilberto with us."

The guard raised his club. "Not if I have anything to say about it."

At that moment Susan could almost hear something in Harmony's brain snap. For the past week Susan had watched her beautiful blonde cousin grow paler and weaker. Now Harmony's cheeks flushed a dangerous pink. She stepped up in front of the guard in her clingy yellow sarong, placed her feet slightly apart, and said, "Hit me with that stick of yours. Please."

Susan knew what was coming.

The guard must have suspected something was wrong too, because his lip trembled. "I don't want to hurt anyone."

"Go ahead. Really. Take a swing at me, anywhere you like." Harmony taunted him, shrugging with one shoulder. "Give me your best shot, or get out of the way."

The boy hesitated a moment, but his authority was on the line. He swung at her legs.

With a sudden swirl of yellow, Harmony jumped up, caught the guard's wrist, spun him about, and wrenched his arm behind his back.

The preschool teachers gaped. One of them managed to ask, "How did you do that?"

"It's our kindergarten lesson for today," Harmony explained. "Always keep the children safe. And get a black belt in the martial arts."

The guard tried to break loose. Harmony twisted his arm until he winced. "Dregs, could you take his handcuffs? I think he needs help chaining himself to the shelter. We have business elsewhere in Raja today."

Dregs unhooked the handcuffs. "Yes, ma'am."

Meanwhile Susan had picked up the guard's fallen walkie talkie. She held it out to Harmony. "Any message for the Tico trolls?"

Harmony pushed the TALK button. "Tico Bob? Are you listening out there?"

The device crackled a moment. "This is Bob. Over."

"Well, this is Harmony. Yes, that Harmony. Try to stay out of hot water from now on, will you? Over." She flipped the walkie talkie into the pool with a splash. Then she turned to Dregs. "So, Susan tells me you're a physicist. How would you suggest we unlock a shipping container?

"With explosives." Dregs grinned, bulging his eye. "I've saved up some fireworks from the Plaza shows."

"Let's go." Harmony and Dregs headed for Nirvana's gate, but Susan stayed behind, frowning.

Dregs turned. "Aren't you coming, babe?"

"I'll catch up later."

Harmony asked, "Why? What are you going to do?"

Susan stared at the ground. When she needed words most, they failed her.

Words failed Neil that morning, too. Working his way through a bowl of Wheaties in his hay barn he glanced at his phone and noticed a missed message from Singapore.

"Good evening, Mr. Ferguson." The recorded voice had an Asian accent Neil could hardly understand. "This is Nguyen Tran, of the Tran Investigative Service. I am sorry to report disappointing news. We have had much difficulty receiving official records for the Rajneesh Commune. It is not owned by people from Costa Rica, as you had thought. It is a three-person partnership of nationals from India, Mexico, and the United States. Their legal names are —"

The three names were pronounced so oddly that Neil had to replay the recording several times. Then he sat there, speechless.

Almost by reflex, as if he were pushing an emergency escape button, he speed-dialed Connie.

"Neil, you asshole." Her exhausted, grumbling voice was at once a relief and a threat. "I felt like crap after talking to you last night. By 3 a.m. I gave up trying to sleep, got in the car, and drove south. If I can stay on the road, I'll be at Fort Klamath in a few minutes. Tell me you've got coffee."

"Uh —" Still struggling for words, Neil walked outside. Perhaps the fresh air or the bright morning sky might clear a path through the underbrush that seemed to have filled his head.

"Neil? Are you there? And yes, I've got this on speakerphone, so my hands are on the wheel. Neil?"

"Connie?"

"Yeah, it's me. Did you call just to breathe at me?"

"Connie, I —"

"You what?"

"I know who the killer is. And his motive is not what we'd thought."

"Oh, really?" She sounded sarcastic. "Is it Erik Hamsby? The dead Bhagwan? The Russian mafia? Your brother Mark?"

"No, it's —" The boom of an explosion cut his words short. Across the road, skyrockets were bursting into colored sparks above the tent roofs of Raja. "Jesus!"

Connie groaned. "Not him again."

"Something's wrong in Raja. It looks like the drilling rig is blowing up. How soon can you be here?"

"Three minutes."

"A big cloud of smoke is blowing this way. The highway's going to be jammed. I'll ride my bike and meet you at the intersection in front of Zorba's. Maybe we can find out what's happening there."

Neil signed off and grabbed his bicycle. Across the highway, Raja looked like it was erupting. Most of all, he feared that his daughter Susan might be at the center of that volcano.

Chapter 42

Susan was nowhere to be found, and they were running out of time. Harmony had disabled two more Tico guards in the drilling yard, leaving them to limp away for reinforcements. Then Dregs had strapped fireworks to the padlock on Gilberto's shipping container. The resulting blast had knocked Dregs off his feet. For a full minute, geysers of colored fire lit up the drilling quadrant of Raja. Concussive white bombs burst atop rocket arcs. Pinwheels of sparks writhed across the dusty storage lot.

When the smoke began to clear, Harmony unwrapped the fold of her sarong that she had used to cover her face. Much closer to the shipping container, Dregs was raising himself to one elbow. His wild hair was singed and his face black, but his eyes blinked white and wide. "Holy crap. It didn't work."

"Are you all right?" Harmony helped him to his feet.

"Yeah, but look." He pointed a sooty finger at the charred metal door. "The lock's intact."

From inside the shipping container they could hear Gilberto coughing. "*Armonia?* Are you trying to kill me?"

"I'm trying to rescue you, Gilberto."

"Don't! Not me," Gilberto called back. "I tell you, it is Roger who must be saved. The reincarnated Bhagwan."

"One thing at a time." Harmony scowled. Already a crowd of red-robed sannyasins had begun to encircle the yard, drawn by the fireworks. "Any more bright ideas, Dregs?"

Dregs was staring at her. "Has anybody ever told you how beautiful you are when you're angry?"

Harmony clenched her fingers into claws. "Has anybody ever told you that you're an ugly homeless wino?"

"Yeah, I get that all the time," Dregs admitted. "But you're not like me. You're persuasive. Talk to these people. Convince them we're the good guys."

Harmony surveyed the ring of onlookers skeptically. She was about to speak when a voice boomed above them.

"This is Jesus speaking."

Bewildered faces looked up at the sky.

Dregs sighed. "I got the loudspeakers for the public address system working this morning."

"As your swami," the gigantic voice continued, rumbling throughout the tent city, "I am speaking to you because Raja is in danger. Everything we have built is being threatened by Harmony."

The faces in the crowd looked even more confused.

"Sannyasin Harmony and her conspirators have stolen the treasure of Nirvana."

This time even Harmony and Dregs exchanged a puzzled glance.

"Sannyasins of Raja!" the voice boomed. "Seal the gates of the city. Do not let Harmony escape. You must stop this traitor and her thieves at all costs."

Finally the crowd seemed to understand. They formed a ring around Harmony and Dregs. Slowly the circle began to close. The only sound was the faint, distant growl of machinery.

Dregs asked, "Have you got an aikido move for this?"

"We need a miracle," Harmony replied.

"Unfortunately, our only Roman Catholic is locked in a box. Hey Gilberto, can you pray?"

Gilberto did not respond. Meanwhile, however, the clanking of heavy machinery had grown much louder.

"Perfect," Harmony said. "Now they're sending tanks after us."

But the vehicle that emerged from the smoke and dust, its engine roaring in low gear, was not a tank.

It was a garbage truck.

In the driver's seat, Susan didn't make eye contact with anyone. She did not appear to hear the shouts of the crowd as she slowly bore down upon the circle of Rajneeshees. The truck's motor whined higher. The red line of sannyasins wavered, and then scattered. Harmony and Dregs swung up on the running boards. Dregs shouted through the closed window, "The fireworks didn't open the lock."

Susan's only reply was to push a lever. The truck's hydraulics swung out the two large metal prongs used to hoist Dumpsters. Without stopping, Susan rammed the prongs under the shipping container. The truck smashed into the box with a jolting crash. For a moment the container skidded forward, plowing up dirt. Then Susan touched another hydraulic lever and the forks began to lift. The box was so heavy that it briefly tipped the entire truck forward, wheels spinning in the air. Then the truck teetered back. The tires bumped the ground, bounced a bit, and found traction. Now the ten-ton truck wobbled forward with the giant box tipped in the air. The engine's whine made it hard to tell if the shouts they were hearing were Gilberto's.

Susan rolled the windows down to listen, but instead got an earful from her hangers-on.

"Thanks for the lift, babe," Dregs shouted.

"How can you see where you're going?" Harmony asked.

The sixteen-foot metal box in front of the windshield did block most of Susan's forward view, but she had driven Raja's streets enough that she had created a map in her mind. There was no point in explaining that her peripheral vision filled in sufficient clues to find the way. She could see enough of the ground directly ahead to avoid running over anything unexpected.

"They've sealed the gates, babe," Dregs said.

Again Susan didn't comment. She had heard the announcement about the gates.

"Can't you go any faster?" Harmony asked.

Why, Susan wondered, would her cousin want to go faster if she thought they were driving blind? And yet the question did have a genuine mechanical answer. "Rajneeshees are cheap," Susan said.

"Cheap?" Harmony repeated. "So what?"

Susan swung around a corner, ripping out the wall of a tent. She frowned. She needed to focus. Still she explained, "They bought a Dumpster truck with a broken transmission. First gear is all I've got."

Dregs squatted on the running board to peer out under the shipping container. "Uh, babe? You're missing the East Gate by one block."

When she didn't respond, he shouted, "Babe! This street's a dead end. There's no gate."

Susan pressed the accelerator, her grip on the wheel steady. She thought: There will be a gate soon enough.

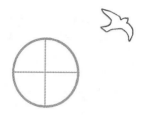

Chapter 43

Neil was wrong about the traffic jam. Raja's gates were closed, so Dawson's streets didn't have many vehicles. Instead the streets were crowded with people. Everyone was curious about the fireworks and the commotion in the Rajneesh city. Modoc construction workers in hard hats, Baptists from the Real Jesus Refugee Center, and even the drunks from Captain Jack's Casino had ventured outside, blinking at the morning sun to see what was going on. All of them seemed drawn to Raja's East Gate.

Neil had bicycled too fast, and now stood by the "Escape from HELL" sign, doubled over with pain. Even with the bandage and a week of healing, his broken rib could still hurt like a sword in his side. He managed to straighten up, lean his bike against the signpost, and talk to a few passersby before the black Buick from the Portland Police Bureau pulled up beside him.

Connie stepped out in a black jacket and slacks. She went straight to give him a hug.

"Yow!" Neil winced.

"Oops. Forgot about the rib. You look so much better."

"I was." He managed a pained grin.

She pointed to the crowd of people. "So, what's going on?"

"Some say there's a riot. Others say a robbery. Raja's sealed off."

Connie stood on tiptoes, trying to see over the crowd. Raja's main gate was not only locked with chains, but barricaded with trucks, pallets, and even furniture. Connie turned to Neil. "You think the killer's in there, don't you?"

Neil nodded.

"So it's a Rajneeshee after all. But which one?"

"My brother called from Costa Rica. He said the Rajneeshee farm down there was run by three people: El Hermano, El Guerrero, and El Viejo. Swami Bhrater must have been El Hermano, the Brother."

"And Guerrero would be Juan, the other Rajneeshee who was shot. So who's El Viejo? Is he the killer?"

Neil nodded. "But he's not that old. They called him Viejo because of the sound of the letters."

"I don't get it. Who is he?"

"Victor James."

Connie still looked lost.

"V. J. Collins, the commune's operations manager. He went by the Indian name of Vijay, but his initials really are V. J. He's El Viejo."

Connie sat back on the bumper of her car. "How could Vijay Collins possibly be the killer? He was almost shot himself that night at the Moda Center. The sniper hit Swami Bhrater right next to him."

"That confused me too," Neil admitted, rubbing his temples. "Vijay must have convinced Juan Guerrero to assassinate the swami. It was a precision shot by an expert."

Light dawned in Connie's face. "Guerrero was mixed up in the Mexican drug cartels. He knew all about weapons. And he's about the only Rajneeshee who didn't have an alibi for that night. But why?"

"Back in Costa Rica, Swami Bhrater was the spiritual leader, Juan Guerrero knew how to smuggle marijuana into the States, and Vijay knew how to run everything else. Once they moved their operation to Oregon, where marijuana is legal, they didn't need Guerrero anymore."

"And when they discovered a reborn Bhagwan named Roger Nash, they didn't need the old swami anymore."

"Vijay must have convinced Guerrero to shoot the swami first. But Vijay had a bigger plan. A week later he got in a car, packed the sniper rifle and a .22, and drove down Burnside to give Juan Guerrero a ride."

Connie covered her eyes with her hand. "God. We wondered why Guerrero would get into a car. The driver was his partner."

"What a surprise when Vijay pops him in the back of the head with the pistol. Vijay must have hoped the police wouldn't notice such a small bullet hole, especially after he drove up Wildcat Mountain and blasted the corpse in the chest with a rifle."

Connie uncovered her eyes. "OK. It's possible. But there's no proof."

"That's a problem," Neil admitted.

"And no motive. Even if Vijay didn't need his colleagues anymore, why would he want them dead?"

Neil lifted the cell phone from the pocket of his cowboy jacket. "I asked a detective in Singapore to find out who owns Raja's business operations. It turns out that the Rajneesh Commune is owned by just three partners: Vijay Collins, Swami Bhrater, and Juan Guerrero. The last man standing gets it all."

"What about Tico Bob and Swami Jesus?"

"Henchmen, working for Vijay."

Connie frowned. "But what about Roger? If he's really the reborn Bhagwan, wouldn't —"

A metallic crash cut her words short. The crowd surged toward Raja's main gate to see what was happening. Connie and Neil followed.

A block north of the gate, behind Captain Jack's Casino, a garbage truck with a shipping container over its hood had smashed into the metal fence of Raja's outer wall. The wire mesh stretched, screeching. Razor wire snapped, whipping through the air. The truck's tires exploded one after the other. But by lowering the shipping container to mash down the fence, the truck managed to clank onward on its rims. Sparks flew as it turned a corner toward Vishnu Way. Hydraulic prongs lifted the metal box back into the air. When the truck turned the next corner, the box caught the edge of a shed behind Jack's. An entire wall ripped loose, splintering clapboard. Startled gamblers scrambled for cover. The street crowd retreated too, leaving Neil and Connie to confront the truck alone.

"Susan?" Neil asked.

Dregs waved from the running board, his face black and his hair burnt. "Hi, Pops. We need a bolt cutter to get Gilberto out. Susan thinks they'll have one at the construction site."

The truck swerved onward, narrowly missing the ex-Zorba tent, the parked Buick, and the Escape From HELL sign. At the far side of the intersection the truck's battered wheels finally ground to a halt against a curb. The engine died. Hydraulic hoses hissed. The huge shipping container gently lowered, crushing the construction site's plywood fence.

Tom Shontin, the stocky Modoc tribal elder, strode out from the construction office trailer, flanked by half a dozen men in hard hats. He crossed his arms, surveying the scene. "What is the meaning of this?"

Neil limped through the hole in the fence. "Sorry about the mess. My daughter wants to borrow a bolt cutter."

Shontin studied him sternly for a moment. Then he jerked his head toward one of the workers. "Get Mr. Ferguson a bolt cutter."

The worker ran to retrieve the tool. Meanwhile Dregs, Susan, and Harmony climbed down from the truck. Connie stepped through the fence, but then held out her arms to keep the crowd on the street at bay.

Shontin's gaze fell on Harmony. "The beautiful Harmony. You won many converts for Raja. Now you have decided to leave paradise?'

"Uh, yeah." She shrugged with one shoulder. Then she blushed, embarrassed that her first response would be the casual shrug of a hippie. She lowered her eyes. "I mean, yes sir."

Shontin raised an eyebrow.

"They were poisoning us," Harmony continued. "The new well they drilled under the national park? The water's hot, but it has arsenic in it."

"What!" Neil said, alarmed.

"Poisoning everyone?" Shontin asked.

Harmony shook her blonde hair. "Mostly they used the hot water for heating the marijuana greenhouses. But they also piped it in for Roger and me to drink."

Shontin's expression darkened. "They cannot do this on Modoc land."

A workman came jogging back with what looked like an oversized pair of garden loppers. Meanwhile a small, tinny voice had been complaining in the background. When the bolt cutter snipped the padlock and the shipping container's blackened doors swung open, Gilberto stumbled out into the daylight.

"Gilberto!" Harmony cried, clutching him. "You came to rescue me."

"No, *Armonia*. You rescued me."

"You came to rescue me first."

Gilberto had grown stubbly whiskers, but his black hair seemed perfectly in place and his slacks still seemed pressed.

"Who is this man?" Shontin demanded.

"Gilberto Montale," Harmony explained. "They locked him up because he found out about the crooked drilling. They were going to deport him to Italy."

"This is not important!" Gilberto's hands flew up like agitated birds. "Before *Armonia* arrived I heard the security guards saying that Roger Nash is going to die. He is the one you must rescue."

Shontin worked his jaw as if he were chewing on a thought. "The young Bhagwan drove to Crater Lake this morning, alone, to calm the angry spirit there."

Dregs added, "I saw a dozen red cars leave the North Gate half an hour ago, headed toward Crater Lake. Would the Tico trolls want to help Roger?"

"Maybe." This time it was Susan who spoke. She unzipped one of the cargo pockets of her overalls and took out a small wooden box, loosely wrapped in a sheet of white paper.

"The Bhagwan's case!" Harmony exclaimed. "How —?"

"Nirvana was unguarded. I wanted to give this box back to my father. Roger's mother gave it to him to seal a promise."

Susan looked down as she handed the box to Neil. "I found it on Swami Jesus's table, holding down this letter."

Neil scanned the pages, raised his eyebrows, and then read it aloud:

Jesus, my Swami —

I am not the reincarnation of the Bhagwan Shree Rajneesh. Rather than continue to live this lie, I have decided it is more honorable to fall from the edge of Llao Rock. I will die knowing that Raja is safe in the hands of you, the Bhagwan's true spiritual heir.

— Roger Nash

"Bullshit!" Harmony objected. "Rog wouldn't say that. He wasn't suicidal. He was meditating. He was getting closer and closer to some kind of enlightenment."

Neil held up the paper. "His note isn't signed. The whole thing is printed with a computer."

"Rog wouldn't do that either," Harmony said, her hands on her hips. "He made everyone write journals by hand."

"I have the feeling," Dregs said, "That those carloads of Tico trolls were not going to Crater Lake to rescue Nash from suicide. They were going to assist."

Shontin frowned. "This is evil upon evil."

Dregs added, "And with a thirty-minute head start, there's nothing we can do to stop them."

Neil thought for a moment, and then asked Shontin, "How long does it take to drive to Llao Rock?"

"Maybe three-quarters of an hour. By now the red cars will be past park headquarters. It is the last ranger outpost on the way."

When Neil still looked thoughtful, the Modoc elder asked, "What are you thinking now, Mr. Spirit-of-Coyote? You are the one the Rajneeshees keep knocking down. Did you imagine that you could stand up this time too — perhaps by turning yourself into a snake, like Skell?"

"Maybe." Neil put the Bhagwan's box in his pocket.

Shontin shook his head. "You are not a god, Mr. Ferguson."

"No, but I know where to find superheroes when I need them." Neil limped back toward the hole in the fence. "Connie, put the blue lights on your car."

Chapter 44

With the siren wailing and lights flashing, Connie threaded her way through the crowds on Dawson's highway north. "We won't get to Crater Lake in time, no matter how fast I drive."

Neil took out his cell phone, but the screen stayed black. "Dang. The battery's dead."

Connie fished a white cable out of the padded box between the two front seats. "Here's a recharger."

"Whew, thanks." A red battery icon appeared on his screen. While he waited for it to turn green, he said, "Don't drive over seventy. I've had bad luck with high-speed chases."

"Don't remind me. Instead tell me about Vijay. I understand why he'd want to kill Swami Bhrater and Juan Guerrero to get their shares of the Commune. But why kill Roger? He's just a barista."

"Exactly. At first Vijay liked Roger because he was harmless. He was a useful tool to win more converts. But then it turned out that Swami Bhrater had made a will, signed by two witnesses and notarized by Harmony's mother. It left the old swami's shoes to Harmony, and everything else to Roger Nash."

Connie saw where this was leading. "We thought Swami Bhrater didn't have possessions. But he was actually a one-third owner of the commune, a partnership worth millions. If Roger inherited —"

"Then Vijay would need to murder one more person before he owned it all." The icon on Neil's phone turned green. He flicked through his recent calls and tapped Dennis Milovic. The phone rang a moment.

"Hello, Dennis? This is Neil Ferguson in Dawson." Neil listened a while and then spoke again, "Sure, the town's totally ready for two thousand bicyclists. The streets are full of eager spectators. Where are you guys now? The Watchman? Where's that? Say, I've got a really big favor to ask. You know that murder investigation I've been working on? Well, I'm in a Portland police car right now, heading your way at —" Neil paused to look at the speedometer, and winced — "Eighty-three freaking miles per hour. We're trying to catch up with about a dozen red Priuses. They're full of Rajneeshee security guards who may have been accomplices in the first two murders. We think they're on their way to commit a third one. Could you have Cycle Oregon clog up the Rim Road? If you stop them for maybe twenty minutes we'll be there to arrest them."

Another pause. "No, they shouldn't be armed, at least I don't think so. Maybe one little pistol. Yes, it's really important. And no, I'm not kidding. Don't get hurt, but don't let any red cars through either."

When Neil put away his phone Connie asked, "Do you think they'll really be able to stop the Tico trolls?"

"Two thousand people in Spiderman outfits? You don't mess with superheroes."

"Still, we might want to call the Klamath County Sheriff too." She pulled out her phone. "Oops. Down to one bar. We won't get coverage again until we're at the Rim Road." She handed him the phone and floored the pedal.

The Buick flashed past the old wooden *Crater Lake South Entrance* sign so fast they left it swinging on its chains. The posted park speed was forty-five, but Connie swerved past California travel trailers and Utah pickups as if they were standing still. Tires squealed as she turned off Highway 62 at Mazama Village. With the siren blaring, Connie zoomed through the *Employees Only* lane at the fee both, where rangers in Smokey Bear hats were handing out park maps to tourists.

Traffic was thicker, and much slower, on the switchbacks up to Rim Village. Neil drummed his fingers on his knees as they crept up the hill at twenty-five miles an hour. At the rim itself the astonishingly blue lake suddenly spread out before them, a colossal inland sea in a circle of cliffs.

All of the tourist traffic was turning off to the right toward Rim Village. The Rim Road north toward The Watchman and Llao Rock had a big orange warning sign, *Closed Due to Bicycle Race.*

Connie accelerated past the sign. "You'll find him under Tolufsen."

"What?"

"The county sheriff."

"Oh, right." Neil called the number on Connie's phone. When the sheriff answered, Neil didn't bother to explain about the murders. There was still no proof, and no time. Connie had rounded a corner and braked to a sudden stop. Red cars and bicycles completely blocked the route ahead, where the road traversed a steep mountainside.

"Sheriff?" Neil said, "Lieutenant Wu tells me you don't have jurisdiction to arrest illegal aliens on the Modoc reservation. Well, we've got two dozen of them driving without licenses here in the national park. That's right, they're bottled up at a Cycle Oregon roadblock by The Watchman on Rim Drive. If you can get here fast enough, they're all yours."

With the blue lights still flashing, Connie backed the Buick sideways to block the road. Then she checked the service Glock in the shoulder holster under her jacket.

"Ready?" Neil asked.

She nodded nervously. This was the part she liked least about her job: arresting a suspect who might be armed. If the Rajneeshee operations manager really had shot Juan Guerrero with a pistol, he could have it with him now.

"Let's go talk to Mr. Collins." Neil and Connie opened the car's doors simultaneously. They walked up the road past the jumble of red cars and bicyclists, ignoring shouts and questions, focused on finding a bald man with Gandhi spectacles.

Neil had been right about the Rajneeshees in the cars. Almost all were Costa Ricans. He recognized several of them as guards he had fired from the security team in Portland.

But he didn't see Vijay Collins. At the front of the parked cars, Tico Bob was arguing with Dennis Milovic and a group of Cycle Oregon people in brightly colored stretch suits. Neil tapped the tall, skinny security chief on the shoulder.

Bob whirled around, his face almost as red as his beard. "You can't—"

Neil cut him short. "Where's El Viejo?"

Bob stopped, his mouth open.

"Didn't Vijay come with you this morning?"

Tico Bob drew himself up. "Maybe."

Neil turned to the Cycle Oregon organizer. "Did any cars get past you?"

"No red cars, no."

Neil felt a shiver of foreboding. "What about black cars?"

Dennis shrugged. "There was a Rolls Royce, but the driver was this black guy from Portland, and you didn't say —"

"Damn! How far is it to Llao Rock?"

"Three or four miles. Why?"

Neil looked around. The Buick was stuck on the wrong side of the roadblock. A bicycle would be too slow. Whoever had driven the first of the red cars had left the key on the seat. Neil climbed in and pushed the power button. "You coming, Connie?"

She got in the passenger door, slammed it, and held her badge out the window. "Police! Clear a path!"

As the car whirred through the crowd, Neil shouted back to the bicyclists, "Hold the rest of these clowns as long as you can. The county sheriff is on his way to arrest them."

When they finally reached open road Neil pushed the accelerator to the floor. The hybrid hummed harder up a half-mile hill. Then it rolled like a skateboard down the far side. Ahead, Llao Rock hunched above the lake's rim, as steep and grim as Yosemite's Half Dome. Even at this distance Neil knew that the two dots in the roadside pullout at the mountain's base must be Roger's red Prius and Vijay's black Rolls. Connie unholstered her Glock and rolled down her window.

When they finally pulled up alongside the Rolls, Neil recognized the frightened face in the driver's seat.

"Bear!"

"Boss?" The big driver waved at them frantically. "Get inside, quick!"

"Why?"

"There's a sniper out there, boss! I'm not kidding, I saw him. Get inside, man. This thing's armored."

Neil and Connie got out warily, scanning the forested slopes of the mountain ahead. Neil crouched beside Bear's door. "Who did you see?"

"Erik Hamsby, man! The sniper in the news. He's up on the left side there with a backpack and a rifle."

"What about Vijay?"

Bear rolled his eyes. "He's out there trying to stop Roger Nash from jumping off a cliff. Vijay started up the right-hand side of the mountain before I saw Hamsby."

Connie crouched beside Neil, using the car as cover. "You didn't bring a gun, did you?"

Neil shook his head.

"Then I'll go after Vijay. If you're right, he may be armed."

Neil kept shaking his head. Looking at Connie, he recalled a rainy night in an East Portland library parking lot. They had been on a stakeout together at the start of the Cooper case. Connie had volunteered to walk out alone, toward a man who later tried to kill her. Neil had let her take the risk. He had regretted that moment ever since.

"Go after Hamsby," he said. "He's more likely to trust a woman. I'll hold off Vijay until you get there."

"With a broken rib?" Connie asked skeptically.

"With anything I've got." Before she could object he ran across the parking lot and scrambled up the slope to the right until he reached the cover of the first trees. His rib stabbed at his lungs, doubling him over in pain. He gritted his teeth to keep from crying out. Before straightening, he picked up a hardball-sized rock to use as a weapon. But the rock was pumice. All of the rocks strewn across this mountain slope were pumice, volcanic froth so light it floats. Throwing a rock like that would be as effective as throwing a popcorn ball.

He tossed the rock aside and climbed onward, holding his side, pacing himself. After ten minutes he was drenched with sweat, but the forest had thinned to a few struggling whitebark pines. The open summit of Llao Rock was almost in sight. He picked up a bent branch that could serve as both a cane and a cudgel. By now the knee he had injured in his bicycle fall was sparking pain down his leg with every other step. He limped up another few hundred yards, his heart pounding so hard he had to rest. He collapsed behind the last tree — a dead, gnarled snag. In falling, he snapped the end of his cudgel.

The dry wood cracked so loudly that it might as well have been a gunshot.

A moment later a bald head appeared above the summit rocks,

hardly a hundred feet away. Sunlight glinted from round spectacles as if they were searchlights. Neil scrambled behind the snag, but he was too tired and too hurt and too slow.

"Sergeant Ferguson," Vijay called out, peering from the cover of the rocks. "Your persistence amazes even me."

"Give it up, Collins," Neil called back. "We know you're El Viejo. We know you shot Guerrero."

"You're not convincing anyone, Ferguson, by using the word 'we'." Vijay came out from the rocks and walked a few feet downhill until he was in full sight. He held out his hands to either side, the mountain breeze luffing the folds of his loose shirt. "Go ahead, arrest me."

Neil struggled to his feet, wheezing.

Vijay laughed. "You've always been a loner, Ferguson. And you never did like guns. So this time you're going to lose."

Vijay lifted his shirt and withdrew a small handgun from the pocket of his baggy trousers. "You see, I don't like guns either. I don't know much about them, but I've found they can be useful." He waved the pistol's nose toward Neil. "Come on out. You can leave your broken stick behind."

"Did you already kill Roger?"

"Not quite yet." Vijay waved the pistol to his left. "Walk this way, around the side of the hill. I want you to see him. Both of you will have to be recycled to new lives today."

"The county sheriff is on his way."

"Walk, Ferguson. Don't make me kill you here."

Neil walked ahead, his hands half-raised. "You won't be able to cover this up."

"You don't think so? The trick is to tell people a story they want to believe. That's why I put myself in the crosshairs, right beside Swami Bhrater. But you have to set up the story in advance. People expected a sniper because they'd already seen the Bhagwan in crosshairs."

Neil stopped, dumbfounded. "It was you! You're the one who paid for the streetcar ads attacking the Rajneeshees."

Vijay shrugged. "That little campaign raised millions."

"Then why did you want more?"

"An interesting question. Maybe it's something about growing up in a ghost town."

"Valsetz," Neil said.

"You remember! My home town isn't even on the maps anymore. At least Raja is a city I can keep safe, for my own. It's different, you see? It's not like one of those dreams that slips away when you wake up."

Vijay stared past Neil at the blue lake.

Neil used that moment to spring forward, rushing at Vijay for a tackle.

But Vijay calmly pulled the trigger.

The bullet struck Neil in the side of his chest, spinning him to the ground. He writhed on the cinder slope, gasping with pain.

"Drat," Vijay said. "Now I'll have to work this into my narrative too. I suppose you struggled with Roger before you both fell off the cliff."

Neil gagged, breathless from the pain. He pulled his hand away from his chest and saw that his palm was red. The bullet had gone through the bandage over his broken rib. The slug must have lodged in his lung.

"Yes," Vijay mused. "That would fit. The media has already played you up as a rogue cop. They'll want to believe that a desperate loser shot Juan and later tried to use the same gun on Nash. The disgruntled former employee attacks his boss."

"You — can't —" Neil struggled with each word. He tasted blood.

"You're right. I need your help. Can you crawl? I want you there when I shoot Roger. He's just around the corner, in a world of his own. Wrestling with the Modoc gods in his mind, I suppose."

Neil rolled onto his face and struggled to lift himself to his hands and knees. Blood dripped into the cinders beneath him, a steady red leak. Dust and tears smeared his face. But he had made a promise. His own daughter Susan had reminded him. Neil had sworn an oath to Roger's mother that he would keep her son safe.

And that reminded him of one last option.

Neil crawled forward.

"Good boy," Vijay said, urging him on with a wave of the pistol. "You know, hiring you was a stroke of genius. If I had installed the Costa Ricans as my security team right away, sannyasins would have been suspicious. But by setting you up to fail first, everyone agreed we can't trust outsiders. It's another example of how I've exceeded the master."

Neil wheezed for air.

"No, not Shree. Rajneesh was just a puppet. The real mastermind behind Rajneeshpuram was Ma Anand Sheela. She taught me the art of using a swami to rule a city. People called her the Bhagwan's lieutenant. I called her Ma Chiavelli. Do you know where Sheela is now?"

Pain clenched Neil in the middle. He vomited.

"After serving a mere two years in a rather nice penitentiary she cut a deal and moved to Switzerland. I think she's a nurse in an alpine chalet helping Alzheimer's patients. Escorting souls from one life to the next. Appropriate, don't you think?"

Neil clawed forward through his vomit and blood. He could see a dark-haired head over a rise.

"But Sheela was sloppy," Vijay continued. "She poisoned hundreds of people without actually killing anyone. She bused in thousands of voters without winning an election. No, Sheela taught me the need for planning. By devising the streetcar advertisements and hiring you, I became invisible and untouchable."

Roger Nash was sitting cross-legged, facing them with his eyes closed, perched on the edge of Llao Rock's cliff.

Vijay raised his pistol.

"Rog!" Neil gasped. "He's going to kill you!"

The young Bhagwan half opened his eyes.

"Do you —" Neil coughed. "Do you want to die?"

"Do I still want?" Roger asked. "That would be the final hurdle."

Vijay leveled the pistol at Roger.

Neil reached into his pocket, took out the wooden case, and tossed it toward Roger.

Off balance, on his knees, Neil threw the box too high. It arced up over Roger's head.

But just as the case was about to sail off the cliff into Crater Lake, Roger reached up with his left hand and caught it.

"Wonderful!" Vijay exclaimed. "The case of the reborn Bhagwan. This is simply too perfect."

Roger turned the elegant little wooden box in his hand. In Sanskrit, the cover text read, *Open Only In An Emergency*.

"Open it!" Neil said.

"Yes, do," Vijay agreed, laughing. "Let's see what gem the old Bhagwan left for you in your hour of need."

Roger broke the wax seal with his thumbnail. Then he slid the latch and lifted the hinged lid.

Neil crawled forward and wiped his eyes. All he could see was polished wood. It wasn't a box at all. It was a piece of wood that had been sawed in half and hinged back together.

Vijay rocked back on his heels, laughing. "It's empty!"

"No, don't you see?" Roger held it up, his eyes wide with marvel, as if he had just awoken to a new world. "It's full! Completely full. It is the Uncarved Block."

Neil groaned. He sank to the ground, finally overpowered by pain, shock, and loss of blood. He managed to turn his head to watch the end.

Roger tossed the hinged block back toward Neil. "It is the Bhagwan's key to everything." He closed his eyes and exhaled slowly.

"Good bye, Roger," Vijay said. He aimed the pistol at Roger's forehead and pulled the trigger.

Click.

Roger touched his thumb and middle fingers together.

Click.

Vijay shook the pistol and pulled the trigger again, but it merely clicked. When he turned to look at Neil, his eyes told the story: He really didn't know much about guns. He had forgotten to reload the pistol after its last use. There had been only one bullet left in the chamber. And Neil had taken that slug instead of Roger.

"I never liked guns." Vijay tossed the pistol aside. "We'll end this the way it was always meant to be. Wrestling on top of Llao Rock."

Vijay held out his hands like a football blocker. "Sorry, Rog."

Then he charged forward to push Roger over the cliff.

Chapter 45

The winds that sweep over the Cascade Range seem puzzled by Crater Lake's missing mountain. They swirl about the caldera, writing cryptic cursive messages black against the blue waters. Even if you have seen the lake a thousand times you cannot help but stare into the deep, trying to read the choppy, wordless writings of invisible spirits. And it doesn't help that the winds whisper along the cliffy rim, because they lie. The stories they tell are full of sunny pine woods and fields of sweet lupine, not death.

Neil never fully understood what happened atop Llao Rock. One moment Roger Nash had closed his eyes, seemingly at peace with the prospect of death. The next moment Vijay Collins had run at Roger to push him over the edge.

But before Vijay reached Roger, the young Bhagwan's maroon robe began to shimmer. Somehow Vijay seemed to pass directly through Roger, as if the barista were a ghost.

Without so much as a cry, Vijay Collins had stumbled off the cliff and into the void.

Surely he must have tripped and missed Roger!

Where Vijay had vanished, a Clark's nutcracker slowly flew up on a draft. The big gray jay landed on a rock, eyed the young Bhagwan, and screeched a caw.

Roger blinked at the bird. Wherever he had been in his trance, he was now back. He stood up and stretched.

"Neil!" A voice carried on the wind across the summit. "Neil?"

The nutcracker cocked its head.

Roger turned and saw a bloody body, lying prone in the cinders, its eyes still open. "Good God!"

"Neil?" Connie's voice was louder now.

"Over here!" Roger scrambled to Neil's side.

Connie emerged over the crest of the hill, her semi-automatic in hand. "Neil!" Behind her followed a shy young man with a backpack, a dirty face, and a stubble beard.

Roger helped Neil roll onto his back. "Quick, I think he's been shot."

Connie dropped to her knees and opened his sheepskin jacket. She paled at the sight of his blood-matted shirt.

Neil wheezed. "It was just a .22."

"We'll get you to a hospital." She looked about and noticed the gun in the cinders. "Was Vijay here?"

Roger frowned. "I'm not sure. I was — somewhere else."

"You had your eyes closed," Neil said, wincing as tried to raise himself to one elbow. "Vijay fell off the cliff."

"He just fell?" Connie asked skeptically.

"Yeah, he just fell."

She stood up and peered cautiously over the edge of Llao Rock's sheer, two-thousand-foot drop. "I don't see anything but water down there. We can deal with that later. Right now, you need a doctor. How are we going to get you to the car?"

"I can walk." Neil finally managed to prop himself up by an elbow.

"Like hell you can." Connie looked to Roger. The young barista had never been athletic, and the recent weeks had left him even more frail. Connie herself was strong but short. They couldn't carry Neil a mile by themselves.

Roger nodded as if he had heard her thoughts. He waved to the young man cowering behind the summit of the hill. "Erik? Is that you?"

Hamsby ventured out a few steps.

Neil grunted. "Is he armed?"

"Just scared," Connie whispered. "It was all I could do to convince him to follow me up here."

Roger called out, "We've got a man down, Erik. We need your help. I need you on our side."

Erik shifted from one foot to another. "On the Rajneeshees' side?"

"Life is a puzzle, Erik. Everyone has a place where they fit." Roger held out his hand. "Come and help save a life."

Neil knew Roger's speech shouldn't work. Erik hated Rajneeshees. The Army sniper had always been jealous of Roger. And yet there was magic in the barista's voice.

Like a timid animal under the spell of a whispering keeper, Erik Hamsby walked down from the summit to help.

Neil's head began to spin, and not merely from the pain, and the loss of blood, and the elevation atop Llao Rock. Who was this Roger Nash, a barista who seemingly had the power to catch bullets with his bare hand?

Dim voices cried out in alarm. Connie's face flashed past, her mouth open. And Neil sailed into another world.

Chapter 46

Ding.

When Neil awoke in the back seat of a speeding Rolls Royce he could see the back of Bear's head.

Ding.

Groggily, Neil pulled his phone from the pocket of his bloodied sheepskin coat.

"You're awake!"

His head was on Connie's lap. He tried to focus his eyes on the white letters of a text message. The sentence was short, and at first impossible. But then, suddenly, everything made sense.

"We're getting you to a doctor," Connie said. "You're going to be OK."

"Vernonia." Neil's voice was little more than a croak.

"What?"

"The Buddhists —"

"Don't try to talk." She stroked his hair. "We're almost to Dawson."

"In Vernonia." He cleared his throat. "Have you got the number of the Buddhists?"

Connie tipped her head, drooping the black curtain of her hair to one shoulder. "At the retreat center in Vernonia? I think so. Why?"

"Call them. Now."

"You're hurt, Neil."

He managed a crooked smile. "I want to try your masseuse."

The Modoc doc had had a busy day, with a heart attack and a drug overdose before noon. The heart attack, at least, turned out to be a false alarm — a victim of acid reflux from a hot dog at Jack's. Still, it took her more than two hours to fit in Neil's x-ray, prep, and surgery.

By then a worried cluster of well-wishers had gathered in the clinic's waiting room. For once, there were no recovering patients on cots. The white-washed walls smelled of antiseptic and old milk. The waiting group had already compared notes about the day's revelations. None of them had imagined that the Rajneeshees' own operations manager could have been behind the "Never Again" advertisements. Neil had solved that riddle, and he had paid for his discovery with a bullet in the chest.

Connie fiddled nervously with her phone. Susan sat by herself, fastidiously drawing perpendicular lines on a page of classified ads. Harmony and Gilberto huddled on the edge of a cot, holding hands and whispering in each other's ears. Roger Nash sat with Erik Hamsby, discussing Iraq. Erik kept looking across the room shyly at Susan. Seemingly unaware that Erik might be a rival, Dregs had cornered Tom Shontin and was expounding on the geology of hot springs.

All of them fell silent when the door to the back room opened. The doctor closed the door behind her and began washing her hands at a stainless steel sink.

"Well?" Connie asked. "How is he?"

The doctor dried her hands with a paper towel. "I think you could shoot him a few more times."

Indignant, Connie propped her hands on her hips.

"The bullet hit his broken rib," the doctor explained. "His coat and the bandage had already slowed it down, so it didn't get to his lung. I took it out with tweezers and a towel."

"A towel?"

"To bite on. We don't use much anesthetic in Dawson."

"Can I talk to him now?"

"Could you ever?"

Connie didn't have an answer, in part because the door behind the doctor had opened.

Neil leaned in the doorway, a fresh white bandage on his chest and a towel over his shoulders. "She says I'm a lousy patient."

"You —!" Connie had been about to call him an asshole. She wanted to hug him or hit him — she didn't know which, and she couldn't do either. Instead she just stood there, her fists balled, her eyes tearing up.

Outside, a distant horn faintly honked, as if from an overlooked car alarm.

"You were shot!" Harmony exclaimed. "Doesn't it hurt?"

"Only if I breathe."

"He was in shock when he arrived," the doctor said, "but he seems to have worked through it."

"Dad's engine runs hottest on fumes." Susan spoke with her head down, as if she were reading the classifieds aloud. "I think he also knows something we don't."

Meanwhile the honking outside had grown louder, and was joined by the tinkling of bells. Dregs looked out the window toward the highway. "Whoa, dudes! It's Cycle Oregon."

Neil pushed off from the door frame, weaving slightly. "This I have got to see."

Connie took his arm, helping him across the room to the front door. Outside, he sagged onto a plank bench against the old dairy's front wall. The others came outside too, mostly worried about Neil. But everyone ended up watching the spectacle coming down the highway from Crater Lake — a mile of bicyclists in racing silks.

At the front a white van flashed its headlights and honked its horn. The army behind had lined up as if in battle formation, five abreast in hundreds upon hundreds of rows. Teardrop helmets hunched over low-slung handlebars. A neon kaleidoscope of shiny cloth stretched over taut muscles.

Tom Shontin nodded. "Even Skell needed a host of minions to stop Llao."

Neil cast the tribal leader a critical glance. "You plan to shut down Raja, don't you?"

Shontin pointed to Roger and Harmony. "The red-robed Indians tried to poison these two." He turned his hand to Gilberto. "They locked this one up for telling the truth. And you, Mr. Spirit-of-Coyote," he lifted his chin toward Neil. "They just keep trying to kill you."

Neil looked to Connie. "Did the sheriff find Vijay?"

She shook her head. "Tolufsen had his hands full with the Tico Patrol. The state police wound up securing the crime scene on Llao Rock. They've taken the pistol in for tests."

Neil watched the armada of bicyclists ride toward the center of town. A crowd had formed along the roadside, cheering. Evidently word had spread that the bicyclists had blockaded the Tico Patrol. He wondered how much people knew about Vijay Collins.

"You didn't answer my question. About the body."

Connie shrugged. "So far the state cops are calling Vijay a person of interest."

"Not dead?"

"You're the only one who saw what happened. If he's in Crater Lake, he might be hard to find. It's a quarter mile deep."

Shontin added, "Evil gods don't ever die. But I think the treaty is broken between the red Indians and the red-robed ones."

"Who's running Raja now?" Neil asked.

"No one," Harmony said. "Swami Jesus is still in there, but who'd listen to him now?"

"What about Tico Bob?"

"At the county courthouse," Connie said. "He may not have broken any laws, but they're holding him for questioning."

"Chaos," Susan said.

"The Rajneeshees earned it, babe." Dregs put his hand on her shoulder so gently that she did not flinch.

Harmony crossed her arms. "They lured us in with their talk of peace and love, but it was all just a front for the same old crap — greed, power, and jealousy."

Neil watched his niece from the side. Hate was a poison more insidious than anything in the water. But Neil had seen other powers at work that day too. He closed his eyes. He would need a bit of that strength now.

When Neil reopened his eyes Shontin and Connie were talking about the Modoc reservation's fledgling tribal police force — a handful of untrained recruits. They would have to be deputized to start rounding up the sannyasins in Raja and sending them home, wherever that might be.

"Stop," Neil said.

"Stop what?" Shontin asked.

"Stop talking and listen." The exertion made him pause for breath. More quietly, he said, "I was hired by Harmony to find out the truth about the Rajneeshees. I warned her that I don't quit easy."

Harmony managed a small smile. "That's for sure."

"I also said you might not like what I find out about your new friends."

"That also turned out to be true."

"We learned that Vijay Collins was as ruthless as Ma Anand Sheela. But were they really typical Rajneeshees?" Neil nodded toward the town across the road. "Thousands of good people are living in that tent city. Think of the preschool teachers in your class. They work hard. They're not like Vijay."

Harmony bit her lip.

"Think of Swami Bhrater. He had been a con man in India. When he came to Oregon he changed. He regretted his past. You could sense that he found a better way."

Neil pointed to Roger Nash. "Things changed when they found this young man in a Portland coffee shop."

The barista blushed. "I'm no longer certain." His black beard had grown long and square, but his eyes still made him look boyish.

"You have a gift," Neil said. "People who are lonely, who don't fit in — they listen to you. Instead of worrying about themselves they start working together. You've built a city out of the sagebrush."

"Yes, but —"

"And now you own most of it."

"I do?"

"You do." Neil sat back. Evidently Connie had not told them everything.

Tom Shontin frowned. "How is this?"

"The Rajneesh commune is a partnership registered in Singapore. I found out it was owned by three men: Juan Guerrero, Vijay Collins, and Swami Bhrater. Now they're gone. But Swami Bhrater left a will. It says Harmony gets his sandals and our young barista inherits everything else."

Harmony interrupted. "That's what I've been saying."

"Yes, and now it means that Rog will be the sole owner of Raja's business operations."

The group fell silent as they considered this news.

Roger looked dazed. At length he asked, "You're sure?"

Neil nodded. "You can run Raja or close it down."

Dregs ventured, "You wouldn't have to grow marijuana in those greenhouses."

"Organic coffee might be good," Harmony said.

Roger held up his hands. "Too much has happened. We've hurt too many people. I don't know anything about running a city."

Neil took out his phone. He flipped through the messages until he found the text he had received a few hours earlier, on the drive back from Llao Rock. He held it up so that only Roger could read it.

The barista's expression shifted from doubt to confusion. "But how —"

Neil switched off the phone. "You know it's true, don't you?"

Roger ran a hand over his face.

"You've got a city full of people over there," Neil said. "Like it or not, you are their leader. What are you going to do?"

Roger drew in a long, breath through his nose. When he slowly exhaled, anxiety seemed to drain away from him. He lifted his head and turned to Tom Shontin. "Do you believe in reincarnation?"

The Modoc leader grunted noncommittally.

"It's about correcting mistakes," Roger said. "Perhaps the same is true of a challenge like Raja. You only fail if you don't get up and try again."

The Modoc leader frowned.

Roger asked, "Would you give us one more chance?"

And here Neil knew that Tom Shontin should say no. The Modocs had been dragged into crimes by their allies. The Rajneeshees had already wasted a second chance after Rajneeshpuram in the 1980s. But such was the power of Roger's calm confidence that the Modoc leader hesitated.

"I might ask the council for one more month, as a trial."

"Would they say yes?" Roger asked.

"You'd have to cap the well under the park."

"Agreed."

"And help pay for the new tribal police."

Roger held out his hand. They shook, and Roger gave him a grateful bow.

Then Roger turned to Dregs. "Could you have the Plaza Stage wired for a presentation by seven o'clock tonight?"

"Tonight? I guess so."

"Good. I have an announcement to make. Stream it live everywhere you can."

Dregs grinned. "I'm on it."

"Harmony?" Roger looked to Neil's niece. "I can't do this without you."

"No way," she protested. "They tried to poison me."

"Us, Harmony. They tried to poison us both. That's why I need you there tonight. To help me explain what went wrong."

"They think I'm a traitor. This morning the loudspeakers told them that."

"People remember you from the revival at the Moda Center. You danced to fill time. You introduced Swami Bhrater. You invited everyone to wear red scarves and join us. If they see you, they'll believe we're all willing to make a fresh start."

"But what if I don't want to make a fresh start? I mean, even my parents walked away from Rajneeshpuram. I joined the Rajneeshees dreaming of rainbows. Now I realize Raja's not a place for everyone." Harmony looked down. "I want to go back to teaching kindergarten in Eugene."

"Then say that on stage. Be honest. But please, tell me you'll be there to introduce me."

Harmony turned to Gilberto. The Italian physicist wiggled his hands uncertainly in mid-air.

"OK." Harmony shrugged with one shoulder. "I'll go if Gilberto can be on stage too."

Gilberto struggled for words to object.

"Agreed." Roger smiled. "I want everyone there."

"Everyone?" This time it was Connie who spoke.

"That's right, Lieutenant. We'll open the gates of Raja. The people of Dawson are welcome to come. The bicyclists too."

"Then you'll need security," Connie cautioned. "The tribe's police force isn't ready."

Roger raised an eyebrow at Neil. "Sergeant? Do you want your old job back?"

"Nope." Neil gave him a dry smile. "I'm retired."

"How much did we pay you?"

"Twenty grand a month, before I got fired."

"As far as I can tell, you never quit. We'll send you twice that in back pay."

"That's fine, but you'll still have to find someone else."

"And I know who to ask." Roger looked around the faces gathered in front of the Modoc clinic. To everyone's surprise he put his hand on Erik Hamsby's shoulder.

Erik stammered, "But — they think I'm a killer."

"You're a watcher, old friend. Today you told me something few people seem to know. After your stint as a sniper the Army rotated you out of combat to serve with the military police in Baghdad's Green Zone. You're trained as a lawman. I need a watcher like you at that stage tonight."

"Would I have to wear red?"

Dregs said, "Actually, the stage crew wears black."

"Black. I see." Erik knit his brow. Had he somehow just agreed to work for the Rajneeshees?

"Susan," Roger said, turning to Neil's daughter. "I don't suppose you'll be staying?"

"We left a mess in Raja," Susan said. "It will take me a week to clean up the garbage. Then I want to go back to my recycling job in Portland. They need me there."

Roger nodded that he understood. "And Bear, what about you?" He looked to the big chauffeur. "Would you rather drive a Rolls Royce here or a Radio Cab in Portland?"

"I like the Rolls a lot, boss."

"Then let's go. We've got four hours till show time." Roger looked around the group. "Let's drive in the front gate and retake the city."

Chapter 47

Hier ist das erste deutsche Fernsehen —

On his laptop computer, Dregs flicked through the channels that had uploaded the live stream.

. . . the BBC World Service. Officials of the Rajneesh International Center in Poona, India are distancing themselves yet again from Roger Nash, the self-proclaimed "reborn Bhagwan" in the American state of Oregon. Police have accused one of Nash's supporters of committing last month's murders. Officials cautioned —

Flick

. . . Hampton with a special live report for KPDV news. In a moment we're expecting a statement from the Rajneeshee commune in Klamath County, where a third member of the cult is missing and presumed dead. Angela, what else do we know so far?

Well, Marcus, the man who apparently fell from a cliff at Crater Lake this morning was Victor James Collins. He was operations manager and part owner of Raja, the group's controversial partnership. Police now believe Collins may have been responsible for the Portland murders that had been widely blamed on outsiders.

Why would a Rajneeshee kill his own people?

Police haven't yet discussed a motive. But they raised the possibility that Collins may also have been the author of the "Never Again" advertising campaign. In June, billboards began appearing on streetcars, depicting the

Bhagwan in the crosshairs of a rifle. The ads sparked nationwide outrage, but they also brought the Rajneeshees a lot of donations.

I wonder if some of those people will want their money back?

It seems likely, Marcus. The state attorney general has already announced that she's launching an investigation of fraud. The cult's non-profit tax status —

Harmony leaned in behind the backstage curtain. "We're ready." She had tied her blonde hair up in a bun. With a plain blue vest over a long-sleeved white blouse, she looked like a kindergarten teacher, not a Rajneeshee entertainer.

"Live in sixty seconds!" Dregs called out. He typed the words on his computer and hit SEND. Then he dialed up the volume of the sitar music on the stage's loudspeakers. Time for preparation had been short. They hadn't worked out an actual program. Dregs had found one person to run the lights and three others with video cameras, but they had no intercom. No matter what happened on stage, all Dregs could do was switch from one camera view to another, editing on the fly.

"Live in five!" He called. "Spotlight! And — curtain!'"

He dialed down the music to make way for applause. Where the hell was the audio? The Plaza was as silent as a mountain lake. Two of the cameras had focused on Harmony, standing alone, lit up in the middle of the dark stage like a startled fawn. He switched to the third camera, panning the crowd. In the low orange glow of evening a sea of people stretched across the square and down Vishnu Avenue as far as the open East Gate. Today the sannyasins in red were outnumbered by construction workers, bicyclists, and curious civilians.

The audio was on. There was no sound from this crowd.

"Hi."

Harmony's breathy voice swept out across the multitude.

"I'm Harmony Ferguson, the one you've been warned about."

There were a few tense laughs, but only a few.

"It seems like a lifetime ago that I stood before an audience like this to open the Rajneesh Revival in Portland."

She looked back nervously to Gilberto, in the shadows of the stage wing. He nodded encouragingly.

"Back then I asked you to open your hearts to the possibility of happiness, enlightenment, and a shared future."

Boos began rising from the back of the crowd.

"I'm not going to ask you that today," Harmony continued, louder now. "Many of you are disillusioned and angry. Well, so am I. A month ago, none of us knew that the Rajneesh Commune was owned mostly by one shadowy man, Vijay Collins."

Backstage, Dregs was searching his computer files for a photo of Collins to put on the screen, but he couldn't find one. Why had nobody thought to take a picture of their operations manager? Instead Dregs cut to a closeup of Harmony.

Harmony's eyes were damp. Perhaps because of those tears, the boos began to diminish.

"For twenty-five years," she said, "Vijay twisted the teachings of the Bhagwan. He used the commune to smuggle marijuana from Costa Rica into the United States. When marijuana became legal in Oregon, he sold the farm in Central America and moved here, hoping to corner the marijuana market. To Vijay, sannyasins were free labor. The Modoc reservation was a place to dodge state laws. Swamis were puppets, and enlightenment a sham.

"Through his security guards, the Tico Patrol, Vijay ruled Raja with fear. He built a wall, confiscated our phones, and threatened us with snipers of his own invention. This morning — "

Harmony stopped to wipe her eyes. "Oh, damn. I'm sorry."

The camera cut to the side, closer still. Her lower lip was trembling.

"This morning Vijay shot my uncle, Neil Ferguson. I had recruited him as a private detective to find out the truth. After shooting Neil, Vijay tried to push Roger Nash off of Llao Rock. I think there must have been a struggle. Neil says there wasn't. Anyway, it was Vijay who fell. He is not missing. Unlike Ma Anand Sheela, the woman who once ruined Rajneeshpuram, Vijay Collins is dead. Even with a thousand lifetimes of penance, I don't think either of them will be able to restore their karma."

Harmony held out her palms. "So where do we go from here?" Dregs switched to a wide-angle shot.

"As for me, I'm going home. I've realized that by joining the Rajneeshees I was trying to run away. I was running away from my job, from my responsibilities, from growing up — " she glanced back to Gilberto. "And from the man I love."

When Harmony turned back to the audience, a smile dimpled her cheek. What a difference! Even Dregs, watching a camera scan the faces in the crowd, could feel the anger ebb.

"Roger Nash, the reborn Bhagwan, asked me to introduce him tonight by telling the truth as I see it. All right, here it is. The Rajneeshee way is not for everyone. As far as I'm concerned, Raja either needs to be shut down or it needs a complete fresh start. But this is also true: The experiment here should not fail because of hate. It's all too easy to be suspicious of foreign faces and foreign ideas. The children in my kindergarten classes don't have this problem. They play with everyone. Mistrust is something we learn as we grow up. So maybe it's something we can unlearn with the right teacher."

Harmony held out her hand toward the curtain at the back of the stage. "And that brings me to Roger Nash. Yes, he's a coffee shop guru. But he's also an honest man and a teacher of truth. He is the one person I would trust with the impossible job of rebuilding Raja."

Roger parted the curtain and walked out onto the stage. Instead of robes he wore blue jeans and a white T-shirt that set off his square black beard. He raised his arms in greeting, a cordless microphone in one hand. Then he bowed to Harmony. The applause was thin.

Before Dregs could turn off Harmony's audio, her lapel mike amplified the whisper, "Break a leg, Rog."

Roger staggered to one side, mimicking a limp. At last the audience was able to laugh. But were they laughing with him?

"Sannyasins!" Roger called out. "Modoc friends! Cycle Oregon bikers and guests! Raja is dead. You have just heard Harmony Ferguson tell you what she feels. I think we all share her disappointment. She says to trust me, but why should you? I'm twenty-six years old. This swami gig is pretty much my first real job. So tonight I want to introduce you to some people you don't know — people who have real answers. Are you ready?"

When the audience didn't respond, Roger repeated the question louder. "Are you ready?"

The crowd managed a half-hearted, "Yes."

Roger shook his head. He shouted, "Are you ready!?"

"Yes!"

"Much better." Roger walked to the front of the stage. "Our first surprise guests are eight folks sitting right here in the front row. Please, would you join me on stage?"

The cameras had not been positioned for a view of the seats below the stage. Dregs eventually cut to a wobbly, hand-held unit that caught a group of middle-aged men and women in business suits looking for a dignified way to clamber up the stair-stepped stack of pallets that formed the stage.

Roger held out his hand to help them up. "We've got a civil engineer, two architects, a lawyer, a school administrator, an emeritus professor, a housewife, and a retired CEO. I don't know much about running a city, but these folks might."

They formed an awkward line, the women smoothing their pin-striped skirts and the men straightening their red ties.

"Allow me to introduce the board of the Rajneesh Foundation, a non-profit charity that owns the dormitories, cafeterias, schools, and meditation centers of Raja. While I won't trouble you with all of their names, let me give the microphone to the board chair, Ellen Statlinger."

A woman with a bob of hennaed hair, Mrs. Statlinger wore a navy blue pantsuit and a short necklace of red beads. After she accepted the microphone she put a pair of half-frame glasses on her nose, squinted at the crowd, and then took the glasses off. "I'm the civil engineer on the board, so I'm not used to speaking to large groups."

Dregs cranked up the volume to boost the woman's voice.

"First, I should confess that the Foundation has had very little to do with the business operations of the commune, which was under Mr. Collins' purview."

Roger borrowed the microphone briefly. "Do you regret that?"

"Yes, but we had our own responsibilities. Since June we've had to deal with over $7 million in donations. About half of that is now in a reserve fund to meet future rent payments."

"You pay rent?"

"For our share of the Modoc reservation. Our agreement with the tribe was to finance construction of a development project for them. They've started work on a complex that would include a casino and a cultural center. Frankly, I'm relieved to hear that the tribe may be willing to extend our agreement. Their project is less than ten percent complete."

Roger started to borrow the microphone again, but changed his mind. "Can we get a second mike out here?"

Harmony came back on stage, unpinning her lapel mike.

Roger attached the mike to his shirt. "So the tribe wants someone here to pay rent, but preferably not a psychotic dictator. Any other options?"

Mrs. Statlinger glanced down the line of board members. "We met this afternoon and decided we might try to incorporate Raja as a real city."

"What would that entail?"

"Well, it would be democratic. Any resident of Raja who is registered to vote could cast a ballot. The next feasible election date is November. Some of us on the board might run for city council, but anyone else could too. And of course we'd need a candidate for mayor." She smiled at Roger.

"No, no. I'm a swami. I'm not into worldly business."

A faint voice shouted from the crowd, "Like hell!"

Roger's face lit up. "Hecklers? I've been missing my protesters. Please, tell me it's Mr. Hamsby." Roger shaded his eyes as he scanned the crowd. "It is! Here, can we pass him back the cordless microphone?"

Backstage, Dregs was scrambling to keep up. The spotlight and two of the cameras were roaming the crowd. All manner of noises were coming out of the handheld mike as it bumped its way from hand to hand through the audience.

Finally the mike, the spotlight, and the cameras converged on an angry Baptist minister with a bow tie and slicked-back hair.

"Have you got my son up there?"

Erik Hamsby, dressed entirely in black, stepped out from the stage wing and waved.

"He's not a hostage, Mr. Hamsby," Roger said. "This morning your son carried a wounded detective down from Llao Rock. It turns out that Erik and I are old friends from Sunday school. He served in the Army years ago, but now he dislikes violence as much as I do. I offered him a job in Raja and he said yes."

"You've brainwashed him like everyone else. Let me talk to him."

Roger unclipped his lapel mike and held it out to Erik. But the young man only shook his head and retreated into the shadows.

"You and Erik can talk about this later," Roger said. "Maybe he'll show up at your refugee center tonight. Right now we're talking about incorporating Raja as a legal city. Do you have a problem with that?"

Mr. Hamsby grumbled a while before he continued. "Yes, I do. A Rajneeshee city council would be window dressing for the same old scam. The whole business operation is privately owned. Whoever takes over for Vijay Collins could run the same marijuana racket."

"You're exactly right. After Collins disposed of his partners, he owned the Rajneesh commune outright. That included Raja's greenhouses, two restaurants, an airline, a Portland hotel, and a coffee shop. Altogether, he was worth about $4 million."

"See?" Mr. Hamsby turned around in the spotlight, gesturing to the crowd.

"Except for one thing. Collins is dead. And when they settle up his estate it looks like I'll end up inheriting the whole mess."

"You see? You see?"

"But I don't want it. The Bhagwan Shree Rajneesh might have. He grew up in poverty in India. Even as he preached against materialism he couldn't resist collecting Rolex watches. Me, I grew up in a middle-class neighborhood in Hillsdale. I was happy with a job in a coffee shop. I didn't even have a car until two guys in red robes showed up on Killingsworth and offered me a Rolls Royce."

"You took it, didn't you?"

"You know, I might keep the Rolls. It's armored, so it's practical for official trips. But everything else — the greenhouses, the hotel, the airline — all that stuff I'll donate to the Rajneesh Foundation. No, better yet, I'll turn it over to the City of Raja. Let the city council deal with running the business. That way everybody in town will have a job, and nobody will have to pay taxes."

"Seriously?" One of the foundation board members had asked the question so loudly that it was picked up on Roger's mike.

"Seriously. I'm not a businessman. I'm a swami."

"You're a fake!" Mr. Hamsby shouted, his face red. "You're a Sunday school dropout, a barista with a blog. You're a fraud."

Roger lowered his head. "You're right again, Mr. Hamsby, but in a way you don't expect. To explain that, I'd like to introduce my final guests of the evening. But first, please, a round of applause for Mrs. Statlinger and the board of the Rajneesh Foundation."

The audience responded by clapping a little harder than they had yet that evening.

As the board members climbed down from the stage Roger told them, "I hope you don't run unopposed this November."

Roger shaded his eyes. "It looks like my next guests are just coming through the gate. Could everyone please make way for the wheelchair? And Mr. Hamsby, it's been a delight, but perhaps you could hand them your microphone. Any parting words?"

Backstage, Dregs remembered exactly what Mr. Hamsby had said before yielding his microphone a month ago at the Moda Center: "They're going to kill us all." Dregs' finger hovered over the mute button.

Hamsby glowered a moment. Then, to Dregs' relief, he handed over the microphone without comment.

Dregs flicked through the live channels. Most had already switched to commercials or other programs. Whatever surprise Roger had saved for the end of the presentation would run live on KPDV, the Raja website, and not much else.

Dregs cut to a camera that had zoomed in on the new arrivals making their way through the crowd. Riding in the wheelchair was Neil Ferguson, dressed in the cowboy gear he had worn for most of the past week — a black Stetson, jeans, boots, and even the sheepskin jacket, although it now had a blotch of blood on one side, as conspicuous as a state fair's red ribbon.

To Neil's' left was Connie Wu, wearing a police uniform instead of civilian clothes. But the woman pushing Neil's chair on the right, with rimless spectacles, a lop-sided ponytail, and a long purple dress, was someone Dregs had never seen before.

Roger announced, "Arriving in a wheelchair tonight is my own new personal hero, Neil Ferguson. He not only puzzled out the Rajneeshee murders, but this morning he took a bullet that I think was meant for me."

Applause swelled across the Plaza.

"Assisting him tonight are my Aunt Patricia from Vernonia and Lieutenant Connie Wu, the Portland police detective who's been handling this case. I'm sure she'll be glad to see it closed."

At the foot of the stage, where there was no wheelchair ramp, some of the men in the front rows offered to carry Neil. He waved them away and stood up, grimacing. Then he took off his cowboy hat and climbed up the stack of pallets on his own. When he finally stood beside Roger the entire audience had risen to applaud.

Ten seconds, twenty seconds — Dregs let the ovation stream out at full volume.

By then spectators had carried Neil's empty wheelchair up onto the stage. Connie and Patricia held Neil's arms as he lowered himself into the seat.

"Now here's the surprise about my hero," Roger said. "Long before he figured out the murders, Sergeant Ferguson had a laboratory run DNA tests on me and the old Bhagwan. How did you do that, anyway?"

Connie held a microphone to Neil.

"I'd rather not say."

"And why is that?"

"Because it's not legal for a retired cop to take DNA samples without permission."

"Well, you have my permission now. The lab reports explain something that has troubled me all my life."

Dregs switched to an extreme close-up view.

Roger's brown eyes had a strange, sad gleam. He spoke with a catch in his voice.

"I am not the reincarnation of the Bhagwan Shree Rajneesh."

A murmur spread through the audience.

"I am his son."

Backstage, Dregs held his earphones closer. Had he heard this right? The audience too seemed to draw in its breath.

Roger held out his arms to the woman in the long purple gown. "Aunt Patricia?"

Tears were running down her face. Wisps of light brown hair had come loose from her ponytail. She stepped forward hesitantly, her lips tight. Then she buried her face against Roger's chest.

Neil was the first to clap his hands. Applause slowly spread through the crowd. But it was an uncertain wave that crested early and died out when it lapped against the Plaza's far shore.

At length Patricia stepped back, wiping her eyes.

"Forgive us," Roger said, clearing his throat. "The mother listed on my birth certificate refused to let me meet with Aunt Patricia after I turned twelve, so we have some catching up to do."

Patricia laughed through her tears, nodding.

"Aunt Patricia," Roger said. "I think this is your story to tell."

Connie gave her the hand-held microphone.

Patricia brushed back the wisps of hair. "I'm embarrassed to say that I've done foolish things in my life. I'm probably not done making mistakes. But standing here tonight is not one of them. I am Roger's birth mother."

"I've felt this all my life," Roger said. "But how is it even possible? Were you with the Bhagwan at Rajneeshpuram?"

"I was too young to leave home then, although I wanted to." She shook her head as if to loosen the memories. "When I was eighteen I set off around the world, hitchhiking with a backpack, looking for answers. I spent half a year in a cave on Crete. Did you know Zeus was born in a cave there? George Harrison, the moody Beatle, lived there looking for enlightenment."

Patricia sighed. "I left Greece to pick fruit on a kibbutz in Israel. It was 1990. That's when I heard that the Bhagwan was back in India, teaching under the name of Osho. A group of us from Israel went together on a cheap flight to Madras. It turned out that the Rajneesh ashram in Poona charged more in tuition than we could afford. But Osho caught my eye. He picked me out to mentor in person."

"In person?" Roger asked.

She blushed. "He was older by then, worn out by the years in Oregon. But he still liked nice things and free love. People say he hated children, but he must have changed. He knew he didn't have much time left. Anyway, when I became pregnant he didn't ask me to have an abortion. Instead he bought me a plane ticket back to Portland."

"Then why did you hide what had happened?" Roger asked.

"I was young, a wanderer. I couldn't imagine raising a child. My older sister Catherine had been trying to start a family for years. She had a home and a car and a husband. It made sense to let her claim the baby. And Catherine was so excited. We arranged a home birth at her house. Her husband didn't like doctors and I was all into the natural thing, so no one else knew."

"Still, the timing seems crazy," Roger objected. "I was born three days after the Bhagwan died, on the exact minute he predicted."

"Maybe not the exact minute." She gave him a sly smile, a look that awakened an impetuous charm. "It was a home birth, so when I heard that Osho had passed away, I fudged a little on the birth certificate to make things match. You see, by then I was starting to regret my decision. It made me a little naughty. I suggested that Catherine name her son Roger, knowing that her husband was a huge fan of Roger Maris, the baseball star. I knew they'd never realize that Rog Nash sounds like Rajneesh. Then I offered to babysit every Saturday, knowing that they wanted that day off for their church work. That allowed me to take you to Saturday Market, where I ran a massage booth. I started introducing you to the teachings of the East. I saw those Saturdays as an antidote to your Baptist Sunday school. But when you were twelve, my sister got mad and cut us off."

Patricia's smile vanished. "Nothing had ever hurt me so much. I had given my sister my own child, and she refused to let us meet. Osho had tried to teach me to let go of my emotions. But I never did forgive my sister.

"And so this winter, when I heard that a splinter group of Rajneeshees were coming back to Oregon, I sent them an anonymous email. I suggested that they just might find the reborn Bhagwan in Portland as predicted. All they had to do was look for a twenty-six-year-old blogger serving mochas in a shop on Killingsworth."

She turned to Roger, her eyes damp. "Just look at all the trouble I've caused. I'm so sorry, Rog."

"Sorry? I've been blessed to grow up with two women who loved me as their son. And today I've learned that I have two fathers as well. I have to admit, it explains a lot."

"But not everything," Neil objected. He looked to Patricia. "What about the box?"

"What box?"

Neil raised his hands as if they held an imaginary case. "A little wooden box sealed with an imprint of the old Bhagwan's ring."

"Oh that." Patricia laughed. "Osho gave me a little box before I got on the plane. He said it was for the baby, so I slipped it in among the presents at my sister's baby shower. I guess that was another example of my passive aggression. What happened to it?"

"Your sister never gave the case to Roger."

"That sounds like her."

"Instead she gave it to me."

Patricia looked at the detective in the wheelchair, puzzled. "Why you?"

"I don't know. But after Vijay shot me this morning, the box was the closest thing to a weapon I had left. The inscription on the lid said to open it in an emergency. So I gave it to Roger to try."

"And what was inside?"

"Nothing."

"Oh." Patricia looked disappointed. "I'd always imagined Osho might have put one of his expensive watches in there."

"Actually, it wasn't a box at all," Neil said. "It was a single piece of wood that had been cut in half and hinged back together to look like a case."

"How peculiar. I supposed it was another one of Osho's pranks."

"No." Roger had closed his eyes. "It was his most important message."

He spoke as if in a trance.

"The Uncarved Block is the perfect whole, both there and not there, the symbol of the transcendence of the material world. It is the one lesson my father never mastered. The Bhagwan gave it to me as a reminder in my moment of doubt."

Backstage, Dregs desperately tried to adjust the screen's brightness. The spotlight seemed somehow faulty, shimmering. Worse, the only microphone still functioning seemed to be the unit on Roger's lapel. Either that, or the audience had vanished.

Roger touched his forehead with his thumb and middle finger.

"I remember now. There was a struggle, but it was not on Llao Rock. It was here, inside. The greatest struggle will always be the one inside of us."

Now all the audio was gone. The lights were dying. Dregs tried all the channels. Nothing worked. Time itself seemed to be holding its breath.

In desperation, Dregs pressed the key on his laptop marked ESCAPE.

Roger opened his eyes, and Dregs was back in control. He breathed a sigh of relief.

Roger bowed to the crowd in the Plaza. "Thank you for coming here tonight, all of you." He bowed again, this time toward his mother and Neil.

"Tonight I ask you to look inside yourselves. And tomorrow, I invite you to return here to start anew at Raja. Our work won't be easy. We will have to make do with Raja's natural hot springs. We will have to rebuild trust and heal divisions. That's a tall order. But if you know in your heart that something is right, don't let anyone tell you it's impossible."

He pressed his hands together. "Now go in peace and friendship. Thank you all again for coming, and good night."

Dregs had no way to signal the light technician, but she took the cue on her own. Floodlights filled the Plaza. Dregs switched to a black screen with the symbol of a single white dove. Below it in white letters, he typed, "You have been watching a live presentation by Roger Nash at the Plaza Stage in Raja."

While the audience blinked in the lights, Roger hugged his mother. Harmony came out and kissed Neil on the cheek. People in the crowd began talking and moving about.

"What happened to the box?" Connie asked Roger. "The state police didn't find it at the crime scene."

"I think I gave it back to Neil," Rog said. "Once I had the message, I didn't need the envelope."

Neil lifted his hands. "I don't remember exactly what happened to it either."

Connie chided, "You lost the case of the reborn Bhagwan?"

Neil shook his head. "I think that box goes wherever it wants."

Roger said, "Or wherever it's needed."

The crowd had begun filing out of the Plaza. Going the other way, however, were two men with crew cuts and dark gray business suits. The men stubbornly fought against the flow, heading for the stage. Finally they climbed up the pallets.

"INS," the older of the two men told Roger, holding out a badge.

"Who?"

"Immigration." The agent took out a paper. "We're looking for an alien by the name of Gilberto Montale."

Gilberto looked startled. "That is me. What do you want?"

"Your visa has been revoked."

"Wait a minute," Connie objected. "The Klamath County Sheriff is already dealing with immigration problems in Raja. He rounded up a couple dozen illegals this morning."

"That may be, but we've got orders from Seattle to bring in the Italian. He's on a watch list."

Harmony clutched Gilberto's arm. "No! He hasn't done anything wrong. He's my fiancé. He came to rescue me."

"Sorry, lady." The agent took a pair of handcuffs out of his pocket. "Let's go, Montale."

"No!" Harmony turned to Roger in desperation. "Marry us!"

"What?" Roger blinked.

"They can't deport Gilberto if he's married to an American citizen."

The agent shook his head. "Marriages of convenience are illegal."

"It's *not* convenient! Do it, Rog."

"Nope." The agent clicked the handcuffs on Gilberto's wrist. "Vows have to be officiated by a judge."

"He's a freaking justice of the peace!"

Roger asked, "Do you guys really want to get hitched?"

Gilberto stammered. "Itched?"

"Married, you dingdong," Harmony said. "*Sposato, con mio!*"

"*Dio mio!* Yes, *si*, really?"

Roger held his hand over their heads. "By the power vested in me by the laws of the land and the unity of all, I pronounce you spouse and spouse. Now kiss the bride, you lucky —"

"Wait!" Dregs jumped out from the backstage control station, his hair wild. "On the count of five. Three, two —"

Harmony grabbed Gilberto and kissed him so hard that the agent handcuffed to his wrist staggered to his knees.

Simultaneously fountains of red sparks began erupting in a semi-circle around the edge of the stage. Skyrockets shot up into the sky, exploding in rayed fireballs that turned the entire city red.

Everywhere people looked up, marveling. Were they celebrating the death of Raja, they wondered, or its rebirth?

Chapter 48

Neil bicycled through the morning drizzle, taking another lap around Portland's riverfront Esplanade to clear his head. For the second time in his life he had spent a night at Connie's house. It had been wonderful, but then she had suggested that he might want to move in with her — to save rent by giving up his apartment.

Moving in with Connie made sense. It's what Neil had wanted for the past year. And yet, the thought of losing his independence left him nervous.

Gilberto had moved in with Harmony, his visa problems solved by a marriage that even the immigration officials had to admit seemed sincere. The new couple were already thinking about buying a house for them in Eugene, close to town where Harmony could walk to her kindergarten and Gilberto could apply for a physics position at the university. Neil's brother Mark was still in Costa Rica with his wife Melanie. They seemed satisfied to stay there teaching meditation classes and building wooden toys. Neil's daughter Susan had remained for the week in Raja to get the recycling system in order. Dregs was still talking about formalizing his relationship with her, but as usual Susan wasn't talking at all.

That morning, after Connie left for work, Neil had paced her empty house as if it were a cage. Even he couldn't explain his uneasiness. He loved Connie. Together they had solved the case. Connie's job was secure. The Rajneeshees had promised Neil $40,000 in back pay. Publicity from his success was likely to bring him clients as a private detective. A doctor had told him to stay immobile to let his broken rib recover. He should be relaxing in bed. Instead he had put on his Lycra outfit and set out on his bike. How many times can you start your life over? Even children aren't the answer. Once Neil had imagined that Susan would grow up perfect, avoiding all the mistakes he had made. Instead she had grown up imperfect in different ways. Perhaps the old Bhagwan, at the end of his life, had pinned similar hopes on an unborn child in Portland. The path to enlightenment was supposed to be a spiral, narrowing toward a black hole of perfection in the middle. But to Neil, life felt more like a helix, a corkscrew that vanished into the weary distance without every reaching the center.

The second time he looped over Tilikum Crossing a streetcar clattered alongside him. Larger than life cutouts of the KPDV news team rolled past with giant white smiles: "Marcus and Angela, Live at Five!"

Around and around, the news repeated itself, an endless loop from Tilikum Crossing to the Broadway Bridge and back. Shootings, hate, suffering — that carousel would spin forever.

Neil had been looking for a sign that morning. Was this it?

His chest hurt. His head hurt. He didn't want to go back to Connie's house, not yet.

At the Riverplace Marina he veered away from the river path into the city. Along Chapman Park, beside the tower of the Federal Building, he saw the flashing neon of the Lotus Café, the bar where he had gone to drink himself into forgetfulness during the dark year after his wife Rebecca had died. Now he narrowly avoided that dive's gravity, but its pull left him off balance.

He wanted a drink. Just something to ease the pain, to escape the cycle for a day, a reward for all he had suffered.

He bicycled into his apartment building's underground garage, left his bike in the middle of his parking slot, and rode the elevator to the eleventh floor. He opened the door and tossed the helmet aside. Then he sat on the edge of his bed.

He knew he shouldn't risk taking a drink. He had made it home without slipping into that downward spiral. But the lure of oblivion was strong. No one was there to stop him.

He was still wrestling with demons, increasingly afraid that they would win, when he noticed that his bedside drawer was closed.

Completely closed.

Neil's heart sped up. He looked around. Nothing appeared to be missing from the apartment. The front door lock had been intact. But he always — *always!* — left the drawer of his night table half an inch ajar.

He used the drawer as a sign. He knew that sloppy thieves might leave it open. Only a careful intruder would close it.

Neil approached the night stand as if it were an unsprung trap. Cautiously, he pulled the drawer open.

The photograph of his wife Rebecca was still there.

And behind it, sitting in the shadows, was a small wooden box with the remains of a broken wax seal.

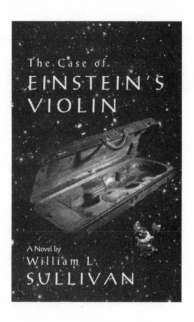

The Case of Einstein's Violin

by William L. Sullivan

When Ana Smyth and her friend Harmony Ferguson find Albert Einstein's violin case they sell it on eBay, unaware that it has been linked to a missing formula for quantum gravity. Soon they are dodging international spies on a race through Europe to discover the truth behind their family's past.